The Mill on Magnolia Lane

BOOKS BY TILLY TENNANT

The Mill on Magnolia Lane

TILLY TENNANT

Bookouture

Published by Bookouture in 2019

An imprint of StoryFire Ltd.

Carmelite House
50 Victoria Embankment
London EC4Y 0DZ

www.bookouture.com

ISBN: 978-1-78681-841-6
eBook ISBN: 978-1-78681-840-9

For Jacquie, the happiest, kindest soul I've ever met.

Chapter One

She'd driven past the old wreck a hundred times or more over the years. There was more sky than roof and more rubble than walls but still it had an indefinable charm, something that had always drawn Lizzie in.

'Makes me melancholy, seeing that old place go to ruin,' her dad would say.

'One day we should fix it and live in it,' Lizzie would reply, and her dad would chuckle. It was never patronising, only with wonder at the beautiful naiveté of childhood, where anything was possible and dreams always came true if you dreamt them hard enough.

'One day,' he'd reply. 'I've often dreamt about owning it myself. One day you and me will fix it together – how about that? A little castle for my princess.'

But that day would never come, not now. No fixing of a castle for a princess, no dad's help, no sage advice. The car she travelled in today drove past the crumbling hulk of the old mill, following the hearse that carried her dad's coffin. Now there was just her and her mum. Once today was over, her younger sister Gracie would go back to her job and boyfriend in London, and brother James back to his slacker mates in whatever dump he was currently inhabiting, and Lizzie would have to pick up the pieces of her mum's broken heart – the dutiful child, the one who always stayed behind.

'It's such an insult,' her mum said from beside her. She dabbed at her eyes with a fresh tissue from her bag. 'That witch in the official car and me trailing behind. He was my husband first.'

'But he was Florentina's husband last,' Lizzie said in an even tone. She'd heard this so many times now it was hardly noteworthy. 'Sorry Mum, but you have to accept that's how it is.'

'Why do I? She stole him from me and she has no right to be the grieving widow.'

'But she is.'

'She didn't know him like I did.'

'But she loved him and he loved her.'

Her mother turned a swollen face to her. 'Well, we all know *you* loved her too.'

This time Lizzie bit back a sharp retort that had no place being uttered in the current circumstances. Her mother was hurt, and she was angry and frustrated, and she was saying things that she'd later regret. If Lizzie reacted in the same way they'd both have plenty to regret when the dust had settled. If they were going to get through these dark days, they'd need each other.

'Please,' she said, struggling to keep her voice level. 'Let's not get into that again. We got along – what else was I supposed to do when she was married to my dad?'

'You could have shown your disapproval.'

'And where would that have got us? Would you have had Dad picking sides? Because if he'd been forced to pick sides, he might have chosen her rather than us. *That's* why I made an effort to get along with Florentina. I didn't want to lose him.'

Lizzie's mum pursed her lips but said nothing. Lizzie supposed that, in some ways, it had all been in vain. They'd lost him anyway – all of them. Her mum turned to face the window and Lizzie reached across to catch a silent tear that tracked her cheek.

'I know it's been hard, Mum.'

'I've borne it without complaint.'

'I know you have. You did it because you loved him. We all accepted things we'd rather have not because we loved him.'

'Because I loved you too and I didn't want to make our break-up harder for you than it was already.'

Lizzie pulled her mum into a hug. 'That's what makes you my absolute hero.'

'Don't be silly,' Gwendolyn said with a sniff. She wriggled from Lizzie's arms and dabbed at her eyes again.

The car slowed. Lizzie looked out of the window to see the evergreen-topped walls of the churchyard come into view. The wiry trees reached from the grey stones into a patchwork sky, their branches buffeted by a brisk November wind. The village of Piriwick was a pretty place and its church was still picturesque, even when dressed for such a sombre occasion. Her dad had returned to the village of his birth as often as he could during his lifetime, sometimes bringing his children to see what few sights there were. Often Lizzie and her siblings had been bored, but now she wished they'd shown more enthusiasm. It seemed only fitting that he should be buried here.

'Looks like we're here,' she said. Her gaze ran over a crowd of black-clad mourners gathered at the gates. All turned at the arrival of the lead car. There were some people she knew, a lot that she didn't. Perhaps they were from his other life, the one he'd shared with Florentina.

'It would have made him happy to see so many people here,' her mum said, nodding approval.

'It would,' Lizzie agreed. 'He liked a good turnout for any social occasion, even more so when it was in his honour.'

'He went to enough of them.'

'He did.' Lizzie laughed through the tears she could no longer hold back. 'He would have gone to the opening of an envelope.'

'I think he secretly always wished he was a celebrity.'

'He was to us.'

Lizzie turned to see her mum was smiling now, even as tears rolled down her own face. For the briefest moment they shared the bittersweet memories of a man who had been as remarkable as he was loved, and it was hard to believe that such a larger-than-life character was no longer among them. His death had been so sudden that they'd all struggled to take it in, even now. But then Lizzie dried her eyes and took a deep breath.

'We'd better go in and get our seats.'

'Behind Florentina, I suppose.'

'It stinks, I know. But hold your head up high and proud. You were his first love and you had a lot more years with him than she did – everyone in there knows it.'

'And we had you and your brother and your sister,' her mum said, stroking Lizzie's face. 'If nothing else good came from our marriage there was always you three.'

It was Lizzie's turn to purse her lips, biting back a reply that demanded to know that if her siblings were so perfect, where were they now? Gracie was in another car with her Hooray Henry boyfriend, having dashed up at the last minute because she had a presentation that was apparently more important than her father's funeral, and James had promised to come but as yet had not reported for duty. Which had left Lizzie alone trying to comfort her mum when she was barely coping herself. What loving children indeed. How blessed her parents must have felt with the kids who could barely trouble themselves with a visit once they'd flown the nest.

She shook away the bitter thoughts – now was not the time for them and they wouldn't help her feel better in the end. James and Gracie had their own lives now and they were free to make choices that suited them, not their parents and not her. It stung, that was all, and it must have stung their mum, though she'd never say it. They were her children and in her eyes they could do no wrong no matter how anyone else saw it.

Lizzie and her mum climbed out of the car and Lizzie linked arms with her. They walked together, arm in arm, as the path that threaded the churchyard crunched beneath their feet. She glanced back to see another car had just arrived. Her sister, Gracie, got out and she had her boyfriend, Frank, with her, but also James – presumably they'd travelled from London together. At least that was something; at least they were here.

Lizzie tugged on her mother's arm and gestured that they should wait for a moment. Once Gracie and James had joined them, they turned again, facing the crowd of mourners and the huge church doors.

This was it.

Showtime, her dad would have said.

Chapter Two

It was May Day. A time of new beginnings, of optimism, of celebration, of new life. A time when thoughts turned away from darkness towards the coming summer. At least that was Lizzie's hope.

She stood now, looking up at the grey stone walls of her new home, the grass-carpeted flats of the Fens stretching away to meet a cornflower sky, the smell of new pasture and the first apple blossoms filling her head. Her fingers were curled around a set of keys in her pocket. Where the decision had come from – as sudden and violent as a tropical storm – she couldn't say. Perhaps it was the memories of her dad, always with her whether asleep or awake, that kept bringing the old mill into her mind, so often that she felt she might become obsessed with the place. Perhaps it was the need of a sea change in her life, of something to aim for, something to give her days meaning when everything had become so dull and repetitive. Perhaps it was just that the place was so achingly beautiful, the sorrow of its current state giving it a sort of handsome, noble tragedy, that once she'd found out who held the deeds she could do little else but try to buy it.

Perhaps it was all those things but none of it seemed to matter now anyway. Once she'd contacted the local authority and they'd been happy to get it off their hands for an incredible knock-down price, it seemed fated. Her mum had said Lizzie was crazy when she broke the news of her purchase, but there had been a glint of something in her eye even as she did. Was it approval? A vicarious sense of adventure? A wish that she'd taken more risks herself when she'd been young and financially independent enough? Lizzie's dad must have mentioned his own love of the place in the past and perhaps her daughter's purchase had brought those moments to Gwendolyn's mind again.

All Lizzie knew for certain was that her dad's death had been the catalyst for long-needed change. Before she'd really thought things through, she'd got a huge mortgage and was handing a significant chunk of her life savings over as a deposit. As a result, she was now the proud owner of the Mill on Magnolia Lane. It stood alone, away from the main village of Piriwick, which was a funny mix of old seventeenth- and eighteen-century cottages with a modern estate of boxy houses tacked onto the outskirts, as if to remind it that the world had moved on. Along the lane that led to the mill sat the stragglers – the odd farmhouse or old worker's cottage, now turned into equestrian centres, pottery barns or farm shops. If Lizzie's mill had a name, nobody knew it, but perhaps it didn't matter; perhaps it was just another sign that it had always been waiting for Lizzie to come and make it hers. She liked to think her dad would have approved, that his spirit was somehow guiding her to make the choice. More likely his passing had made her recognise the fragility of a life that was far too short to be shying away from living it to the full; though with the way Lizzie's life had panned out since her traumatic break-up with Evan twelve months before, it was no wonder she'd begun to shy away from it.

Of course, buying into the romance of rescuing an old shell of a windmill was one thing, but making it habitable was a very different thing altogether. And as Lizzie stood gazing at it now, it wasn't just hope and optimism filling her breast, there was a fair amount of trepidation too.

Now that she looked at it, knowing it was hers and all the responsibility that went with that, the project seemed much bigger and more daunting than it had before. Not only that, but once it had been converted into a place fit to live in, she'd need to make it pay the bills too.

The plan hadn't always been in her mind. She had a perfectly good job writing web content for travel and holiday sites, which paid well and was flexible enough to fit in with her life. It was funny, really, because she'd sort of fallen into the job and it didn't seem to matter that she'd been to barely a tenth of the places she wrote about (though often writing about them made her want to go). What did matter was painstaking research and a bit of imagination, and that she could do. One of these days, perhaps a client would offer to whisk her off to Rio or New York to see for herself what she was writing about, but as yet she was still waiting. However, when she'd decided to take on the mill, she'd had a long chat with a surveyor who had imparted a perhaps inappropriate hope that one day the old place might be grinding corn and wheat again, as it had been meant to do, and the idea had been planted so firmly in Lizzie's head that she'd been unable to shake it.

She'd put her skills to good use and had researched for hours, late into the night, in the evenings, on lunch breaks. She'd soon realised she wouldn't be able to make amounts of flour big enough to supply supermarkets or factories, but she could make enough to produce her own artisan bread products perhaps. Or someone else's artisan bread products, though the idea of a batch bearing her own company label was undeniably appealing. She'd never even considered milling before, which was silly when she thought about it, because what else was a great stonking mill for? But once she'd had the idea, it seemed silly to have the sails of her mill standing idle when a little wind power was all it needed to make it useful again. Of course, the cost involved in getting the sails to a state where they could turn again without flying off into the sunset was a different matter entirely, and it was something she was still working out. Still, working things out seemed to be the motto for her whole life right now.

A shrill ring from her pocket interrupted her thoughts and she pulled out her phone.

'Hello, Mum.'

'Have you been in yet?'

'About to.'

'So you haven't had the chance to realise it's simply the most terrible idea you've ever had?'

'Not yet,' Lizzie replied with a little laugh, recognising her mother's dry humour and not a bit offended by it. 'But it's glorious out here right now. I wish you could see just how beautiful it is in the sunshine. There's just grass and sky for miles and it's so quiet. It's just another reason to be happy I bought the place and when things get tough I'll just look out of my windows to remind myself of that fact.'

'You mean those windows that currently have no glass in them?'

'Yes, those ones. At least summer's coming so I won't mind it being a bit draughty.'

'I hate to break it to you but it won't be warm at night without windows, unless we have a tropical heatwave. So you're still not feeling as if you want your cosy little townhouse back?'

'It's a bit late for that, even if I did.' Lizzie shook her head as her gaze went back to her new project. Besides, even though her little house in town had been home and it had served her perfectly well, there had been too much of Evan in it. It had been home for a while, but it had never felt the same since he'd left and she wouldn't miss it. 'I'm here now and I'm going to make it work.'

'Has that man brought your caravan over yet?'

'Derek? He just phoned to say he's stuck on a narrow road behind a tractor but he'll be with me as soon as he can.'

'That's country living for you.'

Lizzie's mum had never understood anyone's desire to live outside civilisation, and anywhere that wasn't threaded by a decent network of tarmac roads was outside civilisation in her book. Why would anybody want to travel miles for the nearest shop, or have wildlife running riot in their garden, or get snowbound in the winter or cut off by floods when it rained? Why suffer all those medieval inconveniences when the modern world provided perfectly good solutions to those things and a comfortable, easy life safely surrounded by concrete and streetlights? Oh, Gwendolyn liked the countryside well enough, but a quick drive out and back for tea was enough for her. Lizzie's love of the outdoors was definitely something she'd inherited from her father.

She turned around at the sound of a distant engine and watched as the speck of a black vehicle towing another began to grow larger as it travelled the road towards her house, the engine getting louder.

'Speak of the devil – I think the caravan's here.'

'Oh, I'll let you get on then. I'll call back later; see how you're settling in. Don't forget to let me know if you need any help. I expect that caravan will need a good clean given it's second hand and I can always come over—'

'It's fine, Mum. I can do the cleaning and there's no need for you to come all this way just to work for me.'

'I only want to help.'

'I know you do. Thank you.' Lizzie looked towards the vehicles again, almost at her gates now. 'I'd better go.'

'Bye, Lizzie.'

'Mum…' Lizzie drew a breath. 'Do you really think I'm making a huge mistake here? That it's too much for me?'

There was a pause. 'Probably. But you've made your bed now so you'd better get lying on it.'

'That's not the answer I was looking for,' Lizzie said with a faint smile.

'You'll be fine, sweetheart. You're a dreamer, just like your dad was, but unlike your dad, you're a doer too. He drove past that mill a thousand times and I know he always longed to take it on, but he always held back. He dreamt and never did, but you… I have all the faith in the world you'll make it work.'

Lizzie allowed herself to relax a little. She knew her mum hadn't really meant all the sarcastic comments about the mill being a terrible idea, but hearing her say she had faith made all the difference.

'I suppose Dad was scared to take it on. He had a lot more to lose than I do and a family to provide for, which I don't.'

Lizzie tried not to reflect on how very true her statement was. Since her split with Evan, she really didn't have anyone to answer to – nobody else to consider, nobody to tell her she couldn't. It was a valued freedom, but the gift was laced with a little pain too. With the split, and then losing her dad, it had been a tough couple of years.

'I suppose so,' her mum said. 'He'd be pleased as Punch to see you taking it on now, though.'

'He'd be doing the plumbing for me if he was here now. At least trying to.'

'He would.' Her mum laughed. 'And making an almighty cock-up of it too.'

'Probably. Thanks, Mum.'

'I'll speak to you later. Bye, love.'

Lizzie ended the call and mustered her brightest smile for the driver of the 4x4 as he pulled up outside her garden gates. As she'd suspected, it was Derek, the man who'd advertised his old caravan for sale on a local auction site, a caravan which just happened to be exactly what Lizzie needed. She'd spoken to him on the phone and he'd insisted that it was no bother to bring it out, so a smile was the least he deserved.

'Hi, Derek,' she called as he sauntered from the car to join her.

'It's a lovely spot here.' He sunk his hands into his pockets and looked up at the mill. 'Impossible to reach when the road floods, mind you. You might want to watch out for that. It's more often than you might think.' He shot her a sideways look. 'Moved here from the city?'

'It wasn't exactly a city – a bit small,' Lizzie replied. She knew full well that what he really meant was she'd been some city dweller who didn't have the faintest idea how life worked in the country and would be turning tail and heading back to her comfortable suburban existence the minute Mother Nature threw an obstacle in her path.

'Well, it takes a while for things to get through when the water's high, not like it does in town.'

'Honestly, I don't think I'll be that sorry if I do get cut off for a day or two,' Lizzie said, repeating the defence of her decision to move out to the Fens. Derek had a valid point but saying it made her feel more than a little foolish. Once again came the needling sense of annoyance that he was passing judgement on her life choice and her capability when he didn't have a clue about any of it. 'It'll give me a good excuse to stay indoors with the telly and a mug of cocoa.'

'It will that,' Derek said, appearing not to have noticed the offence he'd caused. 'Your boss at work might not be so pleased when you can't get in, though.'

'I'll be working for myself so my boss will be just fine about it.'

'Oh, what's that doing?'

'I do web content right now.'

'What's that?'

'I basically make stuff up for websites.'

'Right!' Derek chuckled. 'Sounds like a fine way to make a living.' He scratched his head as he studied the skeleton of the windmill. 'And what is it you plan to do with this?'

'I'm going to get the old place going again.'

'As a mill?' he asked, unmistakable incredulity in his tone.

'I think it's doable.'

Derek whistled through his teeth. 'On your own?'

'I'll get workmen in.'

'And running it long term?'

'I haven't worked that bit out yet. Maybe I'll have to employ someone.'

'It's finding someone who has the skills that might be a problem. There's not much call for windmilling these days.'

'I know. But I'm sure we can learn on the job together.'

Derek scratched his head. 'Well, it's not for me to pass judgement. As long as you're happy. Are you hooked up to the grid here?'

'No, there's a generator. Has its own water supply too, takes it from an underground spring or something.'

'Got all your certificates for that?'

'I've asked the local authority to come and carry out a risk assessment, but I do know when it was last checked it was fine.'

'I'll bet it was a long time ago.'

'That's why I thought I'd get it rechecked.'

'Well, it sounds as if you've thought of everything.'

'I wouldn't quite say that but I'm doing my best. I've done enough research.'

'It seems to me you've got most everything you need.'

'Apart from a roof, upper floors, large portions of wall… and some windows wouldn't go amiss either.'

Derek grinned as he angled his head at the keys now in her hand. 'Don't think you'll be needing them to get in. Blow on the front door and it'll probably fall down.'

'Probably,' Lizzie agreed with a smile. Despite his implicit questioning of her sanity, she rather liked Derek. She'd only bought a caravan from him but she had a feeling he was a man you could rely on if you were ever in a fix for anything else. He hadn't been under any obligation to tow the caravan out for her but he'd been happy to do it anyway; in fact, he'd insisted. Although it was possible he'd only come to take a closer look at the madwoman who'd bought the old wreck that had stood empty and decaying on the side of the road for as long as anyone in these parts could remember.

'It's a heck of a task you've got yourself there. I suppose your husband is quite handy?'

'I'm afraid I don't have one of those.'

'Sorry, of course you're too young to be married.'

'Hardly,' Lizzie said with a little laugh. 'I wish I could say that but I'm thirty-two. I think that might have qualified me as an old maid in days gone by.'

'My Caroline says she wishes she was an old maid sometimes. Says her life would be easier if she didn't have to wash an old man's socks every week.'

Lizzie giggled. 'You're not that old!'

'I know. I'd like to know who this fella is – they're not my socks…
That said, she puts up with a lot and she probably does wish she was
an old maid at times. I'd be lost without her, though.'

'No one to wash your socks?'

'Exactly.' Derek looked up at the mill again. 'You've got a builder
on board? If not I might be able to help.'

'That's kind of you but I've got a decent quote and I've said yes; I
just hope he turns up.'

'Who've you got?'

'Lundy and Sons.'

'Ah, Tim Lundy. He'll turn up alright.'

'You know him?'

'I know of him and he's got a good reputation.'

'Well, that's a relief.'

'I should imagine it is. Pay much for this place?'

'Enough.'

'Right…' Derek jingled some loose change in his pocket. 'None of
my business, just curious. So where do you want this caravan then?'

As they began to discuss the best location for her temporary home, Lizzie
looked back at the place that would one day become her permanent one.
Hopefully. It was barely a dwelling at all right now – good reliable ventila-
tion, her dad had always said, which meant hardly any walls at all. From
within the bare rafters of the old roof, birds flitted to and fro. It looked as
if there was a fair little colony in there, and goodness knew what else had
settled in. Renovating this old place was a huge task, perhaps bigger than
she was capable of tackling, but still it made her smile like nothing had ever
made her smile before. It was almost as if the mill had been waiting for her
all these years. As she stood and looked, it seemed to say *Welcome home.*

Chapter Three

It didn't take long to turn a caravan into home. A few knick-knacks, the odd photo, a couple of throws, the kettle and the television plugged in, and Lizzie was done. Most of the belongings that she would eventually transfer from her old place to the new one were still in storage, and she'd go over to her mum's to collect the clothing she'd stashed there when she'd sold her old house as and when she could fit it into her tiny temporary wardrobe.

Derek had stayed for a quick chat and a tour of the crumbling ruins she was planning to call home (hard hats included) and he'd left mid-afternoon, much later than she'd envisaged, but she'd enjoyed the company in the end and had been proud to show her mill off. She had some actual paid work to do, but it would have to wait because she could barely concentrate while the heady mix of excitement, trepidation, hope and downright terror was rushing through her veins like the craziest drug.

So she'd spent a restless evening alone in her new/old caravan listening to the unfamiliar sounds of the countryside at dusk just outside her flimsy door, followed by an equally unsettled night in a strange bed. At least she'd been able to sleep in late the following morning, having no demands on her time first thing and having finally drifted off in the wee small hours. The builder was due to bring supplies so he could start early on Monday morning, but he wasn't coming until the afternoon. So Lizzie sipped tea from her favourite mug and sat by her caravan window, gazing out onto the rolling meadows, backlit by a climbing sun that lifted a sea of golden mist from the lazy river, and contemplated how breathtakingly, achingly beautiful her new home was. Though she'd never been fully able to express or understand just what had drawn her to this spot over the years, why it had featured again and again in her dreams of the perfect life, she could see all those reasons spread out before her now.

A rap at the door of her caravan made her jump. Were the builders early, or had she really lost track of the time to such an extreme? At least she'd had the foresight to get dressed because she was no stranger to days in her little house in town spent entirely in her pyjamas.

Straightening herself out briefly as she passed the mirror, she went to the door and opened it to find a teenage boy grinning up at her.

'Hello,' he said, waving enthusiastically. 'I'm Charlie. Do you live here now?'

'I, er…'

'I live at the next house with my brother. We saw you yesterday with your suitcases. Jude said you were hot.'

Lizzie stepped back, uncertain how she was supposed to reply to the report that someone named Jude, presumably Charlie's brother, had said she was hot. And that they'd taken such an interest in her arrival.

She tucked her chestnut hair behind her ears. It needed washing and, not expecting anyone to visit, she simply hadn't bothered. It had been like that a lot since Evan – little things had slipped, things that she would have always made certain to do because he'd notice if she didn't, like making sure she always had make-up on and that her hair was neat and clean, and that her eyebrows were always trim and her pores nice and clear, and that she pedalled away the cellulite on her exercise bike for at least twenty minutes a day. Those things had seemed to matter a lot more back then than they did now, but that was because she had nobody now to care whether she did them or not. Part of her rather liked that she could sit in a pair of jeans so grubby they might develop the capability to walk to the wash basket by themselves, but part of her would think about that and feel a little lost. It was no way for a 32-year-old woman to feel; though faced with the alternative of letting Evan back into her life, maybe she'd find a way through it all eventually.

'Can you come to our house?' Charlie continued, barely registering her hesitation. 'We have a dog and a cat named George and Mildred. My dad called them George and Mildred. It's an old show, you know. He's dead now; it's just me and Jude at our house. Jude looks after me. He makes me beans with the toast on another plate by the side.'

Lizzie opened her mouth to speak but no sound came out.

'That's the way I like beans and toast,' he continued. 'I don't like it when the beans are all over the toast, makes it mushy…'

'Oh, well…' Lizzie began. 'I mean, it's lovely to meet you, Charlie, but…'

As she was grappling for a reply, a figure in the distance caught her eye. He was running down the lane towards the open gates of her house. Noticing her distraction, Charlie whipped around to see what she was looking at. And then he gave an excited wave.

'Jude!' he shouted. 'I've asked her to come to our house!'

'Charlie!' the newcomer panted as he tore through the gates and towards the caravan. As he slowed to a halt he looked up at Lizzie.

'I'm so sorry,' he said. 'I hope he hasn't disturbed you.'

'Not a bit.' Lizzie gave a bemused smile. She couldn't help but recall now that Charlie had reported Jude saying she was hot, and she couldn't help but notice that he was pretty hot himself. He was tall and well built, dressed in T-shirt and jeans with a hoodie thrown over the top. His dark hair was cut short but it was thick and perhaps had a natural wave when allowed to grow. The blue of his eyes looked almost indigo in the morning sun, the irises ringed with grey, and they had a quality about them that made it hard to stop looking. At least, they seemed to be having that effect on Lizzie. What she wouldn't have given for a mirror right now; she felt certain that she was probably having the worst hair day ever and that there was probably dried toothpaste or possibly even something worse on her top. Impulsively, she glanced down and was relieved to see that there didn't seem to be anything too horrific.

'So, can you come to our house?' Charlie asked, turning to Lizzie again. 'We have Snakes and Ladders. I love Snakes and Ladders. Do you like Dolly Parton?'

'Charlie…' Jude put a gentle arm around his brother's shoulder. 'We talked about this, didn't we? You can't just go to strangers' houses and invite them to ours. And you can't just take off out of the house unless you're with me. I was worried sick when I saw you were gone just now.'

Charlie's gaze went to his shoes. 'I'm sorry, Jude. I only wanted to ask. You said—'

'I'm not angry; just don't do it again.' Jude looked up at Lizzie from the bottom of the caravan steps while she stood on the top one, wondering if she ought to go down to them. It was a bit weird to be looming over them like the queen of the castle.

'I'm so sorry about this,' Jude continued.

'It's OK,' she said. The relationship between them was clear enough – it seemed as though Charlie needed a little more care than the average teenage boy and Jude had taken the role of carer on himself.

Lizzie decided to throw caution to the wind. 'Listen, I don't know anybody around here yet. If you've got time I'd love to invite you in for a cup of tea.' She smiled at Charlie. 'I feel as if we're friends already after your lovely welcome, and it would be nice to get to know you both a bit better.'

Charlie clapped his hands. 'Can we, Jude?' He switched his broad smile to Lizzie. 'I don't like tea. Do you have milkshake?'

Jude started to laugh. 'You do like tea; you're just after a crafty milkshake because I told you no earlier today!'

'I only wanted one strawberry one.'

'It was breakfast time! You can't have milkshake for breakfast!'

'Oh, I don't know,' Lizzie cut in with a smile. 'I don't have milkshake in right now but I promise to get some in for you next time you visit. I can do tea, though, as your brother says you like it, with as much sugar and milk as you want.'

'I have four,' Charlie said emphatically, clambering up the caravan steps without further invitation. Lizzie moved aside to let Jude follow, and he gave her an apologetic look, to which she returned a reassuring smile.

'It's really fine,' she said. 'I'm happy to have company.'

'As long as it's OK,' he said. Then he lowered his voice. 'He has two sugars; he only thinks he has four because I tell him that's how many he's having. Any more than two and he'd be clinging to your ceiling with his fingernails.'

She laughed. 'Two it is. Welcome to my humble abode.'

She watched as Jude climbed the steps and then followed after him. When she got back inside she saw that Charlie had already plonked himself on her sofa and was examining her TV remote, very much at home. Jude hovered in the doorway.

'Take a seat,' Lizzie said.

'Want some help?'

'No. But give me a few minutes because I literally just put everything in my cupboards yesterday and I can't remember where anything is yet.'

'That sounds like our house and we've lived there for years so we don't have that excuse. Charlie has a habit of putting things away in strange places and they're never seen again.'

'Oh,' Lizzie said with a little laugh. 'So you're already at home then!'

*

'So, you're the first neighbours I've met,' Lizzie said, placing the teapot she'd surreptitiously washed clean of dust before filling with tea on the table they were now gathered around.

Charlie grinned through a mouthful of Jammie Dodger. 'I like these,' he said. 'My favourite biscuits.'

Jude laughed. '*All* biscuits are your favourites.'

'Not Rich Tea.'

'Well, they're not even really biscuits,' Lizzie said, sharing a smile with Charlie. 'They might as well be tea coasters for how much taste is in them.'

'What's a tea coaster?'

'One of those things you put your mug on to stop it making rings on the table,' Jude replied. 'Not that you'd know because you never use them.'

Charlie let out a cheeky laugh. 'We don't have any of them.'

'Yes we do. Dad put them away in the cupboard years ago because he gave up trying to persuade you that that was where your cup was supposed to go.' He turned to Lizzie as Charlie reached for another biscuit from the plate. 'So you're the person taking Mad Lady Mill on?'

'Mad Lady Mill?' Lizzie asked with a look of disbelief. 'Is that what it's called?'

'Yeah. Well, it's a nickname anyway. I don't know where it came from but it's the one my dad always used. Others too when I was growing up. I suppose something a bit tragic must have happened here once. That or a mad lady lived here.'

'Is that why it's been empty for so long?'

Jude shrugged. 'No idea. All I know is that no one's ever lived here as far back as I can recall.'

'We used to drive past it a lot when I was growing up,' Lizzie said. 'My dad always said he wanted to buy it and give it a bit of love but he never did. I suppose it was too much to take on with a family. Anyway, I'll have to find a new name for it. I can't call it Mad Lady Mill.'

'How about Magnolia Mill? As it's on Magnolia Lane?'

'Oooh, I like it!'

'Is your dad going to help you fix it up as he fancied buying it himself?'

She hesitated, memories flooding back. Where did she even begin telling the story when it was so painful? She kept it short and hoped that would keep the tears at bay. 'He died. The end of last year.'

'God, I'm sorry.'

Lizzie gave a slight nod. 'Your dad died too?'

Jude blinked. 'How on earth did you know that?'

'Don't worry…' Lizzie smiled at his sharp look. 'I'm not psychic or anything. Charlie told me.'

'Charlie ought to start his own newspaper,' Jude said, throwing his brother a sideways look. 'He loves spreading news, especially ours.'

Charlie simply grinned before slurping at his tea.

'I'm sorry to hear it, though,' Lizzie said gently. 'Was it long ago?'

'Five years. I'd not long finished university. It was unexpected – a sudden heart attack – nobody saw it coming. I had plans but…' He shrugged.

'What about your mum?'

'We lost her when I was twelve. Cancer. Charlie was still a baby.'

Lizzie was seized by the sudden urge to reach across and pull him into a hug, but she pushed the impulse away. 'God, I'm sorry. So it's just you and Charlie?'

'We're alright. We're happy enough now that we're settled into a routine.'

'It must have been hard at first.'

'It always is – there's nothing easy about losing a loved one. You must know that as well as me.'

Lizzie nodded.

'You still have your mum?' Jude asked.

'Yes, thank goodness. I'd hate to be without her.'

'That's good to hear. So, you're going to be living here by yourself?' Jude flushed a little.

Lizzie could feel her own cheeks burning. While she was happy to be here, alone or otherwise, this wasn't the future that had been in the original plans for her life. If things had worked out differently with Evan, she'd still have been in their safe little house in town. The crumbling windmill on Magnolia Lane might have been rescued eventually, but it wouldn't have been by her.

'It's just me. For now at least. I tried to persuade my mum to come with me but she's having none of it.'

'It's a big place to live in by yourself.'

'I know. I expect I'll get used to it.'

'What made you buy it? If you don't mind me asking, that is. It must have been a hell of a task trying to find out who owned it to buy it from.'

'That wasn't the problem; it was getting the purchase through – that was definitely a task and a half.'

'So why go to all that trouble when there are some nice little cottages on the estate down the road all ready to move into?'

'I suppose it reminded me of my dad every time I drove past, reminded me of happier days, of childhood. I don't know really. It was like something drew me here and wouldn't let go.'

'And I thought you were just going to say you liked a challenge.' Jude looked over the rim of his mug and raised his eyebrows.

'That too,' Lizzie laughed. 'And it's certainly a challenge.'

'It's crazy,' Jude continued.

'So, do you live in one of those cottages on the estate?' Lizzie asked.

'No, we're in the big house on the road into the village. You might have seen it – you have to pass us as you turn into Magnolia Lane. We're not that far from you actually… we drove past and saw you going into the caravan with some boxes yesterday.'

'Our house has big chimneys,' Charlie said, his mouth full of biscuit and jam.

'And I think you've had enough of those,' Jude replied, sliding the plate out of Charlie's reach.

'I don't mind if he wants more,' Lizzie said.

'That's very kind but you don't know him like I do. It's fine now but it won't be pretty later on when he's running circles around his bedroom like a hamster on crack.'

Lizzie smiled.

'So how about that invite to our place?' Jude asked. 'Want to take us up on it now you know us better or will you be running for the hills?'

'I think I'd be running a long way to find hills round here,' Lizzie said, her smile suddenly shy now. 'It's about as flat as you can get. I'd love to come over.'

'Great,' he said. 'What are you doing tonight? I'm about to make too much lasagne and I'll need an accomplice to help dispose of the evidence.'

'That sounds amazing.'

'Seven OK? The dress code is smart casual and I'll make sure your name is on the VIP list.'

Lizzie smiled, her stomach doing little cartwheels while all thoughts of staying clear of men were forgotten.

'Seven sounds great.'

*

Lizzie walked down Magnolia Lane, heading towards the big house that Jude had described. She'd noticed it a few times over the years when she'd driven this way with her dad, and it was strange to acknowledge – not for the first time – the unexpected course life could take. Not once on those journeys could she have even imagined that she'd one day be sitting in that house as a dinner guest.

She'd decided to walk, confident that it wasn't too far and figuring if a little Dutch courage was on offer when she got there, having no car to drive back would make it easier to indulge. Jude had offered to pick her up, but she hadn't wanted to put him out. Besides, it was a lovely evening – the clouds burnished in saffron and orange as the sun sank low, the full moon still a promise. The hedgerows were thick with the peppery scents of wild grasses and foxgloves, birds darting and soaring, going home to roost or making a meal of the gnats circling in the air above the road. And a little Dutch courage would certainly go some way to steadying the hyperactive butterflies in her tummy.

Back in the caravan, dresses, trousers, skirts and tops were strewn across the bed. The occasion was less formal than a proper dinner party – like the sort you'd throw for a boss you were trying to impress (not that Lizzie had ever had a job important enough to need to impress a boss) – but it was more formal than a slobby takeaway on a friend's couch. What the dress code was here was anyone's guess. Not only that, but a good deal of her clothes, her make-up, hair-curling wands, rollers and straighteners were stored at her mum's house until she could make the room for them and it was really too far to drive up there to get any of it for this… whatever it was. Still, what she wouldn't have given for something to smooth the nest on her head that had been towel-dried and blasted with the hairdryer to no good effect at all.

Part of her was annoyed at the notion that what she wore tonight and how her hair looked mattered so much, and even more annoyed at her inexplicable nerves. It wasn't a date. Of course it wasn't a date. So why did it feel like it might be?

The invite to dinner had been thrown out, a nonchalant gesture of friendship that didn't mean anything. Jude was just being a good neighbour, and probably looking to give Charlie a bit of entertainment too. Lizzie was beginning to wish now that she'd made up some excuse not to go.

It's not a date and he won't care what you look like, Lizzie kept reminding herself. Except that it didn't matter how many times she told herself that, because *she* cared what she looked like and she cared about what he might think.

In the end, she'd stepped out in her cleanest jeans and a pretty smock top – she hoped that the compromise between casual and feminine would be about the right balance. She didn't want to look as if she was making too much effort. But then again, she did.

With these thoughts circling the runway of common sense, the flats of Suffolk rolled away before her, mile after mile of greens and taupes, fields of crops and fields of fallow, meadows of wild grass, boundary fences and hedgerows, broken only by the road that ran and ran until it met the coast. Somewhere, away in the distance and out of sight, lay the sand dunes and marshes of Southwold and Walberswick, where Lizzie's dad used to take her and her siblings crabbing during the summer holidays. Gracie would complain, Lizzie would follow her dad's instructions to the letter – always the child who wanted to please – and James would be doing his best to get stranded in the oozing mud of the estuary. They'd spent many happy hours there but Lizzie barely had time to think of them these days. Perhaps it was another promise she'd make to herself now that she lived so close – to go and visit, to sit on the little wooden jetty quietly dangling her crab line once again, for old times' sake. Or perhaps she'd walk the promenade watching the waves break around Southwold pier as the North Sea wind whipped them up. It wouldn't make life that simple again, but it would make her feel free and light, if only for a short while. Who knew, if things went well with Jude and Charlie, maybe she'd even have new friends to take along?

In the other direction was the village of Piriwick with its chocolate-box houses and a quirky village hall so wonky it almost looked drunk. There was a farm shop, an independent convenience store, a couple of quiet pubs, a tea room and that was about it – at least, if Lizzie's memory served her correctly. Bolted onto the village was a tiny estate of new houses. It was meant to be part of Piriwick, but it was neither here nor there, and nobody in the village could quite decide whether it sat within their borders or not. Jude's house occupied a strange spot even further along the road – too far out to be part of village life but too close to be anything else. In fact, Lizzie's own mill was probably the first building on that road to really lay claim to the accolade of being 'somewhere else', though Lizzie wasn't sure where that somewhere else was. If the new estate was suffering an identity crisis, Jude's house and Lizzie's mill were having mini breakdowns.

Lizzie became aware of a thrumming engine. Moving aside and off the road, she waited for the car to pass. But it slowed and she recognised Derek as he pulled up alongside and wound down his window. In the passenger seat next to him sat a woman with steel-grey hair in corkscrew curls tied back by a scarf. Lizzie wondered if it might be his wife, Caroline. It seemed like a safe bet.

'Need a lift?' he asked.

'Hello, Derek,' Lizzie said with a smile. She offered a tiny wave to the woman in the passenger seat. 'I'm fine but thanks for stopping to ask.'

'It's really no trouble at all,' he said, eyeing her curiously.

'Really, I'm OK. If I'm honest I'm quite enjoying the walk and I'm only going as far as Piriwick anyway.'

'We're going that far. You're not going to the Golden Lion, are you? Only we're going there – wouldn't bother with the other pub, ale's always a bit off – and you'd be welcome to join us.' Derek looked at his passenger. 'Lizzie could join us, couldn't she? She doesn't know anyone local.'

The woman smiled. 'Of course you could. I know a pair of old fuddy-duddies aren't much excitement, but you'd always be welcome.'

'That's kind but I sort of have plans. Another time, maybe?'

'Oh, of course, you just let us know. We visit the Lion most weeks. I'm Caroline, by the way. Pleased to meet you.'

'You too,' Lizzie said. 'Derek's told me all about you.'

Caroline turned to Derek. 'It had better have been good.'

'Oh, it absolutely was,' Lizzie said with a grin. 'He made you sound like an angel.'

'Now I know someone's telling me little white lies. And you're quite sure we can't tempt you into the car?'

'That sounds very sinister, dear,' Derek said.

'She knows what I mean!' Caroline slapped his arm playfully.

'Quite sure,' Lizzie said.

'I mean, it really is no bother,' Derek pressed.

'Derek!' Caroline said with a little laugh. 'Lizzie might not want you to know where she's going – did you ever think of that, you old gossip!'

'Oh, it's nothing like that,' Lizzie protested, not really wanting to tell them despite this. She'd only just moved in and she wasn't keen on being the subject of rumours so soon. 'I'm just off to visit someone.'

'Anyone we might know?' Derek asked, while Caroline slapped his arm again.

'Don't give in to his demands,' she said with a warm smile. 'Honestly, and people say it's the women who are nosey! You have a lovely evening wherever it is you're off to.'

'Well then,' Derek said, 'if you're sure then we'll be on our way. Don't forget, you have my number and you can call if there's anything you need.'

'Thanks, I will. Enjoy your evening too.'

Derek lifted his hand in an airy wave and Caroline smiled warmly as he pulled away from the side of the road. Lizzie watched the car grow smaller until it finally disappeared.

*

If she'd been forced to hazard a guess, Lizzie would have said that Jude's house was a Victorian build, though she was hardly an expert in these things. Standing in a garden of prim and proper rose bushes and mature plum trees, bordered by hefty leylandii, it was double-fronted with steeply angled roofs and tall chimneys, the weathered red brick embossed with an abstract wave design in a row beneath the eaves. The sash windows were tall and the front door painted a slick black. It was handsome, in an austere sort of way, but it didn't seem to suit what she knew of Jude so far at all. Lizzie wondered how much of it was to Jude's own taste and how much still remained from when his parents had lived there. Perhaps he was one of those people who didn't really care all that much about houses, only that he had one to live in. It was funny not knowing, and Lizzie wasn't sure whether she liked it or not. But then, she'd thought she'd known Evan, and it hadn't made any difference in the end.

She took a moment to smooth her hair (for what it was worth) and collect herself. Then she knocked and almost immediately Jude was standing before her, smiling and looking a lot more relaxed than she felt she did.

'You found us OK then?' he asked.

'It wasn't that hard when you're practically the only house on the road into the village,' Lizzie replied, suddenly feeling shy. Now that she saw him again, he was so much more than handsome. He seemed to have this strange effect on her that she couldn't explain, but it was all she could do not to stare hopelessly into the depths of his eyes. She wondered whether he could tell – if he could then he certainly wasn't showing it.

'You say that…' His easy smile broadened. 'But you'd be surprised how many people say we're hard to find when they haven't been before.' He stepped back and threw the door open. 'Come in. Charlie's in the kitchen laying the table; he's really looking forward to seeing you again.'

Lizzie stepped in and Jude shut the door, instantly intensifying the rich, herby aroma that had faintly tickled her senses on the doorstep.

'It smells amazing in here.'

'Let's hope the product lives up to the advertising then.' Jude gave a soft chuckle.

The kitchen was bright and airy and a lot less imposing than the outside of the house had suggested, with high ceilings and French doors leading to a paved area and the garden beyond. An archway to the left revealed a more intimate dining area, with a large armchair stuffed into a nook by the window and a glossy rosewood table, but there was a more casual pine table in the kitchen, the scuffs and scratches telling of comfortable meals with a lively family, and Lizzie was glad to see it was this one that was laid out for their meal.

Charlie turned and waved as Lizzie walked in. 'I'm making salad! Do you like salad? I don't.'

Lizzie couldn't help a little laugh. 'People only eat salad because they grow up being told they have to.'

'The trick is to mush it in with everything else so you can't taste it,' Jude said.

'It makes you wonder why anyone buys it at all.'

'Because we're supposed to care about the vitamins or something?' Jude offered.

'Probably,' Lizzie agreed.

Charlie brought an overflowing bowl to the table and carefully set it down before taking a seat and beaming at Lizzie. By the looks of things, there was a market garden somewhere that had been stripped clean, which was strange when you considered that they'd all just agreed they didn't like salad. Despite what she'd just said, however, the salad did look fresh and crisp and actually pretty good.

'Take a seat,' Jude said, gesturing to Lizzie. 'Can I get you a drink? I've got wine.'

'Wine would be lovely.'

Jude nodded and went off to the fridge. A moment later he returned with a bottle of white. The cork was popped deftly and he filled a glass in front of Lizzie before leaving her the rest and going to the oven. When he returned to the table this time, he was carrying a bubbling lasagne, browned and crisp on top. He placed it on an iron trivet at the centre of the table.

'Don't touch it, Charlie; it's hot,' he said mildly, and Charlie's hands immediately went under his knees.

'It looks amazing,' Lizzie said.

'It'll be OK. It's about the only thing I can cook well.'

'That's not true.' Charlie wagged a finger at his brother. 'You can make beans with toast at the side.'

'Oh, I can do that,' Jude replied cheerfully. 'I'm quite good at driving out for takeaway too – that's cooking, isn't it?'

'If this tastes as good as it looks I'd be happy to eat it every day and I wouldn't worry about being able to cook anything else,' Lizzie said.

Jude scooped out a mound and put it onto a plate for Charlie before offering to do the same for Lizzie.

'Is it cheeky to ask for the corner bit?' she asked. 'It won't get me thrown out, will it?'

Jude grinned. 'It won't get you thrown out as long as you leave me some. The crunchy bits are by far the best.'

'They are, and of course I wouldn't want to deprive you of your crunchy bit. Or Charlie, for that matter.'

'Oh, Charlie only eats the pasta sheets anyway,' Jude said. 'I don't even know why I bother putting the rest on his plate. And I'll eat pretty much whatever's going. You wouldn't be depriving anyone.'

Jude continued to dish out a portion for Lizzie, taking care to scrape a large section of the edge of the dish for her, and handed it over. As Lizzie reached for the salad, Charlie began to fire questions at her. His curiosity knew no bounds, particularly as he'd already quizzed her quite exhaustively earlier that day when they'd had tea at the caravan.

Do you have a dog? Are you going to get one? Do you like cats? How many CDs do you have? Do you like country music? Can you sing? Why haven't you got a job?

Lizzie did her diligent best to answer each one, finishing by patiently explaining that while it might look like she didn't have a job, she did, in fact, work from her caravan. At this point, Jude hinted strongly that perhaps Charlie ought to get on with eating his meal and give Lizzie a rest. Charlie looked a little disappointed but he went back to picking the pasta sheets from the lasagne while a little cairn terrier padded into the kitchen. He looked old, with grey whiskers around his mouth and wiry eyebrows.

'George!' Charlie cried, as if he'd never seen him before. He turned to Lizzie. 'This is George!'

The little dog was followed by rangy looking cat.

'And here comes Mildred too!' Charlie announced. 'This is our cat, Lizzie!'

Mildred looked imperiously at the gathering, decided she couldn't be bothered with making the acquaintance of the new person at the table and skulked off again. George, on the other hand, gave Lizzie a brief sniff, and then decided he liked what he smelt and sat down by her chair, gazing up at her.

'Oh, he's smelt dinner,' Jude said. 'Even George knows if it's lasagne he'll get the meat from Charlie's plate.'

'It looks as if he thinks he might get it from mine too,' Lizzie said.

'Hmm, clearly he's decided you could be a soft touch.'

Lizzie laughed softly. 'Is he allowed to have some?'

'A little won't hurt, but we have to watch his diet these days – he's an old boy and he doesn't get the exercise to work it off like he used to.'

Lizzie broke off a piece of cheesy pasta sheet and offered it to George, who sniffed before taking it gently from her fingers and then wolfing it down.

'Friend for life now,' Jude said.

'If someone fed lasagne this good to me then I'd be their friend for life too.'

'I'm glad to hear it,' Jude replied, and suddenly Lizzie realised just what she'd actually said. She blushed.

'I mean… if I was a dog…'

'It's OK – I know what you mean.'

'I mean, it's really good,' Lizzie continued, unable to stop herself digging in deeper. 'Better than my sister's and that's saying something because she's an amazing cook.'

Jude took a sip of his wine. 'You have just the one sister?'

'Yes, Gracie. And a brother, James.'

'Do you get on well?'

'We get on great because they both live in London,' Lizzie said with a little laugh. 'It's much harder to argue with someone when they're a two-hour train journey away. What about you? Is it just you and Charlie? No other siblings? Half-brothers or -sisters?'

'It's just us.' He chewed slowly as he studied her. 'So is there anyone else… significant?'

Heat spread to Lizzie's cheeks again. 'I don't have a boyfriend, if that's what you mean.'

Was that what he'd meant? God, how she wished she was better at reading these situations.

'Jude's got a girlfriend,' Charlie offered cheerfully. Lizzie turned to him, trying not to let the disappointment crush the air from her lungs. There it was in one sentence – her answer.

'That's nice,' she managed to say.

'Charlie, Harriet is not my girlfriend now – you know that.'

Charlie looked confused for a minute. 'But you have Artie,' he said, brightening again, and Lizzie felt that boulder weigh down a little heavier. She had a feeling she might know who Artie was.

Jude turned to Lizzie. 'Harriet's my ex. And Artie…' He shifted, his expression losing some of its relaxed ease. 'Artie's our son.'

'Oh.'

Why did Lizzie suddenly want to leave? Was it because of the echoes of a past of her own she'd been trying to forget, now clanging out a new warning?

'We're just friends now,' Jude continued. 'We have Artie to think about so it makes sense.'

Lizzie nodded. 'How old is he?'

'Almost three.'

'Do you see him much?'

'As much as I can. I don't want to miss out on Artie's childhood, even if we're not together. Harriet gets on really well with Charlie too – they're very close. We've both known her for a long time.'

Great, Lizzie thought. Not only a child together but a long-standing friendship too. Why did she always pick the complicated guys? She liked Jude, and she was beginning to feel confident that he liked her too, but already she wondered whether anything more than a friendship with him could withstand the threat of a constantly present ex and the child they had.

Lizzie pushed the idea firmly out of her mind and inwardly chided herself for being so paranoid and ridiculous. Her heart was still fragile and uncertain after the break-up with Evan – that was all – and if Jude said it was over with his ex, then it must be over.

'Your house is lovely,' Lizzie said, doing her best to move things along. 'Did you decorate it yourself?'

'Some of it. For so many years I wanted to make structural changes – thought I had all the answers to make the spaces work best for the family. I thought I knew everything back then... Dad wouldn't have anything changed, though. He liked it the way it was because that was the way Mum had liked it. Now that they're both gone I can see what he meant and I'd rather keep it how they liked it too. We've painted and done other bits and pieces, of course,' he added, taking a gulp of his wine.

'Structural changes?' Lizzie asked with a half-laugh, recognising that the pain of his memories was private and they didn't know each other well enough yet to openly discuss it. 'If you want structural changes you're welcome to go crazy at my place.'

'Actually, I'd love to help if you'd like me to. You see, it's what I do – I'm an architect.'

'Really?' Lizzie's face split into a broad smile. 'Wow, that's what you call good fortune – at least on my part. Fancy me meeting an architect during my first week at the mill!'

'Did you have plans drawn up for your renovations?'

'Actually...' Lizzie began, suddenly feeling silly. She hadn't had anything drawn up professionally, assuming that she could manage alone.

'It's expensive – I realise that,' Jude said, taking her hesitation as the answer to his question. 'I can see why most people would try to get along without hiring someone to do that. I'm sure you've got it all covered, but if you need any help or advice, don't think twice about giving me a call – no charge, of course.'

'Really? It would be OK?'

'I could come up whenever you like and size it up, give you a few ideas about what you could do with it.'

'Wouldn't it put you out? I mean, you must have paid work to do.'

'I've always got paid work to do but I can always make time in my schedule to help a friend.'

Lizzie blushed again. She liked the sound of that, even though she probably wouldn't do much to change the existing layout of the mill, and she especially liked that he'd called her a friend.

'And you're sure it would be OK?'

He reached for his drink. 'Of course it would.'

'Thank you,' she said, her insides fizzing at the warmth in his smile. 'I'll do that.'

*

Lizzie might have guessed that the evening would end with kissing. It did, in the shadow of Magnolia Mill as Jude had seen her to her caravan door, Charlie waiting impatiently in the car for him.

'May I?' he'd asked, a perfect gentleman, his eyes dark and inviting like new worlds to get lost in. Lizzie had nodded eagerly, her breath quickening, and their lips touched with a spark, a jolt of desire that shot through her body. There'd been a fierce attraction that had grown with every moment in his company, and if Charlie hadn't interrupted them, finally sick of waiting in the car, there was no telling where the kissing might have led. Lizzie had never been a bed-on-the-first-date kind of girl but there was a first time for everything and some attractions that were too strong to fight.

When she thought about it now, lying in her own bed in her tiny caravan after the last echoes of his car engine had faded, she replayed the moment of their kiss in her head. Only this time, the conclusion that might have been had they not been thwarted by Charlie played out. She realised that the direction the day had taken was unusual, but then everything about her life was unusual right now so why not this?

Chapter Four

A light drizzle kissed the window as Lizzie woke. For a moment she was confused, until she remembered that her comfortable pad in town was gone and now she lived in a creaky caravan that dripped and wobbled on its bricks and smelt a bit odd in damp weather. She also remembered that she sort of liked it that way. If it was easy and comfortable then it wouldn't be an adventure worth having.

Reaching for her phone to check the time, she smiled to see a text message from Jude already, even though it had only just gone eight. She opened it and her smile broadened as she tapped out a witty reply that really had no right to be in her head at such an hour. He made her feel clever and witty; he made her want to be sparkling and sexy.

Can't wait to see you again, came the reply. She couldn't wait to see him again either, though somewhere in the dark recesses of her brain an impatient little voice told her to beware, to keep her cool, to focus on what really mattered. She'd had her heart broken before and not so long ago… Meeting someone like Jude almost as soon as she'd arrived at Magnolia Lane certainly hadn't figured in her plans.

Tapping out another brief reply, she put the phone to one side and pushed herself out of a bed that was far too warm and comfy. There was a ton of rubble and litter to be cleared and only her to do it.

*

Lizzie twiddled with the dial on her portable radio until she found a station playing old nineties house music that would do nicely as a backing track to her day's work. The delivery driver had just left a huge empty skip and the first plank of wood echoed satisfyingly as it hit the bottom with a clang. She threw in another and another, and with every hunk of wood there came a growing sense of optimism, of excitement about her new project and the life she had always dreamt of without even knowing she'd wanted it until now.

An hour saw a good layer of debris lining the bottom of the skip and a good sheen of sweat on Lizzie's brow. Pausing to catch her breath and take a sip of water, she leaned against the container and shielded her eyes against the glare of a sun that had chased away the morning's drizzle. She watched with a vague frown as a car approached in the distance, winding its way up the shimmering ribbon of the road perhaps faster than it ought to. After a moment she pulled off her thick gloves and made her way to the gates. As she'd expected, the car pulled in.

'So this is where you are, *cara mia*,' the driver announced as the window wound down. 'It's not very easy to find, is it? The satnav wanted to take me to Wangford for some reason and it wouldn't have anything else.'

Lizzie looked in surprise at her stepmother and uttered a silent prayer that her mum wouldn't choose this moment to spring an unexpected visit...

'Florentina! I wasn't expecting to see you. It's a bit rural up here for you, isn't it?'

Florentina gave a vague shrug. Nobody who knew her could deny that she didn't do countryside well – she was even less suited to it than Lizzie's mum was. It perhaps had a lot to do with her upbringing in the exclusive streets of Milan, where her father had worked in a leading fashion house, followed by her stint in Paris and a couple of years at a finishing school in Switzerland. Suffolk was a million miles from the world she'd come from as it was, even the less remote parts, but Florentina was never going to be content with her family's plans for her future. So, as they'd plotted to get her married off to a wealthy Italian banker, she'd run away to England to take a job that by their standards was positive drudgery. When she'd then had the audacity to fall in love with an older Englishman who already had a family, it had been an insult too far. From what Lizzie knew (which was only what Florentina chose to make public), they weren't exactly on speaking terms. Florentina had settled with Lizzie's dad in Norwich, and she'd always seemed content with their life there.

Lizzie had often wondered if that were really true, and she'd thought that perhaps her stepmother might go back to Italy after her dad's death. So far, there had been no signs of that happening, but she supposed that Florentina was still adjusting to life without him, as they all were. Perhaps big changes would be hard to think about for a while.

'Well,' Florentina announced, 'I thought to myself that I haven't seen your new house yet. In fact, I've hardly seen you at all lately.'

'Sorry about that. It's just… awkward. You know…'

'Of course I understand. You've got to be loyal to your mum. But I do miss our chats.'

Florentina got out of the car and surveyed the mill in all its decaying glory. '*Oddio!* What a beast!'

Lizzie laughed. 'You could say that.' She was always tickled by Florentina's odd little outbursts of Italian, no matter how often she heard them. 'I like it, though.'

'I'm sure it'll be lovely when you've finished. How long do you think it will take?'

'I'm aiming for six months, though I realise that the best-laid plans don't always… well, they become non-plans. I'd like to be in for Christmas, though, one way or another.'

Florentina gave a meaningful look at the skip, and at Lizzie's filthy overalls. 'It looks as though you could do with some help.'

'There's a lot to do, but I was expecting there to be.'

'I'm at a loose end today. I could help. I'd probably be useless but I'm happy for you to take advantage of my services, for what they're worth.'

'I don't know…' Lizzie began. 'I mean, it's sweet of you and everything but I'm mostly just clearing out today and it's heavy work.'

Florentina frowned. 'What is your famous saying…? I may have the body of a weak and feeble woman… but I can work as hard as anyone.'

Lizzie grinned. 'I'd feel very guilty working you like a pit pony.'

Florentina clamped her hands on her hips and her frown deepened. 'Lizzie… I helped my uncle build his new house when I was thirteen. I know how to do these things.'

'Wow! Did you?' Lizzie frowned.

'Well, I passed him a hammer once – it was very heavy…'

Lizzie giggled. 'What about your clothes?' she asked as she ran a meaningful gaze over Florentina's outfit. She was wearing a beautiful midnight silk blouse tucked into indigo jeans that showed her hourglass figure to its best effect and some expensive-looking leather boots – probably Italian. She always liked to look her best, but then, being a buyer for a high street department-store chain, Lizzie supposed that sort of came with the territory. That, and her parents' influence.

Though Florentina was hardly a stick and was only ten years younger than Lizzie's 57-year-old mum, she had a certain magnetism and spirit that was hard to ignore. It was easy to see how Lizzie's dad had been completely beguiled by her. Mum could say what she liked about Florentina, but the fact was she was smart and warm-hearted with a wicked sense of humour. And despite the nagging sense that she was somehow betraying her mother, Lizzie did like her. Even at the start, when her father had left her mother, though Lizzie had made a point of trying to like Florentina for the sake of her dad, Lizzie and Florentina would still have got on well anyway. And Lizzie had guessed that her dad had been unsettled at home for a long time before Florentina came into his life, something he'd later admitted in a surprisingly frank moment. He'd told her that he hadn't been in love with Gwendolyn for many years and that he'd stayed with her for the sakes of Lizzie, Gracie and James.

By the time he'd met Florentina, supplying wine from his merchant's store for a corporate bash she was organising for her boss, his children had all been old enough to cope without him. Florentina wouldn't have been 'the other woman' for anyone, and he guessed that too, very quickly after meeting her. If he was going to have a last shot at happiness, it would have to be all or nothing. So he went with all, and although it broke Lizzie's heart to see her mum go through the split, where was the rule that said her dad wasn't allowed happiness? Someone was always going to suffer in this scenario; someone was always going to lose out. It wasn't fair, but then not much in life was.

'I'm all prepared, don't you worry about that,' Florentina said, striding around to the boot of her car and popping it open. 'I went around the sales and got some *favoloso* work boots and a pair of very fetching overalls.' She shook out an orange boiler suit and Lizzie let out a snort.

'It looks like you're off to prison!'

'Well, they do say orange is the new black.' Her stepmother grinned. 'What do you say? You can tell me all the gossip as we work.'

'OK,' Lizzie said, trying to ignore the little voice of guilt that whispered there would be trouble if her mum found out about this. 'I'd love some help.'

'*Bene!*' Florentina rested her hands on her hips and looked up at the house. 'You know, I really do believe this place could be quite beautiful when you've finished.' Her eyes misted and for a moment she was somewhere else, far from where she stood. But then she shook herself and sniffed hard.

'Dad would have loved to see us here, working together on this,' Lizzie said softly. 'He would have loved to see you helping me.'

'He would have loved seeing me break a nail,' Florentina said briskly. She gave another almighty sniff and rallied. 'OK, I will change my clothes and I will be ready to work.'

*

Working alongside Florentina proved to be a riot. There were moments of reflection, of course, and times where their thoughts turned to the man they had both loved, grief still raw and the presence of one another reminding them of what they'd lost. But Florentina had a sharp wit and an energy, a way of turning sadness into optimism and hope, and Lizzie was glad of the company even without the physical help. She knew she'd pay for it later with guilt when she spoke to her mum, and, sure enough, half an hour after the sun had begun to sink behind the hills and Florentina had kissed her goodbye, her phone rang.

'How have you got on?' her mum asked. 'I've been thinking about you all day.'

'Mum, you really don't need to worry.'

'I know, but I do. I wish you'd let me come over and help.'

'It's pretty back-breaking stuff; I wouldn't want you to hurt yourself.'

'I'm fifty-seven, not one hundred and seven! Anyway, when are your builders due to start?'

'Next week. They dropped a lot of stuff off yesterday.'

'Met any of your neighbours yet?'

Lizzie blushed at the memory of her evening with Jude and the things she'd thought about doing with him, and was glad her mum wasn't in the room with her.

'I've met a guy who lives in the village with his brother,' she said, keeping her voice carefully casual. It was no good – her mother had picked up the scent.

'Is he nice?'

'Seems it.'

'Eligible?'

'Mum!'

'I'm just asking. Can't I ask? I'm just curious.'

'No, because asking will lead to asking some more.'

'Just so long as he doesn't turn out to be like Evan.'

'Thanks for reminding me. I think I can spot another Evan if I meet one, and this one is definitely not another Evan.'

'Well, if you're sure.' Her mother's voice had softened. 'In that case it's up to you who you invite to share your life, as long as I'm the first to hear about it.'

'You will be; you know that. There's nothing to report right now – I've only had one meal with him and his brother was there for that – and really I've got enough on my plate without worrying about it.'

'Are you managing OK in the caravan?'

'It's small but as long as I don't want to throw any lavish dinner parties it's fine.'

'You're cooking? And eating enough?'

'Now you sound like a mother.'

'I *am* a mother. And if I don't remind you to eat properly you won't.'

'That's where you're wrong because all this physical work is making me constantly ravenous.'

'Speaking of work, how are you managing that?'

Lizzie wondered if this was the point where she could ask whether anyone was expecting the Spanish Inquisition, but she resisted the temptation. She had to count herself lucky that her mother cared enough to ask because neither of her siblings had bothered yet.

'I don't have too many demanding clients on the books right now so that's lucky,' she said. 'I can sneak off and see to builders and stuff on site and get my articles written in the evening when they've all gone home.'

'Good,' Gwendolyn said. 'Listen, there was a reason I was phoning. I'm making a big cottage pie tomorrow. I thought I might bring some over. You'll be in?'

'Well, I'd love to see you but it's a bit far, isn't it?'

'Forty-five minutes or so… I've done it plenty of times before.'

'It's an hour in traffic, and an hour is a bit of a drive just for cottage pie,' was Lizzie's hesitant reply until her sluggish brain realised that the visit was probably about more than cottage pie. 'I mean, I think I'll be in. Perhaps you could let me know before you start out so I'm sure to be here. Mum…' she added, 'is everything OK?'

'You mean, am I lonely now you're not just down the road? Of course I've always known that you'd all leave eventually, and I was blessed to have you nearby for as long as I did, even if James and Gracie are in London.'

'That's not what I meant. I know you expected me to move away but that doesn't stop you from being lonely.'

'Well, you're not coming back and I expect I'll get used to it in time. You have your new place and that's important to you – don't you get worrying about me.'

'Only I was thinking… I wondered if … Oh, never mind. I just want you to be OK.'

'I am. There's no need for you to worry.'

There was a brief silence, Lizzie trying to frame an argument that she didn't really believe that was true. Perhaps her mum was right, though. Perhaps they all needed to get used to this new arrangement, because this was life and it was what people did. Other children moved away from their parents and it was all fine. But then Lizzie's stomach growled and it was so loud that she wondered if her mum could hear it.

'I'd better get something to eat,' she said. 'I haven't had much time to shop today.'

'You *are* looking after yourself, aren't you?'

'Of course I am!' Lizzie laughed. 'And I won't die of starvation if there's a massive cottage pie to get through tomorrow evening if you're coming up.'

'You can be sure of it,' Lizzie's mum replied. 'Goodnight, sweetheart. See you tomorrow.'

'Looking forward to it. Love you, Mum.'

'Love you too.'

The line went dead and Lizzie put the phone down. Then she picked it up again and scrolled through the contacts. At the entry for Jude she paused. Perhaps calling so soon after seeing him would come across as needy, even though she did want to see him, very much. Giving herself a little shake, she put the phone firmly on the table again and headed to the little kitchen area to drop some bread into a toaster.

*

The day had started with blue skies, stretching endlessly towards the Fens and the coast beyond. Lizzie had been woken by the sound of a bumblebee at her bedroom window. She'd lain awake, listening to it for a while until it apparently decided that the caravan wasn't a giant flower and went on its way. She'd taken a little longer over breakfast today – toast with jam but no butter because she'd run out and, frankly, the shop was just too far to go to for one thing – and then she'd got dressed in her overalls, determined that just because it was the day of rest for everyone else, that wasn't going to apply to her. But then had come the knock on the door, Charlie chattering like a locomotive engine beyond it, and even though Lizzie was faintly annoyed at the idea of her plans being disrupted, her stomach was also fizzing with anticipation at the thought of seeing Jude.

'You know I'm supposed to be working on the house today?' Lizzie asked now, arching a brow.

Jude grinned, the sun burning down on them as they stood on her overgrown lawn. 'You can't work today. Who's working today? On a beautiful day like this?'

'Me. It's alright for you – you already have somewhere to live with a roof and everything.'

'Alright then, when we get back I'll help you – how's that?'

'I'll help too!' Charlie put in. 'I'm good at helping!'

'I'm sure you are,' Lizzie said. 'It's just that…'

She'd promised herself she wouldn't get distracted. The mill would never be fit to inhabit if she kept dropping everything at the first sign of something more fun. But fun had been in desperately short supply since her dad's death and Charlie looked more hopeful for her answer now than Jude did, if that was possible. She had things to do, but she hated to disappoint Charlie.

'An hour,' she said finally. 'And only because it's Sunday and it's supposed to be the day of rest anyway. Don't come and do this on another day because I won't be swayed.'

'Absolutely,' Jude said, giving her a mock salute. 'And anyway, I'm serious about helping, you know.'

Lizzie blushed. 'Thank you.'

Jude clapped a hand on Charlie's shoulder. 'So, Charlie boy, we have a picnic to get ready.' He looked at Lizzie and the way he smiled took her breath away. She hadn't been ready for it, and if he was going to do that a lot he might have to start warning her for the sake of her health.

'We'll come back in a couple of hours to pick you up,' he added. 'Sound OK?'

Lizzie nodded. 'More than OK. I feel bad that I don't have much to offer towards it, though. I don't even have butter for sandwiches!'

'Don't worry about it.'

'Maybe I could get off my lazy bottom and drive to the shops?'

Jude held his hand up. 'Forget it, honestly. Once you're settled in your swanky windmill pad you can make me dinner. How's that sound?'

'IOU one dinner. Sounds perfect.'

*

Lizzie was full and happy as she lay back on the blanket, losing herself in the gentle gurgling of a nearby stream and the hum of bees that balanced on the wildflowers carpeting the meadow. The sun was warm and kind, and she could have drifted into a pleasant doze had it not been for something tickling her nose. She opened her eyes to find Jude grinning down at her, a length of reedy grass between his thumb and forefinger as if he were about to perform some delicate surgery. He waved it around before reaching to tickle her again with it, but she intercepted and knocked it out of the way with a giggle.

'Don't you dare!'

'OK, I won't. Only if you let me do this instead, though,' he said, bending to kiss her. The most delicious tingle rippled down her spine.

But then she sat up, afraid that if she let him do it again she'd lose the self-control she was barely holding onto. She hardly knew Jude, and even though the attraction was strong, she had to remember that.

'Where's Charlie?'

'He's just over by the river watching for the heron.'

'There's a heron there? I've never seen one in real life before.'

'I'm not sure if it's still there but we saw it a few times in the early spring so I wondered if it was nesting close by. It's white – really rare. Want to go and look for it?'

Nodding, she brushed herself down as she got to her feet. 'I'd love to!'

Bird watching, Lizzie thought wryly as she followed Jude through the long grass to the river. How lame would Gracie have thought that? When they were kids Gracie was always the one bored by everything, the one who wanted to be off having adventures in the world while Lizzie was happy to sit crabbing or hunting for creatures in rock pools or feeding the birds in their garden. But then, Gracie wasn't here, and neither was James, and maybe Lizzie could be as lame as she liked and not have to give a damn anymore. She couldn't help but feel that being lame with Jude and Charlie was going to be a lot of fun.

They'd just started out in the direction of the riverbank when Lizzie heard a distant voice – someone was shouting Jude's name. She turned to see a couple picking their way through the tall grass, heading their way. The man was lugging a rucksack. Lizzie took a closer look and could see that he was in his mid to maybe late twenties, but that perhaps puberty had never really finished with him – his hair a floppy mess, a denim jacket covered in patches and badges and trainers that looked like they'd been distressed for fashion rather than by time. The girl was around the same age. Jude shouted back with a cheery wave.

'What are you doing here?'

'I think we had the same idea as you,' the girl said. 'I'm not sure our picnic is quite as impressive, though.' She angled her head at the rucksack, which the man opened to reveal a sorry-looking tangle of crisp bags, and then looked meaningfully at the tubs and packs still out on Jude's blanket.

'You can have some of ours if you like,' Jude said. 'We've got plenty of leftovers.'

'If they're going begging then we'll take them off your hands,' the man said with a grin. He wasn't bad-looking, but Lizzie suspected that he was the sort of man she'd find irritating pretty quickly – a pathological need to look cool and probably full of poorly informed but quite strident opinions on just about everything. He clearly knew Jude pretty well, though, so perhaps he wasn't all bad…

Jude shoved his hands in his pockets and glanced between Lizzie and the girl. For the first time, he appeared to feel awkward.

'Harriet, Damon… this is Lizzie,' Jude said. 'Lizzie… Harrie and Damon are… my friends.'

'Pleased to meet you,' Lizzie replied, understanding suddenly flooding in.

'Oh, so you're the new girlfriend?' Harriet laughed, and she threw a look of pure flirtation at Jude that made Lizzie stare. She didn't have time to dwell on it, though, because Charlie's voice came from behind them and he ran to fling himself at Harriet.

'How are you, Chuckles?' Harriet laughed as she ruffled his hair. 'Missed me?'

Charlie frowned. 'I only saw you both yesterday!'

Damon stepped forward and offered Charlie a fist bump, which had him grinning. And then it faded.

'Where's Artie?' Charlie asked.

'Oh, he's having a little day out with his grandma and granddad,' Harriet said.

'Where's he gone?'

'The zoo.'

'I love the zoo,' Charlie said.

'Don't we all?' Harriet replied.

'Why didn't you go then?' Charlie asked.

'Well, there wasn't much room in the car and I thought I might as well come for a picnic with Damon instead.'

'We've had a picnic,' Charlie said. Harriet looked at the blanket.

'I can see that. I bet you ate most of it as well.'

'No I didn't.' Charlie looked deeply offended.

'Yes he did,' Jude said, grinning at Charlie, who now grinned back.

'Lizzie had the little fish things,' he said. 'I didn't like them.'

'Sushi?' Harriet asked. 'Oh, I know your feelings on sushi well enough.' She turned to Jude. 'Remember that time we went to that Japanese restaurant in Norwich and all Charlie would eat was the sweet mochi? We must have spent about twenty pounds on plates and plates of the stuff just to fill him up!'

Jude laughed. 'God yeah! That day was such a laugh. Wasn't that the day you ended up dancing with that busker who then tried to give you his phone number?'

'And as I recall you pretended to get all tough to see him off, but even he wasn't convinced by the act, and he didn't know you!'

Jude chuckled again and gave Harriet such a look of affection that it rattled Lizzie even more than the flirtatious eyes that Harriet had thrown at him only a moment before. 'I must have "softy" tattooed on my forehead.'

'You do,' Harriet said. 'Don't I always say, Damon, that Jude is the biggest softy I know?'

Damon didn't seem to be anywhere near as unsettled by the exchange as Lizzie felt, and she began to wonder whether perhaps she was being a little paranoid about it. He just grinned and nodded. 'Nicer than me.'

'Not nicer than you, just more gullible,' Harriet said.

'Oi!' Jude cried, but he was laughing still. 'Just wait! I'll give you gullible!'

Lizzie cleared her throat. She hadn't meant it to be such an obvious reminder of her presence but Jude turned to her now and he looked suitably reminded anyway. His laughter faded and he took Lizzie's hand.

'We were just on our way down to the riverbank,' he said to Harriet.

'Oh, Irma at the Lion says there's a white heron hanging around somewhere near this bit,' Harriet replied. 'I think it might be an egret actually, but if it's a white heron that would be amazing. We thought we'd have a look for it – I want to get some photos for a wildlife photography competition I've seen.'

'We saw it a few weeks ago so it's definitely been nearby,' Jude said.

'Brilliant!' Harriet said, hitching her backpack up onto her shoulders. 'Can you show us where?'

Jude nodded. 'Yeah, come down with us – the more the merrier!'

Without so much as looking at Lizzie for her approval, Jude turned and beckoned them all to follow. Lizzie's hand had slipped from his as they began to walk. So much for their idyllic day together.

Every word, every sentence, that passed between Lizzie and Harriet seemed to contain some subtext, some guarded meaning. They sat comfortably enough on the riverbank together in the warm afternoon sun, eyes trained on the river, Jude, Charlie and Damon unaware of the storm clouds in Lizzie's head and of how Harriet seemed to be going out of her way to contribute to her unease. Lizzie tried to keep her misgivings in check and get the measure of Harriet to work out how she fitted into Jude's life, but she was finding it hard. Harriet and Jude, and even Damon, were saying one thing, but Lizzie couldn't help sensing something very different.

But Harriet was giving nothing away. Outwardly, she was perfectly sweet and saintly and it was easy to see why Charlie and Jude loved her so much. She was pretty in an edgy sort of way, with dark cropped hair, heavy brows and mesmerising hazel eyes flecked with tiny shards of brilliant jade. She wore her jeans and red checked shirt well, managing to look sexy in an outfit that Lizzie would have worn to work on the mill and wouldn't have looked sexy in at all. She was witty and comfortable in her own skin, smart and interesting and funny and all the other things that made Lizzie feel inferior. It grew more and more apparent that she had been a huge part of Jude's life for years and years and that Charlie adored her more than he adored anyone else in the world.

Harriet snapped photos on a bulky digital SLR camera that wouldn't have looked out of place in the hands of a professional, and it seemed to Lizzie that most of them were of Jude. It did nothing to alleviate her sense of unease at the way Harriet and Jude were with each other. They laughed together like a couple of teenagers, like people who knew each other's souls intimately from years of friendship, and it was Harriet who constantly reminded him of shared anecdotes, encouraging him to recount them and finishing them for him with punchlines that often became private in-jokes. Lizzie would steal a look at Damon every so often, but he didn't seem bothered at all by it. Then again, Damon looked as if he wouldn't know an emotional crisis if it slapped him across the face and Lizzie couldn't work out what Harriet saw in him anyway. He was so different from Jude in so many ways that it didn't make sense.

Perhaps an hour had passed in this way when Charlie suddenly leapt to his feet and pointed at the trees overhanging the far bank of the river.

'I saw it!' he cried.

'Shhh!' Harriet hissed, pulling him down to the grass again. 'You'll frighten it away!'

Charlie blushed and crossed his legs on the ground again.

'Harrie didn't mean to shout, Charlie,' Jude said, giving her a pointed look as he spoke.

Harriet pouted. 'He was loud enough to scare away every bird for miles.'

'And he didn't mean it,' Jude said firmly.

Harriet ignored him and got to her feet, camera poised, keeping low to the ground as she moved closer to the riverbank. When she was right at the water's edge, she began to snap. Lizzie fought the urge to run over and push her in. They'd only just met, but even though she couldn't really have said why, already Harriet was winding her up.

Jude touched her hand, and instantly she calmed.

'See it?' he whispered.

Lizzie followed the line of his outstretched finger as he pointed to the trees at the far riverbank. It took a moment, but then she saw it, and all her ire melted away.

'It's gorgeous!' she breathed. 'Beautiful!'

'Isn't it?' Jude smiled at her and she met his eyes. He leaned forward as if to kiss her, but then Harriet's voice cut into the moment and he jerked back.

'It does look like an albino heron,' she said, and Lizzie looked around to see her flop down on the grass next to Jude. 'I'll be so pissed off if it's an egret because that won't win anything. I'll show Grandpappy later and see what he says.' She stretched to kiss Jude on the cheek and grinned. 'Thanks for letting us crash your party.'

'We don't mind, do we, Lizzie?' Jude said blithely.

'Of course not,' Lizzie said. How could she say anything else?

Chapter Five

'I've never been so excited to see scaffolding!'

Lizzie pulled the old cardigan tight around her. The sun had barely risen but, as promised, the builder and his subcontractors had arrived Monday morning, bright and early, to start work. There was little Lizzie would be able to do herself now without getting in their way so she was planning a day locked in the caravan catching up on the work that actually paid her bills.

But she stood now in her garden with Tim Lundy, the builder, while he explained what the immediate plan of work was and then waited for her approval. She didn't really care which way round they did things as long as they did it and as long as they didn't take too many months – the thought of winter in her creaky little caravan wasn't an appealing one.

Tim grunted, which interrupted her train of thoughts. She'd found him rather stony-faced, but he seemed honest and straightforward, and he said things plainly, which was all she could ask for.

'So you want us to work on the extension first?' he asked.

'The house bit? Yes.'

'Right.' He nodded curtly.

'So I can move into that bit while the mill is being restored.'

'Have you found your specialist for the workings yet?'

'No. I was sort of hoping you might know someone?' Lizzie said hopefully. She'd already posed the question to Jude, but he didn't have anyone in his architectural contacts who knew about windmills. If Tim didn't know anyone then it was going to take a bit of research.

'No, but I can put the word out if you like. I'm not promising anything, though, mind.'

'That would be brilliant,' Lizzie said.

'It'll likely take most of the day to get this lot up,' he added, angling his head at a growing stack of scaffolding at the base of the gable wall. 'But you can't do anything without it, not on a place as unsafe as this.' He turned a flinty stare on her. 'You've not been playing about inside, have you? Not the safest place to be.'

Lizzie shook her head forcefully, and she decided very quickly that she wouldn't mention going in to clear the place out. Or the tour she'd given Derek the caravan vendor. Or the time she'd taken Jude and Charlie in. Or the half-dozen times she'd stood in the ruins dreaming of what they might look like when all the work was done.

'I'll have to put notices up,' Tim continued. 'In case you get any daft kids snooping around. Don't want to get sued if one of the little buggers breaks a leg or something.'

'There was nothing up all the years it was empty before,' Lizzie said tentatively.

'Then somebody was a bloody fool.' He dug his hands in his pockets and strode away to speak to the scaffolders before Lizzie had a chance to reply.

'So, I'll be in the caravan if you need me for anything,' she called. Whether he heard her or not there was no reply. Feeling strangely redundant after her previous few days of intense activity, she hesitated for a moment before finally heading inside, out of the way.

*

It was hard to concentrate knowing what was going on outside. Sitting still didn't come naturally to Lizzie and what she really wanted to do was get stuck in herself. Instead, she had to be content with going to the window every so often to see how things were progressing. There was a team of men out there now, radio blasting, the sounds of metal poles clanging together, whistles for attention and good-natured banter crossing back and forth across the site. The sun was shining and there was nothing to hamper the work, and Lizzie had to be grateful for that. She'd gone out with a couple of trays of teas that had been gratefully received, but even that wasn't making her feel very useful. Maybe she'd drive out later and fill her car boot with biscuits – her dad always said there was nothing like a steady supply of tea and biscuits to get a workman on side.

For now, to take her mind off things, she'd clicked into a search engine and typed in 'antique furniture', narrowing the search to the local area. She hadn't really made any solid plans for the interior décor once the shell of the building was done, but she'd daydreamed of what it might look like: a vague sense of a light-filled space sympathetically furnished in a style that suited the solid stone build and the period of the mill. There were large windows to consider, high ceilings and circular rooms in the main body of the mill, while the extension where the mill owner and his family would once have lived was smaller and the ceilings much lower, and it would take a lot more imagination to bring light and space to these rooms. Jude had already said he could help there, though his expertise was more architectural than interior design. It was easy to get fired up anyway – help or no help – because the possibilities were endless, and every time she looked through a house magazine she saw another style or theme that she loved. She couldn't have them all, and she guessed that in the end she'd wind up with something quite eclectic, a mishmash of the best bits that she hoped would still look beautiful and put-together enough to work.

According to the search engine there was a salvage/antique yard less than five miles from where she was now, tucked away down a secluded lane. Lizzie clicked on the link and went onto their website, scrolling through photos of household detritus in various states of repair. Some items were rough, like the stone bird tables with chunks missing and bits of rusting Victorian fencing, and some were more delicate, like the pair of exquisitely carved wooden benches and a bed frame fashioned from scrolled ironwork. On the home page of the site there was a photo of the yard as a whole, row upon row of treasure – or trash, depending on how you felt about old furniture. It looked like a fairyland to Lizzie, though she knew plenty of others who would probably disagree. But this was going to be her home and only she got to decide what went in it.

Her gaze went to the caravan windows again, where the scaffolding that would hug the outside walls of the mill was going up apace. Suddenly it all looked more real than ever – this was actually happening. Maybe it wouldn't be too premature to go on a little shopping trip and if she only bought smallish things she could store them with her mum for a while.

Putting the postcode of the yard into the map function on her phone, she checked the location to find that it was pretty much where she'd thought it would be and it wasn't really much of a drive. Then she dialled her mum, who picked up on the third ring.

'Are you doing anything for the next couple of hours?' she asked.

'Hello to you too.'

'I just wondered if you fancied a shopping trip?'

'I thought you had the builders starting work today?'

'They have, which means I'm pretty much redundant. So do you fancy it? I'm going to look at a reclamation yard.'

'What for?'

'I don't know. Bits of stuff.'

'Bits of what?'

'I'm not sure yet. I think I'll know what I want when I see it and fall in love with it.'

Lizzie's mum chuckled. 'That's no way to shop.'

'It's the *only* way to shop.'

'In that case I'd better come; there's no telling what you might buy without a steadying influence.'

'Brilliant! I'll pick you up in an hour!'

Lizzie smiled as she ended the call. She was suddenly excited at the thought of spending some time with her mum. Over the past few days, when she'd been sitting in her caravan in the evening watching the sun dip behind the horizon, she'd realised that, although this was everything she'd ever wanted, she missed her mum. She missed her little house in town being close enough to jog around the corner to borrow a cup of milk, just as an excuse to call for a chat with her mum, or to call anyway, not really needing an excuse at all. It was so quiet out here, so removed from everything she'd known all her life, and even though it was glorious, it was going to take some getting used to. The only thing she didn't miss about her old town was Evan. As far as she was concerned, the town could keep him.

*

It was almost two hours later by the time Lizzie and her mum were picking their way through the aisles of furniture at Reg Astley's reclamation centre. Her mum had got distracted by a stray cat in the garden and wasn't ready when Lizzie arrived to pick her up, and then they'd got lost on the seemingly simple route to the yard. Now they wandered up and down the lot inspecting things that caught their eye. There was that peculiar smell of sun-baked varnish and brass polish layered with a fusty aroma that always came with unheated warehouses full of old junk. Lizzie didn't mind it – she'd soon get the smell out of anything she purchased once it was brought into a warm, dry interior and renovated.

'Most of this is absolute rubbish,' Lizzie's mum said, running her fingers along the top of an old fireguard with a look of bemusement and then inspecting the dust it had left on them. 'Surely people want to get rid of this stuff, not buy it.'

'You do have to do some rummaging,' Lizzie agreed.

'*Some?*'

'OK, a lot,' Lizzie replied with a laugh. 'It's part of the fun. It's exciting when you find something good because you've had to work for it.'

'We'd have been better off spending the afternoon in IKEA. At least they have a nice café. And no dust.'

'I'm sure they have dust; they just have more people to keep it at bay. It's a different kind of dust too – this is the dust of history. That's just the dust of… IKEA.'

'Does that mean your dust has cholera in it?' Lizzie's mum raised her eyebrows.

'I hope not! Anyway, if my dust has cholera then yours must have meatballs in it.'

'Meatballs?' Gwendolyn looked confused.

'Meatballs… because it's IKEA and they sell those Swedish meatballs?' Lizzie shook her head with a grin. 'Never mind.'

They carried on walking and she pointed to what looked like a church pew. 'This looks nice and solid. Could work in the kitchen with a big scrubbed pine table.'

Lizzie's mum shook her head. 'Too low. And if someone wanted to leave the table before your other guests they'd have to ask everyone to get up and let them out.'

'So you don't like it?'

'Not especially. Reminds me of Sunday school as a girl.' She gave a theatrical shiver. 'I hated Sunday school.'

'I know, I remember you telling me the stories when I was little. I was terrified of nuns until I was about twenty; didn't realise they were actually supposed to be nice.'

'I wish I could meet one of them now – I'd give them a piece of my mind.'

'I expect most of them would be dead by now.'

'Then point me to the graves and I'll dance on them.' She pointed to a huge mirror leaning against a wall. The intricately designed metal frame of loops and swirls was tarnished and the glass grimy, but nevertheless it was an eye-catching item. 'That's quite nice, I suppose. It would reflect a lot of light if you hung it in an entrance hall or somewhere.'

'It's lovely,' Lizzie agreed, making a beeline for it. 'Let's put it on the maybe list – I expect it would clean up a treat but I can't just bring to mind where the right wall to hang it would be.'

'Let's see what they've got inside the warehouse. I think we're done out here, aren't we?'

'I saw a lovely armchair on the website, actually,' Lizzie said. 'I'm hoping that's inside because I haven't seen it.'

Lizzie's mum raised her eyebrows. 'I expect they wouldn't want to keep something with upholstery outside.'

They went inside and began to work their way around the crowded warehouse. It was clammy, despite the warmth of the sun outside, and the unmistakable smell of ageing furniture Lizzie had detected before was present again here, only stronger. An attractive young woman was sitting at a mahogany desk in a glass-walled office tucked in the corner of the hangar. She glanced up, and Lizzie immediately recognised Harriet. Her heart sank.

'Oh, here's the chair!' Lizzie said, hurrying over to it and trying to ignore the knot of anxiety in her stomach. Now that they were here and Harriet had seen her, she couldn't very well leave, even though she wanted to. She looked back to see Harriet motion to her with a smile, to indicate she'd be with them in a minute. Lizzie turned her attention back to the chair. She didn't have the will to explain to her mum right now that Jude's perfect ex-girlfriend was about to assist their purchase. The chair was upholstered in a faded tweedy check, high-backed with elegant curved legs and scrolled arms, and wouldn't have looked out of place in a hunting lodge somewhere in the grounds of Balmoral.

'That?' Lizzie's mum asked with a vague note of disbelief in her voice.

'Imagine it reupholstered,' Lizzie said. 'Don't you think it has a lovely shape?' She bent to inspect the base. 'Looks solid enough too; just a bit tatty on the outside. Some new fabric and it'd be perfect.'

'If you say so. I would have thought something like that would be better,' Gwendolyn added, pointing to a chintzy three-piece suite.

Lizzie shook her head. 'Too twentieth century.' She turned her attention to the chair once more and ran a hand along its back. 'This is a lot less… generic.'

'Common, is what you want to say. Lots of us do perfectly well with a sturdy sofa and matching armchairs.'

'I'm sure I'll get a sofa too,' Lizzie said wearily.

'Where's that going then?' her mum asked, nodding at the chair.

'I don't know yet. Maybe in the entrance hall or somewhere. Perhaps one of the bedrooms. Honestly, I love it so much that I'll make a space for it wherever I can; I just want to get it.'

'I can't see a price tag on it. Let's ask the girl in the office.'

Her mum began to march across the warehouse. Lizzie might have known this would happen. At the office, she rapped on the open glass door. Harriet smoothed a fleeting look of annoyance from her expression.

'Lizzie, hi! Fancy seeing you here. What can I do for you?'

Lizzie's mum shot a questioning look at her.

'This is Jude's friend,' Lizzie said, wanting this to be over as quickly as possible. 'The man I told you about.' She turned to Harriet. 'Could we get a price on a chair please?' Lizzie asked. 'It's the high-backed one over by the teak bureau.'

'The taupe one?'

'Yes.'

'I think it's two hundred, but let me check.' Retrieving her phone from the drawer of her desk, she dialled a number. 'Grandpappy, it's me,' she said after a pause. 'The taupe wing-back, it's two hundred – right?' There was another pause and then she nodded. 'I thought so but I wanted to check… Yes, we're fine here, don't you worry; it's been pretty quiet… OK, see you later.'

Ending the call, she looked up at Lizzie and her mum. 'Yes, two hundred pounds. We can deliver too if that helps, providing it's not too far.'

'Magnolia Lane… out towards the river,' Lizzie said. 'I'm actually in the old mill.'

'Oh, that would be no problem.' A faint line scored Harriet's brow as she hesitated.

'Mad Lady Mill, as it's apparently known,' Lizzie added, slightly thrown by her hesitation. 'Although I didn't have a clue when I bought it or I might have thought twice about putting the offer in.'

Harriet's eyes widened now. 'You've bought *that*? Jude never said!'

At this point, Lizzie's mum cut in. 'I'd just like to clear up that madness doesn't run in the family.'

Harriet laughed. 'I would imagine you know what you're doing,' she said, but her tone implied she would do nothing of the sort herself, which irritated Lizzie.

'Would you be able to do a discount if we took two items today?' Gwendolyn added, shushing immediately with a lifted finger the argument that Lizzie was about to offer. 'We rather like that huge mirror outside in the courtyard. If we take that and the chair today, what can you do for us?'

Lizzie stared at her mum, mortified at the request, but Gwendolyn looked the other way.

'Oh…' Harriet began, reaching for her phone again. 'I'll have to ask my grandfather – it's his place; I just help out.'

'That's OK, we can wait if you want to call him,' Lizzie's mum replied serenely.

'If you show me which mirror you're interested in first I'll see what he says.'

Lizzie turned to her mum and lowered her voice to a fierce whisper as they followed her out of the office. 'I can't believe you just asked that!'

'It's called haggling,' Gwendolyn whispered back.

'I know what it's called but nobody does it anymore!'

'I bet you he knocks some off when his granddaughter phones. Places like this, run by the older generation, expect their customers to drive a hard bargain – they set their prices accordingly. It's how business was always done before.'

'Well, I wish you'd warned me you were planning to do it. Besides, I'm not sure both of those things are in the budget. I'm not even sure I should really be buying the chair because by rights I don't even know what my furniture budget *is* while building is still ongoing.'

'It doesn't matter anyway, because you won't be buying the chair or the mirror. I will.'

'No!'

'Oh, shut up! You're my daughter and if I can't treat you every now and again then it's a poor showing.'

'Mum… I thought we'd sorted this…'

'We have. I'm sorting it now and I don't want to hear another word about it.'

Lizzie opened her mouth, another argument on her lips, but then she relaxed into a smile.

'I can't let you buy both. One or the other.'

'We'll see,' her mum replied briskly. 'If he quotes a good price for the two it'd be silly not to buy them both now. No point in taking one at full price and then deciding you want the other after all and having to come back and pay full price again.'

'Mum, you're impossible!'

'I'm allowed to be.'

Lizzie frowned, but she was never going to win this argument and so it was probably easier to give up. 'Do you work here full-time?' she asked Harriet instead.

'Most days. My grandmother used to do it, but she's not well now and had to stop. Mum and Dad have their own business to take care of but Grandpappy needs the help and I don't mind. It suits me to work for family rather than elsewhere.'

'Here it is,' Gwendolyn said, stopping at the mirror Lizzie had been admiring.

'Oh, I like this one too,' Harriet said. 'If you want to give me a minute, I'll have an answer for you quick as I can.'

Lizzie watched as she dialled her grandfather again. She was less irritating today than she had been at the river. Maybe they'd just got off on the wrong foot? Maybe Lizzie hadn't read Harriet right after all? She hoped so, because this was the mother of Jude's child, and it was likely she wasn't going to be disappearing from his life in a hurry, so it would be a lot easier if she and Lizzie could get along.

After a brief conversation, Harriet ended the call and turned to them with a professional smile. 'He says he can knock twenty pounds off but any more will mean he won't be able to eat next week.'

Gwendolyn laughed. 'We'll take them both then and we wouldn't dare ask for any more discount!'

＊

'What a sweet girl. Very helpful,' Lizzie's mum said as they got back in the car.

'Very helpful because she managed to get the price you wanted?' Lizzie asked with a wry smile, her eyes on the gates ahead as they negotiated the gravelled driveway. Sweet or not, she was just glad to be leaving the yard.

'And because she agreed to store it for you.'

'That's true. Though I suppose a sale's a sale and if they've got the room to keep it then the money's better in their pockets… at least from their point of view. Thank you – it was naughty of you but I'm ever so grateful.'

'With a discount that good I was hardly going to walk away from it.'

'I know, but it was still a lot of money and I appreciate it.'

'You're welcome, and let's say no more about it. If any of you three need help I'll always do my best to give it. It just so happens that the other two never call me, and I don't get to find out they need help until they don't need it anymore. So I get to spoil you instead.'

Lizzie slowed for a red light. 'I tried to call James the other day but he didn't reply and he didn't get back to me.'

'I expect he's busy,' her mum said, and left any further musings on the subject hanging in the air of the car like a speech bubble from a cartoon for Lizzie to read. What was left unsaid was that it was far more likely James had spent the last two days on a floor somewhere, incapable of speech after a marathon bender. Nobody had really been able to figure out what had led him down the path he'd chosen to take for most of his adult life – aside from his parents' divorce, at which point he'd really been too old to be affected by it to any great extent, he'd had the same happy upbringing as the rest of the Lovell children. Gwendolyn had blamed it on the wrong friends at the right time, and Lizzie had always been inclined to agree. Whatever had happened, Lizzie and James were very different people.

'Come on,' Lizzie said as the light changed to green again and she let off the brake. 'When we get back to the caravan I'll make you a cup of tea and we'll score all the builders out of ten.'

Chapter Six

It felt like a long time since Lizzie had eaten so well. The restaurant was bright and airy, fitted out in chrome and gunmetal grey, the kitchen open to allow customers to see their food being prepared, and beyond the wide windows was a wooden terrace dotted with tables and parasols and perfectly manicured pot plants. She was wearing her favourite Laura Ashley tea dress – nothing fancy and an old wardrobe staple, but as she'd been in grubby jeans and T-shirts almost exclusively for the previous fortnight she still felt vaguely overdressed now that she was wearing something else.

Jude smiled across the table. They'd met a few times since that first date-that-wasn't-really-a-date at his house, and they were getting along well. In fact, Lizzie felt already that they might be entering a more serious phase in their relationship. Though things were still relatively new and it made her a little nervous, she couldn't help but feel excited by the prospect.

'Did I say you look gorgeous?'

Lizzie reached a hand to her hair and smoothed it down self-consciously. She hadn't felt particularly gorgeous when she'd left the house, but the simple act of Jude saying it suddenly made her feel like a supermodel. 'You might have done.'

'I clearly haven't said it enough. You do.'

'Thank you. Although I feel weird. Like the girl from My Fair Lady when she first goes posh.'

He grinned and drained his wine glass. 'Do you know what else feels weird? Not having Charlie with us. I think the fact that's even a thing is weird too. Most people don't have their brother with them everywhere they go. But I'm so used to him being with me that I feel as if I've left an arm at home or something when he's not here.'

'I worry when he's with us both that I might do or say the wrong thing. Especially when we get a little close…'

His brow creased as he filled up their wine glasses. 'Does it bother you that he's always there? It's just that, with his learning disabilities—'

'God, no! I didn't mean that at all! I just don't want to make a situation that might be awkward for you or something you have to deal with when I've gone home. God, I completely understand how hard it is for you and how much you worry about keeping him safe. It's just funny when he's not here because I can do and say what I want, and I'm so used to that not being the case. Charlie's a sweetheart and I really don't mind him spending time with us.'

'There aren't many people I can trust with him, that's for sure. There aren't many who understand him.'

'I'd be the same, I guess. It's really nice that Harriet is happy to sit with him occasionally, though,' Lizzie said, trying to beat down the tentacles of jealousy. The more she heard about Harriet, the more perfect the woman sounded. Jude had made it clear that what they'd once had was over, and that she was really just a part of his life because she'd become so embedded in it through Artie and, to a lesser extent, her connection to Charlie. Although Lizzie believed him, it was hard not to feel insecure about the situation.

'Yes, Harriet's amazing with him, but she's known him for years so she gets his little quirks,' Jude replied, completely oblivious to the way his innocent praise only turned the knife.

'That's good,' Lizzie said stiffly.

And then it seemed that Jude, perhaps for the first time, really saw how things were. He reached across the table for her hand and held it tight.

'She's a friend. A good friend to me but especially to Charlie. But she's nothing more than that.'

'I know.'

'Do you?'

Lizzie sighed. 'If I said not really would that make me sound a bit needy?'

'No, it would be nice. I don't want you to worry about her but I can't deny that it makes me secretly happy because it means you quite like me.'

'I like you a little,' Lizzie said, a smile creeping across her face.

'Only a little?'

'You'll do for now.'

Jude wove his fingers into Lizzie's. 'I like you a lot.'

'You do?'

'You can't tell?'

'Maybe you need to make it more obvious.'

Jude gave a soft chuckle. 'Harriet says she can stay over with Charlie if she needs to.'

Lizzie raised her eyebrows. 'No curfew?'

'Nope.'

Lizzie took a slow gulp of her wine and studied the glass for a moment. This felt like a big moment. It *was* a big moment. She looked up at him. 'So you could come back to mine?' she said.

'I could.'

'And you could stay all night?'

'If you wanted me to.'

'I like the sound of that.'

'I was hoping you would.'

*

Lizzie lay in Jude's arms, head resting on his chest. The wind was up outside, howling around the caravan, and every so often a branch from a nearby tree would crack and groan. On another night, Lizzie might have been mildly alarmed by the change in weather – living alone in a little tin box sometimes made her feel more vulnerable to the whims of the elements than her old place used to – but tonight she felt safe and warm and protected. She was also more content than she could ever recall being before. She felt as if every inch of her had been kissed and stroked and teased and satisfied. Sex with Jude had been everything she'd imagined, and even as their bodies cooled passion stirred again. Let the wind do its worst – right now she had something much wilder occupying her thoughts.

'That was something else,' he said, trailing a finger down her arm.

'Good, that's exactly the right thing to say.'

He laughed softly, and then they fell to silence again, their two bodies feeling as natural pressed together as if they were one. Jude stroked Lizzie's hair from her face and gazed at her, the only sounds their light breathing and the wind snapping the tree outside, until a new noise cut through it.

Lizzie giggled.

Jude laughed. 'Was that your stomach grumbling?'

'It might have been. But then I'd been saving myself all day for dinner and we didn't get the chance to have pudding.'

'We could have stayed for dessert.'

'We could have done, but you ruined it by mentioning sex. After that, cheesecake went out of the window.'

'I didn't actually mention sex; I simply pointed out that I didn't have to be home tonight.'

'It's the same thing in my book.'

He pulled her closer still and gave her a squeeze. 'Want me to order pizza?'

'No pizza delivery wants to drive here tonight in this gale.'

'I could drive out and get some. Wouldn't take me long.'

Lizzie propped herself up and kissed him hard. 'How about you don't get pizza and stay in bed with me?'

Rolling them both over, he slid on top of her with a lazy grin. 'Don't blame me if you die of hunger.'

'At least I'll die with a smile on my face.'

'Fair enough,' he said, dipping his mouth to hers once again. She let out a sigh, expectation tingling deliciously in her gut. She could live without food, but she was quickly beginning to realise that she couldn't live without this. Being with Jude felt so right and natural that it scared her a little. She tried to remind herself that Jude wasn't Evan – he was nothing like Evan – but the scars on her heart would always be there. The break-up had made her stronger, and she'd come out of the relationship far braver and more capable than she'd ever imagined she could be, but it had also made her wary.

*

The sound of engines outside woke Lizzie. She rolled over to see Jude asleep beside her and she leapt up in a panic, casting around for a pair of jeans to pull on. They'd overslept, and the last thing she needed was to be caught in a post-coital doze by a nosey builder.

As she yanked a T-shirt over her head there was a tap at the caravan door. Lizzie pulled on some jeans, shut the bedroom away from view and raced to answer it.

'Tim!' she said, trying to sound airy and not at all like she'd only just woken after a night of passion.

'Alright,' he said. 'Just letting you know we're here.'

'I'll make some tea,' she replied hastily. 'The usual?'

'That'd be much appreciated,' he said, looking at her sternly.

With a curt nod, he sauntered off to organise his men. Lizzie let out a sigh as she closed out the noise. But as she turned a strong pair of arms folded around her.

'Gotcha!' Jude said.

'Good morning,' she said, instantly relaxing into his embrace.

'Isn't it just?' he replied, kissing her.

'I can't believe we slept in so late.'

'Who was that at the door?'

'You mean you couldn't tell by the noise? It was the builder. He always lets me know he's arrived. Like all the shouting and banging wouldn't tell me that.'

'He's just doing his job I suppose.' Jude kissed her again before going to the window and moving the net curtain aside. 'I should probably get back,' he said, looking out. 'I hadn't realised how late in the morning it was. Charlie… you know…'

'I don't suppose you can expect Harriet to stay there all day, especially with Artie to take care of too.'

'More's the pity,' he said, crossing the room to take her in his arms again. He was warm and smelt good, and she laid her head on his chest for a moment, listening to his heartbeat. Then he tilted her chin up and kissed her, and she could have happily forgotten that she needed to get dressed and make tea for her army of workmen outside. But then he pulled away with a look of regret.

'I wish we didn't have so much to do,' he said.

'Me too. If you need a shower before you leave, feel free to use the facilities. I'll have to water the troops before I can get one.'

'That sounds good,' he said, grazing his lips over hers, lightly this time, though her own lips tingled with the imprint of his for a long time afterwards. 'You're incredible – did I tell you that?'

'You might have mentioned it about ten times last night,' she said with a smile.

He lifted her hair from her neck, a delicate touch that sent shivers of delight through her. 'Well, I'm saying it again. You are incredible.'

'Go and get your shower,' Lizzie groaned, as desperate to fling him back into bed and ravish him as she knew he was her. 'If you don't go soon I can't be responsible for my actions.'

*

An hour later, Jude kissed her again before she opened the caravan to let him out. She watched with a smile and an ache of longing as he strode to his car. And then Tim Lundy called across.

'Alright there, Jude! How's Harriet and the nipper?'

Jude nodded shortly. 'They're fine.' He glanced back at Lizzie. Her brow creased into a vague frown. She watched Jude walk back to the car, throwing her a last brief smile before he started the engine and pulled out of the drive.

Tim came over as the car disappeared. He handed over a handful of mugs he'd collected. 'You're good friends with him, then?'

Lizzie paused, slightly taken aback by the bluntness of the question.

'Yes,' she said. 'He's my boyfriend,' she added, making a fist of putting the record straight.

Tim grunted a noncommittal reply before turning and walking back to the construction site. Lizzie watched him for a moment before heading back inside. She had a lot to do and a late start wasn't going to help.

Chapter Seven

Lizzie's mill was beginning to live up to its Mad Lady nickname. If things had been this disastrous for that inauspicious occupant, it was no wonder she'd gone mad. During the weeks that followed her first night with Jude, Lizzie had started to dread the knock at the caravan door that would see her listening to Tim, the colour draining from her face as he explained yet another problem they'd found: dodgy foundations, rot in the roof timbers, ancient lead water pipes that weren't remotely legal or healthy, a snag in planning permission, a supplier who'd gone bust without delivering goods they'd been paid for…

The initial excitement at the start of Lizzie's grand, once-in-a-lifetime project had ebbed away. She kept a fearful watch on her bank balance and her finances dwindled at a rate she had never reckoned on. Jobs were coming in, of course, but it often took a while to see the income from those because each one would involve planning, completion, sign-off from the client, invoicing and then – if the client was a prompt payer, and many weren't – finally payment. If things continued at this pace she'd seriously have to consider selling her caravan to raise extra funds, leaving her faced with the prospect of camping out in the shell of her nowhere-near-finished mill. She wondered how much trouble it would be if she asked Tim to concentrate on one corner that she could inhabit without too much discomfort, though she suspected that the answer to that question wouldn't be what she wanted to hear. Even with her limited experience, she guessed it wouldn't be so simple to separate the building into chunks fit for living in and those not, because one bit was always connected to another in a way she wouldn't have the building knowledge to foresee, making it impossible to work on that section without disturbing another.

She was trying to explain all this to Jude one Sunday as they sat watching a Disney film with Charlie.

'If you get the plans from Tim I could take a look and maybe give you some advice,' Jude said. 'That's assuming he's working from proper plans.'

'I haven't ever asked,' Lizzie admitted.

'Maybe you should ask him.'

'But do you think my idea could work?'

'Without seeing the layout it's hard to tell, but I suspect you might find it's as difficult to do as you fear. I mean, you can live in pretty much anything really if you're prepared to have building work going on around you, but I'm sure you don't really fancy that.'

'I might not have a choice,' Lizzie said in a dull voice. She pressed her fingers to her forehead and closed her eyes. 'I might have known it would go this way, I suppose.'

'You could stay with us,' Jude said.

Lizzie glanced across to see that Jude's brother was engrossed in the movie with a broad smile stretching his face. That was a relief, because Charlie's enthusiasm for any plan that involved them seeing more of Lizzie would doubtless sway her on an issue that she needed to stay clear-headed about.

'That's really nice of you,' she began carefully. 'It's just…'

'You don't want to?'

'Not that I don't appreciate the offer…'

Jude turned his attention back to the TV. 'It was just a thought; I was trying to help you out – it doesn't matter.'

But his hand had slipped from hers and Lizzie got the distinct impression that it did matter.

'I'm sorry,' she said. 'I didn't mean to sound ungrateful.'

'Why on earth are you sorry?' he asked, his gaze still trained on the screen.

'I don't know. It's just that…'

'I said it was OK,' he replied, but his tone said otherwise.

'I just don't want to rush anything. It's best for all of us.'

'I know it is. There was nothing in it – just trying to do you a favour.' Jude's jaw was set.

'I realise that but it's more… Maybe we'll see how the build's going over the next few weeks?'

'Look!' Charlie shouted, interrupting them, pointing at the TV. 'He's fallen out of the boat!'

Lizzie smiled as he turned to her with a grin. She'd never been so grateful for one of his enthusiastic outbursts as she was right at that moment.

*

Luckily Jude's strange mood hadn't lasted for long and, by the time they'd parted, it was as if nothing had happened. Except that it had happened, and Lizzie had been left wondering what it all might mean. She'd gone to bed that night with the matter tapping at her consciousness, like a sharp tooth that kept being found by a tongue, and she'd woken up with the same vague sense of the same conundrum still troubling her. But it was a new day and the builders would be here again soon, and Lizzie soon found herself considering what new misery Tim could inflict on her instead of worrying about Jude and his funny turn.

As she sat on the caravan steps with her first cup of tea of the day, gazing up at the mill – which looked oddly romantic in the early morning light, despite the scaffolding – she reflected that, with all the stress, it was easy to forget that they had made some progress. The old building was beginning to look like a house rather than a shell, from the outside at least. The walls of the long living quarters standing adjacent to the mill tower looked solid, the brickwork had been cleaned up to reveal dove-grey stone, the roof was watertight and a glossy new front door hung at the entrance. The windows had yet to be replaced, and there was still a great deal of work to be done inside, such as electrical rewiring and fitting a new boiler, bathroom and kitchen. Right now, however, the main priority was making sure old floors were safe and ceilings weren't about to come down on someone's head.

Putting down her cup, she crossed the garden as the rising sun turned the meadows beyond golden. The front door was unlocked and Lizzie pushed it open to step inside. Her tread echoed on the bare floor, sunlight skimming the windowsill as it flooded the entrance hall. She took a deep breath and appreciated that the house smelt of chemicals and unprimed wood and damp – it was the smell of a work in progress, of her home coming together, warts and all.

But perhaps it was overly optimistic to imagine herself living in here any time soon, and her thoughts returned to Jude's offer the previous day. Perhaps she'd been too hasty when she'd refused it. Now that she thought about it, his reaction troubled her more than she'd really admitted. He'd seemed genuinely hurt and offended, and she hated that, but why should she feel guilty when all she'd been doing was deciding for herself what she wanted? Their relationship was good just the way it was, wasn't it? She hadn't come to Magnolia Lane wanting or looking for love, but what if love had found her regardless? And if it had, what was she supposed to do about it? She'd almost forgotten how she was supposed to behave in a proper relationship.

Damn her stupid mistrust. Damn the betrayal that had split her from Evan and made loving anyone else that much more difficult. If only she'd never met him. If only she had a time machine that would take her back to the moment she'd first walked into the bar where Evan played pool every Saturday night so she could tell her past self to run – run fast and far. Jude had done his best to put Lizzie at ease when it came to Harriet, but Lizzie was finding it harder to let go of the shadow Evan had cast over her life.

She needed to speak to Jude. But then her intention to go and fetch her phone from the caravan was diverted as the sound of a throbbing car engine reached her. Not Jude's car – she knew that sound now like her own heartbeat, she'd listened for it so often – and not the grumbling engines of the work vans arriving. Ordinarily the sound of a car out on the road wouldn't have concerned her, but it seemed as if it was pulling to a halt close by. Going out, she spotted the low chassis and gleaming red paintwork of her sister's sports car, now parked outside her garden gate. A vague frown creased her forehead. Gracie didn't do spontaneous visits. She was usually so wrapped up in her whirlwind life in the city that she barely had time to worry about her family in the wilds of Suffolk. Sometimes it was easy to forget that she had a sister at all, and, true to form, Gracie hadn't bothered to come and see Lizzie once since she'd bought the mill.

She watched as Gracie climbed out of her car, and as her sister looked up and their eyes met, Lizzie's breath caught in her throat. Not since their father's funeral had Lizzie seen her sister look so distraught. Flinging open the gate, Lizzie raced to throw her arms around her.

'Gracie... what's wrong?'

'It's...' Gracie swallowed, caught by a heaving sob. 'It's Frank...'

'Frank?'

'I've... I've driven... all the way... from London...'

'In this state?' Lizzie cried, horrified at the thought of what could have gone wrong. Gracie could barely speak, let alone drive. 'What's happened; what's Frank done?'

'He's...' Another sob. 'He's dumped me!'

*

'Of course you must stay with me,' Lizzie said, handing Gracie a hot, sweet tea as she sat at the little table in the caravan. Then she crossed to the gas fire. It was summer and even though the mornings out here often had a chill, it was hardly enough to bother Lizzie. She'd noticed that Gracie was shivering, however. It was difficult to know whether this was down to her mental state or whether she was simply feeling the cold that bit more. Gracie had always been thinner than Lizzie, slender and delicate, with hair more auburn than chestnut and paler skin, but she looked very wan and thin to Lizzie now. Perhaps that had something to do with the shivering. 'There's not a lot of space,' she continued as she struck a match and put it to the gas, 'but I can make room for you.'

'Really?' Gracie took a sip of her tea and gave Lizzie a watery but grateful smile. 'I'm sure I'd be a terrible nuisance.'

'Weren't you always?' Lizzie asked with a sideways look.

'I suppose so,' Gracie said. But whereas an inside joke like this would usually have provoked laughter, now it only sent her sorrowful gaze to the depths of her teacup.

'How long can you stay off work?' Lizzie asked. She couldn't imagine the stern-looking boss who stalked the gleaming glass corridors of the advertising agency where Gracie worked on Canary Wharf being very happy that one of her client managers had disappeared into the ether.

'I don't know. I haven't even told them I won't be in today – I came straight here when I got Frank's text.'

'Bastard,' Lizzie said, reminded again of the cowardly circumstances of Gracie's dumping. She'd always thought Frank too old for Gracie (he was fifteen years her senior), and she'd always thought him arrogant too, but Gracie had always been so smitten and so in awe of the man that she wouldn't hear a word said against him. Not that she'd have ever listened to Lizzie about anything anyway. Besides, no matter what anyone thought about Frank, he had always seemed to make Gracie happy, and it looked from the outside that he was taking good care of her – paying the rent on their flat, treating her to exotic holidays and generally making sure she had everything she needed. Lizzie didn't know exactly what had happened here yet, but she guessed nobody would have seen it coming, least of all her sister.

Lizzie stood and wiped her hands down her jeans before joining Gracie at the table with a tea of her own. 'You could ring in sick later maybe? Pretend you were throwing up or something to explain why you didn't do it earlier?'

'Yes, yes, I suppose I could do that.'

'And you can self-certify for a week too so you wouldn't need a doctor's note.'

'Yes. And by then Frank and I might have fixed everything and I'll be back in our flat again and back to normal.'

Lizzie forced a bright smile. 'Perhaps,' she agreed. 'Have you got much with you?'

'A couple of bags in the car. Probably nothing that I need, but I wasn't thinking straight and I picked any old thing up to pack.'

'Anything you don't have we can sort here.' Lizzie paused, taking a slow sip of her tea. 'Does Mum know?'

'Not yet – didn't want to worry her.'

'She's going to find out.'

'I can't stay with her,' Gracie added. 'We'd kill each other inside a week, you know that.'

'I wasn't going to suggest it,' Lizzie said. 'I think we ought to tell her sooner rather than later, though. She'll be ever so hurt if she's the last to know.'

'If it all blows over and Frank has me back then there's no point in worrying her.'

'You don't want to tell her at all? What if it came up in conversation by accident?'

'You wouldn't tell her, would you? Not after I asked you not to?'

'I might not mean to but who knows. And do you really think it's that certain that you'll be back with Frank so soon?'

Gracie nodded thoughtfully. 'Perhaps I'll tell her later then. But if she tries to persuade me to move back in with her you must back me up that it's a bad idea.'

'Maybe it won't be as bad as you think,' Lizzie said, looking doubtfully around at her tiny caravan. 'I mean, there's a spare bedroom but it's really small, and we'd have to buy some bedding for you…'

'You don't want me here? I knew it was going to be a problem—'

'Of course I want you here!' Lizzie said, hoping she sounded suitably convincing. 'And if you *are* right about Frank then it wouldn't be for long anyway.'

*

On reflection it ought to have been obvious from the start that the same tensions that had crept between Gracie and her mother in the years before she finally left home would end up featuring in Gracie's new arrangement with Lizzie. Out of the three siblings, Lizzie was least like her mum, and Gracie was perhaps the most like her, but this was why Gracie and her mum often clashed. James hardly counted at all – he was most like no one any of them had ever met.

It's only a week, Lizzie kept telling herself as she forced yet another smile and bit her tongue as Gracie used all the milk without telling her, or all the hot water so that Lizzie had to wait for the tank to refill, or signed for parcels and took them in but then couldn't remember where she'd put them when Lizzie asked, or answered her phone when Lizzie was perfectly available to answer herself, or hovered around the caravan like a lost spirit, talking whenever Lizzie needed to concentrate on a project or a piece of important work. Though she understood Gracie's need to offload, it was hardly helpful. And she could have told her sister that it wasn't helpful and about just how distracting all that stuff was, but Lizzie was afraid that the criticism, however mild, might have Gracie bursting into tears.

And all of that was without taking Jude into the equation. Where on earth she was going to get a moment's privacy to spend time with him was beyond her right now. After the first couple of days, it had become quite apparent that there was no reconciliation to be had with Frank, who (Gracie had on good authority) was happily banging an intern at the advertising agency where they both worked and had probably been doing so for some time. And so Gracie was left with the conundrum of where she was going to live long term.

'I always thought you ought to have got a place of your own instead of chucking your lot in with Frank,' Lizzie said one day as she abandoned an article she was trying to write about the hidden paradise of Majorca's rustic interior while Gracie wept again.

'That's not helping me to feel better,' Gracie snapped. 'If you're going to tell me that I was wrong and you were right all along then I might as well go and live with Mum. I'll hear it there just as often but at least she has a decent bathroom.'

Lizzie clenched her teeth. She didn't have the energy for another spat. 'All I meant was it makes things hellishly difficult for you now.'

'Don't I know it.' Gracie sniffed. 'You know,' she continued, more pensive now, 'the longer I stay here and see how happy you are without all the confusion of somewhere like London, the more I wonder if I might be happier here too.'

Lizzie opened her mouth to begin a reply, with a dread suspicion of where this conversation was going, but Gracie jumped in.

'Obviously I didn't mean *here*. I meant somewhere *like* here. Somewhere quieter, where life isn't quite so competitive.'

'What about your job?'

'Perhaps there's a way I can do it away from London. Or maybe I'll chuck it all and work freelance like you do. It can't be that hard finding work just writing little bits and pieces here and there, can it?'

'There's a lot more to it than writing little bits and pieces here and there,' Lizzie said, fighting to keep her voice level. 'And it takes time to build up a client base,' she added, making a mental note to keep all of her current clients away from any kind of contact with Gracie. And under no circumstances could she mention her eventual plans to start producing her own bread, made with flour ground at the mill. One word about that and she'd have Gracie as a partner before she'd had time to sneeze. 'In a few months perhaps you'd begin to get on your feet but it wouldn't be an instant salary, not like you're used to.'

'But *you* did it.'

'I had the luxury of living with Mum when I started out – I didn't need to worry about a steady income in the beginning.'

'Oh,' Gracie began. 'Well… what if…'

'What?' Lizzie prompted, though if anyone had asked her to bet on what was coming next she was pretty sure she wouldn't get great odds on it.

'Well… you said this mill business was costing more than you'd imagined, and you said that it's even conceivable you might run out of money to finish it…'

'Yes,' Lizzie said slowly, beginning to wish that she hadn't been quite so open with her sister about her financial predicament.

'And since I might need somewhere to live and I might even leave London I thought perhaps…'

'That you could live at the mill? With me?'

'Well, yes. And I could pay rent, so that would help with your costs,' she finished brightly.

'The mill isn't fit to live in yet, that's the first problem. I need the cash to finish it way before I can consider anyone living in it.'

What she didn't add was that if she was considering anyone but her living in it at all, the last person she'd ask was Gracie. You could love your sister but it didn't necessarily mean you could spend prolonged periods of time in their company without wanting to throttle them.

'But I could help you there too,' Gracie said.

'But I thought you didn't have any money. Frank used to pay—'

'I have a little left from the bits Dad willed to us and bits I managed to save from work bonuses and stuff. Not fortunes, but a nice pot.'

'Oh. Well, wouldn't you be better putting that towards a place of your own – wherever that ends up being?'

'Yes, but I thought perhaps—'

'Gracie, it's kind of you, but I wouldn't be able to accept your money.'

'But I'd be living here so it wouldn't be charity, it'd be rent. It would solve both our problems at once.'

It would be the beginning of my problems, Lizzie thought. She shook her head.

'I just don't think it's the best way for you to use what you must have worked very hard to save. Trust me; you'll see I'm right in time. I mean, what if you meet another man? You might want to move in with him, buy a place together this time instead of relying on a man letting you into his home. And where would you be if you'd used all your savings on my house? Upset – that's where.'

'I could never be upset with you.'

Lizzie raised her eyebrows.

'That was when we were young,' Gracie said, ignoring Lizzie's look of scepticism. 'We're alright now, aren't we?'

Again, Lizzie was dying to argue but she held her tongue. The only reason they were alright now was because she'd held her tongue a lot over the past few days.

'And,' Gracie continued, 'I'm absolutely finished with men for good.'

'I seem to recall hearing that before Frank. And when you'd finished with the one before that.'

'This time it's different. Frank has honestly smashed my heart to bits and there's no way I can put it back together. I'll die a lonely old spinster with a house full of cats and cobwebs between my legs if you make me go and live alone.'

'You know I love you?' Lizzie said gently. 'And it's because I love you that I'm saying no to this and I'm not changing my mind. Take as long as you need to get over Frank, but then I'm shoving you back out into the world and, one day, you'll thank me for it.'

'Easy for you to say with this gorgeous old mill and your perfect secret boyfriend that you won't even let me meet.'

'It's not that I won't let you meet Jude, it's just that the opportunity hasn't presented itself,' Lizzie said. Perhaps the opportunity had presented itself, but Lizzie hadn't tried very hard to grasp it. Gracie was an acquired taste for most people, and it was still early days with Jude. 'I didn't think you'd be up to it so soon after breaking up with Frank.'

'I actually think it might help cheer me up. Maybe we can have dinner with him? That would definitely cheer me up.'

'Charlie would have to come too.'

'Charlie?'

'His brother.'

'Oh, well that's OK,' Gracie said cheerily and Lizzie could only hope that when she met Jude and Charlie she'd think before she spoke – something she wasn't exactly famous for.

'You do remember what I told you about Charlie, don't you? About his special needs…?'

'Of course I do. I'm not a complete idiot.'

'And I'm not sure there's enough room in the caravan for all of us and it seems a bit rude to invite ourselves over to Jude's place.'

'You've got tons of space.'

'The mill is nowhere near finished,' Lizzie reminded her.

'Not the mill – the garden.'

Lizzie blinked.

'Borrow a big table,' Gracie continued, 'some fairy lights in the trees, a patio heater... *Voila*!' She clapped her hands together, a smile spreading across her face. 'You've got the makings of a lovely al fresco dinner! It'll be just like dining in Naples!'

It was amazing how the prospect of a little bit of Neapolitan glamour could cheer the apparently broken-hearted Gracie. But Lizzie couldn't help a smile of her own. It did sound rather idyllic, even if the countryside of Suffolk was about as far away from southern Italy as you could get.

'Alright,' she said grudgingly. 'I suppose you ought to meet Jude and Charlie.'

'Absolutely. I need to see who this man is! After all, you said after Evan—'

'I know what I said after Evan, but I didn't mean it,' Lizzie said, though she'd meant every word at the time.

'Let me arrange it all!' Gracie said, her eyes shining with a sense of purpose. Perhaps this was just the thing to stir her into action and set her on the road to recovery. Lizzie could only let her get on with it and hope she was right.

'OK,' Lizzie said. 'I'll call Jude and see when they're free.'

Chapter Eight

Gracie had thrown herself into full party mode. She'd already been to IKEA to buy a cheap but cute dinner table that wasn't going to fit with Lizzie's décor plans for the house one bit, and that would either have to leave with Gracie or be sold. She'd also bought a stack of dinner plates, cutlery, glasses, napkins, chairs and seat covers; a new dock and speaker for her iPod; a patio heater that was capable of accelerating the rate of global warming all by itself; and fairy lights in a quantity large enough to confuse any passing alien that a new constellation had exploded into the night sky where that funny little planet they called Earth had once been. But, though Lizzie was faintly alarmed that her sister might be taking this dinner business a bit too seriously, Gracie seemed proud of her achievements and the activity was making her happy. More importantly, it was keeping her out of Lizzie's way, though the builders weren't quite so pleased when Gracie asked them to move a great deal of heavy equipment out of the way so she could set up under the shade of a couple of spreading pear trees.

Dinner was arranged for the following Saturday night. Lizzie had pointed out that it was going to be difficult to cook in the caravan but Gracie had replied brightly that she watched Gino D'Acampo cook outside all the time on TV and it would be easy to tootle off and buy the same equipment he used. Lizzie had also wanted to point out that Gino

D'Acampo didn't often have to do battle with the rains of the English countryside when he cooked outdoors – he was usually on some beach or surrounded by sun-ripened orange groves – but instead she suggested Gracie buy an awning as well and set up her stove underneath it to prepare for any eventuality. Her sister had decided she would be chef, cooking from her station as the party got started, where she would be able to chat to Jude and Charlie without too much intensity or awkwardness, and Lizzie (who only really cooked when she had to) was just fine with that.

Friday arrived and Gracie was out getting the last fresh ingredients together. Lizzie had been savouring the peace of her absence – a silence she'd begun to wonder if she'd ever enjoy again – when she heard a car pull up outside the gates of the house. Taking herself down the caravan steps, she smiled and waved as Florentina appeared at the gate.

'What brings you out here?'

'Tiles,' Florentina replied with a grin. 'Very cheap and very nice. I thought you might be interested.'

'And what lorry might these tiles have fallen off?' Lizzie raised her eyebrows.

'No lorry,' Florentina laughed. 'The DIY branch of our sister business is selling them off. I picked up a few samples, wanted to give you the chance to snap them up before anyone else.'

Lizzie looked at her stepmother's hands. They were empty, save for her keys and phone.

'They are in the car,' Florentina said. 'There's far too many to bring out so you'll have to look at them in my boot.'

'Right – I don't need telling twice!' Lizzie grabbed her hand and marched her back to her car.

'I don't even get a welcome drink after driving all this way with your samples?' Florentina laughed.

'Not until I've had a good nosey. I wouldn't want you to feel you'd had a wasted journey or anything.'

With a grin, Florentina opened the boot. Amongst the jumble of the spare tyre and jack, de-icer and old shopping bags lay a treasure trove of glossy-coloured ceramic tiles housed in grubby, open-topped display boxes. Lizzie almost squealed with excitement.

'And there's enough of any of these currently in stock to do a bathroom or kitchen?' Lizzie asked, gazing down at the hypnotic array of colours and designs.

'Of course it depends on the size of the room but there's more than enough for an average one, I should say. I would take a few more than you need in case you break some because these are end of lines and you'd probably struggle to get more.'

'And are they all different prices?'

'All one price to you, *cara mia*.'

Lizzie looked up. 'And what's that?'

'Free.'

'What?'

'My gift to you. And do not complain; they're hardly anything to me and your dad didn't leave me poor, so…'

Lizzie was silent for a moment. She felt guilty about the prospect of accepting such a gift, and with anyone else she might have offered an argument, but this was Florentina. Besides the fact that she was a formidable force when it came to any arguments and rarely lost them, Lizzie understood that sometimes her stepmother felt she had to make amends for the role she'd played in splitting Lizzie's parents up.

'I don't even know where to start choosing,' Lizzie said, looking down at the boxes again. 'They're all gorgeous.'

'Well, you must have some ideas on your colour schemes.'

'It's all a bit vague at the moment really.'

'Then how about something neutral?'

'Ugh, I hate neutral anything!'

'I know,' Florentina said with a laugh. 'Maybe start with the colours you absolutely don't want then and put them to one side? At least that will help.'

'Sounds good to me.'

Together they discarded all the beige, some dark greys and deep reds that Lizzie knew straight away would suck the light from any room, some navy blue that she thought would do the same and some pink florals that they both agreed were far too eighties.

As they laughed and chatted, going through what was left and discussing the virtues of each colour and design, Gracie arrived back. The first Lizzie was aware of it was a cold greeting from behind them and, instantly, the temperature of the air around them seemed to drop twenty degrees with it.

'Hello, Florentina…'

'You're back!' Lizzie said, rather obviously and with unmistakable guilt in her voice as she spun around to face her. Because, while Lizzie had been able to forgive and move on from Florentina's relationship and eventual marriage to her father, Gracie hadn't dealt with it quite so well, adopting her mother's outraged stance on the matter. It was perhaps because Gracie had never been quite so close to her dad as Lizzie was. After all, Lizzie and her dad were interested in a lot of the same things – they both loved quiet days on the coast or walking in the countryside, whereas Gracie loved the brash, brightness of city life. So it was only natural that Lizzie would be more desperate to hold onto any sort of contact with her dad and make compromises to do so that Gracie could just not accept.

'What are you doing here?' Gracie asked, addressing Florentina and ignoring Lizzie's statement.

'I came to see if Lizzie wanted any of these tiles.'

'I'm sure Lizzie can go to a shop when she's ready to buy tiles,' Gracie said crisply.

'Gracie…' Lizzie began. But Florentina stopped her with a slight gesture and forced a smile.

'It's alright… I should go anyway… somewhere to be… sales meeting…' Gathering the tiles that Lizzie hadn't yet dismissed into a single box, she loaded it into Lizzie's arms. 'Let me know which ones you choose and I'll sort it out for you.' She turned back to Gracie. 'It's good to see you looking so well. Are you on holiday?'

Gracie offered no reply but aimed a look at Lizzie that was capable of frying her on the spot.

'I'm going to put this food in the fridge,' she said.

With that, she marched to her car and lugged the bags of shopping out. Lizzie and Florentina watched as she took them to the caravan.

'I'm so sorry—' Lizzie began.

'I should have phoned ahead. I wanted to surprise you and I didn't realise…'

'Frank's left her,' Lizzie said, knowing that it was the only excuse she could offer that might cut her sister some slack for what amounted to unforgivable rudeness. 'She's really cut up about it.'

'So she's staying with you?'

'Until she gets back on her feet.'

'Good,' Florentina said firmly. 'Family is important at times like these.'

Lizzie paused, taking in the full meaning of her stepmother's statement. 'I suppose you haven't heard from…'

Florentina shook her head. 'My parents? No. Apparently it doesn't matter that your dad died, I still defied them by marrying him against their wishes. Screw them – that's what I say. My family are old-fashioned snobs. But I have lots of lovely friends instead…' She reached to embrace Lizzie. 'We'll get that drink another time, *cara mia*.'

'I'd like that.'

She watched as Florentina packed up the car, giving her a small smile and a wave as she pulled away from the house. And then she turned and stormed towards the caravan.

Gracie was sitting on the sofa with a magazine.

'There was absolutely no need for that!' Lizzie said, snatching the magazine away and throwing it onto the sofa.

Gracie's eyes blazed. 'I don't have to like her. Especially now that Dad's dead – she's not even proper family anymore.'

'Dad loved her. Maybe one of the ways we can respect his memory is by being kind to the woman he loved – did you ever think of that?'

'What's the point? He knew when he was alive we didn't like her so why would it be any different with him gone?'

'Gracie—'

'I know, I know… I'm out of order.' Gracie snatched the magazine up again. 'I can't help it. She's the reason we're all scattered to the four winds. We were happy before she turned up – a happy little family.'

'She never made you leave for London – you'd have gone anyway.'

'And James?'

'What about James?'

'Would he have become such a loser?'

'You can't blame Florentina for James's benders!'

'But if he'd stayed with Mum perhaps he wouldn't have—'

'He's twenty-six! How much longer could Mum have protected him? He's an adult and he's made his own choices, and you can't blame anyone for those but him. In fact, James would probably agree with me on that point.'

'He's too drunk most of the time to agree on anything.'

Lizzie mentally counted to ten and drew in a long breath. 'Gracie,' she said, struggling to even her tone, 'you're a guest in my house. Florentina was also a guest. Guests don't get to say which other guests are welcomed in – only I do that. Next time I won't send her away.'

'So you'd choose Florentina over your family?'

'I shouldn't be forced to make that choice! My own sister shouldn't be putting me in that situation! Don't forget that you're also here because I'm letting you stay.'

'You'd kick me out?'

'That's not what I'm saying!'

'That's what it sounds like to me!'

'I don't think anyone would blame me if I did – you're such a bloody pain in the arse!'

'What's that supposed to mean?'

'Do I actually have to tell you? Do you really need me to point out every annoying thing you do?'

Lizzie heaved in breaths, aware of how control was slipping away from her when she'd promised herself it wouldn't. If she lost her temper now she might say things it would be hard to take back, but she was close.

'Please do,' Gracie said with a scowl. 'Because I'd love to learn the secret of being perfect, and you clearly have it down to a T.'

Lizzie stomped to the kitchen area and filled the kettle. She didn't want a drink but it would be something to take her mind off the things she was dying to say to her sister. But Gracie didn't want to let go now the argument had started.

'I mean, you're so perfect and wonderful and lovely that I'm surprised nobody has written a musical about you. Lizzie Lovell, the wonder of Piriwick, who rescues all the lost souls. She skips down the street and birds flock to her and fluffy bunnies spread rose petals on the path as she walks with her perfect man and perfect life and who is oh so clever and never ever gets it wrong—'

Lizzie slammed the kettle down. 'Stop it!' she screeched. 'Nobody says I'm perfect!'

'Then stop acting like you are!' Gracie shouted.

'At least my boyfriend isn't shagging the intern!'

'At least mine wasn't going after sixth-formers like your ex was!'

Lizzie froze, tears pricking her eyes. It was clear that Gracie knew instantly she'd crossed the line, but perhaps Lizzie had been asking for it.

Gracie was silent. She opened the magazine at random and began to rip through the pages, so fast that she couldn't possibly be reading anything. But then she looked up. 'I don't like her but I'm sorry I upset you. That's all I can say.'

Lizzie recognised a white flag. 'Could you at least be civil if she comes again?'

'Do you want me to leave?'

'Of course I don't!'

'Because I will.'

'Where would you go?'

'What do you care?'

'I do care – you know I do.'

'Looks like it. I suppose if it was Florentina sitting here now it would be alright, wouldn't it? I don't suppose she'd be annoying you half as much.'

'Gracie, please… don't be like this. I'm not going to stop being nice to Florentina, but you're my sister and I love you, and I would never want to see you with nowhere to live.'

'Well you're hardly making me welcome pointing out all the reasons why you hate having me here, are you?'

'I don't hate having you here… but even you must realise that we're not kids anymore and it's going to be harder to live under the same roof than it used to be.'

'It's hard for me too,' Gracie said, and Lizzie could see the pain in the truth of that as she looked at her now. 'I've lost everything in the blink of an eye. Do you think it was easy to turn up at your caravan and ask for help? Don't you think I felt like a terrible failure? I knew I'd look pathetic to you. But I came here because you were the best person I could think of to help.'

Lizzie let out a sigh. 'I know all that. I'm sorry I shouted at you.'

Gracie wiped a hand across her eyes and nodded. 'I'm sorry I was horrible to Florentina. You know I can't ever like her, but if she comes again then I'll try not to be rude.'

Lizzie walked around the worktop and sat on the sofa next to her sister. 'Can I get a hug? Or do you still hate me too much?'

Gracie reached across and they embraced. It felt good, tensions draining away even as they were in each other's arms. Life was hard in the caravan together sometimes, but it had taken Gracie real guts to admit her humiliation and come to Lizzie for help, and Lizzie had failed to see just how much wind had been taken from her sister's sails. While she'd tried to be upbeat and optimistic, she must have been dying inside, just as Lizzie had been after Evan.

After a moment, Gracie broke free and Lizzie could see by her expression that she wanted to put the argument behind them too.

'Did you get everything you needed from the shops?' Lizzie asked, a question designed to draw a line under the incident and move them on.

'Apart from the cut of beef I wanted. I might have to go to Waitrose for that.'

'There's a farm shop not far from here – they have lovely meat. Want to take a walk down there before it closes?'

'How far is not far?'

'Would take about twenty minutes.'

'OK.'

Gracie yanked on a pair of trainers that had been lying under the table. They happened to be Lizzie's but in light of their current truce Lizzie didn't see the point in making a fuss about it. Instead, she headed to the bedroom to get another pair of shoes for herself and grabbed her keys, glad they'd managed to call time on their disagreement. Perhaps, once the weekend was over, it might be prudent to broach the delicate matter of Gracie's departure date. They would be into their second week together by then and really, if they were both being honest, that was more than enough of each other's company for either of them. There was a reason the Lovell siblings were scattered to the four winds, and right here in this caravan was a huge part of it.

Chapter Nine

Their spat could have soured the evening, but Lizzie was determined not to let things fester, and they'd cleared the air during their walk to the farm shop. Or rather, the air had cleared them, because the pleasant afternoon sun as they trekked down country lanes, their heads filled with the scents of wild grass and heady scarlet roadside poppies, had worn them both into a stupor of contentment, and the incident with Florentina hadn't been mentioned again. So by the time they'd got back to Magnolia Lane they were friends again, and Gracie's chatter was like machine-gun fire as she described what she was going to cook with their meat.

Now, twenty-four hours later, the fairy lights had been strung through the old pear trees, the canopy erected to shade the table and temporary stove, the patio heater was burning and the places were set with sparkling new glasses and dinnerware. Gracie stepped back with a satisfied smile as she inspected what she'd done and what Lizzie had been only too happy to let her take charge of, because a busy Gracie was a happy one. Then she disappeared into the caravan to chop some vegetables.

Bang on time, Jude arrived with Charlie, and after a kiss which Lizzie wished could have lasted a lot longer, he was led to the clearing beneath the trees.

'Wow!' He ran his gaze over the preparations for dinner. 'You didn't tell me this was an actual event. I feel woefully underdressed.'

'Don't.' Lizzie laughed. 'It's not an event; it's just that my party organiser got carried away. Don't think you'll get this kind of treatment every time you visit me.'

'I won't,' Jude said, giving her a grin that made her heart gallop.

'This is nice,' Charlie said, mouth open and eyes transfixed on the twinkling lights and pristine place settings, as if he'd been transported to a fairy grotto. And Lizzie had to admit that perhaps they had gone a tad over the top for what was supposed to be an informal get-together. But Gracie had been revelling in the whole process so much, and she'd barely mentioned Frank while she'd been absorbed in her plans, so Lizzie had thought it easier to let all that slide, content that her sister was enjoying herself.

Just then, Gracie emerged from the caravan with an armful of candles.

'Oh, hello!' she called. But then she stopped as she focused on Jude, seemed to stare for a split second before checking herself, shaking her head and smoothing her puzzled expression into a smile. The whole episode had been brief, though not brief enough for Lizzie to miss it, and she could see by the expression on his face that it had clearly thrown Jude too.

'This is my sister, Gracie,' she said cautiously. 'And Gracie, this is Jude and Charlie.'

'Hello!' Charlie called with the same excited wave he had given Lizzie the first time he'd come knocking on her caravan door.

Gracie smiled. 'Pleased to meet you. And you too, Jude… Don't mind me; get comfortable at the table. I want to get these candles going – they keep the midges away, you know.'

'I could do that,' Jude said, stepping forward to take them from her. Gracie looked as if she might refuse but then seemed to think better of it.

'Thank you; that would be lovely.'

Jude took the candles and, with direction from Gracie, began to dot them at strategic points around the table before lighting them. In a matter of minutes, the air was filled with the sharpness of citrus and lemongrass, which wove into the existing scents of freshly cut grass and the night-blooming honeysuckle around the old fencing.

Charlie hovered at the fringes of the activity, suddenly and uncharacteristically shy.

'Why don't you sit down?' Lizzie asked gently. 'You can have a drink if you like while we get everything ready.'

'Or you could help?' Jude cut in, firing a glance at Lizzie that asked for approval.

'Why not?' Lizzie said. 'It's not the norm to set your guests to work, but if you want to get stuck in you can.'

Charlie, normally needing no encouragement to undertake a task, shook his head uncertainly. Lizzie wondered if the apparent formality of the setting might be putting him off, despite it not really being that formal at all. Whatever it was, he wasn't quite his usual enthusiastic self.

'Don't worry,' Lizzie said. 'Sit down and I'll get drinks.'

Jude joined Charlie at the table and rubbed his back to reassure him while Lizzie went to the fridge in the caravan. In the tiny kitchen space, Gracie was unwrapping slabs of glistening steak from sheets of greaseproof paper.

'What do you think?' Lizzie asked as she reached into the fridge for bottles of juice and wine.

'He seems nice,' Gracie said, but Lizzie immediately detected some unspoken caveat to that statement.

'I'm glad you approve,' she replied, choosing to ignore it. Instead, she grabbed her bottles and left Gracie slamming a mallet down onto the steaks. Though it might threaten to, Lizzie wasn't going to let whatever random misgiving Gracie seemed to have about Jude and Charlie ruin her night. Perhaps her sister was still feeling vulnerable after her break-up with Frank and their recent argument about Florentina, more than Lizzie had realised, and perhaps her trust levels of men in general were pretty close to zero. It was true that Lizzie's had been just as low after her split from Evan. Perhaps Gracie was even a little resentful that Lizzie had found someone who made her happy at a time when she had just lost her man. Frank hadn't been a bit interested in winning Gracie back, and Lizzie suspected that had wounded her sister more than if he'd tried to lie his way back into her affections as Evan had once done with her.

More than once Gracie had been tempted to contact him, but Lizzie had talked her out of it, citing all the reasons why it was a bad idea. Her sister had taken the advice grudgingly, though Lizzie suspected that she might have been stalking him on social media because Gracie seemed to know an awful lot about what he was up to and even more about what the intern he'd had the affair with was up to. Lizzie didn't want to ask, and if Gracie had wanted to tell her she would have, so Lizzie had left it at that. All she could do was be there for Gracie, and she was doing her best in that regard. She knew nights like this would help. Gracie really sparkled in social situations, and nothing made her happier than playing hostess. Once the dust settled and she got into her stride, Lizzie was sure her sister would find this evening a welcome distraction from her woes – as long as everything went to plan. That wasn't always quite so easy to predict...

✻

As Lizzie had hoped, Gracie seemed to rally. She proved herself a skilful and entertaining chef as she cooked steak to order at the outside griddle (and a burger for Charlie), while Lizzie dealt with the side dishes. Afterwards, she grilled slices of pineapple sprinkled with brown sugar and topped them off with whipped cream, and Jude declared it the best thing he'd ever eaten. Lizzie looked on with pride at her talented sister. Growing up, she'd always felt Gracie was more capable at pretty much everything she turned her hand to and this evening had proved it – Lizzie was sure she couldn't have pulled off such a cool and fun dinner party with quite the same panache. She tried not to dwell on Gracie's first reaction to seeing Jude, even though part of her was desperate to ask. Asking, however, might well lead to another argument and, as much as it bothered Lizzie, there were all sorts of reasons why she wanted tonight to be a success. If Gracie was going to spill the beans, it would have to wait.

After dinner they sat in the latticed shadows of the old pear trees with blankets on their knees as they chatted, getting to know each other, until Charlie began to yawn and Jude stood up.

'It's been amazing but I'd better get my brother to bed. He's been up since the crack of dawn.'

'Why?' Gracie asked.

Jude smiled. 'He was excited about tonight.'

'Oh, Charlie!' Lizzie said with a fond chuckle. 'You've been here tons of times now.'

'I think maybe there was a slight difference tonight,' Gracie reminded her, which only made Lizzie laugh again.

'OK, point taken. Sorry, Gracie!'

Jude and Charlie both took their leave, Charlie with a warm hug and Jude with a kiss given in the shadows of the trees while Gracie and

Charlie tried to pretend they weren't looking. And then they left and it was just Lizzie and her sister again.

They shared the last of the wine in comfortable silence, Gracie insistent that it was pointless leaving the last drops in the bottle to turn to vinegar. The clear sky glinted above them with stars in numbers it had always been impossible to see whenever Lizzie had looked up from her house back in town, and the breeze rustled through fields of wild grass and trees heavy with summer foliage. But as Lizzie began to feel sleepy and wondered if she could be bothered to go to bed, or whether she might just stay where she was in front of the heater all night, Gracie finally made a move, stifling a yawn of her own.

'This stuff won't clear itself,' she said, gathering up the dirty glasses.

'It'll wait a minute,' Lizzie said, stretching like a cat. 'Talk to me, Gracie. We never get times like this anymore.'

'I should think you're sick of me by now. I've done nothing but talk to you this past week.'

'I know, but I don't feel as if you've actually told me anything.'

'What does that mean?'

'There's been plenty of crying over Frank, insulting Frank, wishing all sorts of foul mishaps on Frank, but it's all been about Frank. What about *you?*'

'There's nothing much to say about me – everything the same as ever. Decent job, enough money, hoping for eventual marriage to a man who won't turn out to be a complete shit.'

'You might not have that decent job for much longer.'

Gracie was pensive as she took another sip of her wine. 'Maybe I really don't want it anymore anyway. After all, when I go back I have to face Frank, don't I?'

'You might have to face him sooner or later regardless. Don't you need to go to the flat and get more of your things?'

'I don't think any of it is stuff I really need.'

Lizzie doubted that was true but she remained silent on the matter.

'Maybe we should talk about you instead,' Gracie said. 'I hardly know *you* these days.'

'Don't be silly.'

'It's true. This place…' Gracie swept a hand towards the broad shadow of the construction site. 'Where did this suddenly come from? The need to live out here? To pour everything you have into a wreck? It's such a huge gamble.'

'I don't see it as a gamble.'

'You've said yourself you don't know whether you'll run out of money before it's anywhere near finished. I'd call that a gamble.'

Lizzie shrugged. 'When Dad died I just realised how short and precious life was. If you dream of something, why just dream? Why not make it happen? If you fail, at least you can say you tried instead of wondering what might have been.'

'OK,' Gracie said slowly, clearly not seeing Lizzie's logic. 'And Jude. You like him?'

'Of course I do. But Jude is separate from all this – incidental. I met Jude because I was here. He's certainly not part of the gamble you think I'm taking.'

'And you're certain about him? His intentions?'

'Of course I am.'

'Only, after what happened…'

'Not Evan again. Can't I be allowed to forget about him? I'm not stupid enough to be caught out like that again.'

'That's good.'

Lizzie picked up the placemats and together they began to walk back to the caravan. 'So go on, because I know you want to tell me. Why did you have a moment when you first met him?'

'A moment? Did I?'

'You know you did. Like you already knew him from somewhere.'

'Oh, that,' Gracie said, with what seemed to Lizzie forced carelessness. 'I thought I recognised him.'

'What? Any idea where it might be from?'

'Not really.'

'Might it be recently?'

'Perhaps…' Gracie said carefully.

'You *do* know. Tell me, what's there to be cagey about?'

'I saw a man at the supermarket the other day who looked very like him. Not with Charlie, though, and you said he goes everywhere with Charlie.'

'He could have been without Charlie, I suppose,' Lizzie said. 'They're not joined at the hip, and I know he spends a lot of time with Harriet.' Why was she suddenly so uneasy about this? Why did she feel such a pressing need to get to the bottom of this mystery?

'Harriet?'

'His ex. The girl he has a son with.'

'Hmm.' Gracie was uncharacteristically short of a reply and Lizzie's stomach dropped.

'Was he with Harriet at the supermarket?'

'He was with a woman and a child. I expect that was her.'

'I expect they go out a lot together.'

'Do you really think that's OK?'

'They have a child together.'

'But she doesn't need him to go shopping with her just because they have a child together.'

'He's just like that. He likes to help people.'

'They looked very friendly.'

'They are good friends.'

'Lizzie…' Gracie paused. 'They looked like a couple.'

'What makes you say that?' Lizzie asked sharply.

Gracie shrugged.

'Gracie, you can't serve me half a tale! If you know something or you've seen something then I deserve to know it too! What makes you say that they looked like a couple? Were they kissing? Holding hands or something?'

'No, of course not,' Gracie said, looking a little more uneasy in her evaluation now. 'They were just… close. You know, comfortable with each other. Laughing a lot. Like couples do.'

'They're old friends; I suppose they have a lot of history and they're comfortable with each other because of that,' Lizzie said firmly, though her performance of conviction was more for herself than Gracie. 'Harriet spent some time with us at the river recently and I could see for myself that they get along brilliantly.'

'And they used to be a couple as well, didn't they?' Gracie asked. 'Perhaps…'

Lizzie shook her head. 'They're not now. Harriet's got a new boyfriend and Jude says she's really into him. Harriet and Jude are just not interested in each other in that way anymore.'

But she paused, her gaze suddenly concentrated on the scene of the half-cleared table just visible through the caravan window, warm lights bathing the space, the candles on the table now burned down to stumps, and she felt her world shift, just a little. She'd know, wouldn't she? She'd know if Jude was keeping secrets? She wasn't stupid enough to get caught out again – that's what she'd just told Gracie.

She gave her head a tiny shake. Surely Charlie would have given the game away if there was anything to know, even if Jude was trying to hide anything from her. Charlie couldn't keep a secret if his life depended on it. Jude and Harriet had been close that day at the river, but it was nothing more than friendship. And there was Damon too. Harriet might have been good friends with Jude, but she had a new boyfriend now.

'Listen – ignore me,' Gracie said, forcing a smile. 'Frank's done nothing for my faith in men. I'm sure if Jude says it's all over then it is. And I didn't see any actual physical contact as such…'

'But if you thought I could be wrong? If you had any doubts—'

'I'd tell you – of course I would. I'm sure it's fine.'

Lizzie nodded slowly. Gracie studied her for a moment, but then she got up.

'We'd better get cleaned up or every fox for miles around will be sniffing round after the leftovers,' she said.

Lizzie watched as she went outside and started to gather up the detritus of their dinner party. Did Gracie think she'd said more on the matter than she ought to? Did she think she ought to keep her nose out? It wasn't like her if that was the case – Gracie usually had an opinion and she usually loved to express it. Maybe Lizzie needed to hear it this time too, but she wasn't sure she wanted to push it. It might lead to another disagreement, and there was no telling where this one might end. Even if it didn't lead to an argument between her and Gracie, it might just raise doubts about Jude that were unfair and unfounded. She'd talk to him again, ask him if he was being completely straight with her about Harriet. He might not like it, and he might be annoyed that he was constantly being asked to prove himself, but it was the only way to put Lizzie's mind at rest once and for all. She'd already been burned by one man; she wasn't about to let it happen again.

Chapter Ten

Lizzie dialled Jude's number and picked at a loose thread on her sweatshirt as she waited for him to pick up. Through the window, she could see her builder, Tim, having an animated discussion with one of his team. At least, the worker was being animated – Tim would fail to look animated even if he was plugged into a live socket. As she watched them, a vague dread took hold that they were discussing another problem with the build. But then they seemed to reach an agreement and the worker went away looking happy. Lizzie allowed herself the briefest sigh of relief, but then the phone was answered.

'Hello. This is Charlie speaking.'

'Charlie!' Lizzie said. 'How are you?'

'I'm very well. Who are you?'

'It's Lizzie.'

'Oh. You sound funny.'

'That's probably because you don't usually hear me on the telephone. Is Jude there?'

'Yes.'

'Can he come to the phone?'

'No, I don't think so.'

'Why not?'

'He's running after Harriet. It's his turn to be it.'

'Running after Harriet?' she repeated.

'Yes,' Charlie replied. 'We're playing.'

'Is Artie playing too?'

'Oh yes,' Charlie said cheerfully.

'So you're all playing tag? Is Damon there too?'

'Tig,' Charlie said. 'Not tag.'

'Yes, sorry… it's all the same to me. Is it just Jude and Harriet with you?'

'But this is tig.'

'Yes, sorry, Charlie. What about Damon?'

'Artie's here.'

'Yes.'

'Not Damon.'

Lizzie couldn't decide whether this information made her more or less uneasy. 'Could you just get Jude for me?'

'But he's it.'

'I know he is but I need to speak to him.'

'Shall I get him?'

'Yes please.'

Lizzie caught the snatch of a woman's laughter in the background. Though the fun and games were clearly all for Artie's benefit, the situation was hardly helping to settle Lizzie's current doubts. If anything, it was stoking the flames of jealousy and mistrust higher than ever. Jude had never pretended he wasn't still good friends with Harriet, but Lizzie was beginning to realise that she was struggling with the concept more than she'd even admitted to herself. Since her conversation with Gracie the night before, it was like her eyes had suddenly been opened. When she woke, the first thing she'd wanted to do was call him and clear the air, but then Tim and his team had arrived, and Gracie had needed her, and before she'd known it half the morning had gone.

Before she'd been able to say anything more, the phone went dead. Charlie must have somehow ended the call.

Lizzie's finger went to the screen to repeat the call, but then she paused, her gaze going to the window again, wrestling anew with a monster that was getting stronger with every minute that went by. She'd never been wronged by Harriet but she could quite cheerfully punch her in the face right now.

They looked like a couple. That was what Gracie had said. What if Harriet was always going to be the most important woman in Jude's life? What if anyone else would always be a poor second? Who had ended the relationship? Lizzie had never asked Jude because she'd felt it showed distrust on her part, but now she wished she had. What if Harriet had ended it and Jude was still in love with her?

The phone rang and she looked to see his name on the screen. She swiped to receive it.

'Lizzie?' Jude sounded out of breath. 'Charlie said you wanted me.'

'I'm sorry to call in the day. I thought you might be working, but I just wanted—'

'I'm taking the morning off. Artie's visiting.'

'I know; Charlie said.'

'We had a great night last night, by the way.'

'We did too.'

'Tell Gracie thanks from us both.'

'You thanked her enough last night.'

'Yes.' Jude laughed. 'Well, you can thank her again. She's an amazing cook.'

'I will.'

Lizzie fell into silence. What was she supposed to say now? How could they have the conversation she'd wanted to have if Harriet and

Artie were right there with them – everyone playing together and having a lovely time? Enter Lizzie the green-eyed witch who couldn't keep her suspicious thoughts in check and made sure everyone else's day was ruined by airing them.

'Are you OK?' Jude asked.

'Yes,' Lizzie replied, forcing a bright tone. 'I just wanted to make sure you'd had a good time, that was all. And maybe ask if you wanted to do it again.'

'We'd love to do it again. Just let us know when.'

'Is Harriet there?'

Lizzie couldn't help it. Her question sounded needy and wheedling, but it came out anyway.

'She's here with Artie.' Jude paused. Perhaps something was clicking into place. 'Are you busy right now?' he asked.

'I'm supposed to be working.'

'I was just thinking it might be good for you to come over and meet Artie… It doesn't matter if you're busy, of course…'

Lizzie tussled with an answer. She ought to meet Jude's son and she wanted to, but that little boy was also a flesh-and-blood reminder of what Jude had once had with Harriet. She'd have to one day, of course. But today was definitely not the day.

'That would have been lovely,' she said. 'Another time, maybe? Things are kind of busy right now and…' Her reply trailed off.

'Of course,' Jude said, though Lizzie suspected that her excuse had sounded as lame to him as she herself knew it was.

Lizzie heard Charlie's voice, calling him, and Harriet's voice joining in.

'So you're OK?' Jude asked.

'Oh yes. You get back to your… whatever it is you're playing with Artie.'

'Oh, we're all playing. I think the adults are taking it more seriously than he is,' Jude said with a laugh.

'Fab,' Lizzie said, beginning to feel the smile she was forcing twitch and crack under the pressure. 'Have fun. I'll speak to you later.'

'OK, bye. Don't work too hard.'

'Bye.'

Lizzie ended the call. She needed to offload. She needed to find Gracie.

∗

'You'll never be able to settle if you don't get to the bottom of it,' Gracie said, pulling the spoon out of the ice-cream tub and sticking it into her mouth. Then she licked it clean before wagging it at Lizzie. 'I can't believe you haven't cleared this up with him already.'

'I have. I mean, I thought I had. But then you went and told me that last night.'

'So it's my fault your boyfriend's having his cake and eating it?'

'He's not. I don't think…'

'Well, there's no smoke without fire.'

'Will you stop it with the proverbs?' Lizzie stabbed her own spoon into the tub. It was hardly a nutritious lunch but desperate times called for desperate measures. 'It's not really helping. And you said last night that it was only a vague feeling you had and that you were probably wrong and I shouldn't take any notice.'

'Oh, Lizzie, if you believe me when I say those sorts of things then you really will believe anything!'

Lizzie swallowed a squeal of frustration. Really, Gracie ought to come with a translation manual because, otherwise, how was anyone supposed to work out what she meant when she said anything?

'So you're saying I ought to be worried?'

'Yes.'

'But last night you said the opposite!'

'But last night you hadn't told me he was messing about with her having a great time at his house – which he never bothered to tell you he was planning to do. And that it appears to be a regular thing.'

'Does he have to tell me everything he's planning to do? And does it matter if it's a regular thing?'

'When it involves her, perhaps yes.'

'I can't ask him about it – how crazy and possessive would that make me sound?'

'Well, then I don't really know why you've come to ask me about it. I'm offering you my opinion, and if you don't want me to be truthful then you shouldn't have asked.'

'But you never said any of this last night.'

'Last night you were completely in love with him and you wouldn't have wanted to hear it.'

'I was not and I would have.'

'I think you are a little bit in love with him and that's why you're so bothered.'

'Nobody wants to play second fiddle to an ex. Being in love has nothing to do with it.'

'I think you should cut your losses and leave before it gets too messy. Once you're really smitten it will be horrible having to break it off.'

'Who says I want to break it off?'

'Well, you will if he's still close to this Harriet girl, won't you? You've just said you don't want to play second fiddle to her.'

'I don't, but I don't want to break it off.'

Gracie sighed and shoved her spoon in the ice-cream pot. 'You need to make up your mind.'

'But she's always going to be lurking around if they have a child together, isn't she? I can't do anything about that.'

'True. But then you need to tell him straight that you need boundaries.'

'What kind of boundaries?'

'Between him and Harriet. It's all very well him having access to his son, as long as he isn't having too much access to the mother. He needs to show you that he's keeping it to the minimal, appropriate contact – just enough to parent and no more.'

'OK. How does he do that?'

'How should I know? That's for him to work out if he's serious about you. I'd give him an ultimatum. Either he does that or it's over.'

'I can't ask him to stop being friends with Harriet.'

'I really think you'll have to. I don't see any other way of settling this.'

In the back of her mind, a little voice was telling Lizzie that perhaps Gracie's advice was coloured by her own recent experience with Frank. The problem was, the voice was hardly a whisper at all, and it certainly wasn't loud enough to compete with the unreasonable roar of her own insecurities. Wouldn't it be so much easier to be with Jude if Harriet was out of the picture? Could she ask him to make that kind of sacrifice? Though if he cared for Lizzie at all, then surely he'd understand her need for reassurance?

But then she shook her head and stood her spoon in the tub.

'No,' she said, getting up from the table. 'I have to trust him. If I can't, then I haven't moved on from Evan at all, and if I haven't moved on from him there's no future for me and Jude anyway.'

Gracie gave a nonchalant shrug. 'OK. But don't say I didn't warn you.'

Chapter Eleven

Lizzie didn't sleep well. She hadn't called Jude the previous evening and he hadn't called her, but she wondered if that was perhaps a good thing, given that the conversation she'd had with Gracie was still fresh in her mind. Despite this, it also forced her to muse, more than once, on the possibility that he hadn't phoned her because he'd been busy entertaining Harriet all evening. Hadn't Charlie told Lizzie that Harriet was Jude's girlfriend when they'd first met? It wasn't the case but it was easy to see how it might look that way if she was always there. But then, where did that leave Damon? Surely he'd be as unhappy about the possibility of that scenario as Lizzie was? Surely he would have something to say?

She'd forced herself to work this morning, despite not feeling up to it, because she had a job for a cruise company that she really needed to finish, and then, instead of having lunch, she'd dared to look at her accounts. Now, an hour later, she closed the lid on her laptop and rubbed at her temples. She'd known her savings had been disappearing quickly enough, but once she'd sat down to face the arduous task of working out what was owed to who and how much she still needed to set aside for essential repair work, even she'd been shocked at how depleted they actually were. She might well be living in the mill by Christmas, but there would be no carpets, no paint on the walls, no interior doors and no window furnishings. As for Christmas itself, she might just stretch to a cut-price chicken for dinner but that was only if she abandoned the idea of a flushing toilet in the bathroom.

Gracie placed a cup of tea on the table next to her. 'I thought I'd make you one while I was getting mine.'

Lizzie looked up to thank her but then frowned. 'Have you only just got up?' she asked, looking into a face that was uncharacteristically grey and shadowed and realising that she hadn't actually noticed Gracie's absence that morning. She'd been so absorbed in what she'd been doing that she hadn't noticed much at all, apparently. But she was noticing now, and she could see that her sister was far from her usual bouncy self. It was true that two weeks on she still wasn't over Frank, but as her default setting was usually Tigger on sherbet, even taking that into consideration she wasn't back on form. At least, she didn't look it.

Gracie ran a hand over her stomach. 'Something I ate, I think. I thought I'd try to sleep it off.'

'We both had the chicken last night and I'm fine.'

'Maybe you've got a stronger constitution than me,' Gracie said. 'I knew I shouldn't have bought that stuff out of the reduced fridge but you insisted.'

'The stuff in that fridge is fine – the dates don't mean anything.'

'Yes, they do – they mean don't eat it.'

'We ate it *in* date, though. It wasn't set to go off at midnight.'

'Still…'

'Maybe you've picked up a virus.'

'Maybe, but I don't see how. I've only been here and you're fine.'

'I may yet get it.'

'You might be a carrier. Like those people who gave everyone else the Black Death but didn't get it themselves.'

'Wow – thanks for that.' Lizzie picked up her tea and took a sip. She regarded Gracie over the top of her mug. 'Are you sure it's nothing else bothering you?'

'Yes – I'm just under the weather. I'll be fine.'

Lizzie didn't felt entirely convinced by the denial, but with enough problems of her own to think about she let the matter go at that. However, there was something else she needed to bring up, though that conversation promised to be awkward. Gracie had been with her for two weeks and she hadn't shown any signs of budging. As for time off from her job, Lizzie had no idea when Gracie was thinking of going back to work, but she couldn't imagine that whatever leave arrangements Gracie had in place could last for that much longer either.

She put her cup down and cleared her throat. 'Gracie—'

'Lizzie—'

They both began to speak over one another. Lizzie gave a tight smile. 'You first.'

'Promise you won't shout?'

Lizzie said nothing, but the opening gambit didn't fill her with confidence. If Gracie had the slightest notion that what she was about to say would cause Lizzie to shout, then Lizzie probably wasn't going to like it. It was Gracie's turn to clear her throat and take a deep breath.

'I've quit my job.' She wrapped her arms around herself and gave Lizzie a beseeching look of a quality not seen since the time she'd accidentally knocked Lizzie's favourite snow globe from the bedroom shelf aged fourteen, where it had, rather predictably, smashed into microscopic pieces that they'd still been finding under the bed five years later.

'You've done *what?*'

'You said you wouldn't shout.'

'Believe me, this isn't me shouting. Why would you do that?'

'I'm getting out of the rat race,' Gracie said, her tone taking a defensive note. 'Like you.'

'I was never in the rat race! What even is a rat race? Isn't that some crap people say when they want to excuse the fact that they can't be bothered to work?'

Gracie pouted. 'Don't be like that. It's not just you who can make fresh starts and take chances, you know.'

'But... my circumstances are entirely different from yours!'

'How?'

'Of course they are!'

Gracie gave a nonchalant shrug that she would have known of old would irritate the hell out of Lizzie when they were having a serious debate. 'Perhaps. But it's my life and this is what I've decided to do.'

'OK,' Lizzie said, drawing a slow breath and fixing her sister with a steady gaze. 'So, good for you if it's what you really want. Is it, though?'

'Absolutely.'

'In which case, congratulations.' Lizzie took up her mug again. 'What now?'

'See, you're giving me that disapproving voice.'

'What else do you want from me? I'm doing my best to be understanding about this, but I can't help it if I think you're making a mistake.'

'How come when you do it, it's breaking free, but when I do it, I'm making a terrible mistake?'

Lizzie sighed. 'OK, sorry then. I'm listening now and I'm not judging. So, what are you going to do?'

'I haven't really thought that far ahead.'

'Of course you haven't,' Lizzie shot back. She'd said she wasn't going to judge, but it was hard not to.

'It's alright for you. You're so happy here, and I was so miserable in London—'

'You were happy before Frank dumped you, so is this more about Frank than your job?'

'Frank was only part of it.'

'And you think what I have here is the answer?'

'You're happy.'

'I wouldn't go that far,' Lizzie said, her mind going back to the spreadsheet of expenses she'd just closed.

'But you can slow down, enjoy life.'

Lizzie raised her eyebrows. 'With this old wreck of a mill to renovate and a living to earn on top of that?'

'You know what I mean. It's not the same as having a demanding job.'

'My hustle and bustle is just different, that's all. I still have responsibilities and deadlines and all that stuff. I still have to work.'

'I know, but they're calmer, less fraught.'

'That's only how it looks from the outside. Everybody else's life always looks better from the outside.'

Gracie sat down next to Lizzie. She seemed defeated, and despite everything, Lizzie hated to see her low.

'Do you have any plans at all?' she asked, her tone softer now.

'I just needed something to change, you know?'

'That's all very well, but there's a lot to think about. Like, where are you going to live with no job to pay rent?'

'Well, I had thought…'

OK, here it comes…

'I had thought,' Gracie continued, 'I might be able to stay here with you for a while longer. Just until I work out what I want to do with my life instead of advertising.'

'I'm just not sure that's practical, all things considered.'

'You've had enough of me…'

'I didn't say that.'

'Perhaps Mum will have me for a while.'

Lizzie almost spat out her tea. 'You said yourself you'd kill each other inside a week.'

'Well, that would be two less people for you to fret about,' Gracie said with a faint smile.

'I'd love to say you can stay with me,' Lizzie replied, but only with the conviction of one who can make an offer knowing it wasn't possible to make it good, 'but I don't think I'll have the caravan for much longer and, with the best will in the world, I just don't think you're cut out to slum it in a damp, draughty old windmill.'

Gracie frowned.

'Money's running a bit short,' Lizzie replied in answer to her sister's silent question. 'I think I might have cocked up on the calculations.'

'Everyone always cocks up on the budget,' Gracie said with a solemn nod. 'I've never seen an episode of Grand Designs yet where they didn't have to mortgage a kidney to get some bespoke patio doors shipped in from Germany. So you're selling the caravan?'

'It had occurred to me.'

'What will that raise?'

'Not enough.'

'A ballpark?'

'I don't know. Maybe about ten thousand.'

'Is it enough to finish?'

'I don't know that either.'

'Will the bank give you more money?'

'I don't think so.'

'Oh.'

Lizzie picked up her tea again and took a sip. God, Gracie could cook but she certainly couldn't make a decent cup of tea.

'Couldn't you go and live with Mum until this place is ready to live in?' Gracie said into the gap.

'I had thought about that, but I don't want to mess her around. Besides, it's a long drive to do two or three or even four times a day. I'd rather be on site if I can.'

'It's only forty minutes or so.'

'More like fifty – an hour when the traffic is bad. And that's each time. That soon mounts up to a lot of petrol.'

'I see. So you're staying here come what may?'

'Yes.'

'Sleeping in a survival shelter fashioned from clematis branches and turf from the garden centre?'

'Sleeping in a relatively sound corner of the mill. When I say corner, I mean…'

'Yes.' Gracie smiled.

'I was going to ask Tim if there's any chance the workmen could concentrate on a couple of rooms I could use while they carry on with the rest of the build.'

'Will you have everything you need? Like flushing toilets and stuff?'

'Probably not everything just yet, but I can make do for a few weeks.'

'Weeks?'

'OK, more likely months. Don't cite Grand Designs again – I know these things always run over.'

'So you sell your caravan. What if *that* money runs out?'

'Then I'll have to mortgage a kidney.'

'So it looks as though we might both have to go home to Mother Dearest.' Gracie gave a wry smile. 'Won't she just love that?'

'Actually, I think she probably would. I'm not sure how long it would last before she changed her mind.'

'Well, I don't suppose I've got a lot of choice, even if you have,' Gracie said. 'Although I don't envy your alternative much either…' But then there was a moment of illumination and Lizzie immediately wondered whether she ought to be worried about the look on her face.

'Here's a thought,' Gracie said. 'Don't dismiss it out of hand. What if I bought your caravan and we both carried on living here? You'd have your money and I'd have somewhere to live that I actually liked.'

'Where would you get that kind of money?'

Gracie gave a slight shrug. 'I said I had a little put by.'

'That much?'

'I could get it. Maybe I'd even ask Frank; it's the least he can do for tossing me out like garbage.'

'OK…' Lizzie said slowly, 'but it would still only be temporary.'

'Of course. I couldn't stay camped in your garden for the rest of my life. It's only until you're ready to move into the mill.'

'And then what?'

'Then I'd sell the caravan myself and use the deposit for a flat or something.'

'I'd imagine you'd make a loss rather than a profit,' Lizzie said doubtfully. 'Caravans hardly increase in value the more they're used. You might lose a lot.'

'I know I'd lose a little money on it, but it might not be as bad as you think. And it would probably only amount to the same as I'd pay in rent on a flat in London for a couple of months anyway.'

'You've really got access to that kind of money?' Lizzie asked. She was still unconvinced by Gracie's proposal, but she was fast running out of reasonable arguments against it.

'I think I could get it.'

'You quit your job, remember? What about money after you've spent all your savings on the caravan? Honestly, this just makes me even more doubtful that quitting such a good job is the right thing to do. If you're still in your notice period you could withdraw your resignation if you wanted to.'

'I could, but I'm not going to.'

'You really might want to think that over.'

'I really don't want to.'

Lizzie drank the last of her tea and set down the mug.

'So, what do you think?' Gracie asked.

'You really want to buy my caravan and live out here with me?'

'Absolutely.'

'You know how mad that sounds?'

'I know.'

Lizzie sat back and appraised her sister. If she let Gracie do this, she'd almost certainly come to regret it. They both would. However, it would solve the problem of her dwindling funds without the need to get into more debt. At least for a short while anyway. She let out a sigh and Gracie, recognising that she'd given in, clapped her hands together.

'Brilliant,' she squeaked, looking like her normal self again. 'It's going to be brilliant!'

'You know you think this caravan is crap?' Lizzie reminded her. 'I don't think brilliant is what you'll be saying in three months when the weather starts to turn cold.'

'Oh, but your place will be ready and by then I'll be away some-where new!'

Gracie hugged Lizzie, who gave a weak smile. If only things went to plan like that in the real world.

Chapter Twelve

'Oh my God, what is wrong with you?'

Lizzie frowned down the phone at James. He could be so irritating at times, so facetious, so damn… right. He'd never been blessed with common sense where his own life was concerned, and half the time he didn't know what day it was, but when it came to family matters he was often depressingly, annoyingly perceptive.

'I suppose you got railroaded into saying yes,' he continued with a lazy chuckle.

'You know what Gracie's like,' Lizzie said, and her voice had the same whine she used to adopt when they were kids and Gracie would steal her favourite doll. 'Once she gets an idea in her head, she sort of hypnotises you with her enthusiasm until you think it's a great idea too. Once you've said yes the magic wears off and you see the plan with all its flaws, but by then it's too late.'

'I couldn't have put it better myself. Why do you think I work so hard to avoid her?'

'You work hard to avoid us all.'

'Well, I'm not the one complaining because I'm stuck with Gracie, am I?'

'I'm not complaining exactly.'

'Then why did you phone me?'

'You're my brother. Can't I phone my own brother for a chat?'

'You could if the first subject you decided to rant about wasn't Gracie.'

'I didn't rant.'

'OK, so you were getting your frustrations off your chest.'

'They're not frustrations either. They're… misgivings.'

'OK. *Misgivings*. Fine, good. Glad we got that cleared up. So where is she now?'

'Out. She seems to think the caravan needs more candles.'

'And does it?'

'If we were thinking of performing Catholic mass later tonight, then yeah. Otherwise, the light switches work just fine.'

James gave a warm laugh at the other end of the line. Lizzie suddenly wished she could see him. He was the black sheep of the family, and he caused everyone nothing but anxiety and heartache, but he was her brother and she loved him. She found him funny too, and she missed his irreverent take on life, because his not caring sometimes had a way of making her care a little less too.

'OK.' Lizzie twisted a loose thread on her sweatshirt. 'The subject of Gracie is closed. Tell me what you've been up to.'

'I dunno. Nothing much.'

'But you're looking after yourself?' she asked.

'Of course I am. Big boy now, you know.'

'It's just that… you don't phone me—'

'Not this again…'

'Or Mum either. Or Gracie. We worry, you know. If we nag you it's only because we worry.'

'There's no need to worry. I just get too busy. I think about it and I think I'll phone you, and then I get busy and I forget. Sorry.'

'But you can see it from our point of view? You live so far away and we want to know you're OK.'

'So does Gracie – at least she did – but you don't nag her to call.'

'That's different.'

'How is it different?'

'She had Frank so we knew that even if Gracie couldn't phone us, he'd phone us if there was any trouble.'

'Unless he was the trouble, you mean.'

'Well, yes, that. But at least she had someone looking out for her and…'

'I'm a sad singleton?'

'That's not what I'm saying.'

'I've got mates to look out for me.'

'But they're…'

'What?'

'Well… it's not the same, is it?'

'They're more reliable than Frank turned out to be.'

'Well…' Lizzie cast around for a change of subject that would pull the conversation back from the dark territory it had drifted into. 'When are you coming to see my mill?'

'Said no one ever.' He laughed. 'Who the hell buys a windmill? What are you – Rod Hull? And you all think I'm the weird sibling.'

'It's Dad's windmill. You know how much he loved this place, how he used to talk about it.'

'That doesn't make it a good idea. There's a reason Dad looked but never bought and that's because he was a sane man. Probably the only sane person in the family… no wonder he ran off with Florentina.'

'That means you're not coming?' Lizzie asked, choosing to ignore the jibes.

'I would but it costs money. I don't have thousands to spare like you do.'

'I don't have thousands, not now.'

'That's because you throw it away on stupid things like windmills. They must have seen you coming a mile off.'

Lizzie could have retorted that at least she didn't drink all her money but the phone call would have ended right there.

'Maybe I'll try and see you in the next couple of weeks,' she said instead.

'You can if you want. I expect you're busy, though.'

'Not too busy for you.'

'What about Gracie? Are you bringing her along?'

'If I'm suffering then it's only fair you should too.'

She could hear his warm chuckle at the end of the line again. She was always the one who made James laugh in the same way he made her laugh, and she'd always felt it bonded them somehow in a way neither of them had managed with Gracie.

'You *are* looking after yourself, aren't you?' she asked.

'You know I'm not. It's never been my style. I'll start looking after myself when I get old.'

'That's just it…'

Lizzie stopped herself. What was the point in airing her all-too-real fear that the wayward brother she loved so much might not reach a ripe old age if he carried on living the way he did now?

'Come whenever you like,' he said into the gap, perhaps sensing the need to fill it and spare her the pain of saying what he must have known she'd wanted to say. 'It's not like I have a full schedule.'

'As soon as I can.'

'Don't bring Gracie.'

Lizzie laughed. 'I have to bring Gracie. Imagine how miffed she'd be if I snuck off to see you without her.'

'I know but it was worth a try. At least warn her not to turn her nose up at my flat. And I don't want candles.'

'James – Stig of the Dump would turn his nose up at your flat.'

'Good point. Let's meet at the pub on the corner.'

'Can we stay over at the pub on the corner?'

'I don't think so, but I can ask around, see who's got a spare floor for you. One night, yeah?'

'Don't worry,' Lizzie said, suppressing a sigh of resignation. James was never going to change and perhaps it was easier to accept that rather than keep trying. 'I'm sure there'll be a hotel somewhere close by we can get cheap on a mid-week deal.'

'Mid-week's good, actually. Mid-week is probably best for me too.'

'Right then. I'll text you and we'll fix up a date when I've asked Gracie.'

'Right.'

'And James…'

'Yes, Elizabeth…'

'Phone Mum.'

There was a stifled groan.

'Please,' Lizzie said. 'You know it would make her so happy if, just once, you called her instead of her chasing you down.'

He sighed. 'I'll do it when we've finished here. And only because you've asked me and you're my favourite.'

'Thanks, James. Love you.'

'No you don't.'

'I do.'

'Bye, Elizabeth.'

'Bye, James.'

Stowing her phone in her pocket, she walked slowly back to the caravan. Inside, Gracie was sprawled across the sofa, flicking through the daytime TV shows.

'I thought you were having a nap,' Lizzie said.

'The builders woke me.'

'I was surprised you managed to fall asleep at all with them out there.'

'I know, but I'm just so tired these days.'

Lizzie was thoughtful as she went to the sink. Should she be worried about that? Was Gracie's mood lower than she'd realised? Was that the reason her sister was so tired? Or did it have more to do with her general lack of motivation these days? It wasn't hard to imagine that sitting around in the caravan all day would sap the energy out of her.

'Oh,' Lizzie said, looking at the empty plastic bowl in the sink. 'You washed up.'

'There weren't many.'

'Thanks.'

'What shall we have to eat? I thought I might make a chicken casserole – cook for you for a change as you've done so much cooking for me.'

'That sounds lovely,' Gracie said absently. 'But we'll have to go and get a casserole dish first.'

'I've got a dish; we used it last night…'

Lizzie frowned and, as she opened the bin to see the fragments, Gracie offered a sheepish apology.

'The drilling made me jump and it flew out of my hand,' she said.

Lizzie sighed. 'It's alright.' What else could she say? The way things were going, the best she could hope for was that she'd still have a functional caravan by the time Gracie's stay with her was over, or at least some semblance of sanity. She didn't imagine for a moment she'd manage to keep hold of both.

Chapter Thirteen

Lizzie and Jude had been gifted a rare afternoon alone – Gracie had gone to bed again, citing the same unexplained exhaustion she'd complained about previously. Lizzie had gently asked her if she ought to go to the doctor's, but Gracie had cheerfully informed her that she was sure it was nothing to worry about and so Lizzie reluctantly had to leave it at that. Charlie was spending the afternoon with the saintly Harriet and her little boy. Lizzie was doing her best to keep the green-eyed monster at bay and so far she wasn't doing too badly. The fact that Harriet was sitting with Charlie and Lizzie got Jude all to herself certainly felt like a small triumph, and though Lizzie hated herself for feeling that way about it, she'd take it anyway.

They were sitting under one of the spreading pear trees on a blanket in the garden while Lizzie gazed across at her half-finished mill and tried not to let the sight of a mud-filled hollow right outside the front door and the building equipment that had been abandoned for the last three work days because of an emergency job in Lowestoft stress her out. Instead, right now, she was talking to Jude about Gracie's offer to buy the caravan. Even that was harder than it ought to be, because she couldn't get the conversation she'd had with Gracie about Jude and Harriet out of her mind.

'I'd take the money,' he said. 'You need it and she can't be that bad to live with, surely? She's your sister, after all; how hard can it be to get along? It seems like a win-win.'

'We're not like you and Charlie. On paper we ought to get along but… it's complicated. Gracie and me – *we're* complicated. She's perfectly lovely but she has this…'

'What?'

'A bee in her bonnet, I suppose.'

'About what?'

'Me.'

He had the good sense to stifle any laughter he might have needed to expel at this point. Lizzie certainly detected some.

She sighed. 'I know it sounds ridiculous.'

'Not really,' he said, his expression ironed into respectability again now. 'Sibling rivalry is a thing. Not with me and Charlie, but we're not your average siblings. I imagine it's a thing with others – especially sisters.'

'It's more than that. We bickered all the time as kids. We're OK now, but I don't want the bickering to become something more serious.'

'And you think living together will do that?'

'I don't know. We're just not designed to spend long periods of time together.' Lizzie swatted at a fly. 'The grass is always greener with Gracie, especially when it's my grass. This quitting her job business and moving out here… there's the proof, right there. When she realises the reality doesn't quite live up to the dream it'll be my fault.'

'Your grass isn't looking very green right now,' Jude said, angling his head towards the churned-up ground beyond their safe little corner of the garden.

'Come on, Jude – I'm trying to tell you something serious here.'

'Sorry.'

'While she lived with Frank she had everything she could have wished for – holidays, nice clothes, parties – and she was getting on with a proper life of her own. There's no way she could have compared our lives and wanted what I had. But now…'

'I'm sure it's not going to be as bad as you think. You're both older now, right? She seems pretty together to me.'

'I suppose so,' Lizzie said, though there was no conviction in it. She reached for the glass of lemonade at her side. 'I'm probably being a bit paranoid. Maybe she's just getting used to life without Frank and she's looking to see where it can go next. I suppose it's all very unsettling, having your existence thrown into turmoil like that. All that unsettling is bound to make her want to seize on things she thinks will make it all better.'

'Such as living in an old windmill like the little mouse with the clogs on?'

Lizzie smiled. 'Something like that.'

'Well I declare…' He grinned, and Lizzie nudged him.

'How do you know so much about nursery rhymes then?'

'I was a kid once. I know this god-like form looks as if it must have been sent fully assembled from Mount Olympus on a bolt of lightning, but once upon a time I wore a nappy and drooled just like every other baby. It wasn't pretty.'

'And you have Artie. I suppose you're always singing them to him.'
'Exactly.'

'I can't remember any nursery rhymes at all.'

'I bet you can if you think for a minute.'

Lizzie shook her head. 'Nope, not a one.'

'Not even "Baa Baa Black Sheep"?'

'Oh yeah, that's one.'

'"Three Blind Mice"?'

Lizzie giggled. 'What is it with you and mice?'

Jude pushed her back onto the blanket and kissed her. The leaves on the old pear tree spread dancing shadows over them and a gentle breeze lifted the scents of the wildflowers in the meadows beyond her garden to join them. Lizzie looked up at him. He was so perfect. So perfect for her, so completely and utterly right in every way. It was inevitable, then, that she'd throw a spanner in the works sooner or later because perfect was never quite as perfect as it might seem.

'I thought I might invite Harrie and Damon for drinks with us on Saturday night,' he said, rolling onto an elbow and looking at her. 'If that's OK with you… I thought it might be nice for you and Harrie to get to know each other a bit better, as you're probably going to be running into one another a lot more often.'

'Why will we?'

'Well…' He paused, his smile spreading. 'Because you're both very important to me and I really want you to get along.'

'I'm sure we would get along,' Lizzie said carefully, not wanting to refuse his request but not really enthusiastic about the idea either. 'Will they be bringing Artie?'

'They might,' Jude said thoughtfully. 'Not that they need to because Harrie's mum and dad would be more than happy to babysit, but I guess Artie could stay over – he has a bed in Charlie's room anyway and it would probably make Charlie happy. And it might be a good opportunity for you to finally meet him too.'

'Would anyone else be staying over?'

'You could,' he said, weaving his fingers into hers. 'If you wanted to.'

'What about Harriet and Damon?'

Jude frowned. 'I suppose they would if they were too drunk to go home, but I doubt Harriet would do that if Artie is with us… Does it matter anyway?'

Lizzie forced a smile. 'Of course it doesn't; I was just wondering.'

He moved to kiss her again but she wriggled out of reach and sat up.

'Jude… were you upset when you and Harriet broke up?'

'Well, yes.'

'Did you end it or did she?'

Jude chewed his thumbnail. 'It was sort of mutual.'

'What does that mean?'

'It means we both agreed it was for the best.'

Lizzie knew she should stop but she'd started now. 'Why? Why did you split up?'

'We weren't really working as a couple.'

'So you're better as friends now than you were as lovers?'

Jude frowned. 'I thought we'd been over this. I thought you were OK with Harrie.'

'I am. I'm just curious, because you never said who ended it and I thought maybe she had. Did you plan to have Artie?'

'No.'

'So he was an accident? Is that why you split up?'

'No, we were happy about him.'

'Really?'

'Once we'd got used to the idea. I wouldn't be without him now, not for anything.'

'It's lucky you can be friends still. Not many couples can be such good friends as you two are.'

'Lizzie, what is this? If you're feeling insecure about Harrie again, please understand that you don't have to.'

'Maybe I don't have anything to worry about from you but how can you be sure about her?'

'She's happy for me and she's crazy about Damon.'

Lizzie was stopped in her tracks. For some reason, the possibility of Harriet being crazy about Damon hadn't occurred to her. She just hadn't seen any evidence of that, the day at the river, but perhaps she was wrong after all.

'Oh,' she said. 'That's good. And you like him?'

'It doesn't really matter whether I like him or not.'

'But it does because he'll be around Artie a lot, especially if Harriet and Damon end up together long term.'

'I trust him with Artie, if that's what you mean. Whether I think he's right for Harriet isn't important.'

'You don't think he's right for Harriet?'

'Lizzie… stop worrying.' He leaned over and kissed her. 'You don't need to stress about any of this. I like you and Harriet likes Damon and, like I told you before, we're not interested in getting back together anymore.'

Lizzie tried to smile, but he still hadn't really answered the question that she hadn't quite been able to frame. If anything came between Harriet and her new boyfriend, would that change things between her and Jude? Would he want to go back to Harriet and try again?

'I'm sorry,' Lizzie said.

'Don't be. I understand the way we are might look a bit weird to people on the outside.'

Lizzie tried to ignore the turn of phrase: *people on the outside*. That meant people like her, and that was just the problem. She did feel like she was on the outside. She wondered if Damon felt the same when he looked in on Harriet and Jude's friendship. She tried to dismiss the notion – she was overthinking all of this, and not only was it making her paranoid, it was probably making her bloody annoying too. That was it; no more questioning, no more mistrust. He'd told her more than once how things were, and she didn't need to ask again. She gave him her brightest smile and pushed the matter firmly from her thoughts.

He leaned in to kiss her again but then pulled away as his phone began to ring.

'Sorry… should probably see who it is in case it's a job or something…' he muttered as he twisted for the back pocket of his jeans. He swiped to take the call and Lizzie fought an irrational spike of irritation as she quickly deduced that it wasn't work at all.

'Hey… it's kind of a bad time.' He listened for a moment before speaking again, and this time his voice leapt up an octave in his excitement. 'Seriously? That's amazing! We'll definitely have to celebrate that!'

There was another silence and, as he listened, Jude's grin spread. Lizzie tried desperately to make out what was being said at the other end of the line but there was too much peripheral noise for her to tell. She only knew it was a female voice and it wasn't hard to guess whose it might be.

'It really is amazing news,' he said. 'Lizzie and I were just saying we ought to have you and Damon round for drinks on Saturday night – can you make it? We'll get a few bottles in and toast your success!'

After another brief pause, he bid goodbye and ended the call. He looked up at Lizzie.

'You'll never guess what?'

Lizzie shook her head.

'Harrie's got into the final of that photography competition with the picture of the heron she got with us that day! How amazing is that? You know, she's so good at everything it almost makes you sick,' he added with a chuckle.

Lizzie held in a sigh of despair. It certainly did that alright.

'And they're going to come over on Saturday; it should be a good night.'

'Yeah,' Lizzie agreed with no enthusiasm for the plan whatsoever. 'Brilliant.'

＊

The next morning Lizzie was woken by the sounds of Gracie running the taps in the tiny bathroom of their caravan. She leaned over to retrieve her watch from the bedside cabinet to see that it was five thirty in the morning.

'What the hell…' she mumbled, slamming the watch down again and pulling the duvet over her head. Gracie wasn't exactly known for her early rising – trust Lizzie's contrary sister to find her hidden lark genes when Lizzie had wanted a bit of a lie-in. She listened to the bathroom door close, then Gracie's footsteps, followed by the sound of her bedroom door slamming shut.

Lizzie turned onto her back with a sigh. She'd agreed, finally, to her sister's plan to buy the caravan from her so Lizzie would have the money to pour into the mill, but she was already wondering if it might prove to be a recipe for disaster. Once Gracie owned the caravan Lizzie would be stuck with her, no matter how much they got on each other's nerves – short of leaving herself, which was hardly likely to happen when she needed to be on site to oversee the mill renovations.

As she settled into a doze, these thoughts fading, the sound of Gracie's bedroom door being crashed open woke her again. She listened to her sister's footsteps, running for the bathroom as before. Biting back a cry of frustration, Lizzie threw her covers off and hauled herself out of bed. She was never going to get back to sleep now, even if Gracie could learn to be quiet for once.

＊

'I've been thinking,' Gracie said over breakfast.

Lizzie looked over the top of her mug. A good strong cup of coffee was banishing her sleepiness, and it had always been hard to stay angry with Gracie for long. It was part of the reason that she could be so frustrating, because even if you had a perfect right to be annoyed with her and you really wanted to, you'd find it impossible to sustain. So when her sister had joined her for an earlier-than-expected morning drink, Lizzie had found herself gradually dragged into Gracie's sunny world when she'd been determined to stay under her own comfy little rain cloud.

'Don't exert yourself,' she said.

Gracie folded her arms with a pout. 'Well, I won't tell you what it is I'm thinking if you're going to be like that,'

'Sorry.' Lizzie laughed. 'I really want to know what it is, please tell me.'

Gracie smoothed her irked features. 'I was thinking you don't get much time on your own with Jude.'

'Right…'

'And partly that's because I'm here now.'

'Well, yes, partly it's because we have Charlie to think about too. It's not so easy for Jude to just leave him, and he doesn't get a lot of help.'

'Yes, exactly,' Gracie said, getting more animated now. 'That's what I'm trying to say!'

Lizzie shook her head, nonplussed.

'You know how Charlie's always going on about Harriet?' Gracie continued. 'I mean, he's completely and utterly in love with her, isn't he?'

'Yes…' Lizzie replied slowly, wondering where exactly this was going.

'But she can't be there all the time for him because she has a baby of her own – right?'

'Artie's more of a toddler, as far as I know, but—'

'So you might need a Harriet Two? A spare Harriet?'

'I don't know—'

'That's me!' Gracie squeaked triumphantly. 'I could be the spare Harriet!'

'But you're—'

'Doing nothing much right now. I mean, I have my business to get off the ground and as soon as the work starts to come in I'll have to look after that, but…'

Lizzie thought better than to mention that so far the setting up of Gracie's new business venture had got no further than doodling new logos on her telephone message pad and buying a page on a hosting website, but she thought better of it. After all, it seemed, in her own cock-eyed way, Gracie was trying to do something nice for her. Perhaps it would lessen Harriet's influence in the lives of Charlie and Jude too, though Lizzie tried not to think about how much that might please her.

'But while all that's getting off the ground…' Gracie was still going, and Lizzie forced herself to pay attention, 'I could be getting to know Charlie better; getting used to his ways and then I could look after him. And I'd be much more fun than Harriet because I'd have time to take him for days out and such.'

'How do you come to that conclusion?' Lizzie sipped at her coffee. 'You'll have a business to run.'

'Harriet works too.'

'For her family. I don't suppose they're very strict bosses.'

'True.'

'And she has a baby.'

'Toddler…'

'Still, he takes lots of time and attention. I don't have that to worry about.'

Lizzie resisted the impulse to narrow her eyes. It might well imply that she suspected an ulterior motive to her sister's suggestion and perhaps that was doing Gracie a grave disservice. However, she couldn't deny there was a certain appeal in the idea of Gracie usurping Harriet from her throne.

'It's very nice of you,' she said instead. 'And I know Charlie really likes you.'

'That's what I thought.' Gracie smiled brightly. 'So it would be a good idea?'

'If Jude was alright with it I don't see why not. It would take the pressure off him a bit, and it would mean we could have some more time alone. But don't be offended if he says no – Charlie needs particular care and someone who knows how to give that, and he might not feel comfortable leaving it to someone who's not used to Charlie.'

'I *am* used to Charlie – a little bit anyway. I'm sure it would be OK.'

'And are you sure you're up to it?'

'Of course I'm up to it. I'd probably do a better job than Harriet because I've got nothing else to worry about.'

'But Charlie's known Harriet for a long time so he's far more used to her.'

'Do you think she'll have more children with this new guy she's seeing?'

'I have no idea!' Lizzie said with a laugh. 'What's that got to do with anything?'

'If she has more she'll absolutely be too busy to help out with Charlie and then I'll be able to step up.'

'Why so interested in Charlie all of a sudden?'

Gracie shrugged. 'He's sweet. I was always quite nervous around… you know… people with disabilities before. Now that I know him, he's lovely and lots of fun. And I suppose I just want to feel important to someone. It must be nice to feel someone needs you.'

'I'm not sure Charlie would need you exactly, but he'd always be glad of a new friend. He's about the friendliest kid I've ever met.'

'Exactly. Friends make him happy, so I would make him happy and I'd be important to him, right?'

Lizzie sipped her coffee.

'I'll talk to Jude,' she said.

'Brilliant!'

Lizzie drained the last of her coffee. 'I suppose I should get something done,' she said. She ran a critical eye over her sister. 'Are you going to be alright today if I'm not around much?'

'What do you mean?' Gracie asked, swallowing her water down.

'Well, this morning… you seem a bit under the weather – not quite yourself. And I heard the bathroom door going a few times early this morning. I thought you might be a bit…'

'Oh, that. I just needed the toilet. Anyway, I've got to go,' Gracie said, cutting her off. 'So much to do, I need an early start.'

'Like what?'

Gracie tapped the side of her nose. 'That's for me to know and you to find out.'

'Does that mean you're going out today?'

'For most of it, yes.'

If she'd been alone Lizzie would have punched the air. A whole day without Gracie. Obviously, it wouldn't be a day of peace alone relaxing while all the drilling and sawing and banging happened in the mill across the way, but still…

'What are your plans?' Gracie asked.

'The same as every day, I expect. Listen to Tim Lundy tell me the build is going to cost even more money and that the finish has now been moved to just before the sun explodes and swallows the earth.

And with that distraction, sit at my computer and try to earn some actual money to pay for it all. The usual.'

'Do you think we ought to invite Mum to dinner? To celebrate us moving in together?'

'When?'

'Whenever you say. Tell me when you've had time to check your diary.'

'We can if you like.'

'Great! And I can organise it!' Gracie smiled fondly at her. 'You know, I do love being here now. In fact, I have the best feeling about it all. Later, we should talk about what we're going to do with the mill when it's finished.'

Lizzie tried to ignore the *we're* in Gracie's last sentence, hoping it wasn't a Freudian slip. Was Gracie somehow getting the idea that their current domestic arrangement would continue once the mill was habitable? Lizzie certainly hadn't said anything she could think of that would have given such an impression, and it wasn't what she wanted at all. Magnolia Mill was her house – hers alone. Maybe one day she'd move a partner in (maybe that partner would be Jude and she was hopeful for that), and maybe one day even more distant she'd raise a family there, but until that day it would be her sanctuary. Lizzie loved Gracie but she didn't want to live with her permanently. Surely Gracie got that?

Gracie skipped over and kissed her on the cheek. 'I'll be off out then, before your charismatic life-and-soul-of-the-party builder gets here. I really can't bear to look at his face for another day – he's like a saggy beer-soaked Eeyore.'

Lizzie chortled. 'I must admit looking at him even makes me a little depressed.'

'I don't know how you can bear to have him around the place.'

'But he's a good builder and that's the most important thing.'

'Even though he keeps charging you more money and telling you the job is going to take longer?'

'I don't think those things are his fault, and honestly I have a feeling other builders would be twice as bad.'

'If you say so.'

'I can't swap him now – he's too far into the build and too indispensable – he knows exactly what's what.'

'I suppose he must,' Gracie said. She waved an airy hand. 'Ciao!'

'See you later.' Lizzie smiled, watching her disappear to her bedroom. But then she was distracted by the sound of van engines and she looked to the window to see Tim Lundy's van pull onto the drive.

'Time to start another day of toil, eh, Eeyore?' she said softly with a broad smile. She didn't want Gracie as a permanent feature, but she had to admit that, sometimes, she rather liked having her around.

Chapter Fourteen

While Tim and his crew were hard at work on the mill for what seemed like the millionth day of this interminable build, Lizzie was finding ways to take her mind off talk of hurdles to the new central heating system that she'd proposed and the odd shape of the windows, which didn't lend themselves to any cheap kind of glazing. So she was currently on the phone to a lady named Janet, who owned a working mill fifty miles along the coast. If she was going to get hers working, then she needed all the help and advice she could get, and who better to approach than someone who was already doing it? Sort of anyway, because Janet's mill – Kestrel Mill – was open to tourists only and wasn't inhabited by the family who owned it. They made their own flour to sell in the mill shop, and they baked their own goods in the kitchens below the sails, but the section that would have once housed a miller and his family was now a tiny museum showing just how they would have lived, while Janet and her brood were safely tucked away in a property a mile down the road.

'It's really good of you to spare the time to talk to me about this,' Lizzie said.

'Not at all. It's lovely to see someone else is passionate about conserving our heritage. There are so many of these buildings going to wrack and ruin. In fact, I have to let you into a secret… when I first had the idea to buy a mill, I looked at yours as a possibility.'

'You did? And what decided you against it?'

'Partly the location – it was just a little further from home than I wanted – and partly because it looked so dilapidated that I decided only a madman – or woman – would take it on.'

Lizzie grinned. 'That would be me then – named and shamed. Apparently the people around here nicknamed it Mad Lady Mill. That must have been what they meant.'

'Oh, I might know something about that,' Janet said. 'Nobody's told you the story?'

'Well, no… I didn't think there really was a story.'

'I don't know how long ago, but the miller who owned it at that time had a daughter. They'd lived together alone there after her mother had died. Apparently the daughter got pregnant out of wedlock by a highly undesirable man – at least the miller hadn't been very keen. There was some kind of stand-off – not altogether sure whether it was pistols at dawn or fisticuffs or what – but the young man killed her father in the altercation. She went mad with guilt, lost the baby and spent years wandering around the mill wailing like a wraith, hair wild, dresses torn. Nobody could talk to her, and she saw visitors off with an old sword. So the story goes. It's all very madwoman in the attic, isn't it? If it's not true it's a terrific story to sell the place to visitors.'

Lizzie laughed. 'God, I don't know about that. Maybe if I'd known all that I wouldn't have been so keen to buy it myself.'

She tried not to think about mad girls floating about the house wailing and looking a bit like Marley's ghost.

'So, you'd like to pop over and see Kestrel Mill working? I'm sure it would help to get a solid vision for your own place.'

'You don't mind me opening up Magnolia Mill? I wouldn't be treading on your toes in term of visitors? I mean, we're only fifty miles apart and if I thought for a minute—'

'I think fifty miles is far enough to afford us both a decent living. What are you planning to do exactly?'

'Well, I suppose I'd had some very similar ideas to you. I wanted to sell the flour, but I also wanted to bake artisan bread – different varieties with different kinds of flour – to sell in the shop. I don't know about a café because I don't know how I'd run it yet and my catering experience is limited. I plan to go on a bread-making course – if there is such a thing – but it's something else I need to research—'

'I could teach you some basics if you were able to visit when the mill is closed.'

'You could? That would be amazing! You're sure it would be no bother?'

'None at all. My family say I'd bore anyone to death talking about bread given half a chance so I'd love to go through some basics with you. It might be enough to get you started or even help you decide whether it's the right way for you to go or not. I would imagine people would still visit the mill even if you weren't producing anything just for the historical value – if visitors are what you're after.'

'Well, the tourism is secondary really. What I want to do is make the bread, but I need visitors to buy it – otherwise, what's the point? I like bread as much as the next person but even I can't eat two tons a day.'

Janet laughed. 'I don't think you'll be producing quite that much. But do come and see me whenever you like. I can show you around Kestrel Mill and tell you as much as I know about milling, and then we'll spend some time in the kitchens at my house. In fact, it might take a while to go through it all so you're welcome to stay overnight if you like – we have a guest wing where we sometimes put holidaymakers up, and it's free over the next couple of weeks.'

'Oh, that's so kind of you! I couldn't possibly—'

'You could. It'd be lovely to meet you, and I'm sure Andrew and the kids would love to meet you too.'

'That's your husband? Is he involved in the mill business too?'

'No, he's a banker. Can't be bothered getting floury every day. The mill is my project – keeps me out of mischief, or so he says. I quite like it that way. He's happy enough commuting into London every day, and I think he's as crazy wanting to do that as he thinks I am for wanting to run a mill!'

'I think there are quite a few people around here who think I'm crazy for wanting to take a mill on too.'

'Do you have any idea when it will be finished?'

'I had hoped for the end of the year – before Christmas. That's looking a bit unlikely at the moment, though.'

'These things always take longer than anyone imagines they will. It's wise to manage your expectations, and it sounds as though you have.'

'I haven't had a lot of choice. It sometimes feels hopeless. I wonder if I've taken on far too much and if it will ever be within my power – or budget – to see it through.'

'I felt like that when we were renovating ours. Perhaps it would be encouraging to see Kestrel Mill in action; you'll be able to see that it is possible to achieve your dreams and get Magnolia Mill back to its glory days again.'

'It certainly might be the tonic I need right now. I'll have to look at my diary and talk to my sister, who's staying with me at the moment, to see when I might be free. The builders might need some input from one of us, and I want to make sure she's happy to take charge of the project while I'm missing.'

'Well, you have my number, so give me a call when you have some dates and we'll see if we can get a matching pair, eh?'

'I'd love that,' Lizzie said. 'Thank you so much.'

'Not at all – I'm looking forward to meeting the madwoman who's taken on that old place.'

Lizzie laughed and they said their goodbyes with promises to be in touch again very soon. As she ended the call, Lizzie was filled with a renewed optimism and sense of purpose. Things had been slipping away from her the longer and more complicated the build at Magnolia Mill became. Seeing another mill in action and meeting the person that had been through the same struggles as Lizzie might just be the tonic she needed to help her through the final push on her own place. She'd talk to Gracie about it later and hope that she wouldn't want to come along, because while Lizzie knew that nobody loved a daytrip quite as much as Gracie did, Lizzie needed her to hold the fort back at home.

She could ask Jude to keep an eye on things at the mill, she supposed, but she didn't want to burden him with anything else while he had Charlie to worry about. And perhaps she could ask her mum, but then Gwendolyn might get flustered if anything went awry while Lizzie was missing, and that was too much stress to put her under, while James would complain about being away from his bedsit and his slacker mates. Florentina would have done it, but Gracie would make things so awkward in that regard it wasn't really a workable solution either. Lizzie and Gracie hardly saw eye to eye on Florentina's continued involvement with the family as it was.

Lizzie frowned as she wandered to the kitchen to forage for a quick sandwich. She desperately wanted to visit Kestrel Mill and she'd just have to find a way around it all, somehow.

*

Gracie was sulking, but Lizzie wasn't going to be bullied. Neither was she going to let her sister dictate who visited the caravan while she still owned it. Their temporary home hadn't yet changed hands, but even when it had been signed over, Lizzie would have to remind Gracie, gently or otherwise, that it still stood on her land and that they were supposed to be in a partnership that worked for them both – which meant some give and take. But for now, to save Florentina from the death stares aimed at her (she'd been passing as she toured her sales territory and had taken her life into her hands to call in at Magnolia Mill), Lizzie had taken her out of the caravan and they were currently inspecting the newly rendered exterior of the mill.

'You should paint it pink,' Florentina said with an approving nod. 'Or lilac. Really get it noticed, make it a landmark – you know?'

'Pink or lilac? It would do that alright,' Lizzie replied, arching an eyebrow. 'I'll stick with a nice Cornish cream – it's already enough of a landmark just being a mill.'

'Well, yes. But you could make it look so adorable. Wouldn't you just *have* to stop at a windmill that was painted lilac?'

'It would look like the ride that Disney rejected for Dumbo Land,' Lizzie said.

'Exactly! Completely adorable!'

Lizzie grinned. But then her thoughts turned to more practical matters and her smile faded. 'Look, I'm sorry about Gracie—'

Florentina wafted away the apology. 'I'm used to it by now, and it won't put me off coming to see you. You are my friend. I suppose I have no claim to any goodwill from any of you really, but I'm grateful for yours at least.'

'Believe me, my life would be easier if I could see you as the wicked stepmother and close ranks with the rest of my clan, but I can't.'

'That's because you are a good person.'

'Hmmm, fat lot of good it does me.'

'I believe in karma, Lizzie. Your reward will come.'

Lizzie raised her eyebrows but said nothing. It was good that Florentina believed in karma because sometimes Lizzie wasn't so sure.

'Have you thought any more about using the mill to make money? You said last time we spoke that you had an idea or two.'

'As a matter of fact I have.'

'And would you like to tell me or is it still a secret?'

Lizzie snapped the head from a stalk of long grass. 'I don't know that it's secret; just a bit of a dream, I suppose. I'm still weighing up how realistic it is.'

'Well, why don't you tell me and I'll tell you what I think?'

Lizzie nodded. Florentina wasn't proposing to give her opinion for the sake of being opinionated, and she would never weigh in on matters she knew didn't concern her – she was merely trying to support and encourage Lizzie, as she always had.

'I want to get the mill milling again.'

'Isn't that going to be difficult if you're living in it?'

'The bottom section that runs off the main trunk used to be the miller's dwelling. It's small but I could turn it into a little gift shop or a café or bakery or something. It doesn't bother me to live around and beneath the workings in the main section.'

'It would be noisy and dusty.'

'Only when the mill was running, and I don't think it would be so often – perhaps a few times a week. I've been talking to a lady who owns a mill up the coast – she runs her sails at weekends mostly so visitors can come and see. She says she doesn't get much call for it in the week, but she will start them up for coach parties who book in advance to come mid-week and show them around. She sells the flour she makes in a shop on site and has a café with goods made from the flour she produces too.'

'Wow…' Florentina stepped back and raised her gaze to the great, sweeping walls of the old structure with a nod of approval. 'So you're planning to have a café too?'

'Maybe,' Lizzie said, more animated now with the encouragement of Florentina's response. 'I'm mostly aiming to produce bread for sale, though. Artisan stuff – unusual and historic recipes, rustic, home-produced and completely organic. I could sell to farm shops and specialist food outlets. And I can establish an online presence easily enough too – obviously I've had tons of experience there. I think it's doable.'

'You have thought of everything.'

'Not quite. But I'm arranging to visit the lady up the coast and she's going to give me some pointers so I hope to be up to speed soon enough.'

Florentina nodded slowly. 'And you're planning to run all of this alone?'

Lizzie shrugged. 'Gracie will think I'm nuts when I tell her. So will Mum and James, come to think of it – they already think I'm nuts for buying the mill in the first place.'

'Sometimes, when the mad ideas take off, that's when everyone else wishes they'd had the courage to try them out. How much will you need to get this going? Have you budgeted for it in the build costs?'

'I had – sort of. But I think that will all get eaten up by the build itself now. If I do go down the road of trying to make it a viable business, it'll have to be a bank loan of some kind, I expect. Although God knows what bank will give me that because I'm already up to my neck in debt. I think I'd have to do a pretty persuasive job of selling the idea to them, but I'm willing to give it a go. If I don't get what I need at first, then I'll have to keep trying every avenue until I've exhausted them all. After that…' She shrugged. 'Well, I haven't thought about it yet.'

Florentina was silent for a moment, eyes shielded from the sun as she looked up at the mill, its new render drying into camouflage patches in the sun.

'How would you feel about a partner?' she asked finally.

'Who would that be?'

'Me, *cara mia.*'

It was Lizzie's turn to be silent. She glanced back at the caravan where Gracie was having one of her now frequent lie-downs – or sulking, as Lizzie preferred to call it – and then back at Florentina, who held her in a measured gaze.

'I don't know,' Lizzie said. 'You're really interested? It wouldn't be a safe place for your money at all.' And it wasn't just the safety of Florentina's money that worried Lizzie, though she couldn't say so. Her stepmother's offer was tempting, but Lizzie would have to find some way to make her family accept such a situation.

'I realise that. I can't promise anything at this stage, but I am intrigued. It's just the sort of plan your dad would have liked.'

Lizzie smiled. 'It is that. I think I'd like a partner very much, but I don't want to leave you short or risk money you might need.'

'Your dad made sure I was alright, and I can still work because I would be more of a silent partner – I'd only be involved in the financial side of things. All the hard work would be down to you, I'm afraid; you can't imagine how attached I am to these very expensive acrylic nails…'

Lizzie grinned. That wasn't true, because when the chips were down Florentina always got stuck in, but she loved to give the impression of glamour regardless.

'I must admit it's beginning to sound very doable,' Lizzie said.

'Do some research and find out what we'd need to start up. Then we can talk some more – how does that sound?'

'Brilliant! Maybe in that case you could come and visit Kestrel Mill with me too? It'll give you an idea of where your money might be going and whether you think it's worthwhile or not.'

'Won't Gracie want to do that with you?'

'Gracie will have to grow up a bit and accept my choices. If you're going to be involved in this business then you should come to see Kestrel Mill. I need someone here to look after the build anyway and Gracie can do that.'

Florentina looked doubtful. 'Let's get the basics down first. If you want to go and see the mill to get some idea of whether it's work you feel confident to undertake then by all means go. If it becomes a reality, then we'll see about visiting together. There's no point in me driving a wedge between you and your sister for nothing.'

'You wouldn't—' Lizzie began, but then she looked at Florentina's face and she knew that her stepmother was right, even if she didn't want to admit it. Gracie wouldn't like it at all, and while it wasn't really any of her business, there was no point in winding her up if they didn't have to – things were complicated enough already.

*

Lizzie and Jude were painting an old cabinet he'd bought for her. Lizzie had immediately fallen in love with it, but when she'd asked him where it was from he'd just tapped the side of his nose and told her he had his sources. Lizzie realised that it had probably come from Harriet's grandfather's reclamation yard, and she tried not to let the fact bother her, not least because even she could see how incredibly ungrateful that would be. The cabinet was being transformed with the help of some cream chalk paint, though Lizzie had said more than once she had no idea how she was going to keep it away from the dust the builders were constantly kicking up when it was finished. But they'd both agreed that keeping busy was the only way they wouldn't be texting Gracie every two minutes to see if all was well with her and Charlie. Once they got stuck in, it had been a lot of fun too.

Lizzie put down her brush and wiped her hands down her overalls as the sound of a car pulling up at her gates caught her attention, and she turned to see Charlie tumble out and race to meet them.

'Gracie's car is fast!' Charlie squeaked, setting a look of alarm on both Lizzie and Jude's features. 'And we saw alpacas! They're so fluffy! They scratch a lot and they love grass!'

Jude's features relaxed into an indulgent smile. Charlie's voice couldn't have got much higher if he'd taken a lungful of helium, and you couldn't be anything but happy to see him so excited.

'They were so cute!' Charlie added with a huge grin. 'They said we could buy one!'

'Charlie!' Jude laughed. 'Where are we going to keep an alpaca?'

'They said *people* could buy one,' Gracie cut in, joining them now. 'I don't think they meant us in particular. Though they were utterly adorable…' It was hard to know who'd been more taken by the alpacas, because her sister was wearing a grin as wide as Charlie's.

'Maybe we should get one,' Lizzie said. 'Gracie looks smitten too.'

'Yes!' Gracie cried, taking Lizzie by surprise.

'I didn't actually mean—'

'We should *totally* get one!' Gracie continued. 'More than one! People could come and pet them – they'd pay money… I mean, I would. We could make them an attraction and I bet there aren't any other mills with alpacas. Oh, we could make jumpers from their wool! In fact, we could have lots of animals—'

'Steady on,' Lizzie said, and her laugh was rather less assured and more nervous now. When Gracie took hold of an idea, she really took hold. 'We don't know the first thing about alpacas, and nobody said anything about making the mill a tourist attraction.'

Gracie raised her eyebrows in vague disbelief. 'Well, what else are you going to do with it? What's the point in owning a stonking great windmill if you're not going to let people come and look?'

'I'm going to live in it for a start.' Lizzie exchanged a brief look with Jude. 'And further than that I haven't figured out yet.'

'But you can't just live in a place like this!' Gracie insisted. 'People will drive to see it anyway – they already do and it's not finished yet. At least make some money out of that!'

'Do they?' Lizzie asked doubtfully.

'Haven't you seen the cars stopping to see?'

'Not really.'

'Well they do.'

It wasn't that Gracie was mooting an idea Lizzie hadn't already mulled over herself many times, it was just that her sister had a habit of taking the most tentative, half formed of ideas and running with them. Of course, Lizzie had discussed just this subject with Florentina only a day before, but Gracie was another matter entirely. But it looked as if Gracie had been having ideas of her own after all, and she hadn't needed Lizzie to spark them. She'd expect to play a part in these plans too, and once again Lizzie reluctantly had to admit to herself that it wasn't what she wanted, guilty as the thought made her feel.

While this conversation had been happening, Charlie had gone into the garden to fetch a chair. He appeared with it now and placed it solemnly behind Gracie, giving her a silent, pleading look.

'What's that about?' Jude asked him.

'Gracie needs to sit down,' Charlie said, 'like before.'

Both Jude and Lizzie turned to Gracie now with their own silent questions.

'I'm fine.' Gracie waved a hand for Charlie to take the chair away. But Charlie only looked pained by her refusal to sit down. 'Really,' she insisted, 'I'm alright now.'

'The alpaca lady said you ought to go to hospital,' Charlie said.

Lizzie looked sharply at Gracie now. 'What's this? What happened?'

'It was hot,' Gracie said. 'I had a little heatstroke.'

'You love the sun and you've never had heatstroke in your life.'

'There's a first time for everything,' Gracie said irritably.

'Don't give me that. You've been odd for a while now – tired, moody…'

'I am not moody!'

'Tell that to Florentina.'

'That's not moodiness; I just don't like her. It doesn't matter how I feel, I'll always dislike her.'

'Alright then, you've generally been odd and you can't deny that.'

'I don't think I want to have this conversation in front of your boyfriend,' Gracie hissed.

'What sort of conversation do you think we're about to have?' Lizzie's hands went to her hips.

'She had a funny turn,' Charlie said, taking Gracie's elbow despite her protestations and trying again to lead her to the seat.

'Charlie!' Gracie shook him off, and his look was one of such profound and wounded shock that Gracie's bottom lip began to wobble while Lizzie and Jude simply stared at her.

'I'm sorry,' Gracie said, her voice wavering to match her lip now. 'I'm so sorry, Charlie, I didn't mean…'

Charlie crossed to Jude at his beckoning, where Jude placed a protective arm around his shoulder.

'Gracie,' Lizzie said gently, 'tell me the truth. Are you... could you be pregnant?'

Gracie finally collapsed into the seat Charlie had fetched for her and nodded, eyes misting.

'Yes,' she said in a small voice. 'I didn't want to believe it, but... I'm having Frank's baby.'

Chapter Fifteen

Lizzie had called a crisis meeting. Gracie's news was too big for her to handle alone and, besides, as Gracie would hear no mention of any plan but to keep her baby, it made perfect sense that they break it to their mum sooner rather than later. Lizzie had to agree with Gracie's wish, and she would have been equally surprised to hear anything else from her sister. So they were gathered around the table in the caravan now, Lizzie having driven to fetch her mum once Jude and Charlie had been sent home with apologies and promises to keep them updated.

Lizzie poured tea from the old brown pot for Gracie and her mum. When it was just her and Gracie, she always dropped teabags into mugs and mashed at them like her dad used to when he made tea at the old allotment he'd loved so much, but that would never do for Gwendolyn. It had taken Lizzie a while to locate it, but considering the news they'd just broken to her – both sisters feeling like a pair of wayward teenagers who couldn't be trusted to live alone rather than fully grown women – the teapot was a small approval point that Lizzie could produce to make her mother's mood a little more receptive, so she persevered until it had been found beneath a pile of old rags under the sink.

'I think he needs to be told.' Gwendolyn stirred her tea with a rather more aggressive action than it needed. Surely her one sugar would have dissolved without the need to apply quite so much force.

Lizzie watched and waited until the teaspoon finally went back on the tray, while Gracie looked out of the window, either weighing up what response wouldn't irritate her mother further or reluctant to get drawn into an argument she didn't want to have. To save her further torment, Lizzie helped herself to a flapjack and jumped in.

'She doesn't want to tell him,' she said. 'I've said the same as you, about a million times. By the way,' she added, her mouth now full of syrup-drenched oats, 'nice cakes, Gracie. I don't know how you get them to turn out so well with the crappy little oven in our caravan.'

Gracie returned the compliment with a stiff smile. Lizzie's attempts to lighten the mood weren't having much effect, it seemed. Then Gracie turned to her mother.

'I don't want him in our lives.'

'Why ever not?'

'You know what he did to me? How can I forgive him for having an affair and then throwing me out of the flat? How could I ever trust him not to do something terrible and mean about this? What kind of father is a man like that going to make?'

'He's the father, nevertheless.'

'Mum, he won't care about that. Even you would have to admit from what you know of Frank that he'd make a terrible father. He has no patience whatsoever. He's probably too old to learn any patience now too.'

'He might be different with one of his own.'

'And I might win the lottery this week. I'd say the odds are about the same.'

Gwendolyn sniffed. 'At the very least he should pay his way.'

'I said that too.' Lizzie reached for another flapjack. It was raining, so their plans for tea al fresco had been shelved, but in the circumstances,

Lizzie didn't think the atmosphere would have been any more jovial if they had been sitting in the pleasant shade of the old pear trees in her garden.

'You're your own worst enemy, Grace Lovell,' Gwendolyn said.

'Well, you know what they say about keeping your enemies close,' Gracie returned archly. 'If I'm my own worst enemy then it doesn't get much closer than that, does it?'

Gwendolyn dunked the teaspoon into her cup and began to stir again, and Lizzie resisted the temptation to ask her if she thought she might be able to stir right through the porcelain and into the table beneath. 'Your dad will be turning in his grave.'

'But he'd have been happy at the prospect of a grandchild?' Lizzie said softly. 'Don't you think we ought to focus on the positives? Gracie has said what she wants, and maybe that will change, but perhaps for now we ought to respect her wishes?'

'Whose side are you on?' Gwendolyn said, shooting Lizzie a sideways look.

'Nobody's. I'm on the side of reason and common sense.'

'And for heaven's sake, Mum,' Gracie cut in, 'that tea is stirred! You can't possibly stir it any more without changing its molecular make-up!'

'Don't snap at me just because your hormones are all over the place!'

'Now you sound just like Frank! That's his favourite line—'

'Whoa!' Lizzie shouted. 'Just stop for a minute, you two! Aren't you supposed to be on the same side? Aren't we family? Mum, I know you don't agree with the way Gracie is handling this but it's her choice. And, Gracie, Mum is doing her best to get her head around this, and she's finding it as stressful as you so cut her some slack. OK?'

Gracie pouted, throwing her mother a black look. But then she nodded and their mother did too.

'I'm sorry,' Gwendolyn said. 'I just want what's best for you.'

'I know,' Gracie said. 'I'm sorry I shouted at you, but I don't want to involve Frank.'

'You do realise, however,' Lizzie cut in, 'that Frank is bound to find out sooner or later, and he won't be happy about being kept in the dark when he does.'

'Good!' Gracie reached for a flapjack and rammed it into her mouth. Her mum broke into a small smile.

'I don't think you mean that either,' Lizzie said.

'Well, no. I mean yes.' Gracie's eyes misted and she sniffed back tears, sticking a defiant chin out again. 'He broke my heart, but he only gets to do it once. This time, I call the shots, and he'll find out how it feels to be the last to know something and to be shut out.' Gracie popped the rest of the flapjack in her mouth and chewed rapidly.

'But won't you need some support when the baby comes?' Gwendolyn asked.

'It's a baby and lots of people have them – how hard can it be?'

'I don't think it's the having them that's the hard bit,' Lizzie said with a small smile of her own. 'I think it's the raising that might cause you some headaches.'

'Well, I can do that too. And you'll help me, won't you?' Gracie looked from Lizzie to her mum and back again. 'So I don't need to worry about anything, do I?'

Lizzie forced her smile to stretch. Whether she wanted it or not, it looked as if she was going to be a big part of this baby's life.

'I'm more concerned about the emotional impact of bringing up a child who's the result of a relationship where you can't even bear to look at each other anymore, let alone take joint responsibility for it,' Gwendolyn said.

'I don't know why you're so anxious about Frank being involved,' Gracie replied. 'Honestly, he'd be so useless that I might as well do it alone, and he really wouldn't care either way.'

'I think you'll find he cares more than you might imagine.'

Gracie crossed her arms. 'If he finds out and he wants to be involved then fine, but I'm not going to tell him, no matter what anyone says. And…' she added, wagging a finger at her mother, 'you're not going to tell him either. If he's upset that he didn't know then perhaps he might reflect on the fact that if he hadn't shagged that barely legal girl we would have been together still and he would have known about his baby.'

'I think,' Lizzie began slowly, 'that this is more about getting back at Frank than you thinking he wouldn't be interested in his baby.'

'Well, you're wrong, so it shows what you know,' Gracie returned tartly.

'Don't be like that; I'm only trying to help.'

'I know,' Gracie said, her front crumbling now and tears filling her eyes. 'But it's not helping so please stop trying to psychoanalyse me. I'm just getting used to the idea that I'm going to have a little person totally relying on me for everything and the last thing I want is to think about the bastard who caused it all.'

'You don't really think he's a bastard, do you?' Lizzie asked softly.

'No,' Gracie said. 'That's why it hurts so much to think about him. Please, understand that him being involved would only make things ten times harder. It's better this way.'

Lizzie glanced at her mother. Their silent exchange was the product of many years of fine-tuning their instinctive understanding of what each other was thinking, and this occasion was no different. Neither of them thought that keeping Frank in the dark was the best course of action, but in the end it was Gracie's choice. She wasn't changing her mind any time soon and there was no argument on earth that would do it for her.

'You've got us,' Lizzie said, trying to make her smile as encouraging as she could. 'Whatever you need, we'll be here for you.'

Gwendolyn nodded agreement and then dusted off her hands. 'So, to practical matters. Have you registered with a GP nearby?'

Gracie shook her head.

'You're going to have to, so they can get you on the books of a midwife. How far along do you think you are?'

'I'm not sure.'

'When was your last period?'

'I haven't really been keeping track.'

Gwendolyn rolled her eyes.

'Sorry,' Gracie said. 'I don't suppose I can be very far along – it must have happened just before Frank left me.'

'Well, in that case I'm sure you're going to need to see the midwife sooner rather than later so she can work all that out and make sure you get what you need right now.'

Lizzie smiled. For a moment they'd reverted back to mother and daughter, and Gracie nodded eagerly, obviously grateful for her mum's advice and guidance, as she once would have been as a young girl when mothers knew all and always knew best. With their capable mum on her side and a family who wanted to help, Gracie would be alright… eventually.

*

How Lizzie wished she'd tried a little harder to persuade Gracie to come along tonight. She could understand why her sister – under normal circumstances most likely to be found glowing at the centre of any social gathering – had feigned tiredness to get out of this. After all, why would she want to sit like a gooseberry in between two couples when it would only serve as a cruel reminder that she was no longer part of one? Nonetheless, Lizzie couldn't deny being a little hurt that Gracie hadn't understood her own predicament.

As she dressed, despairing that anything she tried on would compete on any level with Harriet's easy style and effortless sex appeal, she couldn't deny that she was nervous. It made no sense – it wasn't as if she'd never socialised with Harriet and Damon before – but it was almost as if the very intentional nature of this get-together was the problem. She'd only ever been thrown into Harriet's path by chance before, but tonight had been engineered by Jude with the express purpose of helping her and Harriet to become friends. If she was completely honest, Lizzie didn't want to be friends with Harriet, and she suspected that Harriet might feel the same. It was nothing personal, it was just that the last hobby Lizzie wanted to take up was that of sizing herself up in comparison to Harriet on a regular basis, with the likelihood that she'd always come away feeling lacking.

Still, she mused as she fastened the buttons of her trusty old tea dress, Jude had asked her, and it seemed really important to him, and how could she have said no to that? Having Gracie with her would have helped, though. Her sister was so good at diffusing tension, so much wittier and sharper and cleverer than Lizzie, so accomplished entertaining a room full of strangers that she would have had the situation in hand five minutes after they'd walked in. She'd have taken the pressure off Lizzie and they'd have left the gathering a triumph. Now Lizzie was going to have to deal with it alone, and she just knew she was going to cock it up somehow.

Harriet and Damon were already there with Artie when Lizzie arrived. Lizzie had relied on a lift from Gracie to get there, who warned that she'd probably be asleep by eleven and if Lizzie wanted a lift home again she'd have to find it elsewhere. It was good to know that Gracie had her back, she'd mused wryly, but it was pointless to complain and so she hadn't bothered. Charlie was rushing back and forth, carrying glasses and bowls of peanuts and crisps to the table. Jude kept telling him there was enough, but Charlie seemed so happy to be useful that nobody made any huge effort to stop him, even when the table was so full that he'd started to put things on spare chairs.

Harriet was dressed in a black pencil skirt and a fitted black top with long lace-up boots. She wore winged eyeliner and a tiny ruby in her perfectly pert little nose, like Audrey Hepburn gone punk. Lizzie, on the other hand, was like Audrey Hepburn in no capacity whatsoever. As soon as she walked in she felt on the back foot, somehow woefully inadequate against the practically perfect Harriet. Even though Jude greeted her with an enthusiastic compliment, it was a feeling Lizzie found hard to shake.

Damon was in his usual uniform of residual teenage angst, hair over his eyes, dirty black jeans teamed with a lumberjack-style shirt and his distressed trainers. His sleeves were rolled back today to reveal a tattoo that ran the length of his left forearm. It looked like a character from a comic or something; Lizzie couldn't really tell and she didn't like to ask. The more Lizzie saw of Damon, the more she wondered at Harriet's complete turnaround in taste – he really was nothing like Jude at all. Lizzie noted a guitar case standing against the wall of the conservatory where they'd decided to sit to enjoy the last of the sun. Knowing that Jude didn't play any instrument, Lizzie was wondering who it belonged to until Damon leapt up and moved it away from Artie's wandering hands. The look on his face was one of such irritation that she could only assume it belonged to him.

Jude took Artie in his arms and carried him over to Lizzie. 'Say hello to Lizzie, Artie.'

Lizzie couldn't help the way her heart squeezed at the sight of them. Jude looked so good and right with Artie in his arms, such a natural dad, so obviously happy, and she forced herself not to dwell on the thought that he'd already had a life before her, one that was full of love; perhaps one that was better, one he hadn't wanted to lose.

'Hi, Artie,' Lizzie said with a brave smile. 'It's good to finally meet you.'

Artie disappeared into Jude's neck, thumb in mouth.

'I can't believe you've turned shy,' Jude said with a chuckle. 'Come on, Lizzie's not that scary.'

Jude ran a hand over Artie's dark curls. A moment later, the little boy peered out at Lizzie, thumb still in his mouth, his blue eyes almost a carbon copy of Jude's as they measured her up. He didn't speak. Lizzie tried again. It was important that she make a good impression on Jude's son.

'I really like your T-shirt,' she said, pointing to the picture on the front. 'Is that a stegosaurus on it?'

'Ah,' Jude said. 'See, Lizzie knows her dinosaurs too. What do you think of that?' He gave Artie a quick tickle under the chin, which caused the little boy to giggle.

Lizzie smiled as Artie turned to her with a shy one of his own. But then Harriet came over and took him from Jude.

'He can stay up with us for half an hour longer, but then he needs to go to bed,' she said.

Jude nodded, though it was easy to see the disappointment he was trying to hide. Perhaps he'd wanted to give Lizzie more time to get to know his son. She gave him a reassuring smile, trying to telegraph silently that it didn't matter, that they had all the time in the world for that.

As they took their seats, the room balmy from the day's sun, Harriet sat Artie down in between her and Damon on the rattan sofa. Lizzie could have sworn she saw another look of irritation from Damon, but if it was there at all, he smoothed it away quickly. Her attention was drawn to the door, when George the little terrier trotted in. He headed straight for Lizzie, his tail whirring madly, licking her hand as she reached to stroke him.

'Someone's got a fan,' Harriet commented carelessly.

'He must be a good judge of character,' Jude said, smiling warmly at Lizzie, who returned it.

Lizzie then turned to Harriet to reply to her comment, but she was thrown by an expression that said Harriet might not be in total agreement with George's opinions on Lizzie. Lizzie tried to ignore the look – maybe she was seeing too much in it. Harriet seemed so hot and cold towards Lizzie that she couldn't figure out where they stood with each other. But Harriet soon turned back to Artie, fussing over a stain she'd found on his sleeve.

The next half hour was taken up in polite, careful conversation. It was strange, because they'd all met before, but it was almost as if the very act of deliberately pulling them all together had changed the dynamic somehow. A couple of drinks might loosen the mood – at least hers if nobody else's – Lizzie decided, so she took full advantage of Jude's earlier offer to stay over and began with a Malibu and Coke.

Jude had gone into the kitchen with Charlie to mix it, and when he came back and handed it to Lizzie, he had a wicked smile on his lips. As soon as Lizzie tasted it, she realised why, and she gave a grin of her own. There had to be at least a triple measure in there – not that she was complaining. Jude was clearly as keen for Lizzie to stay over as she was. Even better, Harriet was drinking beer watered down with lemonade, just as Charlie had been allowed to do (very watered down for him), saying that she and Damon would be driving back to his place after the party, leaving Artie to sleep over at Jude's place too. Lizzie wondered how much of that had been Damon's idea. He didn't seem to be all that keen on Artie. There was no specific incident that Lizzie could point to that made her think so, just a general lack of engagement that seemed to say it.

Then Artie was duly put to bed in Charlie's room. Charlie had been charged with the task of listening out for the baby monitor that was still in use on the odd time that Artie stayed over. It was a responsibility he took very seriously as he kept leaving the conservatory every ten minutes to listen to it out in the kitchen. He'd return and report the exact sounds he heard, even if that was just snuffling and shifting.

Jude had been in an excitable mood, and the more he drank, the more animated he became. Lizzie could see he was happy to have everyone together in his house. He was up and down – making sure there was enough wine in the fridge, that the beers he'd bought were the brand Damon liked, that Charlie was OK, that Charlie was happy that Artie was OK, that the bowls containing crisps and nuts were constantly overflowing, that the music was loud enough, that it wasn't too loud, that they were warm enough, cool enough… that just everything was perfect. Lizzie was exhausted simply watching him dart around. She'd thought Gracie could get overexcited at the mere sniff of a soiree, but this was something she hadn't expected from the usually laid-back Jude. She supposed it really did show just how much it meant to him that the evening went well, and she resolved to do her bit, no matter what she felt about Harriet.

So she painted on a smile and she tried to be witty and bright, she laughed in all the right places and gave out compliments, and then, as the night wore on and they got drunker, she tried not to notice how close Harriet was sitting to Jude, and how often she touched his leg or his arm as she laughed at a joke, and how they'd lapsed into exclusive anecdotes again, just as they had that day by the river, so that she and Damon could only sit and listen and pretend they got the joke.

But on this occasion, she noticed that Damon wasn't quite as relaxed about it as he'd been the last time she'd met him. When Harriet leaned over Jude and pulled him into a tight hug, Lizzie could have sworn she saw the muscles of Damon's jaw twitch, his smile becoming a little more glassy-eyed than it had been. The thing was, they were all tipsy except for Harriet, so whatever she was playing at, she was doing it stone cold sober. Damon must have realised that too.

'Wanna see my new guitar?' Damon asked.

Harriet offered a withering look. 'Not now – you'll wake Artie. I don't know why you brought it with you.'

'I wouldn't mind seeing it,' Jude said generously. 'You could play it quietly – right?'

'Sure!' Damon leapt from his seat to get it. Lizzie didn't think she'd seen him move so fast all night. He returned a second later with the case and undid the clasps almost reverently to reveal a glossy hardwood guitar. Lizzie didn't know much about guitars, but if it looked that beautiful to her, she could understand the look of absolute love on Damon's face.

'I've never heard you play, you know,' Jude said.

'I didn't realise,' Damon replied. He looked to Harriet, who simply rolled her eyes and shrugged.

'If you must,' she said. 'Better keep it down, though. If you wake Artie I will kill you.'

'I won't wake him – chill,' Damon said, looking and sounding more like an angsty teenager than ever. He shook his fringe from his eyes before taking the guitar from its case.

Jude sat forward expectantly. Charlie almost gasped with anticipation, while Harriet threw a look towards the kitchen, where the baby monitor was sitting on the worktop, listening in on Artie. Lizzie waited with interest. She didn't know anyone who played guitar and really, rock had never been her sort of thing, but she was interested now and a little bit impressed that Damon could play.

Damon stroked his fingers down the strings and then frowned. 'Needs a little tuning,' he said. 'Sometimes they lose it easily while they're still new.'

So they had to wait for a moment while Damon tweaked and twanged and tried to get the strings right. Then he strummed again and this time seemed happier. He began to play a quiet tune, catching each string gently with the plectrum he'd retrieved from his shirt pocket. Jude gave Harriet a look of approval, but she didn't seem quite as in awe – Lizzie supposed she'd heard it all before. Then Jude turned the same look on Lizzie and she had to agree – she was no expert but Damon did sound pretty good.

'Do you know any Dolly Parton songs?' Charlie asked excitedly.

Damon looked confused for a moment, but then he grinned. 'Sorry, my guitar wouldn't let me play one of those even if I did know one.'

Charlie looked disappointed and Harriet reached over to ruffle his hair. 'Some people have no taste, eh, Chuckles?'

'I picked you,' Damon said mildly as he continued to strum gently. 'So I must have some taste.'

'Maybe I picked you!' Harriet countered. 'Who says you got a say in the choosing?'

'Can you play a song?' Charlie asked.

'I *am* playing a song,' Damon said, his head nodding slightly as he strummed.

'A different song,' Charlie insisted. 'I don't know this one.'

'What do you want me to sing?'

Charlie shrugged. His number-one choice had already been vetoed and apparently he didn't have a fall-back position.

'That Smashing Pumpkins song Charlie liked that one time?' Harriet suggested, getting more into the spirit of things now. 'You can play that, can't you?'

Damon paused, but then nodded. 'Yeah, probably.'

His fingers began to move across the strings again, and then he opened his mouth and began to sing.

The look of shock on Lizzie's face was completely involuntary. It was lucky that her hands hadn't also flown to her ears. Damon might have been a competent guitarist, but his voice rasped like a pan scrubber being scratched across a metal pot. Lizzie supposed he might think it was cool and edgy, but it was just offensive to anyone with ears. Even Charlie looked vaguely alarmed, and he was usually happy with just about any kind of entertainment. Harriet alone looked untroubled and unsurprised but then, she must have heard Damon singing plenty of times before. The rest of the room struggled through and suffered it to the end. Damon looked up to forced smiles of approval.

'Any more requests?' he asked cheerfully.

'No!' Jude said a little too quickly. 'I mean, let's save them for later when we've had a few more drinks.' He looked at Lizzie with something like desperation in his eyes. 'Another drink?'

Lizzie downed the last of her Malibu and handed him the glass. She'd gladly take as much alcohol as necessary to drown out the terrible memory of the sound she'd just been subjected to. She'd call it singing, but it would be an insult to singers everywhere.

'I'd love one,' she said.

Jude headed out to the kitchen, leaving Damon to put his guitar back into the case, though he left it open so he could look lovingly at it from time to time.

Harriet reached for a handful of peanuts from a bowl that Charlie had balanced precariously on a side table and popped them into her mouth. With Jude out of the room, the conversation had dried up again.

'Where did you learn to play?' Lizzie asked Damon, more for something to fill the silence than because she genuinely cared.

'Self-taught,' he replied, sitting a little straighter as he did.

'Right,' Lizzie said. 'That's quite impressive. I don't think I could teach myself to play an instrument.'

'You'd be surprised,' he said. 'There are tutorials and everything online now. Anyone can do it.'

That didn't mean everyone should do it, Lizzie thought, though perhaps she was being a little unkind. The guitar playing hadn't actually been too bad. If someone could just have a quiet word with him about the singing, they'd potentially save many people from having to go through what the guests at Jude's house had just had to endure.

Jude returned with more drinks and Lizzie relaxed. At least he could take charge of the conversation again, leaving her to pursue steadily increasing drunkenness.

*

Charlie had been allowed to drink a little beer mixed with lemonade, and while he'd been happy to join in the conversation at first, after an hour or so, he'd wandered off to play on his games console in Jude's little office. Jude and Harriet were taking it in turns to check on Artie now. Sometime around eleven, a tinny little voice came from the baby monitor.

'Mummy!'

Harriet pushed herself from the sofa. 'I won't be a minute. He's doing this all the time at the moment – night terrors or something they call it.'

At this Jude looked alarmed. 'How long has this been going on? It didn't happen last time he stayed with me.'

Harriet shrugged. 'About a week, maybe. He just wakes up all stressed. Apparently it's a toddler thing – nothing to get antsy about. Mum says I used to do it too.'

She left the room, Jude watching her go with a look of concern.

'You heard her,' Damon said mildly. 'He'll be alright in a minute.'

Jude turned to him and now his look of concern had turned to one of irritation. Lizzie knew what he was thinking without having to ask. Damon had no children, hardly took any interest in Artie as far as Lizzie could tell, and wasn't far short of a man-child himself. It was alright for him to offer glib reassurances because – though she could be wrong – Lizzie would bet he'd never had a single responsibility in his life.

'I'll turn the music off for a while, shall I?' Lizzie offered. 'Just until Artie settles off again…'

Jude threw her a grateful look. She went to the iPod dock and pressed pause on the playlist. As she took her seat again, Harriet shouted for Jude.

'Can you come in for a minute?'

Jude got up and went out, leaving Lizzie and Damon alone. Here were two people now thrown together who had nothing more in common than the fact that their partners had once been partners, and if any situation promised an awkward silence, this was it. Lizzie glanced at him and offered a tight smile.

'So…' she began in a bid to fill the gap. 'You never did say what you do for a living.'

'I'm in a band.'

'Really?' Lizzie asked. Considering what she'd heard that evening, she vowed never to get conned into going to see them. 'What are you called?'

'We haven't settled on a name yet.'

'Oh. Where do you play?'

'Haven't actually played a gig yet.'

Lizzie frowned. 'So you're not making money from it? You have another job?'

'Not exactly… I'm helping out on my dad's farm until we get going. We're trying to build up a YouTube audience first, then we'll get on the circuit.'

'Will you try for a record deal?'

Damon's lip curled. 'Give all our earnings to a faceless corporation? No chance! You don't need a record deal these days; you can do it all yourselves and keep all the money.'

'Oh…' Lizzie said, folding her hands over one another in her lap. 'Well, that's good.'

They fell to silence again. Lizzie looked up at the clock. Jude and Harriet had been gone for a good five minutes. She supposed that when you considered they were probably trying to get Artie settled again, five minutes wasn't all that long, but sitting alone with Damon made it feel like a lot longer.

'So how did you meet Harriet?' she asked.

'In a pub.'

'Oh, the Golden Lion?'

Damon snorted. 'Nobody goes in there!'

Lizzie smoothed another frown away. That wasn't what she'd heard from Derek, and the Golden Lion looked quite nice from what she'd seen.

'She was dancing on a table in the Grim Reaper,' Damon said with a grin at the memory.

'Where's that? Is it in the village?'

'God no! I never drink in the village.'

'Why not?'

'Well, it's boring…' he said, as if that were the most obvious thing in the world.

'So where's the Grim Reaper then?' Lizzie asked, deciding it was also somewhere she ought to make an effort to avoid in the future.

'It's out on the A12.'

She nodded and looked at the clock again, wishing harder than ever that Jude and Harriet (but mostly Jude) would reappear. But another few silent minutes ticked by and there was still no sign of them. Doubts and suspicions began to creep into Lizzie's mind, and she shook them away.

'What are they doing in there?' Damon said, clearly beginning to feel as uneasy as Lizzie. 'How long does it take to get a kid to sleep?'

'I have no idea – never had to do it,' Lizzie said.

'He's always doing this.'

'Who?'

'The kid. Always waking up.'

Lizzie shrugged. 'I suppose that's what toddlers do.'

'It's a pain. You can't get a minute alone without him wanting something. He's still staying here tonight, right?'

'As far as I know.'

'Good.'

'You don't like him?'

'Course I do.'

Lizzie paused. She was running out of conversation fast and what there was felt like hard work.

'Do you have to get up early to work on your dad's farm?'

Damon sat back and clasped his hands behind his head. 'Early enough, but it's not like he's going to sack me if I take the odd lie-in, is it?'

'I suppose not. Do you still live with your parents on the farm?'

'Yeah.'

'And they don't mind... I mean, does Harriet stay over there a lot with you?'

'They don't mind. My room's soundproofed anyway for my guitar so...'

'Does she bring Artie?'

'Not if I can help it. Usually Harriet gets someone to babysit if she's coming for the night.'

'How long have you been together?'

Damon scratched a hand through his hair. 'Maybe six, seven months. She's amazing.'

'Seems like it...' Lizzie gave a rueful smile.

'I mean, other than the obvious, she's as close to a ten as you can get,' he said, looking towards the stairs.

'Other than what obvious?'

'You know...' Damon looked at her. 'The baggage.'

'Baggage? You mean Artie?' Lizzie stared at him. She'd always been more worried about Jude's relationship with Harriet than the fact that he had a son, and she'd never imagined that it would be Artie who would present an issue to anyone. She was about to say something to that effect when the sound of laughter came floating through from the baby monitor in the kitchen. It must have been loud because they hadn't been able to make out the indistinct mumbling that had been coming through before, but this was clear. It sounded like Harriet, and something had clearly tickled her.

Lizzie tried to ignore the prickling hairs on the back of her neck and the wave of insane jealousy that suddenly swept over her. Harriet had been doing her best to get one up on Lizzie all night – try as she might, Lizzie couldn't ignore it any longer. Harriet had constantly reminded Jude of how much history they had together, she'd flirted with him despite Damon being there and now she'd taken him off on some pretence of needing him for Artie.

Lizzie glanced at Damon. Would he agree if she spoke any of this out loud? Or was she really seeing things that weren't there?

'What the hell is taking them so long?' he said again, looking at the clock.

'Maybe I should go and see if everything is OK?' Lizzie said.

Just then, Charlie wandered in. 'Can I have some more beer?' he asked, clearly bored.

'Oh,' Lizzie replied. 'Well, maybe we ought to ask Jude first.'

'Where is he?'

'He's helping Harriet. Artie woke up.'

Charlie's expression brightened. 'I know how to get Artie back to sleep!'

'Maybe you could go and help them…' Lizzie suggested, seizing suddenly on a resolution to their current predicament. With Charlie in there, nobody needed to worry about what else might be going on.

Charlie dashed off, and Lizzie exchanged another look with Damon. Only this time she couldn't hide the little lacing of triumph in hers.

Flirt your way out of that, Harrie…

When Charlie came back, Harriet and Jude were with him. Both were smiling broadly and looking as if they'd had the time of their lives in Artie's bedroom.

'Is everything OK?' Lizzie asked. 'Artie's gone back to sleep?'

'He has now,' Jude said. 'He's such a little character, though – messed us around something rotten. He'd got both our full attention and he wasn't wasting that opportunity...' He glanced at Harriet, eyebrows raised. 'I wonder where he gets that from?'

'Not from me!' Harriet laughed. 'You're the needy one!'

'But you love an audience,' Jude countered.

'Oh yeah, right, I forgot that everything is always my fault,' Harriet said with a grin.

'Not everything,' Jude said. 'Just most things...'

'But he's asleep now?' Damon interrupted their banter. 'And he won't wake up again tonight?'

'I think he's settled,' Harriet said. 'I can't promise he won't wake again.'

'So I can't play my guitar?' Damon asked, looking crestfallen.

'Play it quietly, but don't sing,' Harriet said.

Lizzie didn't say anything about the mere fact of them having a drinks party was probably enough to wake Artie again if things got too rowdy. While Harriet was forbidding too much noise, it saved everyone from having to suffer Damon's singing again, even if that hadn't been her intention. For once, Lizzie found herself in agreement with something Harriet had said.

'Can I top you up?' Jude looked at Lizzie's empty glass. She nodded and handed it to him.

'I think Charlie wanted a drink too,' Lizzie said.

'You want one, Chuckles?' Harriet asked, smiling at Charlie. 'Come on, I'll sort yours out while Jude does the others.'

Jude left for the kitchen, with Harriet and Charlie following. Lizzie looked at Damon and tried to hold in the long sigh working its way into her throat. Luckily, he was busy lifting his guitar from the case, gazing at it with such love and wonder that Lizzie was worried he might be about to snog it, but at least it saved her a repeat of the painful attempts at conversation they'd endured moments before. She could hear laughter again coming from the kitchen, but it seemed to be as a result of something Charlie was doing or saying. This time, Lizzie couldn't hold the sigh back. Damon looked up.

'They're always doing that,' he said, angling his head towards the doorway.

Lizzie wanted to ask if it bothered him, but she had the feeling that Damon wouldn't be very good at discretion, and she didn't want anything she said on the matter getting back to Jude or Harriet, so she didn't.

'I suppose they've known each other so long they're like family,' she said instead.

But Damon simply dipped his head to look at his guitar as he began to play, and then Harriet and Jude came back with Charlie and the drinks, and that was the end of that.

Chapter Sixteen

Lizzie had the windows wound down, and the wind whipped her hair into wild tangles as they zipped down country lanes, the slipstream lifting the scents of yarrow and foxglove into the car from the hedgerows. The blue sky was barely troubled by tendrils of high cloud but the warm sun was glorious. Gracie was twiddling with the dials of the radio while Lizzie's eyes were fixed on the road ahead.

'Honestly, there's nothing decent on,' she said as she scrolled through discordant snatches of music that ranged from Beethoven to Katy Perry.

'Then turn it off,' Lizzie said. 'Talk to me instead.'

'I thought you needed to concentrate on the directions.'

'Not for a minute, I'm on a straight road for the next few miles.'

Gracie turned off the radio and looked expectantly at her sister. 'OK. What do you want to talk about?'

'Nothing in particular. It's just nice to chat while we have a bit of time off, isn't it?'

'Lizzie, we live together. We have loads of time to chat.'

Lizzie laughed. 'You know what I mean.'

'Not really.'

'We're always talking when things need doing. We're rarely talking when we have nothing else to think about. We talk about whose turn it is to take the rubbish out or whether we want a cup of tea.'

'Seems to me we've done a lot of talking about other things lately,' Gracie said.

'Well, yes, maybe a little over the last few days. But then you did decide to drop a huge bombshell on us.'

'It was sort of a bombshell for me too, trust me.'

'Then why don't we start with that?'

'I'd really rather not.'

'And that's what worries me. Gracie, you talk incessantly about anything and everything, but then you have something this huge happen to you, and every time anyone wants to discuss it, you clam up. It makes me wonder if you're completely OK with it all.'

'I just don't think there's a lot to say. I'm still a bit in shock, but I expect it will all be alright in the end.'

'But, about Frank—'

'Mum's put you up to this, hasn't she? That's why she was so keen to stay in our caravan to keep an eye on things while you took me to see this other place. I worked it out as soon as you told me we were going to see this other mill because when you first said you were going, you didn't want to ask Mum to stay and hold the fort at all because you thought it would be too stressful for her. I thought it was funny you'd changed your mind. You both must think I fell off a Christmas tree.'

'She's just worried about you. We're both worried,' Lizzie said. It was true, and she was hardly happier about leaving Gwendolyn in charge at Magnolia Lane than she had been when she'd first arranged to visit Kestrel Mill, but she realised that the talk she needed to have with Gracie was bigger than that. Gwendolyn had entrusted the task to Lizzie, believing that Gracie would be more likely to talk frankly with Lizzie than with her, and Lizzie had to agree.

'I don't want to tell Frank.' Gracie turned her gaze to the window. They passed a field of dazzling yellow rapeseed. 'How far is this place we're going to?'

'It's called Kestrel Mill,' Lizzie replied, realising that Gracie had clammed up on the subject of her pregnancy for now and it was pointless to pursue it. 'We've got at least another hour yet. Will you be OK?'

'I expect so.'

'I mean… you're not feeling too sick now?'

'It goes off around mid-morning. Sometimes I get a little light-headed, but if I'm careful I can manage it.'

'Like when you were out with Charlie?'

'Just like that. Charlie was such a sweetheart, you know. He's really lovely.'

'He is.'

'I'm surprised you didn't bring him and Jude to look at this windmill place. After all, Charlie would have loved it.'

Lizzie's expression darkened. She had asked Jude, but he'd told her that he'd already arranged to meet Harriet so they could take Artie shopping for new shoes. She wasn't about to tell Gracie that, though, just like she hadn't told her about the flirting at Jude's drinks party. It would only reopen a debate that she didn't particularly want to have again, and there was really enough to think about without it.

'Well, yes, but… it's sort of work, isn't it? And I wanted to be able to concentrate and take everything in.'

'Work how? It's just another windmill that someone lives in, like you want to do with yours.'

'Actually…' Lizzie took a breath. Gracie wouldn't like it but while they were coming clean with each other about things (at least, some things), now was probably a time as good as any to mention the plans she'd discussed with Florentina. Her sister would find out sooner or later anyway. Lizzie knew she'd be angry, but now that her pregnancy was out in the open, Lizzie had the perfect argument for why Gracie herself wasn't the person to go into business with her – after all, Gracie had enough on her plate just dealing with her impending motherhood, and it was likely she wouldn't even want to think about starting a new business anyway. 'Kestrel Mill is a working mill. They produce flour. That's why I want to see it.'

'Do they? I bet that's noisy.'

Lizzie laughed. 'That's not the response I was expecting.'

'What's that got to do with us? Are you saying you want to make flour?'

'Yes. I've been thinking about it for a while.'

'What will you do with it?'

'Sell some and keep some back to make my own bread.'

'Bread?'

'To sell to shops, and maybe in our own on-site shop.'

'That sounds like a lot of work.'

'It will be. A lot of money to start up too.'

'Do you need some more, because—'

'God, no, Gracie! You need to keep your money – especially now because you're going to need it for your baby. I've got a business partner… at least, interest from a potential business partner. She might put the money in.'

'Mum?'

'Not Mum.'

'Then who?'

Lizzie cleared her throat. 'Florentina said she'd like to.'

Gracie folded her arms, her gaze going to the windows again. 'I bet she would, so she can worm her way into our lives a little more permanently. I suppose she's feeling all at sea now she doesn't have Dad to make excuses for her.'

'I knew you'd react like that.'

'It's your business.' Gracie sniffed. 'Do what you like with it.'

'That's what *I am* doing.'

'Just don't come crying to me when it all goes wrong.'

'Now you sound like Mum. And how is it going to go wrong? It's Florentina, putting a little money into a tiny business. We're hardly going to trouble Alan Sugar.'

'Florentina might not like you quite so much if you lose her money for her. And you might not like her quite so much when she tries to tell you how to run your mill because she thinks a little investment gives her a valid stake in it.'

'Well, a little investment *would* give her a valid stake in it,' Lizzie said firmly, though doubts, unbidden, began to creep in. Gracie could be unreasonable where Florentina was concerned, but what if she was right? What if this partnership did drive a wedge between them? Was it worth the risk?

Gracie pouted. 'That's fine then. As long as you're happy and you know what's what.'

'So you're not angry that I didn't ask you instead? I thought about it but…'

'I know, I'm going to have my hands full. I realise that's the reason. Besides, all my money will go on your caravan when I eventually buy it.'

'About that too… I understand if you don't want to buy it now. You probably need the money for the baby and—'

'That's true, but I also need somewhere to bring up the baby and where better than a place as idyllic as Magnolia Lane? It makes perfect sense to buy the caravan so you can get your building work finished.'

There it was again – the assumption that Gracie was now a permanent feature at Magnolia Mill. Her sister had clearly decided that the caravan would be allowed to stay on the land forever and Lizzie wasn't sure how practical or desirable that would be. But the funny thing was, Lizzie was sort of getting used to the idea of Gracie being at Magnolia Mill herself, despite her misgivings and, to her great surprise, was finding that she didn't actually hate it as much as she'd always imagined she would.

'It might come to nothing, you know – this business plan, I mean. This might all be pie in the sky. I suppose I'll have a better idea when I've learned a bit more about Kestrel Mill.'

'I expect so,' Gracie said sagely. 'So in that case, why haven't you brought Florentina with you today?'

'I had thought about asking her, but I wanted you to come. I thought it might be nice for us to take a trip together – like old times. That's OK, isn't it?'

The darkness in Gracie's expression cleared, like the sun banishing the storm clouds, and she turned to Lizzie with a broad smile now. 'Is that really what you thought?'

'I wouldn't have said it otherwise, would I?'

'That's actually quite lovely.'

'I'm not a total bitch, you know.'

'Of course you're not – I've never said that.'

'I think you might have done a few times over the years.'

'Well… there was that one time when you sabotaged my date with Martin Prosser because you thought he was only after one thing—'

'Which he was,' Lizzie cut in.

'… and the time you took my Clarins lipstick without asking and broke the top off… and the time you grassed me up for taking the chocolates off the Christmas tree—'

'Because you ate them all in one go and threw up in my bedroom!'

'… and the fact that your boobs have always been bigger than mine… and—'

Lizzie laughed. 'OK. So neither of us have been angelic over the years.'

Gracie turned to her with a wicked grin. 'If I haven't then you must have deserved it.'

'Probably. You know, none of us had planned to complicate life at Magnolia Mill with a baby, but can I confess to being a little bit excited now that I'm used to the idea?'

'At least one of us is,' Gracie said, her grin fading.

'Give it time and I think you will be. Look at how Charlie has taken to you. I think you'll be a brilliant mum.'

'We don't have that much time. Spring will be here before we know it and so will the baby.'

'That doesn't change that when the time comes I think you'll step up to the plate just fine.'

'Honestly?'

Lizzie nodded. 'Cross my heart.'

'I think you'll be a brilliant aunt.'

'I already know that,' Lizzie said with a chuckle. 'But you can't go wrong being an auntie, can you? When things are a bit sticky, you just hand the baby back and let Mum deal with it.'

'Oh great, so glad I'm going to get such super support from you.'

'Seriously, you'll be fine. More than fine.'

'It's easy for you to say.'

'Well, it is, but I'm not the one who went and got pregnant.'

'You surely don't think I did this deliberately?' Gracie squeaked.

'No, of course not, I was just agreeing with you. It is easy for me to say, but I can't change the fact that you're the pregnant one and I'm not.'

Gracie's voice dropped and there was an unexpected note of defeat in it. 'Do you all think I'm very silly to want to keep the baby?'

'Why would we think that? I'd be surprised to hear you wanted to do anything else. I think we're more concerned that you don't want to tell Frank.'

'But you understand why? It's hard enough getting over him, and I have to pretend to be tough about it because if I don't I might just fall apart. I loved Frank, you know.'

'I know you did,' Lizzie said gently.

'I really thought we'd be together forever. Now I feel stupid, and I feel like everyone else could see what sort of man he really was and I was just a blind fool who let him walk all over me.'

'Nobody would ever call you that. Don't forget, you're not the only one to have been taken in by a man.'

'Do you still miss Evan?'

'At first I did. And I can't bring myself to hate him even though I should.'

'Then you'll know exactly how I feel about Frank, won't you? I have to keep him out of my life, away from my thoughts, and I can't allow myself to think of him fondly at all. It's the only way we survive, isn't it?'

'You know you're allowed to admit when you're scared. Nobody – especially not me – will judge you.'

'Scared? Of having the baby?'

'That. And other things too.'

Gracie gave a half-laugh. 'I suppose my situation isn't looking too rosy right about now, is it? No home, no job, no boyfriend, and pregnant to boot.'

'But you've got us. You know you'll always have your family.'

'I have, and I'm grateful for that.' Gracie was quiet for a moment, and then she spoke again. 'Lizzie…'

'Yes?'

'This business… I mean. I guess if Florentina is willing to help your dreams come true, I can hardly hold that against her, can I?'

Lizzie threw her a grateful smile. 'Thank you for understanding.' Her eyes turned to the road again and her forehead creased into a vague frown. 'Bloody hell – that's what you get for yakking.'

'What?'

'We've only gone and missed our turning.'

*

As they pulled up in the car park of Kestrel Mill and got out of the car, Lizzie stared up, mesmerised by the sight of the sails turning. She watched for a moment, unable to tear her gaze away, and the mix of emotions she felt at the sight of it was quite overwhelming. One day, this might be her windmill, the old sails creaking and groaning as the gentle wind drove them round, just like they would have done in the days when it was a proper working building. She didn't think she'd ever seen anything as beautiful.

'They're not going very fast,' Gracie said, seemingly rather less affected by the sight than her sister.

Lizzie turned to her. 'They're hardly going to be spinning off into the sky, are they?'

'I just expected it to be a bit more… energetic. You can't imagine them doing anything of use. They just sort of whiz lazily around, don't they?'

Lizzie shook her head with a slight smile. 'Whiz lazily around? Come on, let's go and find Janet.'

✳

Janet was behind the counter of the café in the annexe. Lizzie recognised her immediately from a photo on the mill's website. A couple of families with young children were sitting at tables eating sandwiches and cakes, while a group of half a dozen retirees occupied a long table and bench by the wall with pots of tea and scones.

'Hello, ladies, what can I get for you?' Janet asked brightly as Lizzie and Gracie approached the counter.

'Lizzie Lovell…' Lizzie said, offering her hand. 'This is my sister, Gracie. I'm sorry we're a bit late—'

'Oh, not at all!' Janet cried, grabbing Lizzie's hand and then Gracie's in an enthusiastic shake. 'Not at all! I'll just get Tabitha to come and look after the café…'

Lizzie and Gracie watched her dash off. Moments later, she returned, followed by a teenaged girl – perhaps around sixteen or seventeen.

'This is my oldest,' she said, giving the girl a proud and fond look. 'Slap bang in the middle of A level revision, but you'll be alright to man the till for an hour or so here, won't you, Tab?'

The girl smiled and nodded dutifully. She was blonde, lashes so fair they were almost transparent, flawless skin untroubled by make-up and a willowy figure hidden by baggy dungarees. She was not what anyone would call conventionally beautiful, but there was something quite entrancing about her.

Janet was blonde too, but it was a darker, richer colour, pinned up messily on top of her head, and her brows were darker still. She looked as if she was no stranger to a day out in the sun.

'Can I get you a drink before we start the tour?' she asked.

'I won't just yet,' Lizzie said. She turned to Gracie.

'Perhaps a glass of water?'

'Help yourself to a bottle from the fridge over there,' Janet said cheerily.

Gracie reached into her bag and pulled out her purse.

'No, no,' Janet said. 'Don't worry about that.'

'But…'

'I insist.'

Gracie hesitated, before thanking her and going to the fridge while Janet turned to Lizzie.

'I expect you want to see the mill in action before anything else?'

'Oh, I'd love to! We just saw it from the outside and it's absolutely beautiful.'

'It's been a labour of love. I have photos from when we first got hold of it; remind me to show them to you later. You'll be amazed when you see what a mess it was.'

'Trust me, I might not be as amazed as you think.'

Janet laughed. 'I suppose not with your mad lady place. How's it going?'

'As well as can be expected. I'm not sure I'm going to be finished anywhere near the deadline I'd set but it can't be helped, I suppose.'

'It does tend to be the way of things.'

Gracie joined them again, twisting the cap from a bottle of spring water before taking a sip.

'Are you OK?' Lizzie asked.

'Perfectly,' Gracie replied.

Janet looked from one to the other.

'I'm pregnant,' Gracie said in answer to the silent question. 'Only a few weeks along, though.'

'Oh, congratulations!' Janet said. 'How lovely! I do miss being pregnant. I'd have popped at least twenty out if my husband had agreed to it!'

'I think just the one will do me,' Gracie said.

'That's definitely a more sensible approach,' Janet said. 'Not nearly so expensive. Will you be alright on the stairs? They're a bit steep.'

'I'll be fine.'

She clapped her hands together. 'OK then. If you're both happy to begin, then follow me.'

*

It looked more complex than she'd imagined, but Lizzie was just as enchanted by the inner workings as she had been at the sight of the four great sails outside. A collection of mammoth gears dropped down from the main tower, connected to an iron spindle running into the great millstone. The gears clanked and groaned as they turned, but with the machinery of this mill far more complete than what she had left at Magnolia Mill, it was surprising to see pistons pumping briskly as well. It looked more like an old steam engine than the sedate turning of the sails outside had suggested, and Lizzie could see now that if hers worked in the same way, she might be able to produce her flour on a more industrial scale than she'd imagined.

Janet nodded briefly to an old man who was tipping a bag of grain into what she called 'the hopper', a chute that fed it to the millstones to be ground, shouting to introduce Lizzie over the noise before moving on. Honeyed wooden stairs led to another level where more of the mill's workings were housed, and everywhere the obligatory yellow safety signs sat as incongruous reminders of the modern world.

Gracie looked only mildly interested, but at least she had the courtesy to nod politely every time Janet told her a fact that she clearly didn't want to know. Lizzie appreciated that she'd really only come for the run-out and for a little moral support, so she didn't mind too much that her sister wasn't quite as enthusiastic as she was. But it did make her feel like a massive geek, and Gracie would no doubt tell her she was exactly that as they drove home. Lizzie didn't care if loving this made her a geek or not; she was only excited for the possibilities and hopeful that one day she might see the great cogs and gears of her own mill turning like this too.

'What do you think?' Janet asked as they settled in the café again with cups of tea and sandwiches made from Kestrel Mill's own bread.

'Incredible,' Lizzie said. 'I'm so grateful you could spare the time to show us around.'

'You're welcome to come back any time if there's anything else you need to see. And the offer of baking lessons still stands, as well as the offer of the guest accommodation.'

'We would have loved that but things are just a little too hectic right now, and I couldn't justify leaving the mill overnight,' Lizzie said, thinking of her mother back on site and hoping she was OK. There hadn't been any panicked phone calls, so that was something to be thankful for. As soon as she'd decided to take Gracie with her, she'd known there was no way she'd be able to stay longer than a day and leave her mum with the stress of making sure the building project was staying on track. Besides, Gracie's pregnancy had changed everything. With her sister relying on her more and more, Lizzie couldn't let the building schedule get too far behind, and a night away wouldn't be any help in that regard. She could come back to spend more time with Janet when Magnolia Mill was fit to live in, and, until that time, she'd have to put her dreams of making her own flour on hold and stick to her current day job.

'We've had a lovely day,' Gracie said. 'Your mill is very nice.'

'Thank you,' Janet said with a smile. 'I happen to think so too.'

Lizzie nodded agreement. Kestrel Mill was lovely, but she happened to think that her own mill on Magnolia Lane was the most beautiful thing she'd ever seen. Now that she'd seen Kestrel Mill in action, she couldn't wait for hers to be ready.

Chapter Seventeen

It was early evening by the time Lizzie and Gracie got back from Kestrel Mill and nobody felt like cooking. Gwendolyn offered, but Lizzie was seized by an impulse to go out.

'It's been ages since we've eaten out together, just us Lovell girls, and we might not get many more opportunities in the coming years when our lives get even more hectic than they are now. I vote we go and get a great big meal at the Golden Lion.'

'The what?' Gwendolyn asked, shaking her head.

'The pub in Piriwick. Didn't Dad ever take you there?'

'Your dad hadn't lived in Piriwick for years when I met him and we only really came to visit when we had you kids – we were hardly going to take you to the pub.'

'Oh,' Lizzie replied. 'Well, the man who sold me the caravan says it's very good, so I think we ought to treat ourselves and try it out.'

'What about the money?' Gracie asked.

'Just for tonight, I don't want to worry about money. If we can't have the occasional treat, we might as well go and sign ourselves up for a nunnery or something.'

'I don't think they'd take me.' Gracie raised her eyebrows.

'You'd definitely fall down on the vow of chastity,' Lizzie said with a laugh. 'So shall we go or what? I don't know about you but if they have pie on the menu then I'm in.'

'Do they have pie on the menu?' Gwendolyn asked as she reached for her coat from the peg.

'I have no idea,' Lizzie said cheerfully. 'But it's a pub so I would imagine they've got something of the sort.'

She opened the front door and they filed down the steps.

'Which car shall we take?' Gwendolyn asked.

'We could walk,' Lizzie said. 'That way everyone can have a drink.'

Gracie cleared her throat.

'OK,' Lizzie corrected, 'we can't all have a drink.'

'If I can't then I might as well drive,' Gracie said. 'Come on…'

Everyone followed her to squash into her little sports car. Lizzie reflected that Gracie would probably have to swap it when the baby arrived, and she wasn't sure what would be more of a wrench – giving up her freedom or her precious car.

*

The Golden Lion had to be the smallest pub Lizzie had ever been in. There was barely room for the five tables set out for meals – three of which were already occupied when Lizzie, Gracie and Gwendolyn walked in – but the village of Piriwick was so small, and it already had another pub too, so it probably didn't need anything much bigger. There was a tiny snug off the dining room and a narrow strip of floor that served as the bar area, already packed with locals. The close proximity of the scrubbed wooden tables and the compact nature of the place, with its low ceilings and charmingly uneven wattle and daub walls, gave it a homely feel. Lizzie wondered how it had taken her so long to visit, and she made a mental note to stop by lot more often.

'It's lovely in here.' Gwendolyn took off her coat and hung it over the back of her chair before sitting down. 'You don't get pubs like this these days.'

'That's just what I was thinking,' Lizzie said. 'It was a good recommendation from Derek and Caroline.'

'Who?' Gracie asked as she sat across from her mum.

'The man who saved both our bacon by selling his caravan at an honest price,' Lizzie said.

'Oh,' Gracie said with a smile. 'Hurray for Derek then. I'd buy him a drink if he were here.'

Lizzie picked up a menu. 'Oooh, lamb and leek pie. That sounds good.'

'Oh, I can't eat lamb,' Gracie said. 'The poor things.'

'Well, I'm going to,' Lizzie replied. 'I'll let you have enough conscience for both of us when you choose your meal.'

'Chicken casserole… with shallots, mushrooms and red wine and served with mashed potatoes,' Gwendolyn read. 'That sounds nice.'

'That sounds yummy,' Gracie agreed. 'I'm going to have that.'

Lizzie looked at them both. 'Happy for me to go to the bar and order then?'

Gracie and her mum both nodded and Lizzie got up.

The barmaid, a petite lady, perhaps in her late sixties, was chatting to a customer. She appeared delicate and slender, but Lizzie noticed the knotty muscles of her exposed forearms and wondered if she might be a lot stronger than she looked. Perhaps she was no stranger to hauling the odd barrel around the place. She cut her conversation short and smiled at Lizzie as she approached.

'What can I get for you, my love?'

'Can we order some food?'

'Of course. So what are you having?'

'Two chicken casseroles and one lamb pie.'

'Oh, you'll like the pie,' the man who'd been chatting to the barmaid said. 'Beautiful bit of pie. Local lamb – it was skipping over the fields an hour ago. Isn't that right, Irma?'

The barmaid nodded. 'We sell out most nights so you're lucky it's still on.'

Lizzie smiled and decided that she'd better not tell Gracie about the skipping over the fields business.

'I won't be a tick with this.' Irma jotted the order down on a slip of paper and took it round to the kitchen. The man at the bar looked at Lizzie as she waited for her to come back.

'On holiday are you?'

'No, I live here.'

His eyebrows shot up his forehead. 'In Piriwick?' he asked with obvious disbelief. 'Since when?'

'Well, not quite in Piriwick itself.'

At this he gave a knowing smile. 'Ah… that explains it. I know everyone in these parts, and if someone new had moved into the village I'd soon find out about it. So where are you? On that new estate?'

'Mad Lady Mill,' Lizzie said, deciding that it might be easier to use its local moniker rather than try to explain the imminent name change to Magnolia Mill.

His eyes widened to such a size there was a danger they might take over his face. He swept a hand across a long strip of hair that was valiantly clinging to an otherwise bald head. 'Well, I'll… you're the woman I've heard about!' He swung round at the return of Irma from the kitchen. 'This here's the woman who bought the mill!'

'About time someone did something with that place,' Irma said mildly. 'Do you want to order any drinks, my love?'

As Lizzie gave the order for two beers and a lemonade, the door to the pub opened.

'Here, Derek!' the man at the bar shouted. 'This is her!'

'I know it is,' came the reply. 'I already told you I sold my caravan to her.'

Lizzie turned to see Derek and his wife Caroline smiling at her.

'I knew we'd persuade you to try the Lion out,' he said.

'How are you both?' Lizzie asked.

'Can't complain. Just come for our tea,' Caroline said. 'How's it going at the mill?'

Lizzie grinned. 'I can't complain either.'

'On your own?'

'No, I'm with my mum and sister. They're at the table by the window.' Lizzie pointed and Gwendolyn looked up and smiled. 'Come and say hello.'

'We'll do that,' Derek said. 'Are you eating?'

'Yes, we've just ordered. Don't let that stop you, though.'

'We'll let you finish your meal and we'll come over.' Derek turned to Irma as Lizzie grabbed her drinks to take back to her table, and Lizzie heard him request the lamb pie, only to be disappointed.

'Last one's just gone, Derek,' Irma said.

Lizzie felt a little pang of guilt about depriving Derek of what might be his favourite pie, but she was so hungry and the pub smelt so good that it wasn't big enough to trouble her.

*

Lizzie pushed away an empty plate with a satisfied sigh. 'That definitely lived up to the hype. It was fantastic.'

'Mine was nice too,' Gwendolyn said. Then she looked up at someone approaching the table and smiled. Lizzie turned to see Derek and Caroline carrying a glass each.

'Hello,' Caroline said. 'We did say to Lizzie we'd pop over and introduce ourselves.'

'Mum, Gracie – this is Derek and Caroline. I told you about them.'

'Oh, you did,' Gwendolyn said. She shuffled along the long seat beneath the window to make room. 'You're welcome to sit with us.'

'Thank you.' Derek and Caroline sat next to Gwendolyn.

'How was your meal?' Derek asked.

'Fabulous,' Gracie said. 'Makes me wish I'd moved here years ago.'

'It's very good food here,' Derek said. 'Didn't I tell you so, Lizzie?'

'You did.'

'So how are you settling in?' he asked. He looked at Gracie. 'And you've moved in too now?'

'I'm staying with Lizzie in the caravan for a while,' she said.

'I hope it's not too much of a squeeze,' Caroline said. 'It's not the biggest caravan in the world. We loved it and we only sold it because we needed a bigger one to take the grandkids away.'

'Oh, it's not at all,' Gracie replied with a bright smile. 'It's lovely and cosy.'

'Everyone I speak to is excited about seeing the mill all fixed up,' Caroline added.

'I'm glad about that. My dad was born here, you know. I think he'd be happy to see us back here.'

Derek was thoughtful for a moment. 'Would I have known him?'

'I don't know. Alexander Lovell? He moved away as a young man and that would have been at least forty years ago.'

Derek shook his head. 'No, I don't know the name. But then, we only came to these parts about ten years ago.'

Caroline smiled at Lizzie. 'Tim Lundy says you're going all out to get the mill working again.'

'You've seen Tim?' Lizzie asked.

'Well,' Caroline said, 'I saw Cath, his wife. At the farm shop.'

Lizzie had never imagined Tim being married. She wasn't really sure why, now that she thought about it, only that she couldn't imagine what sort of woman would want to make a life with her surly builder.

'And she says you're having a little fling with Jude Travers too?'

Lizzie felt the smile freeze on her face. She wasn't sure she wanted the whole village talking about her and Jude.

'We're dating,' she said carefully, the smile still stuck to her face, though it was no longer quite so assured. 'It's nothing serious.'

'I think it's lovely,' Caroline said. She turned to Gwendolyn now. 'He's had such a terrible time of it the last few years. First losing his mum and then his dad, and then him being the main carer for his brother, and when Harriet Astley ended things with him there were a lot round here who were very concerned for his health.' Caroline took a swift drink from her pint glass. 'He wasn't himself for a long time. I think if it hadn't been for their little boy he might even… well, of course, he wouldn't have wanted to leave his brother either, but he certainly seemed low enough to do something silly to me. It's about time he found a bit of happiness, and I think you make a lovely couple.' She grinned. 'Even if I have to admit to being a tad jealous. He's an absolute catch.'

'Oi!' Derek cried, but this only made Caroline laugh out loud.

'Harriet broke it off?' Gracie asked, only knowing as much Lizzie had confided in her (which was all Lizzie really knew).

'Oh yes.' Caroline gave a vigorous nod. 'Nobody knows why.'

'I expect there was nothing more to it than they'd got together too young,' Derek said, giving his wife a surreptitious warning glance. 'They'd been courting since they were both at school, and folks can change a lot when they become adults. I expect having a baby changed them too.'

'Oh no,' Caroline said, choosing to ignore, or perhaps just not noticing, Derek's subtle warning. 'I heard Jude wanted to get married before the baby came. It was Harriet who didn't.'

Derek looked askance at his wife. 'Who on earth told you that?'

'Julia. I mean, if anyone would know, Harriet's mum would, wouldn't she?'

'You know Harriet's family?' Lizzie asked.

'I sometimes chat to Julia at choir practise,' Caroline said. 'She has a lovely alto.'

'Well...' Derek sniffed. 'I don't expect Lizzie and her family need to hear about all that now, do they?'

Derek was right. Lizzie didn't want to hear it. And yet she did, and the need to know tore her up. She wished she could go back to her cosy fantasy that Jude wasn't damaged goods, but it was becoming clear that wasn't the case. She glanced at Gracie, who gave her a little look of triumph and her heart sank. Gracie knew the truth too – she'd known all along. Jude wasn't over Harriet at all. So where did that leave Lizzie?

'No, you're right,' Caroline said, leaving Lizzie – at least for now – to marvel at the sudden tact where it had been woefully missing before. 'I suppose that's all water under the bridge now, and he's got you to take care of him now, hasn't he, Lizzie?'

Lizzie nodded and she tried to smile. *Yay*, she thought. *Lucky me.*

*

Gracie had taken Gwendolyn home after their meal at the Golden Lion, leaving Lizzie alone with her thoughts in the caravan. She was reading too much into it, she kept telling herself. Just because Jude had been devastated when Harriet broke things off, it didn't mean he wasn't over her now. People split up all the time and they managed to fall in love again. Perhaps, however, it might be easier to believe if Jude and Harriet weren't quite so close still. Friends, yes, but close friends, even when you considered they had Artie. And this was the bit that kept sticking, that kept pulling at the corners of Lizzie's carefully constructed logic, threatening to unravel the whole lot. There was so much history there, how could Lizzie ever hope to compete? And what about Damon? Was this bothering him as much as it did Lizzie? He'd talked about baggage at Jude's drinks party and he'd seemed as unimpressed at times as Lizzie with the situation, but did he really feel that way? She didn't really think she'd find much of an ally there when it came down to it.

The sound of Gracie's car pulling into the driveway disturbed her thoughts. While Lizzie was glad to have some distraction, there was also a tempered sense of dread. She had a feeling she knew what the conversation that was undoubtedly coming might look like, and she didn't think it was going to make her feel any better. They hadn't really had time to discuss what they'd heard from Caroline and Derek in the pub, but Lizzie guessed they'd be finding the time now.

She went into the kitchen area and poured some milk into a saucepan, setting it on the stove. Gracie came in and flopped onto the sofa.

'I'm exhausted.'

'You want to go straight to bed? I was going to make cocoa, but if you'd rather leave it…'

Gracie waved a vague hand. 'Cocoa would be lovely; it would settle me down.' She gave Lizzie a sideways glance. 'I imagine you might want a bit of settling down too?'

'Why do you imagine that?' Lizzie asked, knowing full well what Gracie meant.

'You can't be happy about what Caroline told us.'

'Caroline told us a lot. Which bit?'

Gracie sighed and kicked her shoes off. They tumbled across the floor. Lizzie fought the urge to pick them up and throw them at her messy sister. 'The thing about Jude being absolutely devastated when Harriet dumped him.'

'You heard Caroline; she did tell us that, but she also said it's all water under the bridge now.' Lizzie reached for two mugs from a cupboard and spooned cocoa powder into them.

'But you're worried he doesn't really love you as much as he loved her?'

Lizzie stared into the blackness of the garden beyond the little kitchen window. She could just make out the shadows of the old pear trees, their branches snapping and creaking in the wind.

'I think he loves me,' she said quietly.

'But you don't think his heart is completely cleansed of feelings for Harriet, do you?' Gracie asked. 'If you're being very honest with yourself.'

'In time that will change. I can help him.'

'You could help him, but can you trust him? What about this other boyfriend? Is Harriet happy with him? Do you think it will last? Do you think that if Harriet gave the word to take Jude back he'd still want you? That's really the question you've got to ask yourself. Do you want to be a back-up plan, because if you doubt it for a minute, then that's what you are.'

Lizzie shook her head. The milk she was heating began to froth and roll, racing for the lip of the pan, and she pulled it clear of the stove just in time.

'I can't keep having this conversation with him,' she said. 'He's told me there's nothing to worry about, and I can't keep on asking him.'

'So you're just going to leave it at that?'

Lizzie poured the milk into the mugs. 'There's not much else I can do, is there?'

'Perhaps I could do some digging—' Gracie began, but Lizzie cut her off.

'I'm not spying on him. Whatever else I'm doing or not doing, I'm not sinking that low.'

'It's not low… it doesn't have to be actual spying. I could just ask a few questions around and about. You could even have a chat with Charlie…'

'No,' Lizzie said firmly. 'That's putting Charlie in an unfair predicament, and besides, he'd go straight to Jude and tell him what I'd asked anyway. And I can imagine that would really make things better…' she added dryly.

'Then how about a bit of snooping around Harriet? Do you know where she lives?'

'Absolutely not,' Lizzie said. 'If I can't trust Jude then I probably shouldn't be with him at all. Nobody's snooping or spying on anyone and that's that.'

*

Charlie was curled on the sofa watching Dolly Parton in concert while Jude and Lizzie cooked pasta together in the kitchen. It was a glorious luxury having a large space to move around in, not having to take every tiny bit of rubbish straight to the outside bins and balancing plates on top of toasters and bread bins to free up space on the worktop. Life in the caravan was beginning to get on top of Lizzie. Sometimes she coped with it better than at others, but while Gracie had reduced the living space with her arrival, her pregnancy now complicated things even further. There was no caravan big enough to contain her black, hormone-fuelled moods – one minute elation, the next utter despair, the next simmering resentment. When her sister was grabbed by one of these, the only thing Lizzie could do was vacate the area and wait for things to calm down.

'So Gracie didn't fancy supper with us?' said Jude, chopping basil.

'I think she feels like a gooseberry. I've told her that we can actually be in the same room without the need to grope one another now, but I don't think she can quite believe it.'

'She's OK, though? No more funny turns?'

'I think her morning sickness is calming down a little. She's not happy about that, weirdly, because she's read that morning sickness often means a stronger ability to carry the baby or something. I don't know, she's obsessed with baby research right now – reads everything no matter how silly. I suppose at least it keeps her good.'

'I thought you said she was getting moody?' Jude brought a handful of chopped leaves over and tossed them into the pan of sauce Lizzie was stirring.

'She is, but even that's like a huge drama that I think she's secretly enjoying.'

'And she still hasn't told Frank? She is going to tell him, isn't she?'

'She knows she ought to, and I think if the relationship had ended any other way she would have done. If you ask me she wants to, but she's getting back at him.'

'For what?'

'For the affair, of course. She's keeping him in the dark to teach him a lesson. He's an arrogant swine and clearly a shit for cheating on her, but I don't believe for a minute he would be the dreadful father she says he would be.'

'Dreadful father or not, surely it's only right he gets the choice to at least try to be a decent one, even if he fails.'

'Well, I suppose so.'

'There's no suppose about it. If Gracie is having his baby, he has a right to know – end of story.'

'But Gracie is the one carrying the baby. It's really her right to involve whoever she wants and keep out whoever she doesn't.' Lizzie was beginning to get irked by his self-righteous tone.

'This is the problem, isn't it?' Jude drained a pan of pasta over the sink, steam wreathing up and out of the open window.

'What?'

'It's all about the mothers. Why don't men get a say in anything? We have no rights at all when it comes to children.'

'That's not true. You have plenty of input where Artie is concerned.'

'Only because I'm friends with Harrie.'

'So it's not true that men get no rights…'

'Clearly it's true in this case. And if Gracie is doing it, how many other women do you think are out there having babies the fathers know nothing about?'

'I've no idea,' Lizzie said, a vague sense of surprise and unease creeping over her. 'At the end of the day, this is Gracie's life and Gracie's choice, and I can't force her to involve Frank.'

'But *you* could tell Frank.'

'No way. It's not my place.'

'It's not your place to stand by and see him excluded from his child's life – Gracie might be right and he might not give a shit but at least give him the choice. And even if he doesn't care at first, he might well change his mind later.'

Jude's mobile phone was out of the way on a windowsill. It began to ring, and he wiped his hands before fetching it and frowning at the display.

'You don't mind if I get this?' he asked.

Lizzie shook her head. It looked like their heated debate would have to go on ice for the moment. Jude swiped the screen to take the call.

'I don't suppose I can call you back—' he began, but then his frown deepened as he listened to the caller.

Lizzie could hear the voice at the other end of the line, even if she couldn't make out what was being said. It was a female voice, and she sounded upset. Lizzie's stomach dropped. Harriet.

'Are you sure that's what he meant?' Jude asked. 'How did you leave things?' He was silent again as he listened some more. 'And that's it?' he asked. 'It's over?'

Once again, Lizzie could make out the tones of the voice in reply but not the words. But then Jude spoke again.

'I can't come right now, but—'

The woman began to speak again, rapid and distraught.

'Harrie… calm down!' Jude's voice rose too, and Lizzie's worst fears were confirmed. 'I'll come over tomorrow but I can't come now because…' He glanced at Lizzie. 'Well, I just can't. I don't think it would be a good idea to come here either,' he added. 'Charlie… you don't want him to see you this upset, do you?'

There was more talking at the other end of the line.

'Where's Artie now?' Jude said, and then nodded, seemingly satisfied with the answer. 'Tell your grandpappy I can come and pick him up early in the morning if he needs me to.'

He threw Lizzie a look of apology. She tried to smile to say it was OK, but she couldn't. It wasn't OK – it was far from OK. Would she always have to share him with Harriet? She realised that Harriet would always claim a part of his life because of Artie, but she didn't want to share him – not like this. And she couldn't be sure that this wasn't some plot to get Jude away from Lizzie. Some people were like that, weren't they – you heard it all the time: *I don't want you but nobody else can have you either…*

'Harrie… Please, let's talk tomorrow. You never know, he might have come to his senses by then and been over himself to fix things with you… I know you don't think so but give it time. He'd be a fool to throw what you have away – everyone knows he's punching way above his weight with you…'

Lizzie's wince was almost physical. If Jude had grabbed a kitchen knife and stabbed her she didn't think it would have hurt any more than hearing him say that to Harriet.

There was more noise at the other end of the line, what sounded like sobbing, and the sound of Harriet's voice unmistakably rising.

'I can't come now,' Jude said. 'I'm so sorry but I really can't…'

After another moment, he said goodbye and ended the call, promising to be there the following day. He turned to Lizzie.

'I'm so sorry. Harrie… I think it's all over with her and Damon.'

'I think I got that much,' Lizzie said.

There was silence. Lizzie looked out of the window. From the living room they could hear the strains of Dolly singing 'Islands in the Stream'. She turned back to Jude and he was watching her, weighing her up, perhaps waiting for a response. What did he want her to say? That she was sorry for Harriet? That she didn't mind Harriet gatecrashing her date with Jude? That it didn't bother her that the woman always seemed to be there, like a dark cloud over their relationship? That she honestly believed Jude was over her? How could she say any of these things when they weren't true?

'You're angry,' Jude said. Not a question, an assumption.

'Why would I be angry?' Lizzie went to the stove and turned off the heat. The pasta sauce had come to a boil, spitting like lava over the surrounding work surfaces.

'You're not?'

'Of course not,' Lizzie said tightly.

'Then why does this room suddenly feel very frosty? Don't tell me this is about Harriet again. I thought we'd sorted that.'

'So did I, but she's here again, isn't she? Demanding your attention. It's like she has this sixth sense where I'm concerned. The minute I start to relax around you she brings something else to the party to make me doubt everything again.'

'That's ridiculous!'

'Is it?'

'The woman's just been dumped! Have a little heart!'

'So now you're making me look like I'm neurotic or something?'

'No! Why are you so threatened by her? She's a friend – why do I have to keep explaining that?'

Lizzie sat down and turned her hands over, staring at them. Then she looked up again. Her heart was beating wildly, and she hated herself for what she was about to say but it had to be said.

'Why didn't you tell me how distraught you'd been when Harriet dumped you?'

'Where have you heard that?'

'It doesn't matter. Why didn't you tell me?'

'I wasn't distraught and she didn't dump me. We're not teenagers. We split up and there's a world of difference.'

'You're saying you didn't go to pieces?'

'Maybe a little but—'

'You wanted to marry her.'

Jude's eyes widened. 'Who told you that?'

'So it's true?'

'Lizzie – none of this matters now.'

'But it does matter. It matters because you couldn't tell me. Why did you have to keep it a secret? Is it because you were afraid I'd find out the truth? Is it because you're still in love with her?'

'No, of course not! I just didn't think it was important.'

'And now she's single… how important do you think that is?'

'What do you mean?'

'I think you know what I mean.'

Jude scraped a hand through his hair. 'No, I don't, Lizzie. Please tell me what it is you think is going to happen.'

'I think you still love her, no matter what you say.'

'Harriet and I will never get back together.'

'You haven't denied it, though.'

Jude threw the dishcloth onto the floor. 'Jesus, Lizzie! What is wrong with you? Why are you so obsessed with her?'

'Because *you* are, that's why!'

Jude raced over to close the door to the living room. 'Keep it down – Charlie doesn't need to hear this.'

'I'm sorry – you're right; he doesn't.'

He came over and reached out, but she shook him off.

'Don't.'

'What do you want from me, Lizzie?'

'You could have been honest about Harriet from the start. I might have understood it.'

'I *was* honest.'

'Not about the effect your break-up had on you. It's no wonder it feels like you had something to hide. How can I believe you don't still have feelings for her now? How can I feel safe that you won't end up back with her now that she's single and I'll be cast aside, nothing more than a casual diversion to while away the time until she was free again?'

'This is crazy.'

'It's not. For once, try to see it from my point of view. How would you feel if the tables were turned?'

'I'd trust you.'

'No, you wouldn't. I'm sorry, but I've been lied to before by a man who said he cared about me. I need to be with someone I can trust, and I'm beginning to feel such a man isn't even out there.'

He studied her for a moment, silently digesting all that she'd said.

'So where do we go from here?' he asked.

Lizzie shook her head. Her eyes glazed with tears and she fought them back. 'I don't know… I need time. I need you to show me that I can trust you.'

'And how am I supposed to do that? I keep telling you over and over there's nothing between me and Harriet now, but you don't believe me.'

'That's because you telling me is not the same as you showing me. Telling is word not deed.'

'You want me to stop spending time with her?'

'I never said that—'

'Because that is not going to happen. Have you forgotten the small matter of our son?'

'Of course I haven't, but that's not what's going on here as far as I can tell. Your friendship with Harriet is about more than just raising Artie.'

'That's bullshit!' Jude cried, and this time it was Lizzie's turn to shoot a cautious glance at the now closed living-room door. He folded his arms. 'If that's really how you feel then maybe we should call it a day right now. Our break-up seems inevitable anyway, or so you say, so why not do it now?'

Lizzie stood up. Eyes full of tears, she dragged her coat from the back of her chair, and as she headed for the back door to leave, she didn't want Jude to see her crying so she didn't look back.

Chapter Eighteen

As Lizzie rushed along Magnolia Lane, she dug her phone out of her bag to call Gracie. She'd left her car at the mill in anticipation of Jude driving her home or them making the walk together hand in hand at the end of the night, Jude seeing her safely to her door like a knight of old. Dusk was bleaching the colour from the day and the temperature had dropped, but that wouldn't have bothered Lizzie ordinarily. Ordinarily, she would have loved walking the lane, taking in every leaf of every hedgerow, every flower, every birdcall with wonder as fresh and new as the first time she'd walked it. Already she was embedded in her rural home, so at one with the landscape that she could never imagine leaving now.

But not tonight. As she dialled Gracie's number, she didn't notice the first shy rabbit emerging into the evening air at the side of the road, or the cloud of starlings flocking to roost, or the fire of the clouds caught by the setting sun. She only wanted her sister to come and rescue her before she changed her mind and went running back to Jude. Whatever else happened now, she wasn't going to do that.

'What have you left behind?' Gracie said with a laugh as she answered the phone. 'Because whatever it is you'll have to manage without it – I'm in my pyjamas and I'm not getting dressed for anyone; least of all you.'

'Oh, Gracie,' Lizzie said, unable to prevent the crack in her voice. 'Can you come and get me? I'm sorry but I really need—'

'Where are you?' Gracie cut in, her voice sharp and full of new urgency now. 'What's happened?'

'I can't talk about it now.' Lizzie sniffed. 'I'm on the lane on my way home, but could you come and get me?'

'I'll be with you in a couple of minutes,' Gracie said. And without waiting for a reply, she ended the call.

Lizzie tipped her face to the sky and tried to sniff back her tears.

Gracie was true to her word, pulling up a matter of minutes later, bundled in a dressing gown. She pushed open the passenger door for Lizzie to get in.

'Don't tell me,' she said as Lizzie fastened her seatbelt. 'It's about Harriet.'

'How did you know?'

'Call it intuition.'

'You were right all along,' Lizzie replied miserably. 'He does still have feelings for her. I suspected it too, but I thought I could be bigger than that; I thought in time he and I would get closer and she'd fade into the background… but that's never going to happen, and I don't think I can be big enough about it. I hate it and I hate her.'

Gracie kept her eyes forward as she navigated the darkening road home. 'I'm sorry.'

'Not as sorry as I am.'

'You really like him, don't you?'

'I think I might have even loved him. At least, it felt like the start of something. What an idiot. I can't seem to get it right with men – I make the most terrible choices.'

'I thought that was me,' Gracie said, flashing a wry smile that faded just as quickly. 'Perhaps we should make a sisterly pact to swear off men for good.'

Lizzie sniffed. 'Perhaps you're right.'

They fell to silence as the car swept into the driveway and Gracie killed the engine. Lizzie was tired and she was confused. She wanted to talk things over, but at the same time she wanted to ignore it and pretend the argument with Jude had never happened. She knew she wouldn't be able to do that, though, because the crux of the argument – Harriet – would never go away. Even if she ignored it this time, the same argument would bubble away beneath the surface and it would keep erupting – at first, small spats like this, until one day it would blow into an almighty explosion that would finish everything. Perhaps, in the long run, ending things now would be less painful for everyone.

Lizzie followed Gracie to the caravan. It was usually Gracie following Lizzie, but tonight Lizzie was happy to let her sister take charge. Inside, Lizzie dropped to the sofa and buried her face in a cushion. A soft touch landed on her arm, and she looked up to see Gracie there, her face full of love and concern.

'You can talk to me,' she said. 'I know what I've said before, and you know what I think about it, but I can listen and not judge – if that's what you need.'

Lizzie shook her head, eyes filling with tears again. 'What's the point? You've been right all along and I was too stupid to see it.'

'Maybe you just liked him a bit too much to see it.'

'But why would he make all this effort to be with me? Why would he pretend he wanted me when it was her all along?'

'Perhaps he really wanted to convince himself that it was you. After all, he thought he would never be with her again and so it would make sense to try to move on.'

'Do you think he might have done? In time?'

'Only you can say that. I didn't see him in your private moments.'

'Do you think he's worth fighting for?'

'I can't say that either. I can only say that you saved me from trying to get back with Frank, and though it still hurts to think of him, I'm beginning to see now that you were right and it was absolutely the worst thing I could have done. I want to do the same for you; I just want to help you make the right choice, even if that's the hardest choice.'

'So you think continuing with Jude would be the wrong choice?'

Gracie said nothing, only rubbed a reassuring hand on the back of Lizzie's.

'I don't want to finish it,' Lizzie said.

'But you don't want to carry on living in Harriet's shadow either. And there's Artie too, don't forget. It doesn't matter what else happens, Jude will never be able to get away from his responsibilities there and that will keep Harriet in his life. You have to ask yourself if you can live with that.'

Lizzie shook her head, tears soaking into the cushion on her lap. 'I really thought we had something.'

'I'll bet that sentence has been uttered in a great many homes over the years,' Gracie said. 'Mine included.'

'All I want is to be happy with a nice man. Is that so much to ask for?'

'It shouldn't be, should it?'

Lizzie gulped in a great breath and tried to swallow her tears. She gave a firm nod, but they kept falling anyway. Let Harriet have him, she thought, seized with a sudden savage resentment. Let him play happy families with her and it will serve him right when she dumps him again. Make Magnolia Mill the most important thing in your life, because it ought to be. Make this dream come true – concentrate on the things you can get right, the things that won't let you down.

They were strong, rousing thoughts, and she tried hard to make her emotions match them. She didn't need Jude Travers, and she didn't care what he did.

So why did that thought feel like a lie? Why did it already feel like her decision to end things was a terrible mistake?

*

It had been a strange week without Jude in it.

She'd needed to hear more, to ask questions and have time to think about his answers. She had a million thoughts whirling in her head like ghostly moths around a streetlight, and she needed someone to help her capture them and give them form. She'd wanted that someone to be Jude – wasn't it the very least he owed her? But he'd sent her away, like he didn't care, and she'd been so angry and hurt and rejected that she hadn't returned his phone calls the next day. Or the day after that or the day after that. If she talked to him now she'd have only words that burned and blistered and were no good at all. Evan had lied to her, but even he'd tried to make it right. Not that there was any making right the thing he'd done.

Lizzie thought back to the day when the girl had come knocking on the door of the terraced house she'd shared with him. She'd looked so young, mascara staining her cheeks. Lizzie had been confused when the girl had asked for Evan, but even then alarm bells had been ringing. She recalled now his face as he came to the door, racing down the hallway having heard the girl's voice. He'd denied everything, but when the girl lifted her blazer and showed him the swell of her stomach, the guilt on his face had told Lizzie everything she'd needed to know.

But the worst was the continued lying. When he'd sent the girl away he'd tried to convince Lizzie that she was making it up, that he wasn't the father, and then that she'd seduced him (telling him nothing of the fact that she was only seventeen) and she must have been tricking him into getting her pregnant. Once she found out the truth, Lizzie had to be thankful that the girl hadn't been any younger, but it hadn't stopped her being disgusted, betrayed, devastated, and a million other emotions. What had she done to deserve it? Hadn't she been a good and loving girlfriend? Hadn't she given him everything he'd wanted and needed? Hadn't their sex life been enough? If there was this girl, how many others? How many more lies? So she wanted to believe that Jude's lie wasn't the same, but it was hard to tell the difference. And perhaps him sending her away, not wanting to talk about it, was more about not wanting to be caught out.

Gracie was doing her best to support Lizzie, but she still had woes of her own, and neither of them was very happy at all, wedged together in their little caravan of misery. It would all pass, Lizzie supposed, but it was hard to see that far ahead. So they kept each other company, the days just as they always were with shopping and cooking and cleaning and watching the painstaking progress of Magnolia Mill taking shape.

Lizzie didn't want to think any further than that – she didn't want to think about how she felt about Jude now, if they had a future after all and if she could trust him – she just wanted to feel OK again, to get her emotions back on an even keel before she turned her mind to more practical matters. When she looked back on these days, sometime in a future that she couldn't yet see, she'd fancy herself almost glad of the distractions that new trials, just out of view on the horizon, were about to bring her. But today, after the usual daily schedule, they'd indulged in a microwave supper followed by an hour of television while they pretended everything was OK. During the last half hour, Gracie's yawns had become more and more frequent, and Lizzie had to admit to feeling tired herself.

'I think it's time to turn in,' Lizzie said.

'I would but I can't be bothered to move. Would you mind if I just stayed here all night?' Gracie was sprawled across one section of the seating that ran around the walls of the caravan, a hand to her still flat belly as if she was ready to pop.

Lizzie raised an eyebrow. 'You might be comfy now, but I don't think you'll be comfy later tonight when it starts to get chilly.'

'Now you sound like Mum.'

'And you sound like a teenager,' Lizzie said.

'I wish I was. Life would be a lot easier than this.'

'Not if you were a pregnant teenager it wouldn't.'

'But I wouldn't be pregnant if I was a teenager because I wouldn't have met Frank, would I?'

Lizzie began to raise the question again of whether Frank ought to be told of his impending fatherhood. The conversation she'd had with Jude a week ago had, amongst other things, made her see the situation in an entirely new light. While she respected Gracie's choice, she was coming round to the idea that Frank should have a choice too, however undeserving he might seem. At least Evan, for all his duplicity, saw the child that he'd fathered and, as far as Lizzie knew, he paid his way and accepted his paternal responsibilities even if he wasn't with the girl. Moreover, it didn't seem fair to Lizzie to deny a young child the chance to know their father. She felt sure that whatever else she might think about Jude and Harriet's situation, Artie was better off for knowing his dad, especially when that dad was a man like Jude.

Her mouth formed the words now as she crossed the room to switch the television off at the wall, but something made her stop. Gracie began to speak again but Lizzie shushed her.

'That street,' she said, looking at the news report now on the screen. 'Doesn't that street look like…'

'Like what?' Gracie said lazily.

'Gracie – look!' Lizzie stepped back to let her sister see the screen. 'It looks so familiar but I can't…'

'Not to me,' Gracie said.

'It is! It's somewhere we know!'

'I'm surprised you can tell at all with that great lot of smoke and fire. I feel sorry for the poor souls who live in that house.'

There was a reporter at the scene, and he was interviewing a fire officer while what used to be a building smouldered in the background, intermittently spitting out flames. Beneath the television picture was a ticker tape headline:

EXPLOSION ROCKS CITY STREET

'The owner of the house is being treated for shock,' the fire officer said. 'Luckily she was away from the premises when the explosion took place…'

Lizzie's eyes widened. 'Oh my God! Oh my God!'

'What?'

'Where's my phone?' she cried.

Gracie flipped herself up now and frowned. 'What is it? Where is it? *Who* is it?'

'Where's my phone… Jesus, holy shit, where is it?'

'Lizzie, calm down! Your phone's right there by the kettle!'

Grabbing it, Lizzie stabbed at the screen to pull up a number. She waited as the phone rang out and the answer service message kicked in. 'Maybe she's with someone,' she said, ending the call. 'God knows but she's not answering.'

'Who?'

'The house…' Lizzie scraped her hair back from her face and turned to the television screen again. 'You must recognise it!'

'There's not much left to recognise.'

'It's—'

The phone in Lizzie's hand began to ring.

'Florentina,' she said briskly in answer. 'Where are you? What's happened?'

'Oh, Lizzie!' Florentina sobbed at the other end of the line. 'I could have died!'

'What happened to the house?'

'I wasn't there… I'd gone to the shop on the corner to get some wine and I'd got chatting to Sev – he always likes a chat when he's there – and if he hadn't kept me so long I'd have been home.'

'Well, thank God for Sev. It looks awful, just terrible. It looks as if there's nothing left.'

'They think it might have been a gas explosion. I don't know how it happened – I suppose the investigators will find out.'

Lizzie's hand flew to her mouth. 'Oh my God!'

'Everyone keeps asking if I need anything, but I don't even know myself.'

'I'm just glad you're in one piece.'

'But everything's gone,' Florentina sobbed. 'All the things your dad ever gave me, all my papers and keepsakes and goods. I'm standing in everything I have left. Some insurance man is going to sort out a hotel for me tonight. Beyond that, I don't know, I—'

'Bollocks to that! You think I'm going to leave you in some hotel tonight, in this state? Hold on; I'm coming to get you.'

'But—'

'Don't argue. We'll be a little cramped here but we can manage. You're family as far as I'm concerned, and family looks after family.'

'Grazie,' Florentina said, and Lizzie knew she must really be distressed to agree to Lizzie's plan without even the feeblest of arguments. 'I'll wait, shall I?'

'Yes, wait. I'll be there as soon as I can,' Lizzie replied, ignoring a black look from Gracie, who had doubtless pieced together the plans from the side of the conversation she could hear. 'Hold tight.'

Lizzie ended the call. As she went to the bedroom to pull some tracksuit trousers over the pyjama shorts she'd been lounging around in, Gracie appeared at the doorway.

'Florentina's house just blew up,' Lizzie said in answer to her silent question. 'What else am I supposed to do?'

'Didn't she say she was sorted with a hotel?'

'Don't, Gracie. Just don't. This is not the time for grudges, and even you can't be that cold-hearted about it.'

If Gracie was offended by the accusation that she might be cold-hearted, she clearly recognised that the situation was too delicate to say so right now. She simply nodded.

'How long will she be here?'

'I don't know, but that's the last thing on my mind right now. I'm just letting you know that I won't be asking her to leave.'

'I expect they'll get her sorted with a new place quick enough,' Gracie said.

Without reply, Lizzie swung past her and out into the main room to fetch her car keys from the kitchen worktop. Gracie wasn't getting her own way this time. If Florentina needed help, and giving help meant the difference between signing the caravan over to Gracie or keeping it a little longer so she could still say who got to stay there, then that was the way things would have to be. If she had to, Lizzie would keep the caravan, whether that meant losing Gracie's money or favour or not.

Chapter Nineteen

'Do you have any more cheese?' Florentina had almost disappeared into the open fridge, her disembodied comment floating out onto the air for anyone to answer who felt inclined to. Lizzie could understand how she'd suddenly been set adrift into a life that was completely alien to her, and that she felt like a useless burden and wanted to do something to make amends and show her gratitude, but she wished her new guest would stop cooking.

Florentina had only been with them for two days and so far she'd cooked at least ten meals – most of them unwanted and unasked for. Not only did they now have enough leftovers to feed a decent-sized battalion, but the food bill was going to be astronomical, and Lizzie would find it hard to take any money that Florentina might want to offer. The caravan was beginning to feel very, very small now, and the atmosphere of cold civility between Gracie and Florentina could have nicely chilled a good chardonnay in minutes. But at least it was all taking Lizzie's mind off Jude.

'Cheese has started to give me heartburn,' Gracie said from the sofa, her new favourite spot. Everything gave Gracie heartburn these days, though Lizzie wondered just how much of this heartburn was imagined, like all the other pregnancy-related symptoms she'd started to develop the minute she'd read about them. 'Don't you need to go clothes shopping or something?' she added. 'You must be fed up with wearing the same two outfits all the time. I'm certainly sick of seeing you in them…' she added under her breath.

'I can go and get some cheese from the farm shop if you need me to,' Lizzie said, ignoring Gracie.

'I can do that just as well.' Florentina's head now appeared from within the fridge. 'You're already doing so much for me—'

'Honestly,' Lizzie interrupted. 'You don't need to keep thanking me, and you don't need to keep doing stuff. I'm more than happy to have you here…' She threw a meaningful look at Gracie. 'We *both* are.'

'I'm sorry, I just *need* to do something,' Florentina said.

Lizzie sighed. 'I realise that. Maybe Gracie has a point about clothes shopping? You do need more, and I'm sure the retail therapy would make you feel better.'

Florentina threw her arms into the air with a heavy sigh. 'I can't think about clothes right now.'

Lizzie gave a small smile. Things were pretty desperate if even Florentina wasn't interested in clothes.

'Perhaps you ought to go into work then?' she said. 'Not that I have any issues with you being here, but it might be good to get some normality back? As you can't have your old house, and you're not really up to shopping, maybe your job is the next best thing to take your mind off everything else?'

'Actually, I was thinking that myself. I know they told me to take the week off, but I don't think I need a whole week, and I'm just getting under your foot here, aren't I?'

'I didn't mean that,' Lizzie said, not bothering to correct Florentina's use of the phrase.

'I know, I know. But it's true, *cara mia*.'

Lizzie forced a smile. 'See how you feel over the next couple of days, then decide.'

Florentina nodded. 'Do you think it's too early to start looking for a new house?'

'Don't you want to go back to your old one? I thought the insurance company were going to rebuild it for you?'

'I've been thinking that maybe it's a sign I ought to be moving on. I shared that place with your dad, and he's not here now, so...'

'It's one hell of a sign,' Gracie put in. 'If God had wanted you to move on he could have popped an estate agent leaflet through your door, not blown you up.'

Lizzie frowned at her and Gracie shrugged. 'Just saying.'

'Is that really how you feel?' Lizzie said, turning back to Florentina.

'I don't know, but I can't stop thinking about it so perhaps there's something...'

'Where would you go?'

'It's nice here, isn't it? Magnolia Lane. Perhaps I'd move closer to your mill – I'd get to see more of you then. That would be nice, wouldn't it?'

There was a time when Lizzie wouldn't have been so sure of that. Apart from wanting to bring her dad's dreams to life, she'd been attracted to Magnolia Mill because of the solitude and peace it represented. That peace and solitude hadn't lasted long, but that was OK because she was getting used to the way things were now. She almost liked it. Sometimes... when Gracie wasn't complaining about heartburn and Florentina wasn't cooking...

There was a knock at the caravan door and Lizzie answered it to find her builder, Tim, on the doorstep.

'Alright, Lizzie,' Tim grunted. 'Need you to come and have a look at something.'

'Oh, right…' Lizzie cast a glance back at Gracie and Florentina. Things seemed peaceful enough right now. Since Florentina's arrival she'd hardly dared to leave them alone for fear they might come to blows, but perhaps that had been a silly fear. After all, they might have had their differences (mostly Gracie was the one with the differences), but they were grown, intelligent women. Surely they could be civil for everyone's sakes? 'Right now?' she asked.

'If you could,' Tim replied. 'It won't take a minute – Gary's just pulled up your floorboards in the milling room and found the joists in a bit of a mess. As your specialists will be coming in after us, he wants to know if you think you can make do with a bit of patching up or whether you want to get all new sooner.'

'Oh, God… I'm coming then.'

Closing the caravan door behind her, Lizzie followed Tim across the garden to the mill. It looked smooth and sleek in the afternoon light with its new render now dry and the scaffolding finally removed. The frames of the vast sails were still damaged, grumbling and groaning like an old man in the light wind, and they would have to be repaired or replaced at some point (repaired, Lizzie desperately hoped, to save some money), but that was a job for the specialist that she'd yet to employ and probably the last thing to be done. The most important thing right now was to make the place habitable, especially in light of the growing guest list at Chez Lizzie. At least Florentina had offered to pay towards the cost of her staying there, and while Lizzie would have loved to say she didn't want or need the money, she was enough of a realist to accept the offer gratefully.

The stairs to the milling floor had no rails and so Lizzie clung to the oily length of rope that served instead as she climbed. Now that Tim had mentioned it, she could smell the damp more strongly than she'd ever done before. Maybe it was in her imagination, or maybe it was the rain they'd had over the previous days – Lizzie hoped it might be one of them and not the confirmation of her worst fears. She'd had enough nasty surprises on this build, and she was running short of nerves to shred.

'Right,' Tim grunted as they finally stood looking at the offending woodwork. 'Holes there – see. Something's had a little chew on them, but we can probably kill that off. But then there's a bit of rot over this side… Water got in, I expect. Middle ones seem fairly sound.' He turned to Lizzie. 'What do you reckon?'

Lizzie stared at the joists. The floorboards were already being replaced and that was expensive enough. God only knew how much more replacing the entire floor would cost.

'If I can save a bit of money by patching up then—'

Tim nodded. 'I thought you'd say that but just wanted to run it by you. Best to ask.'

'Thanks; I appreciate that. It'll be safe enough?'

'It'll be safe for a few years as long as you're not planning to have parties up here.'

'Oh.'

'Probably need looking at again in a few years. We'll do our best for you, though.'

Lizzie continued to survey the floor. 'So if I was using the mill to actually produce flour then it might be a problem?' she asked.

Tim lifted his hard hat and scratched his head. 'Tell you what I'd do – I'd get it patched and then I'd let your specialist look at it.'

Lizzie tried to smooth the frown tugging at her forehead. If ever she'd heard a cop-out, that was it. But she supposed it wasn't really Tim's area of expertise, and he was probably genuinely trying to do his best for her.

'OK,' she said heavily. 'It'll have to do for now.'

Tim gave a terse nod. 'While you're here, there's one or two other bits I wanted to ask you about. You'd best come have a look while we're up here...'

'Right,' Lizzie said, hoping that these one or two other bits weren't going to cost one or two other bits of money that she hadn't budgeted for. 'You'd better show me then,' she said, following him from the milling room, a vague sense of dread building that was bound to ruin her morning good and proper.

*

Lizzie had spent an hour with Tim inspecting and discussing various little details of the job. In the end nothing had been as awful and costly as she'd been expecting, though it had taken some working out as to what solution they were going to employ for each problem his team had run into. But now, as Lizzie made her way back to the caravan, her thoughts were tinged with dread once more as she wondered just how badly Gracie and Florentina might have got on while she'd been missing. While she was there they had a referee, but with her out of the way, it wasn't impossible to imagine that things might just descend into all-out war.

All was quiet as she pushed open the door, and she was relieved to see that they were both on the sofa. Together. Drinking tea.

Lizzie did a double take. There was no screaming or shouting, no frosty glares – in fact, Gracie was actually *smiling* at Florentina.

'Everything OK?' Lizzie asked carefully.

'Do you think I'm blooming?' Gracie asked. 'Do I have a pregnancy glow?'

Lizzie looked at her sister. Gracie's hair needed a wash, she was still in her pyjamas with not a scrap of make-up, and she looked tired. But yes, now that she really looked properly, perhaps she did have a little of something about her that was new. Was it a spark of happiness, a new sense of purpose? Perhaps she was getting used to the idea of motherhood and the notion that she'd have someone new in her life to love, someone who'd love her unconditionally in return. Lizzie couldn't say if it was a pregnancy glow, but there was definitely something.

'I think she absolutely does,' Florentina put in. 'As soon as I got here I could see something different about her.' She turned to Gracie. 'It's a shame we can't bottle it and sell it over the counter because women would be flocking to buy it.'

'I suppose if other women want it they'll have to get pregnant,' Gracie said with a little laugh.

'I'm not sure that would suit everyone,' Florentina returned with a smile. 'And pregnancy doesn't look good on everyone like it does on you.'

Gracie's smile broadened, and she almost seemed to glow like a light bulb turned up on a dimmer switch.

Nicely played, Lizzie thought as she looked at Florentina. Perhaps things weren't going to be as awkward as Lizzie had imagined after all. Florentina had tried with Gracie for years, but they hadn't really had anything to bond over. Perhaps Gracie's pregnancy could be it, and it looked as if their stepmother had already realised the opportunity for herself.

'Anyway,' Gracie said, turning to Lizzie now. 'What did Eeyore want?'

'Mostly to show me things that will cost me more money.'

'Oh, God, can you afford it?'

'None of it is too bad, thankfully.'

'Maybe I can help?' Florentina said. 'You know I said I had some money I'd invest in your business? Well, if you need the money sooner—'

'It's OK,' Lizzie said, and she glanced across at Gracie to see her smile turn into a scowl. It looked as if talk of a business relationship with Florentina that Gracie hadn't approved of had reminded her that she wasn't supposed to like her stepmother. Lizzie suppressed a sigh and supposed that she couldn't expect miracles right away.

Florentina leapt up from the sofa and clapped her hands together. 'Right,' she said. 'Who would like some tasty gnocchi?'

*

Gracie was taking her afternoon nap, Florentina had gone to the farm shop and Lizzie found herself at a rare loose end, unable to concentrate on an article about the best times and places to see the Northern Lights. Instead, she stared absently through the kitchen window of her caravan, elbow-deep in rapidly cooling washing-up suds, her thoughts occupied by Jude. She couldn't deny that she was missing him, even if Gracie had quite successfully convinced her that she was far better off without him. She couldn't shake the feeling that she'd made a terrible mistake, and that she'd thrown away a chance of happiness that she ought to have grabbed with both hands. She'd aired this misgiving to Gracie, who'd instantly pointed out that she herself had said exactly the same about Frank, and that Lizzie had – quite rightly – persuaded her that Frank wasn't the one. Gracie was simply returning the favour by reassuring Lizzie that in time she'd be able to see Jude in the same way.

However much she might want to believe this, she wasn't convinced that she and Jude were the same as Gracie and Frank at all. She wondered if Jude was back with Harriet already, Lizzie and Damon consigned to the past as temporary distractions from the real love story. It hurt to think so, but the possibility was hard to ignore.

She was about to turn her attention back to the washing-up when she saw Charlie bounding up the garden path. Breath held, she waited to see if Jude would follow, a million conversations running through her head, wondering which opening gambit he'd present her with. But then she let it go and her eyebrows went up as she saw that, instead of Jude, Harriet and Artie had got out of a car on the road and were walking across the garden in Charlie's wake. Lizzie frowned, steeling herself as she went to the door to open up before their knock woke Gracie.

'Charlie!' Lizzie said, forcing a smile for him, though her heart was thudding in her chest. She had no idea why Harriet was accompanying him. And although she would have pretended to be cross and angry with Jude if he'd come, she couldn't help a sense of crushing disappointment that he hadn't.

'Lizzie!' Charlie threw himself at her and hugged her tight. 'Why haven't you been to our house?'

'Well…' Lizzie paused. Was she supposed to tell him the truth, or was she meant to sugar-coat a little lie for him? It seemed that Jude hadn't told him, but then, perhaps he didn't know what he was supposed to say either. She and Jude hadn't officially split, but they were doing a good job of looking like a couple who'd broken up. She'd never been in a situation like this before. There had been no messing with Evan and no mistaking that it was absolutely over the minute he'd tried to cover up his betrayal with lies so thin Lizzie could have seen the sky through them.

'I told him you'd probably been busy,' Harriet said, hoisting Artie into her arms. 'Jude told me about—'

'I'd rather not discuss it. But for what it's worth, I'm sorry to hear about you and Damon.'

'Jude was only trying to comfort me, you know. We've been friends for a long time and I tend to turn to him for a lot. The split with Damon… it was a big deal, you know? I really liked him and Jude knows that. But whatever else you might think is… happening… well, it isn't.'

Lizzie was silent. Wasn't it obvious to Harriet that right there was exactly the reason her own relationship with Jude would never work?

'But you're not OK with him?' Harriet added into the silence.

'It's…' Lizzie glanced at Charlie, who was hanging onto her every word. No matter how cryptically she and Harriet had this conversation he might still get more of it than either of them would like – certainly more than Lizzie would like.

'I missed you,' Charlie said into the pause. 'And Gracie too. Is her baby here yet?'

Lizzie smiled now, and this one was genuine. 'Not yet. We have a few months to wait.'

'Will I be able to see it?'

'Of course! You'll be one of the first people to see it.'

'But what if you're busy?'

'We'd never be too busy for you.'

'Is it a boy or a girl?'

'We don't know yet.'

'I hope it's a boy, then he can play with me and Artie.'

'I expect he'd like that. But girls can play with you both too.'

'It's not the same.'

'I'm sure you can work out a game that suits you all – boy or girl.'

Charlie opened his mouth to reply, but then his eyes grew round and his face was a picture of absolute delight as he squealed at something behind Lizzie.

'Gracie!' he cried, throwing himself at her now and hugging her.

'I thought I heard your voice,' Gracie said groggily. 'You woke me up.'

'Oh…' Charlie's face fell. 'I'm sorry.'

Gracie laughed. 'It's alright. If anyone is allowed to wake me up, it's you.'

Gracie glanced up at Lizzie and Harriet and, even though she looked half-asleep, she seemed to make the connection instantly. Gracie turned back to Charlie. 'How about I make us a drink and you can tell me what you've been up to this week?'

Charlie gave an emphatic nod and followed her to the kitchen area, while Lizzie and Harriet stood at the bottom of the caravan steps.

'Would you like some tea?' Lizzie asked. Not because she wanted Harriet to stay but because that was what you did. Although, perhaps a small part of her did want Harriet to stay. Perhaps she wanted to hear something from her that might restore the trust she'd lost in Jude. If only he'd come himself – she'd have talked to him and she'd have listened, despite resolving not to. 'Coffee? And I'm sure I can find some juice for Artie…'

'I don't want to take up too much of your time,' Harriet said.

'Jude sent you?'

'Sort of – but at my insistence. It's not for Jude I'm here, though – it's for Charlie. Jude realises that it's probably over between you and him, but it's hard for Charlie to deal with that stuff. Jude's never really let other girlfriends get close to Charlie unless he was certain they'd stay around for him—'

'Like you?'

'We're friends now, nothing more. The thing is, when you become a part of Charlie's life then you inadvertently make a sort of contract, a deal. You can't abandon him. Once you're in Charlie's life, you owe it to him to stay in it.'

'And Jude sent you to say that to me? He couldn't come and ask this himself?'

'*We're* asking. For Charlie's sake. I came because Jude felt you wouldn't let him speak.'

'He hasn't even tried.'

'He called you and you didn't answer.'

'He could have come to the caravan if he'd really wanted to try and put things right.'

'He didn't come because he has too much respect to hassle you. Jesus, Lizzie – what do you want from him?'

'What do *I* want from him? A little honesty would have been nice. And maybe a sign that he cared about it.'

'He does care about it.'

'Then why are you here instead of him?'

'I told you why.'

'This doesn't help – it just makes it worse. What's the deal with you two? Why are you like this? Like you and Jude against the world? You say you're not together, but you spend almost all your time together. I think he's still in love with you, and it seems to me that you still feel something for him too. Is it still off with you and Damon?'

'I don't think that's any of your business and you're being ridiculous. I can't take the blame for your pathetic insecurities…'

'I'll take that as a yes.' Lizzie narrowed her eyes. 'You do *know* Jude is still in love with you, don't you?'

'He's not. We have a son together and that's all now.'

'So you don't want him back?'

'I haven't come here to try and fix your relationship with Jude. Only you can do that, and even if I could I wouldn't necessarily think it was in his best interests.'

Lizzie's jaw tightened. 'Then why have you come?'

'I've told you why.'

'And that's the only reason?'

'Yes.'

'So you're not getting back together?'

'Of course not!'

'Are you sure about that?'

'I don't see why I have to explain myself to you. What does it matter? You're not even with Jude now. He just wants you to think about Charlie in all this. Charlie's got close to you and your sister, and Jude doesn't want to put him through a painful separation if he doesn't have to.'

What about *their* painful separation? What about the separation of Lizzie and Jude – didn't he care about that? It sounded like the minute Lizzie had left his house that night he'd simply given up on her – on any future they might have had. Didn't he want to fight for her? To hell with his respectful distance – she wanted him to turn up on her doorstep and hammer on the door and demand he talk to her. She wanted him here, thrashing it out. Instead he'd sent the mother of his child – the reason they were in this mess. What kind of message did that send out? He'd clearly confided in Harriet every detail of what had happened between them and Lizzie couldn't believe he'd do a thing like that either. The signals couldn't have been any more mixed up.

Charlie's voice came from behind her. 'Gracie says does Artie want an ice cream?'

Lizzie spun round, suddenly guilty for her thoughts. Jude was right about one thing: whether she was angry or not, it didn't give her the right to cut the people from Charlie's life that he'd grown attached to. The one person who carried the least blame was the one person who had so much to lose and so little hope of understanding why.

She turned to Harriet and forced a tight smile. 'If that's alright with you, perhaps Artie can come in for a little while? My sister would love the excuse to spoil him with a bowl of ice cream.'

Harriet looked as unhappy about the prospect as Lizzie did, but she forced a smile too. 'I'm sure you'd love that, wouldn't you, Artie?'

The little boy plucked out the thumb he'd been sucking and nodded, half shy, half seduced by the prospect of a sweet treat.

'Come on in,' Lizzie said, showing Harriet up the caravan steps and hoping this visit would be over quickly.

*

Lizzie just couldn't bring herself to trust a word Harriet said. Was it pure jealousy, or was there another instinct at work here, telling her all was not as it seemed? Because Lizzie recognised now, even though she'd tried to ignore it, that there was a fairly healthy dollop of jealousy currently lodging in her heart where Harriet was concerned, and there always had been. But as they sat in the caravan together now, Artie giggled and Charlie laughed with him, and Harriet watched over it all with a kind of quiet knowledge in her face that she was the queen of both their hearts. It made Lizzie want to grab Charlie and try to impress him, just as she used to compete with Gracie and James to be their dad's favourite child, and it made her feel silly and ashamed of herself for having such ridiculous thoughts. The longer Harriet sat there, the more Lizzie wanted to tell her to get out. She'd never fought such an unreasonable impulse before, but Harriet just seemed to bring out this strange, madly irrational streak in her.

Things were prevented from escalating by the arrival of Florentina back at the caravan. As she walked in, her eyebrows raised in surprise at the hullabaloo, Lizzie was snapped back to some kind of rational reality.

'If I'd known there was going to be a party I'd have stayed here,' Florentina said with a smile.

'Florentina… This is Charlie – Jude's brother,' Lizzie said, jumping up. 'And this is Artie and Harriet – Jude's…'

'Friend,' Harriet finished for her. 'And we were just about to leave, to be honest.'

'Don't go because of me,' Florentina said.

'We have things to do, and I'm sure you need to get on. And Charlie… perhaps that's enough ice cream for one day, even for you.'

Charlie looked disappointed, but he also looked slightly wrong-footed by the arrival of Florentina. He gave her an uncertain smile before going back to his bowl to make sure he shovelled up the last of it before he was torn away.

Harriet got up. 'Thanks for the ice cream and tea,' she said. 'I hope your pregnancy goes well, Gracie.'

'Thank you.'

'And, Lizzie,' Harriet added, pulling Artie up into her arms. 'Please think about what I said earlier, won't you?'

Gracie and Florentina both looked sharply at Lizzie. They would expect to be filled in later on what Harriet meant, but Lizzie didn't know if she wanted to talk about it. For now she simply nodded at Harriet. 'I will.'

'See you later,' Charlie said, waving madly, a trail of melted ice cream dripping down one side of his mouth. If Lizzie hadn't been in such a strange mood, she might have thought it comical and come to his rescue with a napkin. But she couldn't think about that now.

'You bet.' Gracie stood and began to collect their dirty bowls from the table, seemingly unfazed by the mess on Charlie's face too.

'Bye,' Harriet said, looking at them all in turn, but her gaze resting on Lizzie for a second longer.

Lizzie saw them out and watched as they drove away, and she didn't have a clue what to make of any of it at all.

Chapter Twenty

'Mum wants to talk to you.'

Gracie looked smug as she wandered into the main living space from her bedroom and handed her phone over. A bit too smug, like the time she'd caught Lizzie sneaking her mother's favourite beaded handbag into her own wardrobe aged ten. She'd got the upper hand in the sibling rivalry stakes that time too. Lizzie had the distinct feeling she'd been *grassed up*, a phrase they used to use when they were kids and one that still occasionally came out of Lizzie's mouth – but mostly only where Gracie was involved.

'Hey, Mum…' Lizzie tried to make her greeting as airy as possible. She didn't want to sound guilty before she even knew what she was going to feel guilty about. But she could tell by Gracie's face that she *was* about to feel guilty about something.

'Gracie tells me your stepmother is living with you.'

'Florentina?' Lizzie asked, thankful that Florentina was at the shops. She had to wonder whether this was the reason Gracie had chosen this precise moment to call her mum, knowing that Florentina wasn't there and probably wanting to complain about her. 'Well, yes, but—'

'What on earth for?'

Lizzie glanced at Gracie, who picked up a magazine from the sofa and settled with it. 'I expect Gracie has told you that too, hasn't she?'

'She said something about a fire.'

'It was more than a fire, Mum; her whole house is practically gone.'

'But her insurance company offered to sort accommodation for her?'

'Yes, but I thought it would be mean to expect her to live in some flea-bitten hotel on her own. She's been through so much the past few months and—'

'We've all been through a lot the past few months.'

'Yes,' Lizzie continued patiently. 'But we haven't all lost our homes.'

'She's not exactly been thrown out on the street.'

'But she has lost absolutely everything,' Lizzie said gently.

There was a deep sigh at the end of the line.

'Do you know when she'll be able to go home?'

'Not yet.'

'I suppose it's quite cramped there at the moment.'

'A bit; we're managing for now.'

'I hope she's paying her way.'

'More than paying her way. She's pulling her weight too...' Lizzie shot another glance at Gracie that said to watch out for revenge when this phone call was over. 'And she's been very sweet to Gracie about the baby and everything. In fact, she even bought a whole heap of reusable nappies for her the other day.'

Gracie's cheeks flushed and she scuttled off into her bedroom with the magazine. Lizzie had never seen her move so fast, not since she'd started to complain about swollen ankles. Sometimes, it really was like they were both still kids. *Stick that in your pipe and smoke it, sis*, Lizzie thought savagely.

'When will I be able to visit?' Gwendolyn asked.

'You mean, when will Florentina not be here?'

'Obviously.'

'You can come when she's here, you know.'

'You know I can't do that. It rakes up bad feelings for me.'

'I'm sorry, Mum. She won't be here for much longer.'

'Gracie tells me you're still not back with your boyfriend either. Is that completely over now?'

Lizzie stared out of the window. A light drizzle kissed the panes, and beyond Tim and his team were rushing to throw a tarpaulin over some expensive-looking sawing equipment before the rain really came down.

'Oh, Lizzie – I am sorry. You've had such bad luck.' Gwendolyn's voice brought her back to the room. Her mum didn't add *with men*, but that was what she meant. Lizzie certainly knew how to pick them.

'It's OK. One of those things, I suppose.'

'And there's no reconciliation to be had? What on earth happened? I thought you were keen on this one?'

So Gracie hadn't told her mum the details, and Lizzie had to be thankful that she wasn't entirely devoid of tact. Gwendolyn had been incandescent with rage when she'd found out about Evan, and, in truth, the episode had made everyone in the family a little less trusting of anyone Lizzie had dated since. Not that any of them had lasted long anyway.

'I'd really rather not talk about it,' Lizzie said. 'Not just yet. I'm still sort of getting my head around things.'

'Something must have happened.'

'Something did, but I don't want to talk or think about it now.'

'That doesn't sound like you. Please tell me this one didn't—'

'Honestly, please leave it, Mum. I'm too busy to think about it anyway, even if I wanted to.'

There was a pause, and then Gwendolyn seemed to think better of pursuing the argument. 'Speaking of which, how is the building work going?'

'Good. Sort of on schedule – the new, new schedule anyway.'

'And you're still OK for money?'

'Yes, Mum. And I wouldn't have it off you even if you wanted to give it to me.'

'I want my children to be alright, that's all.'

'That reminds me; I was thinking, as the building work is a little quiet and Florentina is here to hold the fort if the team need anything, I might go and visit James. We could all go – you, me and Gracie.'

'That's a great idea,' Gwendolyn said. 'We'll get him out of that flat for a few hours and take him to a restaurant. I'll bet he hasn't seen a fresh carrot for months. And you can help me persuade him to come back home—'

'He won't, Mum – you know that.'

'He shouldn't be in that awful place with those awful people, and I should have done something about it long before he became so fond of them.'

'Mum, he's an adult; apart from chaining him to his old bedroom at home, you can't control where he goes or who he sees. He made his own choices, all we can do is try to keep an eye on him and make sure we're there for him. Give me some dates you can do and I'll phone him to see if he's free.'

'I can do that right now. Hang on while I go and get the calendar from the wall.'

Lizzie heard a clunk as her mother put the phone receiver down and then footsteps. A moment later she was back, slightly out of breath.

'Right, let's see,' she said. 'How are we doing for next week?'

Lizzie went to her own calendar, pinned up in the little kitchen area. There was a mass of notes scrawled across it – dates for this and that to arrive, phone calls to clients and appointments for Gracie. As they began to work out when they could all get together, Lizzie started to look forward to it. She'd missed James, and a day in his company would help to take her mind off all the trouble and stress here. Not that visiting James wouldn't bring its own kind of stress, of course, but didn't they say a change was as good as a rest?

*

Lizzie had phoned James and fixed a day the following week when she, her mum and Gracie could go and see him. By now, Florentina had used all the compassionate leave granted by her employers for her house misfortune and she was trying to get her head around her workload in a bid to get back to some normality. However, she'd already told Lizzie she would be happy to take some annual leave owed to her and hold the fort at the mill in case Tim and the team needed anything while Lizzie and Gracie went to see James. The plan was to stay overnight in a nearby hotel and try to spend as much time with him as possible to get a measure of his health and mental well-being, and to figure out if any kind of subtle intervention was needed. Speaking to him on the phone was always misleading; he would laugh and joke and tease and sound as if he hadn't a care in the world. It wasn't until you could see him and spend proper time with him that you could see how he really was.

Gracie was now salting a pan of boiling water to throw some pasta in for their evening meal. Lizzie noted with some satisfaction that she had set enough aside for three portions. Since Florentina had been back at work, Gracie had taken on much of the cooking again and had silently adjusted her meal plans to include Florentina. It was progress – a year ago and she would have watched her stepmother starve rather than make any kind of concession at all. They were both trying hard to get along, though Gracie, despite the cooking, was still finding it a lot more difficult than the naturally tolerant and gregarious Florentina. But then, Florentina had made her peace with the fact that almost the whole Lovell family would never forgive her for stealing Lizzie's dad from them a long time ago.

Lizzie looked at her watch and then went to the window. It was almost six. The last contractor's van had just left for the evening and, almost as soon as it had disappeared, Florentina's car pulled up. Lizzie watched her get out and then go to the boot to haul out a huge bubble-wrapped item. Rushing to the door, she raced across the garden to help.

'It's not heavy,' Florentina said. 'Just a bit difficult to carry.'

'Let me grab that end,' Lizzie insisted, taking hold.

Between them they carried it to the caravan. Gracie looked up with an expression of faint surprise as they laid it down on the floor.

'We've got plenty of room for that,' she said flatly, turning back to the pan.

'You do know sarcasm is the lowest form of wit?' Lizzie replied.

'I thought everyone already knew that. Doesn't stop it from being funny.'

Lizzie ignored the comeback and turned to Florentina. If Florentina had been shopping, then she took that as a good sign. As far as Lizzie was concerned, she could fill the caravan to the brim with new stuff if it made her feel better. 'Does this need to go in your room or something?'

'Actually, it's for Gracie.'

Gracie turned back from her cooking now and wiped her hands on a dishcloth. 'For me?'

'For the Little Baked Bean.'

Gracie settled an instinctive hand on her tummy. 'Little Baked Bean' was what they'd christened her unborn baby after seeing online illustrations of how it would look at this stage of her pregnancy. She broke into a smile. 'What is it?'

'Open it and find out.'

Gracie began to tear the bubble wrap off to reveal a beautiful white Moses basket lined with soft lemon fabric.

'Oh, it's just gorgeous!' Gracie beamed. 'Is this one of your samples from work?'

'Actually, no. I was driving home and I saw it in a shop window as I waited at some lights. I couldn't leave it behind.'

Gracie was dumbstruck. It was rare, and Lizzie almost wished she could run to get a camera to record it. But then she put a hand to her chest and stared at Florentina. 'It must have cost a fortune!'

Florentina wafted her hand in the air. 'That doesn't matter.'

'It does!' Gracie pushed it away. 'I can't take this – it's too much.'

'You can, and I want you to. Your baby… Gracie, I don't think you realise quite how much your baby means to me too. I may not be family, but I loved your dad…'

Gracie seemed to wince at the reminder, but Florentina continued.

'And this baby is your dad's first grandchild. If you'll let me – and I know it won't be easy for you – I want to be in the life of your bambino. I know that your dad would want that too if he was here to say it.'

Gracie's eyes filled with tears, and Lizzie could see plainly on her sister's face the internal struggle. How could she reject such a heartfelt plea, and yet it went against everything she'd ever chosen to believe about their stepmother. She'd feel, as Lizzie often did, that friendship with Florentina was a betrayal of Gwendolyn, and yet, in Lizzie's eyes, to do anything else was a betrayal of her father's memory. Dad would have wanted them to look after Florentina, to know that she hadn't been cast out into the cold once he'd gone.

'Thank you,' was all Gracie could say. 'I love it.'

'That's the only thing that matters then,' Florentina replied with a smile that held too much sadness for Lizzie to look. Every time Florentina looked at Lizzie and Gracie she must have been reminded of the man she'd loved and lost too soon, and every time she looked at Gracie's baby in the months to come, she would be reminded even more strongly.

'Well,' Lizzie cut in brightly in a bid to lighten the mood, 'it's not quite the only thing that matters.' She looked at the basket. 'Where the hell are we going to store that for the next few months?'

'Oh, Lizzie.' Gracie laughed, wiping away her tears. 'Trust you to think of that.'

'I'm being serious. One of us might have to get rid of our bed and sleep in that instead.'

'I didn't think about that,' Florentina said, looking genuinely concerned now.

'I'm joking,' Lizzie said. 'Don't worry; I'm sure we'll find some space somewhere.'

'Perhaps Mum will keep it at her house,' Gracie suggested.

'As long as you don't tell her who bought it,' Florentina added.

'Well, yes. I suppose she might just put a match to it in that case,' Lizzie said. After all, there was no point in anyone trying to sugar-coat the truth. Gracie might have come a long way with Florentina, but in a way it had been forced upon her. Gwendolyn Lovell was quite a different matter.

'Oh!' Gracie squeaked, and suddenly rushed off into her bedroom. Lizzie and Florentina exchanged puzzled looks, until she returned a few seconds later with her phone and took a photo of the cot.

'It's to show Charlie,' Gracie said in answer to Lizzie's silent question. 'You know how he loves to be involved in all this stuff.'

That heavy, hollow feeling swept over Lizzie again. She tried so hard not to think of Jude these days, but they'd decided to honour their promise not to cut Charlie out of their lives, and Jude sort of came with the territory. Whether she thought it was good for her or not (and she didn't, which was why she'd decided to keep her distance) Jude was still as much a part of her world as before, even if they weren't a couple. But she didn't need all the angst that he brought with him, all the second-guessing and doubt.

Gracie looked at her, seeming to read Lizzie's emotions on her face. She put her phone down and pulled Lizzie into a hug.

'You really ought to go and talk to him,' Florentina said.

Lizzie stepped out of Gracie's arms and shook her head. 'If he'd wanted to talk there's been plenty of opportunity, and why should I do the chasing?'

'Because you're miserable without him,' Florentina said. 'I bet he's miserable without you too. The two of you are being ridiculous about this.'

'How can you say that?' Gracie countered. 'You know what happened with Evan.'

'Evan was *uno stronzo*,' she said, lapsing into her favourite home-grown insult, 'but Jude doesn't seem like that.'

'I don't know what he's like anymore,' Lizzie said. 'Perhaps I don't really want to know.' She looked at Gracie, who nodded encouragement.

'You're doing fine without him,' she said, firing a warning glance at Florentina that dared her to interfere. Florentina could buy gifts, and they could make real progress in their relationship, but, when all was said and done, she wasn't really family, and Gracie wasn't about to let her forget that. 'You don't need him – you have us.'

Chapter Twenty-One

Tim leaned against his van, cigarette clamped between his lips as he cast a satisfied glance at the mill.

'It's a shame your specialist can't come sooner to get started on the workings, but I suppose it takes time to get someone like that in – there's not many of them and they're in demand all over the country. The good news is, I reckon your living quarters should be ready for you to move in by the end of the month.'

'Really?' Lizzie couldn't help the kick of excitement, though she tried to keep it under control – nothing was ever certain on a project like this, and she'd been disappointed before. Still, it did look as if it was almost ready, even to Lizzie's untrained eye. Already she had colour schemes and soft furnishings whirling round her mind – now came the fun bit.

'Aye.'

He looked at Lizzie with a rare smile. Perhaps her excitement was infectious, or perhaps it was just pride in a long and trying job that was almost done. Whatever the reason, he didn't look quite as much like a drunken Eeyore as usual.

'I expect you'll miss me,' Lizzie said.

'I've got a lot of customers who're sick of waiting for me to get to their jobs, that's for sure. *They* won't miss you.'

Lizzie laughed. 'I suppose not. But I snagged you first so fair's fair.'

'The kitchen fitter wants you to talk to him about the extractor hood when you've a minute.'

'What's wrong with it?'

'Don't know. I expect it's something and nothing – he's like that.'

'Oh.' Lizzie nodded, though she didn't know exactly how to take Tim's statement. 'As long as it's not going to cost me more money.'

'I shouldn't think so; he'd have run that by me first.'

'I'd better pop and see him then.'

Tim gave a short nod and Lizzie made her way to the front door of her almost new home. Inside, it was still full of echoing voices, snatches of music from different radios on different floors, the air full of dust and solvents. But as the sun slanted in through the high windows onto smooth walls and sharp woodwork – blank canvases just waiting for Lizzie to make her mark on them – it was beginning to feel like it could just be her forever home. But the picture had changed since she'd first imagined it, because while she'd always planned to live here alone – at least for the foreseeable future – now, in her mind's eye as she pictured the finished rooms, there were toys scattered around the place, later on maybe textbooks and muddy trainers and the sounds of children playing out in the garden. It had been a family home once, and maybe it would be again. Maybe the old place would never have felt complete without family in it, despite Lizzie's original plans.

She passed one of the smaller rooms that had been earmarked for an office and couldn't help but imagine how perfect it would look painted in bright colours and housing a cot.

Was she actually getting excited about Gracie's baby? She'd reflected more and more with sadness on the day when her sister would leave her – and they'd talked about it at some length, Gracie aware that it was ultimately what Lizzie wanted. But was all this still what Lizzie wanted? Why did Gracie have to bring up her baby alone in some dingy flat when they could share the burden? Not only that, but Lizzie would probably love it. No, not probably – definitely.

It needed some thought, and she'd need to talk to Gracie, but Lizzie was sure that if she decided to ask Gracie to live in the mill with her, her sister would jump at the chance. They could share the childcare for Gracie's baby, and they could share the work at the mill, if Lizzie's business ever got off the ground. Now that Gracie and Florentina were getting on, that possibility might be so much easier to achieve – Florentina as a silent, financial partner and Gracie as an actual extra pair of hands. It wasn't like Gracie was in any rush to get back to her pressured life in London as far as Lizzie could tell, and she'd said more than once how she envied Lizzie's future in the peace of the Suffolk countryside. Together, they might just make this crazy scheme work. Lizzie smiled to herself. She might be making a huge mistake. Then again, she might just be making the best decision of her life.

*

Lizzie looked up to see her brother amble past the vast window of the café on his way to the door. Fifteen minutes late wasn't bad at all considering how late he'd been on other occasions. Lizzie was pleased to note that he looked neat and clean. He would have made an effort, of course, knowing that his mum was coming to see him, and that in itself was encouraging because it meant he was still bothered about what she thought.

The bell on the door tinkled as he opened it. The café was of his choosing – Lizzie, Gracie and her mum had all agreed that given the choice they'd have taken him somewhere far less greasy spoon, but he'd insisted it served the best fried breakfasts in London. So much for

Gwendolyn's plan to get a plate of vegetables inside him. As his gaze settled on their table, he lumbered over with a soppy grin.

James was as ginger as the rest of them were dark, and it had been one of their dad's favourite jokes that he'd scoured the neighbourhood for any sign of a ginger milkman when his son had been born. But nobody who saw them together could deny the shape of the nose and the lopsided smile that they both shared. Even as slight as he was now, James had never lost the roundness of his cheeks, nor had he lost the spark in his eyes that made it seem as if he was constantly plotting his next elaborate practical joke. He'd grown like a weed as a kid too, and by the age of seventeen he had towered over not only his sisters and mum, but over his dad as well. He was over six feet tall as a grown man, almost crouching through the doorway of the café today as he came in.

'Alright?' he asked, folding himself into a seat and tucking his long legs under the table. 'Haven't ordered yet?'

'We thought we'd wait for you,' Gracie said.

'Thought you'd watch me eat first?' he asked, his grin widening. 'Didn't like the look of the place so you decided if I don't keel over then the food must be OK for you to eat?'

'And still not funny,' Gracie fired back, though she couldn't help a grin now too.

'So, I hear you're up the duff,' he replied. 'Is that congratulations or commiserations?' Gracie's smile faltered, but he seemed oblivious to her discomfort.

Gwendolyn leaned over the table to kiss him on the cheek, but Lizzie and Gracie stayed put. James didn't really do kissing and hugging – and the only exception he made in this rule was his mum. Even that was only because she'd been so vocal about it. The nonchalant indifference he showed to Lizzie and Gracie cut his mum to the quick, and she'd told him so, many times. Lizzie didn't worry quite so much about it, because she knew it was really just an act.

'And Frank is over the moon about it, is he?' James grabbed a menu from a rack and glanced down at it before tossing it onto the table.

'What do you think?' Gracie asked, raising her eyebrows.

'I think he's a twat – always have done. Don't really know why you had to ask.' Without waiting for Gracie to reply, James looked at Lizzie. 'What are you having for breakfast?'

'As it's lunchtime, I'm planning on having lunch.'

'Yeah, but they do all-day breakfasts here. You can have your fry-up at midnight if you want.'

'You certainly haven't been in here having fry-ups at midnight,' Lizzie said. 'You're still like a whippet.'

James grinned. 'That's my fast metabolism. I've always been skinny.'

'I could murder a bacon sandwich,' Gracie said brightly. 'In fact, I can't even remember the last time I had a decent bacon sandwich.'

'Well, that doesn't insult me at all, considering I cooked one for you last weekend,' Lizzie said.

'Exactly,' Gracie smiled sweetly. 'I said I couldn't remember the last time I had a *decent* bacon sandwich. Yours has all sorts of rubbish on it.'

'It's not rubbish! That's a Nigella recipe; you were the one telling me to get more creative in the kitchen!'

'A bacon sandwich is bread – the cheaper the better – bacon and sauce. There's no need to mess with the formula. Even Nigella should know better than to break that rule.' Gracie turned to James. 'What do you say?'

'I always knew you were the smart sister,' James replied, his relaxed grin back now.

'Well, you never said a word when you were stuffing it into your mouth,' Lizzie said savagely.

'I'd been having morning sickness for about a gazillion years before that – I'd be stuffing anything into my mouth because I was starving.'

'And I suppose it was so awful that it brought your morning sickness right back.'

'I didn't say it was horrible – just that it wasn't really anything like a proper bacon sandwich at all.'

'I still can't believe you two haven't killed each other yet, living in that caravan together,' James said.

'My thoughts exactly,' Gwendolyn agreed. She reached for the laminated menu that James had dropped and glanced briefly over it before placing it back down and wiping her hands on a napkin from a box on the table.

'We are capable of being adults, you know,' Lizzie said.

'Well,' Gracie cut in, 'one of us is.'

'That's me you're talking about,' Lizzie fired back, 'obviously.'

'Now, now, children.' James grinned. 'Now you see why I haven't come to live in your windmill, Lizzie. Not only is it just plain weird that you want to live in a windmill, but I'd have to put up with you two.'

'Then it's a good job nobody's asking you to move into our windmill,' Gracie said, but then coloured as she looked at Lizzie. 'I mean, *Lizzie's* windmill…'

Lizzie smiled. A few months ago she couldn't have imagined she'd feel so relaxed about her sister's slip of the tongue, but in light of the thoughts she'd been having about asking Gracie if she'd like to stay for good, she didn't mind at all this time.

'You know you can come and stay whenever you want, though,' Lizzie said, turning to James.

'What, with you two there? No thanks.'

'You love us really,' Gracie said.

'That's what you think.' James leaned back in his chair and regarded them both with a wry smile.

'But you will come over occasionally?' Lizzie asked. 'At least to see it? I know you think I'm a nutter for wanting to live in a windmill, but it is pretty spectacular, and I'd love you to visit and see what we've done with the place.'

'And it was special to Dad too,' Gracie added. 'You'd want to see what it might have looked like if he'd ever taken a chance on it, wouldn't you?'

'Dad would never have taken a chance on it,' James said. 'He never took a chance on anything.'

'He had other priorities,' Gwendolyn said. 'Like his family for a start.'

'Not that much of a priority when he ran off with his younger model, were we?' James shot back, and Gwendolyn's lips pursed into a perfect knot as she looked across at the door to the café. Perhaps she was thinking about how easy it might be to escape, because despite the banter, there was a subtle tension in the air. There always was when the family was together like this. Even though they were all blood relatives, they had hardly any common ground at all, and it was only love that kept them coming back to try and get along, again and again.

'So…' Lizzie cut in, her voice brighter and breezier than she felt, 'how about we order one of these legendary all-day breakfasts then? If they're half as good as James thinks they are then maybe we should all try one?'

'Yes,' Gracie agreed, clearly as keen to move on as Lizzie was. 'I think Little Baked Bean is getting hungry.'

'Little Baked Bean?' James raised his eyebrows.

'The baby,' Gracie said. 'That's what we call him.'

'It's a boy then?'

'Oh, I don't know that yet. It's just I don't like saying *it* so I say he, she... but mostly Baked Bean.'

'Only you could give an unborn child a name like that,' James replied lazily. 'Think it might stick?'

They were interrupted by a waitress who couldn't have been older than nineteen or twenty. She exchanged a few pleasantries with James that suggested they knew each other. She took orders for four breakfasts and four cups of tea before leaving them again. James watched her go with some interest, and Lizzie wondered if they'd had some sort of fling.

As she disappeared into the kitchen with their order, he turned to Gracie. 'You know what?' he said. 'It might not be all that bad being an uncle. If it's a boy I can take him to football matches and stuff, can't I? Introduce him to the ways of the Jedi... tell him all about the mysteries of the opposite sex... Might be a laugh.'

'Good God, you don't think I'm leaving you alone with any son of mine, do you? Not even for a minute!' Gracie laughed. 'You'd teach him the most awful things!'

James inclined his head. 'Naturally.'

'You never know,' Lizzie said, 'he or she might actually be a good influence on you.'

James turned to her. 'Are you insinuating I need influencing to be good?'

'Yes.'

'Well, what is *good* anyway?' He crooked his fingers into speech marks in the air around the word *good*. 'How do you know I'm not already good? It might not be your version, but then it's all a matter of viewpoint anyway. If you're sitting me next to Hitler then I'm saintly by comparison.'

'Hmmm,' was all Lizzie could manage in reply.

'I can't believe we're talking about uncles and aunts and grandchildren,' Gwendolyn said. 'I never thought I'd see the day.'

'It's not *that* unlikely one of us would have a child,' Lizzie said.

'With you three it seemed very unlikely,' her mother said. 'You were all interested in other things.'

'Most people have a bit of a life first.'

'Well,' Gwendolyn insisted, 'I can't help feeling that I've been waiting a long time.'

'And Mum's got a point,' James said, turning to Gracie. 'You're only up the duff by accident so it's not like you were planning on giving her a grandchild any time soon. If Frank hadn't done the deed it might have been years.'

'I wish you'd stop calling it that,' Gwendolyn said.

'It might have been never left up to Frank,' Gracie said, her expression darkening.

'Speaking of which—' Gwendolyn began, but Gracie held up a hand.

'No, I haven't changed my mind about telling him. I don't need him, and I don't want him.' She forced a smile and glanced in turn at everyone seated around the table. 'I have all the people I need right here.'

'Why not?' James asked.

'You know Frank,' Gracie said tartly. 'Would you tell him?'

'But you'd get money out of him,' James replied. 'It'd be worth it just for that, surely?'

'I don't need his money. I don't need anything from him.'

'You say that now, but I think you might change your mind.'

'She's made her decision,' Lizzie said. She might not completely agree, but it was Gracie's decision to make, and she, for one, wanted to support her sister at least that far. Especially as Gracie had been such a good support for her since she'd split with Jude. 'We're family and we can be more than enough support for Gracie.'

'Don't expect me to be changing nappies for you,' James said.

'I'm perfectly capable of changing a nappy,' Gracie said.

'You know they don't smell of Parma Violets, don't you?' he fired back.

'Sometimes I wonder why I bother coming to see you.'

'So do I.'

'OK!' Lizzie clapped her hands. 'I'm sure Gracie will find a YouTube tutorial somewhere that explains how to change a nappy, and she'll be fine once we pick up the gas mask.'

'Cheeky cow!' Gracie squeaked, and James threw back his head in laughter.

∗

Lizzie, Gracie and their mother spent a quiet evening at a budget hotel half a mile from James's flat, squished together on a soft sofa in the corner of the bar while they discussed James. On the surface he seemed fine, but then he always did, and they'd learned over the years that his jokes told them very little about how he really was. Perhaps it would have been easier to drive away and leave him in his bedsit with his loser friends if he hadn't tried to kill himself five years earlier. He'd always denied that he'd meant to take quite so many paracetamol and drink so much whisky, but nobody had believed it. He pretended to be resilient, but James was perhaps the least resilient of all the Lovell siblings, however it might look to outsiders. Today, it seemed like he'd well and truly come through whatever issues he'd been having back then, but the fear of a repeat was always there, lurking in the darkness just out of view and throwing a shadow over their relationship with him.

The following morning they'd decided to call on him at home to see him again before they left for Suffolk, but when Lizzie had phoned ahead she'd got no answer.

They stood at the intercom now and buzzed again, but nobody answered.

'I suppose it's quite early,' Gwendolyn said, glancing between Lizzie and Gracie. 'You know how he sleeps – dead to the world once he's gone.'

'You'd think one of his flatmates might have heard it,' Lizzie said.

'Perhaps they went out last night after we'd left him,' Gracie said. 'If they're all hungover it would be no wonder nobody is answering. Try phoning him again, Lizzie.'

'I don't want to wake him,' Lizzie said uncertainly. 'He won't thank us.'

'Oh, for goodness' sake,' Gracie said, getting her own phone out and dialling. She waited, listening until the dialling tone cut off and the answer service message kicked in. 'Buzz him again,' she said, nodding at the intercom as she put her phone away. 'We did tell him we'd call to say goodbye and it's very rude of him not to be up.'

'It's very James,' Lizzie said as she pressed the button again. 'We probably wore out our welcome yesterday.'

'I'll try phoning him again when we get back,' Gwendolyn said. 'Not that he'll answer to me – he'll think I'm nagging.'

'He thinks everyone is nagging,' Gracie said.

'That's because we are,' Lizzie replied as they turned to walk back to the car.

'Still, it's been nice to see him looking so well,' Gwendolyn said.

Lizzie exchanged a glance with Gracie, who climbed into the front passenger seat as Lizzie unlocked the car for them. Their brother had been very chatty, certainly, but nobody could ever say with any certainty that James was well.

'It was nice to see him full stop,' Gracie said. 'It's not often these days we all get together.'

'It's a shame he isn't living closer to us.'

'I'd have him back home in a heartbeat,' Gwendolyn said. 'He just doesn't want to know.'

'That's because you'd be able to keep too close an eye on what he gets up to,' Gracie replied. 'You can't help someone who won't be helped.'

'He knows it's done out of love.'

'I'm not sure he does,' Lizzie said. 'And even then I don't think he cares. James will do what James wants to do – always has done, always will. He was never any different, even when he was a kid.'

'That doesn't mean we have to give up trying.'

'It doesn't, but it means we have to accept that there are limitations on what we can do for him – what he'll *allow* us to do for him.'

'Did you hear him talk about the baby, though?' Gracie asked. 'I think he was actually excited. Maybe that will make a difference?'

'Getting to be an uncle?' Lizzie asked.

'Yes. Perhaps it will be a positive thing to focus on.'

'If he ever gets near enough to undertake any uncle duties, then maybe. We only see him when we make the effort to visit him as it is, but when you have a baby and the mill is up and running, we'll have even less time to make the trip. I can't imagine him doing it instead. Suffolk might as well be Outer Mongolia as far as he's concerned.'

'Then we'll have to make sure we find the time,' Gracie said firmly. 'Once he falls in love with his little niece or nephew I'm sure that will change.'

It was a nice thought – that Gracie's baby might be the saviour of their brother's almost lost soul – but Lizzie wasn't quite as confident as her sister.

Chapter Twenty-Two

'Oh no!' Gracie sucked in her breath as she looked out of the window.

Lizzie looked up from her laptop, biting back a sigh of irritation. While she understood that it was tough for Gracie to get a job right now, she couldn't help but wonder what had happened to her sister's shiny plans to start a business of her own. Being pregnant didn't stop that from happening – at least it shouldn't. But Gracie spent more and more time these days nursing her belly and floating around the caravan like a delicate heroine from a Victorian novel – not doing very much at all except reading the odd chapter of a book (or, in her case, baby magazine), walking the garden and threatening to swoon with every change of the wind. And she wasn't even three months gone yet.

'What is it?'

'Charlie's here… but he's got company.'

Lizzie shot to the window now, expecting to see Harriet with Charlie. But it was Jude. Gracie threw her a sideways look.

'He doesn't usually get out of the car when he drops Charlie off.'

'No, he doesn't,' Lizzie said in a low voice.

There wasn't time to argue the point further, however, because whilst this short exchange had been taking place, Charlie had sprinted to the caravan door and thrown it open.

'Hello!' he cried.

It was tempting to have yet another conversation about knocking – something Charlie seemed to have forgotten how to do since he'd become so comfortable with them both – but there wasn't time to do that either because Jude was hot on his heels. But he did knock – at the open door of the caravan, his expression suitably awkward and sombre.

'Sorry about that,' he said. 'Charlie was insistent that he just comes in now. Says you've told him he's practically family and he can treat this like his home.' He gave a small smile. 'I guess I see now that he does.'

'We don't mind at all,' Gracie said. She looked at Charlie. 'What do you want to do today? I was thinking we might bake.'

'Chocolate cake?' Charlie asked.

'If you like.'

He gave an eager nod.

'Come on then,' Gracie said. 'We'll get the bits out and make a start.'

While Charlie followed Gracie to the little kitchen area, Lizzie looked at Jude. She couldn't deny that she'd missed him, and now, standing in front of her, he looked good.

'You want to come in for a minute?' she asked. Things were already awkward, but she didn't know what else she could do but invite him in.

'If that's OK.'

'Sure.' Lizzie made her way to the sofa and Jude followed. She looked towards the kitchen. 'Gracie seems to come alive when Charlie is here,' she said in a voice quiet enough not to carry.

'I expect it's hard work for her, though, in her current condition. You must say if it's too much.'

'It's fine. The rest of the time she's a right lazy lump so it will do her good to be busy. I guess Charlie brings out that latent maternal instinct. Good for the baby when he or she arrives, I suppose.'

'Charlie loves her to bits. He loves you both. I'm grateful that…
well, you know… that you can both still find time to see him.'

'We wouldn't have done anything else. None of this is Charlie's
fault and you were right – he shouldn't pay for the mistakes of others.'

Jude nodded. 'I thought I'd come and see if you still needed me to
take a look at the layout on your build – offer some advice? Or…' His
sentence trailed off.

'I think I've figured it out,' Lizzie said.

'Oh, right…' Jude glanced at Charlie and Gracie, and then back at
Lizzie. 'I don't suppose you have time for a quick walk?'

'I'm kind of busy… Working on a piece.'

'Oh… right. I just thought…'

Lizzie glanced back at Charlie and Gracie. They had already begun a
fairly disruptive takeover of the kitchen area and, in a place this small,
it wasn't so easy for Lizzie to get away from them to work. Over the
past few weeks she'd been able to charge up the laptop and hide away
in a corner of the garden when the caravan got too much, but as the
daily weather now came with the beginnings of an autumn chill, it was
getting harder to do that.

'Was there any reason in particular?' she asked, turning back to
Jude now.

'I just figured… well, as Charlie is here a lot now and you've both
been so kind to him it's silly for us not to get along. At least be a little
civil with each other – you know?'

'Isn't that what we're doing now?'

'I was hoping for something more like a little friendship rather than
a ceasing of hostilities.'

'It wasn't me who began the hostilities – as I recall.'

'I wasn't the one who ended it between us either.'

'If you're trying to say it was me, then you have some sort of memory malfunction,' Lizzie snapped back. He opened his mouth to reply, but then closed it again, and he looked so deeply hurt that for a moment she felt like the biggest, most unreasonable bitch on the planet. 'I didn't mean that to sound as horrible as it did. Sorry.'

'It's OK. I only wanted to bury the hatchet. I can see why you might not be so keen…'

'And you *have* buried the hatchet. There wasn't really one to bury… Look – wait here a minute.' She went into her bedroom and returned a few seconds later, pulling a thick cardigan around her shoulders. 'I reckon I can spare half an hour if you want to talk away from the caravan.'

Jude nodded. 'Thank you.'

'I'm just popping out for a minute,' Lizzie called over to Gracie. There was a muffled, nonchalant reply from behind her as she pulled the door closed and took the steps down into the garden. A brisk wind was blowing in from the east and heavy grey clouds were massing overhead, bringing a cooler temperature than Lizzie had experienced since she'd first arrived at the mill that spring. It was a timely reminder that winter was on the way, but at least there was real hope now that they'd be living in the mill's annexe rather than the caravan when it arrived, even if the mill itself wasn't working by then. And funnily, this was the first question Jude posed as they left the garden and headed for the bramble-edged lanes.

'Is the build going well?'

'I think we're nearly there. At least, the living quarters are. The mill workings might take a lot longer because we have to wait for a specialist company to get a gap in their schedule, and then when they do it will take ages anyway. In a way it's doing me a favour because the longer they take, the more time I have to get extra finance in place.'

'You found someone, then?'

Lizzie nodded.

'You know, I meant what I said just now – about looking at your building. You can still ask me for help if you need it. With contacts or drawing up plans or anything. I'd like to think we could still be friends.'

'I've made a bit of a fist at drawing up plans but Tim seems to think they look OK.'

'Tim's not really going to say anything else. As far as he's concerned he's just going to act on your instructions and take care of the practical side of those. If he thinks a wall is in the wrong place or you could better utilise a space by moving a door, he's not going to tell you that.'

Lizzie looked at him askance. 'I think you might be a bit unfair to Tim there.'

'He's a builder, not an architect.'

'He's a good builder and I trust him.'

Jude paused, and then he seemed to think better of pursuing the argument. 'Did Gracie end up buying the caravan?'

'No. She needs her money now for other things. I can sell the caravan elsewhere in the next few weeks and that will be something towards the costs.'

'If she hasn't bought the caravan where will she live?'

'With me.'

'In the mill?'

'Yes.'

Jude was silent for a moment. 'Things have changed then,' he said finally.

Lizzie shrugged. 'I've got used to having her around.'

'It's a big place to live in alone, I suppose.'

Lizzie gave him a sideways look. 'That was always the plan to be honest, so it's not that. I want to help Gracie. It's going to be tough for her when the baby comes, and I think she's more scared than she'd have us believe.'

He nodded, lapsing into silence again. Their footsteps crunched on leaves fallen early and littering the lane, and a rook's call echoed across a nearby field. Lizzie had to wonder what the point of this walk was because, if they were supposed to be entering into any meaningful kind of dialogue about their future relationship, it was taking a long time to materialise. But then she had to wonder if they had any future relationship, aside from when Charlie brought them together, and if she was honest, Lizzie could see a time when perhaps even that would stop.

'I didn't want us to end the way we did,' Jude said into the long silence.

'Neither did I. Is that what you've come to talk about?'

'I was hoping we might. Amongst other things.'

'How about we try the other things then?'

'You don't want to talk about us? I don't think it's as simple as ignoring it.'

'We've managed to ignore it well enough for the last few weeks.'

'That wasn't my choice – you wouldn't talk to me.'

'You didn't try very hard to change that, as I recall.'

'I asked Harriet to come.'

'Yes… that was a masterstroke of tact, wasn't it?'

'There's no need for sarcasm.'

'What else do you expect?' Lizzie returned. 'You sent the very person we split up over to try and talk me round? Why didn't you come yourself?'

'I thought you wouldn't talk to me.'

'But you thought I'd talk to Harriet?'

'I thought there was more chance of her persuading you that all there is between her and me is friendship. You wouldn't have believed that coming from me.'

'Maybe I would have.'

'I didn't know what to do. Harriet offered.'

'I'll bet she did.'

'What does that mean?'

'You two – thick as thieves.'

'We have a child together.'

'And how am I supposed to compete with that? How am I supposed to compete with her?'

Jude stopped dead and turned to her. 'Lizzie… you had no need to compete. I loved you.'

She froze too, stopped in her tracks and her train of thought by the words that had come so unexpectedly from his mouth. All the time they'd been together he'd never once told her he loved her.

'I *still* love you,' he added in a voice shot through with hopelessness. 'I don't suppose that counts for anything, though.'

'What about Harriet?'

'Lizzie – you're being so unreasonable! We're friends; how many times do I have to say it?'

'You don't still want to be with her?'

'No! Why would I be here if I did?'

'So she's back with Damon?'

'No. She's single and apparently so am I. But both of us being single, and even being friends and parents, doesn't mean we automatically belong together. If you'd only give me a chance then maybe I could prove it to you.'

'If that's true then I'm sorry I screwed it up. But…' Lizzie paused. Maybe Gracie had been wrong about this? Maybe she was wrong to judge Lizzie's relationship with Jude by the standards of hers and Frank's. Maybe there was still a chance. But maybe they'd already gone too far on their current track now to ever get back what they'd once had. Maybe she didn't want to now, because it had been hard enough getting over him this time, and she didn't know if she wanted to take the risk of having to do it a second time if things went wrong again. She shook her head.

'That's it?' he said. 'You don't want to try?'

'You really want us to try again?'

'Why not? Is it such a terrible idea?'

'It's been too long and things have gone too far to go back. I'm a different person now, and I don't feel the same way I once did.'

'Look me in the eye and say that, because I don't believe it. I don't believe we could have been that good together and not have some of those feelings left.'

'I'm not saying there's nothing left. I just don't think it's enough. I have too much else going on in my life now.'

'I could help you with all those things! I want to be with you when Gracie's baby comes and the mill opens—'

'Won't you be too busy with your own child to worry about someone else's?'

Jude's gaze went across to the wild fields beyond the hedgerow but he didn't reply. Maybe Lizzie had gone too far – but this… *thing*… this situation, had gone too far anyway, so how could speaking her mind make it worse? Thinking it didn't do much to dispel the sudden squirming of guilt in her gut, though. It had been a harsh thing to say, and now she wished she hadn't.

After an agonising minute that felt more like a year, he spoke. 'Why is it so hard to move on from this? Why does it have to be such a big deal?'

'Because I was lied to before and it broke my heart. There… is that what you wanted to hear? Did you want me to drag up painful old memories that I'd tried to bury? I've got trust issues – there – you've got the scoop.' Lizzie turned to walk back the way they'd come.

'Lizzie – please!'

She started to walk again and Jude jogged to catch up.

'Please…'

She shook her head. 'I need time; I've got too much to think about.'

'I get that. OK…' He walked at her side now, his steps keeping time. 'At least let me be involved in all the other bits of your life. You let Charlie stay in yours, and I'll always be grateful for that. So let me return the favour. If you need help with anything, please ask. Please let me help you with the mill, with Gracie… anything you want.'

'No strings attached? I can just ask?'

'No strings attached. I just want to be there for you.'

Lizzie looked straight ahead, the lane twisting into the distance, her beloved windmill standing proud of the grassy flats. It sounded too good to be true that Jude wanted friendship and nothing else. He had to have an agenda other than that; this had to be part of a wider plan to win her back. The question that she had to ask herself was: did she care? Did she want to be won back? The answer from her heart was undoubtedly yes, but did that make it the right answer?

'OK,' she said, turning to him. 'Maybe that would be OK.'

∗

Lizzie tried James's number again as she sat on the caravan steps, wrapped in her fluffy cardigan and watching the sun sink below the horizon. It was the third time she'd tried to call him that day, and she had a feeling that he was watching her number flash up on the screen of his phone and simply choosing to ignore it. After their last visit it had taken two days for him to resurface, Lizzie, Gracie and their mum going out of their minds with worry. The only excuse he'd been able to give them for the fact that he hadn't replied when they'd last called at his flat was that he'd stayed out with some mates and had only noticed all the missed calls on his phone when he got home in the evening.

This time he picked up.

'Hey,' he drawled.

'James?'

'Who else is it going to be?'

'Where have you been?'

'Having a life. Is that OK?'

Lizzie frowned. 'Look, I just phoned to see how you are.'

'I'm fine. How are you? Still got your windmill?'

'Yep.'

'Good. Is that all you wanted to say?'

'Well… I thought we might catch up.'

'I'm a bit busy now, sis.'

'Doing what?'

There was silence on the line.

'James?'

'Yeah, still here…'

'Are you drunk?'

'No,' he said, but then he began to laugh.

Lizzie sighed. She wasn't going to get any sense out of him now.

'Listen, I'm going to call you again tomorrow. It'll be late because we're moving into the mill. You'll be around, won't you?'

'Yeah.'

'Bye, James.'

'See ya.'

'James…'

'Yeah?'

'Please take care, won't you?'

There was more laughter on the line, and then it went dead. Lizzie went back inside, deep in thought. Gracie and Florentina were watching TV, but Gracie turned to her now.

'Did you manage to get hold of him?'

Lizzie nodded.

'Where's he been?'

'I'll give you three guesses.'

'Oh,' Gracie said. She faced the television again. She didn't need to be told anything more, and she probably didn't want to discuss it, just like Lizzie, who knew they ought to be discussing it, but didn't know what on earth they could say or what good a discussion would do. When it came to James, any discussion went round in circles. You could talk about him, worry about him, even try to intervene, but you couldn't actually change anything. James would carry on in exactly the way he'd always done, and nobody but James could change that.

Chapter Twenty-Three

Having Jude around the place again had been strange at first, but Lizzie couldn't deny that his help had been welcome when the time came to begin phase one of moving into Magnolia Mill. Not least because it meant he could go to Harriet's grandparents' reclamation yard to pick up the furniture Lizzie had saved there so that Lizzie wouldn't have to face Harriet again herself.

Florentina (who was still living with them, the projected completion date for her own house rebuild seeming further and further away every day) had said nothing about him being back in Lizzie's life, only to comment that the extra muscle was welcome when it came to moving, because it was amazing just how many large and unwieldy items a small party of women could cram into a tiny caravan. Gracie, on the other hand, had tried to persuade Lizzie that she'd made a mistake inviting him back into her life and affections, but Lizzie replied by insisting that he wasn't back in her life or affections, and that he wasn't with Harriet as they'd thought he might be – and that even if he was, he and Lizzie were just friends now.

Lizzie realised that Gracie and Florentina had probably had private discussions in her absence about the new developments, and in a way she didn't mind that because, if they had, it meant they were getting along better than they'd ever done. Even as little as two months before there was no way they'd have shared that sort of moment – for Gracie especially it would have been all she could do to remain civil. And as much as she appreciated Gracie's support and she understood the reasons for Gracie's distrust of all men, this time she really wanted her sister to butt out. At least Gracie, for whatever reasons, seemed to realise this.

When moving day proper arrived, even though Tim Lundy's vans were still in evidence to get on with work left to be done away from the mill's living quarters, it finally began to feel to Lizzie like the new life she'd dreamt of for so long was about to begin. The early October wind had a chill to it and the skies were low and grey, but it did nothing to dampen her spirits. She even had a bright smile for Jude as he arrived with Charlie, dressed down in old jeans and an outsized sweatshirt complete with holes in the sleeves. It would have looked scruffy on anyone else but (Lizzie had to admit, despite trying hard not to think about it) looked nothing short of sex-on-legs on him. In fact, the more she tried to ignore the pull of attraction, the worse it got. He'd been to visit since their heart-to-heart on the lane, but each meeting had been awkward, every word and gesture chosen with painstaking care, and she'd been able to keep a lid on her feelings. It was difficult to comprehend why things should be so different this time. Perhaps it was the sheer joy of moving into her mill at last that had put a gloss on everything and made her so happy she couldn't keep her defences up. Perhaps something had changed – silently and subtly during their last few weeks as friends – though there was no pinpointing the moment that had led to what she felt today.

There had been a few moments charged beyond reason, a summer storm crackling through leaden clouds: when they'd carried a box between them and his hand had brushed hers; when they'd bumped into each other rushing to and from the caravan; when they'd run for the shelter of the old pear trees as the rain began to fall, realising everyone else had retreated to the mill, leaving them alone there together in the place where they used to spread a blanket and spend sultry afternoons making love. He'd gently lifted a lock of wet hair from her face, his hand against her cheek filling her with an almost uncontrollable urge to pull him in and feel his body tight against hers. For a moment she'd thought he would kiss her, but then he'd given a sad smile and looked towards the sky.

'Seems to have been a short and sharp shower after all,' he'd said, before making his way back to the caravan to resume their moving.

As they broke for lunch, Charlie and Jude headed off to buy supplies from the nearest pizzeria while Florentina poured drinks and set them out around Lizzie's new dining table. After a brief nod of thanks from Gracie, she sat down next to Lizzie with her own glass.

'You and Jude are together again?' she asked carelessly. The nonchalant tone wasn't fooling Lizzie, though; she knew Florentina and Gracie must have shared some theories on the state of her relationship with Jude at some point – possibly even today – and she knew that Gracie had probably put their stepmother up to the casual interrogation.

'You know we're not,' Lizzie said. 'I would have told you both if we were.'

'Did I ever tell you about my friend Sofia?' Florentina asked serenely. She continued without waiting for a reply. 'She was such fun – very wild, always in trouble, and she didn't want a boyfriend. When we were teenagers we would walk the streets of Milan together and we thought we were so sexy and so wonderful that every man must be looking at us. Sofia said she didn't care. She said they could look as much as they wanted but she would never marry, because she didn't think there was a man alive who could tame her.' Florentina paused. 'And then she met

Marco. She looked at him as I see you look at Jude now, *cara mia,* and I knew that her wild ways were over. They were married two years later.'

'I'm not looking at Jude like anything!' Lizzie said, heat rising to her cheeks. 'I don't know where you get these ideas!'

'Don't be ridiculous!' Gracie laughed. 'Do you think we're all that dumb? Even Charlie can see it!'

'He hasn't said anything, has he?' Lizzie asked, a slight note of panic in her voice. 'I'd hate him to get any sort of false hope.'

Florentina looked at Lizzie over her glass. 'But would it be false hope? Nobody would think any less of you for wanting to try again with Jude. It's obvious you both still adore each other, and, for what it's worth, I think he's learned his lesson.'

'It's not about whether he's learned his lesson or not.'

'Then what is it about?' Gracie asked.

Lizzie stared at her. 'You were the one telling me I should steer clear!'

'Yes, but I think he really has realised now just how difficult you found it to see him so close to Harriet. Perhaps he'd be more respectful of your feelings if you were to give him another chance…'

Lizzie's eyes widened, until they were like tiny planets. 'Are you serious?'

'And he hasn't got back with Harriet at all,' Gracie continued. 'A lot of men would have taken the easy route once they'd been dumped.'

Florentina raised her eyebrows. 'Harriet may not have wanted him even if she was the "easy route".'

Gracie waved a vague hand. 'Oh, you know what I mean.'

Lizzie's hands went to her hips. 'So now, after weeks of trying to convince me that I'm better off without him, you're telling me that I ought to get back with him?'

'I'm just saying he seems to have proved his worth.'

Lizzie looked down into her lemonade. Much as she wanted to shake Gracie from time to time, perhaps this time her change of heart wasn't so ill-conceived? Perhaps it was time to let go of this fear and let Jude back into her heart? Any feelings he might have had for Harriet were in the past and he was merely fulfilling his paternal duties with Artie – wasn't he? Maybe Harriet had been pursuing some kind of agenda with all her tricks and flirting, but if Jude was going to get back with her it would have happened by now. Surely Lizzie could get past all that – it wasn't like she'd be the first woman to have a relationship with a man who already had a child by someone else, and almost anyone else she met would have an ex lurking in their past. She took a deep breath and looked up at Gracie and Florentina with a smile.

'Let's see how things go today.'

'You're going to talk to him about it?' Gracie asked.

'Maybe.' Lizzie frowned at the sight of her sister's knowing smile.

'But for now I've got far more important things to worry about,' she added, 'like how I'm going to get my new four-poster bed through that tiny bedroom doorframe.'

Gracie grinned at Florentina, and Lizzie didn't know whether she wanted to slap her stupid, smug face or hug her to death.

∗

Once she'd allowed herself to imagine what life might be like with Jude back in it, all Lizzie could think about was the moment when she could get him alone to tell him how she felt. She was certain he'd still feel the same way as he had on the lane the day he'd tried to apologise, and there was a sense of building excitement for the prospect of putting all the nonsense behind them and trying again. Perhaps they'd be all the stronger for the trials they'd been through to get to this point; didn't people always say that you could never know the strength of a love until it had been tested?

After a lively lunch was tidied away, Lizzie smiled at Jude's tuneless whistle as he screwed together a flat-pack under-sink tidy.

'Happy?' he asked, standing back to admire his handiwork.

Lizzie nodded and rewarded him with a chaste kiss. At first he looked bemused, but then he smiled.

'That's not what I was expecting,' he said.

'But you have no objections?'

He grinned. 'No.'

Lizzie moved closer and, casting a look around to check they were still alone in the kitchen, she lowered her voice. 'I don't suppose you have time to spare later? Maybe we can talk a little… somewhere private.'

'I'd like that,' he said. 'Does this mean…?'

She gave a slight shrug as she looked up into his eyes. 'Who knows? Let's just make that time and see where it goes, eh?'

He studied her for a moment, his hand poised uncertainly. But then he let it trail along her arm and up to her shoulder, sweeping the nape of her neck, and she shuddered as a wave of pleasure ripped through her.

'I've missed you,' he said, his eyes never leaving hers.

'Let's not get ahead of ourselves,' she warned, but her cautious reply didn't match the need she felt at his touch. There had always been an attraction, a chemistry unlike anything she'd ever felt for any man before, and never had it been as strong as it was at this moment. 'I'm not promising anything.'

He nodded, and still their eyes stayed locked. God, how she wanted to kiss him now. She'd missed those lips so much – those hands that could do things she'd never imagined hands could do, the scent that was like a drug, the skin that felt so right against hers.

'So how far along this path might we be?' he asked. 'We're at talking stage?'

'Yes.'

'We're at touching stage?' he asked, his hand resting on the small of her back and gently pulling her closer.

'Maybe a little.'

'This may be a little forward but…'

'What?'

'Are we at kissing stage?' he asked, moving closer still, his voice a hot whisper. 'I really missed kissing stage.'

'Me too.' Lizzie smiled, her insides molten, the ache of need almost overwhelming. She reached up, offered herself, and he dipped his mouth to hers and it was like her veins were full of fireworks.

'Jude! Jude!'

They leapt apart at the sound of Charlie's voice echoing down the hallway, clumsy footsteps speeding towards them. There had been nothing wrong in what they'd been doing, nothing to be ashamed of, and yet even at that moment Lizzie felt ashamed, annoyed with herself that she'd let things get too far too quickly. Didn't her stupid body have any self-control? Did it really have that much superiority over her brain? What had happened to talking things through when they got a quiet moment?

A second later, Charlie was standing at the kitchen doorway with Jude's mobile phone in the air like it was a live grenade with the pin missing.

'Harriet needs us!' he cried. 'Artie's fell off the swing!'

Jude threw a look of despair and apology in equal measure and the drawbridge that Lizzie had been able to lower so easily only a moment before slammed shut again. One thing at a time. There might be a future for her and Jude, but she'd have to accept that it would include Harriet and Artie too. Right now, she still wasn't sure that she could do that.

＊

'Doesn't she have anyone else to run her to hospitals?' Gracie said, stuffing a cookie into her mouth. They were back in the kitchen in the mill, which by now had a lot more furniture than it had at lunchtime. The cupboards were bursting with crockery and pans and the other detritus of cooking and there were new gingham blinds hanging at the windows. It was close to suppertime, but they weren't close to being ready for supper at all. Biscuits and tea were the best they could do for now and everyone was too tired to care anyway.

Jude and Charlie had left them as soon as the call had come through. Jude had phoned shortly afterwards to say they were waiting with Harriet for Artie to have an X-ray and probably wouldn't get back to them that evening. Lizzie could hardly say anything except to express a hope that Artie would be OK and to tell him it didn't matter, but the situation had certainly poured cold water onto her fire. In fact, it had done a lot to cool relations full stop, and even more to add to her initial doubts about letting Jude back into her life.

Lizzie, Gracie and Florentina had agreed that they'd do what they could until dusk fell but that they might have to stay in the caravan overnight and finish moving into the mill the following day now that they were a couple of pairs of hands short. Lizzie was strangely OK with this; it gave her time to reflect on what had happened that afternoon between her and Jude and decide whether her heart ruling her head was really such a wise thing to allow.

'Perhaps her family were all busy,' Lizzie said, chin resting on her fist as she leaned on the table and stared at the opposite wall.

'Anyone would think it's a deliberate attempt at sabotage. She must have known Jude would be here helping us today.'

'I suppose he *is* Artie's dad.'

'That doesn't mean Harriet has to keep calling him for everything.' Gracie reached for another cookie and rammed it into her mouth. Lizzie had heard of expectant mothers eating for two, but Gracie was eating for twenty these days. It was a safe bet that her morning sickness had well and truly dissipated.

'Maybe...'

'I don't see why she has to do it. Do you think she has some weird hold on him? Like she doesn't want him, but she doesn't want anyone else to have him?'

Lizzie sighed. 'You don't think it's crossed my mind? But then, what on earth would she gain from that?'

'Well, he'd be there for Artie no matter what. I suppose if he got close to another woman he might well have another child with her and then Artie might get a little sidelined. I mean, he wouldn't, but I suppose Harriet might think that. Maybe she's just making sure it doesn't happen.'

'She can't expect him to be single forever.'

'I suppose it's easy to get dependent on people, though.'

'So she's going to make sure Jude stays single? Doesn't sound plausible.'

'Perhaps not forever. Maybe just until Artie is eighteen.'

'I don't imagine she needs him to be single. He's not the sort of man to abandon his son and she must know that.'

'Maybe she's realised it's not quite as easy to raise a child alone as she'd imagined it would be. I guess I'll find that out for myself soon enough. It doesn't sound as if her family were over the moon about her choosing to be a single mum either.'

'Well, yes. They help her in practical ways, but I don't know about emotional support. Jude has said they were a bit old-fashioned about it all.'

Gracie narrowed her eyes and studied Lizzie for a moment. 'How come you're suddenly so understanding about it all?'

'I'm not understanding; I think I've just given in. Harriet is just going to be there, all the time, whether I like it or not.'

'Can you cope with that?'

'That's the big question, isn't it? I mean, what if Jude and I did get back together and what if we did end up having a child? Where would that leave everyone?'

Gracie stroked a fond hand over her tummy. 'Lord, I have no idea. I only know there might be a lot more babies around here than there are now!'

'Lucky it's a big place then,' Lizzie said with a half-smile. She looked up to see Florentina wandering in, phone in hand. 'Everything OK?'

'That was the man at the insurance company. One or two snags in the small print of the policy.'

'Anything difficult to sort?'

'I could have done with the documents to check something, but as they burned with everything else in the house…' She flopped onto a chair at the table and reached for the mug of tea that had been left for her. 'How do these people expect you to be able to answer queries about the original policies? Surely they have this information to hand? Isn't it their job to know these things and sort them out? I've got absolutely nothing left and he's asking me about some ridiculous small print on my policy documents! Even if they had not burned, I wouldn't have known anything about it because your dad would have set up the original policy. I only renewed it when it was due.'

Lizzie reached out and gave her stepmother's hand a reassuring rub.

'I'm such an idiot,' Florentina said.

'No you're not.'

'How could I have taken so little notice of the important things?'

'Because none of us ever thinks we're going to need them. Who could have seen something like this in their future, and who wants to imagine it might happen?'

'Well, if I lose everything then I deserve everything I get.'

'Hey…' Lizzie said softly. 'Where has this come from? You've been so strong all this time—'

'It's easy to pretend, isn't it?'

Florentina's eyes misted, and Lizzie, who had never once seen her complain since she'd lost her house, rushed up from her seat and around the table to hug her. 'Oh, Florentina,' she said, holding her tight. 'I'm so sorry.'

'It's not your fault,' her stepmother said with a sniff. 'You've been nothing but kind to me – more than I deserve.'

Lizzie glanced across at Gracie, who looked suitably sympathetic, though Lizzie had to wonder how much of it was real. Gracie and Florentina were getting on well enough these days, but perhaps Gracie would never really see her in the way Lizzie did.

'Don't say that,' Lizzie chided. 'If I'm kind to you then it's because you *do* deserve it.'

Florentina gently pulled from Lizzie's hug and gave her a watery smile. 'Ignore me. It's been a very long day and the last thing I needed was stress from the insurance company. I'm beginning to feel like such a burden on everyone. I just wish they'd hurry and sort things out so I can live in my own house again.'

Lizzie sat down again. 'I've been thinking about that. Do you actually want to live on your own again?'

'I suppose it will be OK.'

'That's just it.' She looked at Gracie and then back at Florentina. 'I want you to stay with me here. Both of you.'

'But it's your house!' Gracie squeaked. 'You said—'

'I know what I said,' Lizzie cut in. 'I've had time to change my mind. I really want you to live with me here in the mill, for as long as you want or need. It's huge, and it's a lot of space to be rolling around in by myself.'

Gracie's eyes were wide. 'You're absolutely sure about this?'

'Yes.'

'You're the best sister ever!' Gracie cried, rushing to throw her arms around Lizzie. But then Florentina interrupted them.

'What about Jude?'

'What about him?' Lizzie asked.

'Perhaps one day, *cara mia*, this will become yours and Jude's home?'

'I doubt it.'

'But you're back together?'

Lizzie hesitated. 'Honestly, I don't know.'

'But I thought…'

'I don't think it's going to work out.'

'But this afternoon you were so sure you were going to try again.'

'But then Harriet called and I remembered that he'll never really be just mine.'

'You want him to be *just* yours?' Florentina said. 'Isn't that a little possessive?'

Lizzie's smile faded as soon as it was formed. 'You know I don't mean it like that. It will always feel like there's another family in our relationship. And if we had a family of our own it wouldn't feel the same because he'd already have another one somewhere else – his first one, which would make them the most important one.'

Florentina shook her head. 'You know you're not making a lot of sense.'

'I suppose I'm just not explaining myself very well. It's hard to express what I mean.'

'I think I might have an idea, though,' Florentina said. 'But if he's worth it, if he's really the one, then surely you can forget those feelings?'

'I thought I could. I was so sure. But…'

'I said it before and I'm going to say it again because I can't watch you lose someone who makes you happy. You come alive when he's near and that has to mean something. Can you really throw that away just because he has a child with someone else?'

'It's not about Artie, it's…'

Florentina raised her eyebrows and Lizzie couldn't help a small smile.

'I don't even know anymore.' Lizzie sat at the table and pulled her mug towards her.

'*Cara mia…* How did you leave it with Jude when he went to the hospital?' Florentina asked.

'I didn't really leave it like anything. He just rushed off.'

'Why don't you phone him now and arrange to meet up tomorrow?'

'I don't know.'

'*Santa Maria*, Lizzie!' Florentina let out an impatient breath. 'Why the sudden caution? Where's the girl who takes chances? What if you'd been wrong about this mill? You weren't, and it took a gamble to find out. So what if you're wrong about Jude? So what if it doesn't work out? Then again, what if it does? The only way you'll ever find out is if you take a chance on him.'

'I know that. I can't explain why I feel so scared. Even I can see now that Jude is nothing like Evan so I can't keep using that as an excuse…'

'Perhaps because this is true love?' Florentina said. 'There's more at stake than ever before because your feelings for Jude are more intense than you've ever had for anyone before – that's why you're scared.'

She glanced at Gracie and seemed to hesitate, tussling with the need to say something she thought they wouldn't like. But then she opened her mouth to speak again. 'When it began with your dad... I'd never felt like that about anyone before. We were both scared because we had so much to lose and we both fought hard to ignore the feelings that were growing but we couldn't... I knew it was going to hurt so many people so much...'

'I understand that but it's still not the same,' Lizzie said gently.

'What I'm trying to say is that the higher the emotional stakes are, the greater the fear. If you are this terrified, perhaps that should tell you that it might be worth taking a chance on.'

'You think so?'

Florentina nodded. 'I do.'

Lizzie was silent again. Then she looked at Gracie, who simply nodded agreement.

'Well, then I suppose I should call him.'

Gracie pushed Lizzie's mobile across the table to her. But as she reached for it, it began to ring. It wasn't Jude's name showing on the display, but Gwendolyn's.

'Mum,' Lizzie answered, a vague frown creasing her forehead as she listened in silence for a moment. 'Slow down... I can't understand what you're telling me.' She listened again, and as comprehension began to dawn on her, every drop of blood seemed to drain from her body. The phone fell from her hand to the table with a dull clunk, and at the other end of the line, Gwendolyn's distraught voice was small and distant.

'What is it?' Gracie demanded. 'Lizzie – what is it?'

Lizzie shook her head slowly. She couldn't speak. She couldn't make sense of anything around her. Only the news she'd just heard filled her head, like a reverb that drowned everything else out.

Her sister reached across the table and snatched up the phone. 'Mum… what's happened?' It was Gracie's turn to listen now, her face losing all colour, just like Lizzie's. 'It's not true. It can't be true!'

Florentina looked from one to the other. 'What's happened?'

Lizzie spoke, her voice small and dull, and she could hear it echo back like she was outside herself.

'James is dead.'

Chapter Twenty-Four

Gracie was wrapped in Lizzie's arms as they stood and gazed at the room Lizzie had earmarked for her and the baby. Her sobs were soaking into Lizzie's blouse and Lizzie envied her ability to cry. It had been three days since the news of James's death, and Lizzie had only been able to stare into a chasm of numbness and wish she could feel something to make sense of the void growing inside her. Her little brother was gone, so why couldn't she feel the loss? She wanted sadness to overwhelm her, to weep and weep as Gracie and her mum were, but there was nothing. She just walked the rooms of her mill over and over, superficial thoughts of paint colours and shelving units masking the real emotions that simmered all the more dangerously without an outlet. When her dad had died Lizzie had been shocked and she'd found it hard to react for many days, but it had been nothing like this. James's death had sent her into a sort of emotional catatonia – she looked like she was functioning, but inside everything was numb and blank.

'What are we going to do?' Gracie looked up at her, her eyes raw and swollen.

'I don't know,' Lizzie said, and she knew they were no longer talking about décor.

'Mum will never survive this.'

'She has to. We all do, because we don't have any choice.'

Gracie dragged in a breath, fighting to stop her tears. 'What was he thinking?'

'I suppose he was trying to do a good thing,' she replied dully.

Gracie began to cry again and Lizzie pulled her close.

'At least it was quick,' Gracie said.

They'd said that many times since they'd had the news, but it had been of little comfort to Lizzie. The policeman kept saying it too, like it ought to make them feel better. James's death might have been quick, but he was still dead. Fast or slow, it made no difference to her world right now because the fact remained that James was no longer in it. Perhaps one day she'd care that he hadn't known anything of the end when it had come, swift and strong from the darkness, but that day wouldn't be for a long time.

Florentina's voice came from behind them.

'I've made a pot of tea if you want some,' she said. 'Your mum's finally sleeping – she must be exhausted.'

'Thanks,' Lizzie said. There was so much she wanted to say to Florentina about her tact and grace and kindness to the very women who had cut her out of their own circle of healing when Lizzie's dad had died, but the words hovered beyond her reach. She was so grateful for her stepmother's presence, but she didn't know how to say it. One day, she thought, when things were easier, she'd find a way to show it.

'Thank goodness I've been able to sleep a little,' Gracie said, smoothing a hand over her belly. 'It wouldn't be good for the baby.'

'It certainly wouldn't be good for you,' Florentina said. 'And that in itself wouldn't be good for your Little Baked Bean.'

'I don't think I want tea,' Lizzie said. 'I've got some measuring up to do in the bathroom for the blinds.'

'That can wait,' Florentina said. 'Come and sit with us. It'll do you good to talk.'

'I don't need to talk – there's nothing to talk about and it won't do any good moping. Things won't change because I'm sitting around talking and I've got so much to do here—'

'Lizzie, please…' Florentina shot a pleading look at Gracie for help.

'You haven't sat down all morning,' Gracie said. 'The decorating can wait.'

Lizzie stepped away to look at Gracie. 'But what's the point? Sitting around talking and drinking tea won't bring him back. James is gone, but we're still here and things still need to be done.'

'It doesn't matter if the mill isn't decorated for a while longer,' Florentina said gently.

'Yes it does!' Lizzie cried. 'How are we all going to live here if it's a mess? I have to make it nice for everyone because there's only me and I have to sort it all out because everyone else is absolutely useless!'

Florentina's eyes widened. She and Gracie stared at Lizzie.

'Sorry,' Lizzie said. 'I didn't mean that, I…' She shook her head. 'Thank you, but I don't want any tea. If you need me, I'll be cleaning the caravan.'

'What for?' Gracie exchanged a look of confusion with Florentina.

'I'll have to sell it and I can't do that if it's dirty,' Lizzie said.

'You have to sell it right now?'

'I can list it. These things can take a while so it won't hurt.'

'But, Lizzie…' Gracie began.

Lizzie didn't wait to hear the rest. She squeezed past her sister and made her way to the kitchen to get cleaning supplies.

*

Exhaustion was getting the better of her, but Lizzie hardly noticed how much she was slowing down. It wasn't until her mum appeared at the door of the caravan that she realised just how long she'd been in there and how savagely she'd rubbed at every surface.

Straightening up, she dropped the cloth into a bowl of suds and closed the cupboards she'd just cleaned. As she rubbed a sleeve across her forehead to mop up the sheen of sweat there, she cast a critical eye over Gwendolyn. She'd never seen her mum so close to a complete breakdown as this. Even the pain of losing Lizzie's dad the previous winter couldn't come close to this for her mum. And the fact was that Lizzie's mum and dad had been divorced for a long time by that point, and though Gwendolyn had loved him until the end, the loss was tempered by the knowledge that, at the end, he had belonged to someone else. Had Lizzie been in a more rational state of mind herself, capable of taking in the full enormity of what had happened to James, there wouldn't have been time to cry, and she wouldn't have allowed herself the luxury anyway because her mum was the one who really needed support. Losing a brother was hard enough, but it was impossible to imagine the pain of losing a child, and Lizzie didn't think that the pain would ever diminish or become less of a thing because that child had become an adult.

'Did you manage to sleep?' Lizzie asked, drying her hands on an old dishcloth.

'Not really. Perhaps I dozed a little,' she added in answer to Lizzie's frown of disapproval. 'I must have done for a while because I lost an hour somewhere, but I don't recall dropping off.'

'You want something to eat?'

Gwendolyn shook her head.

'You've got to have at least a little something,' Lizzie insisted.

'I know, but I just don't have any appetite.'

'None of us has, but we've all got to keep our strength up. If not for yourself, think about Gracie and the baby. If you get ill that's just another thing for Gracie to fret about and the stress won't do her any good.'

Gwendolyn was silent for the longest minute. But then she nodded. 'Perhaps a little soup.'

'Now?' Lizzie asked.

'Whenever. I can get it.'

'I'll get it.' Lizzie took her mum gently by the elbow. If she didn't lead her directly to the kitchen and stand over her as she ate then she knew that Gwendolyn wouldn't eat at all. Three days since the visit from the police and she'd barely eaten a morsel – at least, Lizzie hadn't witnessed it if she had. Gwendolyn had always been a slight and delicate woman, but right now she was more of a shadow than a person.

'You'll have some with me?' she asked as they walked back to the mill.

'Yes,' Lizzie lied.

'Gracie's eating properly, isn't she? What you said about…'

'Yes,' Lizzie replied. Also a lie, although Gracie was at least trying to eat for the sake of her baby. 'Florentina cooked for her earlier.'

Gwendolyn nodded uncertainly, apparently struggling with the concept of owing gratitude to Florentina. It must have been hard for her to accept the other woman's new role in their lives – as a carer and confidante – after all that had gone before. For Lizzie, Florentina was what she'd always been, but this would be all new to Gwendolyn. It wasn't to be forgotten that Florentina had troubles of her own too – more than enough – but all that had been put aside to care for the Lovell women. Karma, Florentina had called it when Lizzie had remarked on her goodness. Karma had a way of paying its debts. Lizzie had been kind to her, and now it was her stepmother's turn to repay that debt, even when Lizzie argued that there had never been a debt at all.

Lizzie led her mum to the table and sat her down before rummaging through the cupboards to find a tin of soup. She barely knew where anything was herself yet, they'd been in the mill for such a short time. After a minute or so, she managed to lay her hands on one.

'Will tomato be OK? It's not very exciting, I'm afraid.'

'It doesn't matter what it is,' Gwendolyn replied in a dull voice. 'Where's Gracie? Isn't she having any with us?'

'I don't know. Maybe she's having a lie-down – want me to check?'

Gwendolyn nodded, and Lizzie left the tin on the worktop and headed off to check the other rooms. Chances were Gracie would be having a rest, or else she might be sitting with Florentina. They'd both liked sitting with Florentina over the past couple of days, as hers was the only voice in the house not drowned in emotion. She could listen objectively, without the anger and shock and raging grief clouding her view, and she offered sensible advice about the most practical aspects of James's death.

In the pocket of her jeans, Lizzie's phone bleeped the arrival of a text. She pulled it out to find a message from Jude. He'd kept in touch, sending regular messages over the days since they'd had the news. She'd asked him not to phone and not to come round because she couldn't trust herself to act in any rational way and, somewhere in the back of her mind, the notion that they'd been getting somewhere in their reconciliation had taken hold. She couldn't risk jeopardising that by doing or saying something screwy that they wouldn't be able to move past, and she didn't think that losing her brother was a legitimate excuse for doing or saying something that would be unfair to Jude. Besides, she had her hands full just holding her own family together and Jude would be an added stress on top of that.

Thinking about you. Just wanted to let you know that the offer of support still stands. Here whenever you need me. No strings. X

Lizzie tapped out a reply.

Thank you. Maybe not yet but I appreciate you thinking of me. X

Her phone bleeped again but she stuffed it back into her pocket. It would be Jude, acknowledging her reply, and she didn't really have time to get into a lengthy discussion with him now. Instead, she turned her attention back to the task she'd set herself a moment before.

Lizzie searched the rooms of her home and found them all empty. With a vague panic, she went outside. Florentina was in the little side garden, bringing in some washing from the line, and Gracie was huddled in an oversized cardigan on a garden chair, talking to her. Though the weather was crisp now, after being crammed into the caravan for so long, everyone had grown so used to making the most of the outdoor space that it had become a part of their daily routine that would probably never leave them.

'There you are!' Lizzie said.

Her voice must have sounded more irritated than she had meant, because both Florentina and Gracie looked around with confused and vaguely guilty expressions.

'Mum's awake,' Lizzie said, smoothing her tone. 'I'm doing some soup for her – she wants to know if you're going to join us.'

Both Florentina and Gracie knew that by 'you', Lizzie meant Gracie, not both of them. So Florentina went back to the washing while Gracie hauled herself up from the chair.

'I suppose I ought to come in and see if she's OK. I don't really want any soup, though.'

'I don't think she'll be happy unless you eat some and I don't think she'll have any if you don't,' Lizzie replied briskly.

Gracie let out a sigh. 'Oh alright then; I'll try.'

'I'll be in shortly,' Florentina added as Lizzie threw her a questioning look. 'You don't really need me just now, do you?'

'You're OK, though?' Lizzie asked.

'I'm supposed to be asking that of you,' Florentina replied with a wry smile.

'I know, but this is all a lot for you to deal with, and, you know, it shouldn't really be down to you to deal with it at all.'

'We've been over this – I wouldn't want to be anywhere else right now. You didn't abandon me…'

'I know.' Lizzie nodded. She looked to Gracie. 'Come on,' she said, a note of dread in her voice. 'We'd better get in.'

Gracie followed her round the house. When they got to the kitchen, the tin Lizzie had left out was open on the worktop. Gwendolyn stood next to it, staring into space. There was tomato soup everywhere. And then Gracie let out a squeak as she saw what Lizzie also now noticed. There wasn't just soup on the worktop – there was blood too. Gwendolyn's hand was extended and it dripped from a deep cut.

'Mum!' Lizzie rushed forward and grabbed her mother's hand. 'What did you do?'

'Huh?' Gwendolyn turned to her, and then looked at her own hand as if noticing for the first time that it was injured. 'I thought I'd open the tin for you.'

'You should have left it!' Lizzie cried.

'I can open a tin – I've done it often enough.'

'But look at your hand!'

'It's just a little cut…'

'It's more than a little cut!' Lizzie turned to Gracie. 'Pass me that tea towel!' Gracie ran to fetch it while Lizzie led her mum to the table and sat her down. Taking the towel from Gracie, she wrapped it around the cut. 'We'll have to take you to the hospital.'

'What about our soup?'

'We can have that later. Right now I'm more concerned about all the blood you're losing.'

'But I've opened it…'

Lizzie looked hopelessly at Gracie. It was clear their mum was losing the plot. How much worse could things get around here?

Just then Florentina came into the kitchen. In a moment she'd taken in the scene and had evaluated it. 'You've got blood seeping through that towel,' she said, putting the wash basket down and marching over to the table. 'You need to wrap it tighter. I'll get another one. Is it deep?'

'It looks it,' Lizzie said.

'Want me to drive her to the hospital?'

'I should go,' Lizzie said.

'I can drive you both if you want to go.' Florentina took off the towel and inspected the wound for a second before wrapping it again. Gwendolyn barely flinched and barely seemed to have noticed Florentina's arrival at all.

'What shall I do?' Gracie asked. 'Should I come?'

'Perhaps you should stay here,' Lizzie said, aware that Gracie had been subjected to enough stress over the past few days and adding to it wasn't going to help her or the baby. 'I shouldn't think we'll be all that long.'

Gracie seemed relieved and she nodded agreement. Lizzie went to fetch another towel to shore up the dressing on her mum's hand and she led her in Florentina's wake, heading for the car.

*

When they got back from the hospital, almost paralysed by exhaustion – physical and mental – and Gwendolyn sporting a small, neat row of stitches in her hand, Gracie met them at the front door.

'You had a visitor,' she said.

'I did?' Lizzie asked, shrugging her jacket off. 'Who?'

'Harriet.'

'Oh.'

Lizzie wasn't interested in Harriet or what she had to say. But as she walked into the kitchen, she saw a huge bouquet of flowers in the middle of the table and, guessing that Harriet must have brought them over, immediately felt horribly ungrateful.

'She did say that Jude had sent you a text to ask if it was OK for her to come over – she just wanted to offer her condolences. But when you didn't reply she just decided to come over anyway and leave the flowers.'

Lizzie took her phone out and now opened the unread text message from Jude. Sure enough he'd sent a tentative enquiry, explaining that Harriet wanted to express her sympathy and didn't want anything but to be able to come over with a gift. She wasn't sure how he would have taken her non-reply but she didn't suppose it mattered now as Harriet had come anyway. Tomorrow, when her thoughts were a little clearer, she'd send him a text explaining what had happened to her mum and why she'd been too busy to respond to his message. She looked up at the flowers. They were simple and elegant and she wished she could feel some gratitude for what was a brave and lovely gesture but she couldn't. That same old numbness washed over her again, exacerbated by the sheer exhaustion brought on by the last few hours, and all she wanted to do was dissolve into the darkness of her own bed. There would be no sleep, of course, but at least there would be solitude.

'I thanked her on your behalf.' Gracie's voice cut into her thoughts. 'She was really very sweet and seemed genuinely sorry to hear about James.'

'That's good,' Lizzie replied absently. 'I suppose I ought to thank her myself.'

'I don't think she was really expecting anything like that,' Gracie said. 'She said not to worry; she just wanted us to know that she was sorry for our loss.'

'Isn't that lovely?' Florentina said, glancing between Lizzie and Gwendolyn, who had collapsed silently into a chair, staring at the flowers while nursing her newly dressed hand.

Lizzie nodded but Gwendolyn offered nothing but more silence.

'Cup of tea?' Florentina continued. She must have known she was swimming against the tide but she kept on trying, and for that Lizzie was grateful.

'Tea.' Lizzie nodded, though it was the last thing she wanted. But what else were they supposed to do? James was dead, Gracie was about to be a single mother with no job and no prospects, Gwendolyn was lost to them, walled up in a reality of her own making, Florentina had nowhere to live and it looked as if Lizzie would never make things up with Jude now. Things were about as bad as they were going to get, so what else did you do when all hope was lost? You drank tea.

Chapter Twenty-Five

Everyone talked about closure. When the funeral was over the family would be able to move on from James's death, that's what they said. The mourning would never really end, of course, but it would mark a point where the shock ended and the readjustment began.

The closure began on a crisp November morning. Almost a year to the day since they'd buried Lizzie's dad, they found themselves in another procession of black cars, travelling to that same churchyard, those same evergreen-topped walls of grey stone, the same wiry trees reaching into a watercolour sky. Lizzie and Gracie sat on seats opposite Gwendolyn, who was thinner and paler than ever. If closure was coming, Lizzie could only hope it would happen soon, because the real fear now was that her mother wouldn't survive this ordeal. Lizzie wasn't about to lose another member of her family, not if she had anything to do with it. Florentina followed in another car, and somewhere in the line, in his own car, Jude had come to pay his respects. Not because he'd ever met James, but for Lizzie.

The congregation was bigger than Lizzie would have expected. She counted perhaps two hundred as she walked hand in hand with her mum and Gracie to the entrance of the little stone church. Old school friends, ex-teachers, neighbours – Lizzie spotted them all gathered in the churchyard, a sea of black suits. They nodded recognition as the

Lovell women joined them, but not a word was spoken; instead, every eye was turned to the coffin now being pulled from the hearse. They watched as it was carried into the church on sombre shoulders. Lizzie dragged a breath from the depths of her lungs – it contained every ounce of strength and courage that she had – and she threw her shoulders back. A couple of hours would see this ordeal over, but that couple of hours looked like a lifetime right now.

She threw a last glance back at the gates of the churchyard and saw Jude walk in. She'd never seen him wear black before and he looked strange – like Jude but not like Jude, like a Jude from an alternate universe. Their eyes met and Lizzie could sense the strength and support that he was doing his best to transmit across the old stones that formed the pathway into the chapel. He gave a hesitant half-smile, and Lizzie returned it. Then, she gripped Gracie and Gwendolyn's hands a little tighter and together they went inside to say goodbye.

*

The pub – ivy snaking around its chimneystack, ancient roof sagging in the middle and yet somehow still defying collapse, the remains of summer roses clinging to the trellis at the front door – had been the venue of James's christening celebration twenty-six years before. Now, they were back once more in his honour, though the clothes were darker and the conversation more subdued. Gwendolyn was holding up remarkably well, listening politely to each old friend who came to express their sorrow at her loss, smiling sadly in all the right places and even managing a little food from the buffet that Lizzie had organised. Gracie was sitting in a corner with Florentina, who seemed to have become something of a spare mum these days. It was a role Lizzie would have played gladly, but perhaps Gracie unconsciously recognised that Lizzie was struggling more than she'd have anyone know. Whatever the reason for Gracie's sudden closeness to her former enemy, Lizzie was content that perhaps they'd seen the end of hostilities. Nothing good could ever come from James's death, but perhaps this was as close to it as they would get.

As she stared into space, Lizzie became aware of a familiar, comforting scent. She turned to see Jude behind her.

'Jude…'

'Hi.'

'Hey. I'm glad you could come. I wanted to say I'm sorry I haven't asked before now – how's Artie's arm?'

'Healing nicely. It wasn't a bad break. He's a tough little nut and it won't be long before he's back to normal.' He gave a warm smile. 'Thanks for asking.'

Lizzie shrugged. 'I should have asked before.'

'I think you can be forgiven for being a little distracted.'

Lizzie smiled tightly.

'So… How are you holding up?' he asked softly.

'I'm fine.' She took a sip of the brandy she'd been clutching and not drinking for the half hour since one of James's old classmates had bought it for her. It was warm and syrupy and strangely consoling.

Jude raised his eyebrows slightly. 'This is me you're talking to. Tell me the truth.'

'Honestly, I'm OK.'

'Am I allowed to say that I know you better than that?' He looked towards the door of the pub. 'Want to get some air and find somewhere quiet to talk? You can tell me again how OK you really are.'

'I'm alright in here.'

'In here you have to put on a brave face – at least *you* think you do. Brave faces are all very well but they don't help anyone in the long run.' He gave her a crooked half-smile and, even in the darkness, a little light flared in her heart for him. 'I thought it was us men who were supposed to bottle everything up.'

'It is. If James had been a bit more open…' Lizzie let out a sigh. 'Who am I kidding? James had been on a path of self-destruction for a long time. If it hadn't been this accident it would have been something else. Disaster was always going to be waiting for him in some form or another.'

'You don't really believe that. My Lizzie would never feel that way.'

'*Your* Lizzie?'

'The woman who used to be my Lizzie.'

'You're saying I'm not the same as I used to be?'

'I don't know. With all you've been through I wouldn't blame you for changing.'

'Well, I haven't changed. Life has changed and shifted the landscape around me, and it's made me look different, but I'm the same.' His gaze went to the floor. Lizzie placed her brandy on the bar. Whatever else had happened between them, he was here for her now and that meant everything. 'Maybe it would be good to go outside after all.'

*

Clouds were tumbling in from the east, bringing a keen wind with them, and dusk was already creeping across the fields beyond the pub gardens. Lizzie pulled her coat tighter, wishing she'd worn something thicker beneath.

'It's a bit chillier than it looked,' Jude said. 'Want to go back inside?'

Lizzie shook her head and perched on a wooden bench. The windows of the old pub were warm with yellow light, but they were deceptively cheerful. The atmosphere inside was anything but inviting. Jude sat next to her, close enough to be a comfort but far enough to maintain a respectful distance. But as his scent assaulted her senses again, she wasn't sure she wanted that respectful distance anymore. He smelt of familiarity and good humour, of lazy days spent under the old pear trees and picnics in the sun, of sultry evenings entwined in her bed. He smelt of hope and optimism – his scent was a reminder of happier times. She took in a deep breath and tried to draw comfort from it.

'The hardest thing to accept is still the stupid way he died,' she said. 'Hit by a car, shoving someone out of the way like he was some cheesy superhero.'

'It wasn't stupid. He was being a good person. He saved that old man's life.'

'I'm supposed to be proud of him, aren't I? I know he was doing a good thing. A bloody marvellous thing… I just wish this marvellous deed hadn't killed him. Is it very wrong that I wish the old man had died instead?'

'You don't mean that…'

'No, I don't. But why did anyone have to die? Why did the choice have to be made? If it was God or whoever, why did he even create the situation in the first place?'

'I wish I knew the answer to that.' Jude gave a slight shrug. 'Lizzie… I don't know what to say.'

She sighed. 'Neither do I. One day I suppose I might be able to see it as a noble deed. It's quite ironic when you think about it – our James a hero. The times we've complained about his waster friends and his lazy lifestyle, and then the first time he decides to do something good it gets him killed. He should have carried on to the pub instead like he would have done before.'

A shiver ran up from the bottom of her spine to the back of her neck as a fresh gust blew in from the east. 'I just feel like we somehow failed him.'

'He was a grown man – you couldn't be there every second of every day. Believe me, I feel the same way about Charlie sometimes, but we're all just doing our best, aren't we?'

Lizzie nodded. 'Did Charlie ask where you were going today?'

'I told him the truth. I try to be as honest as I can about things. Sometimes he struggles to understand, but that's no reason to keep him in the dark. He wanted to come today, but I explained that it was going to be pretty sad and he seemed to get that he would be better off staying at home. Harriet's with him.'

'Brothers, eh?' Lizzie gave a wry smile. 'I never really saw before that it was one big thing we had common – brothers to worry about.'

'I think we had a lot more than that in common.'

'I suppose we did.'

Lizzie wanted to ask if he thought it was too late for them now, but maybe the question had answered itself, simply by existing in her head. Her thoughts quickly turned back to James. The reason they were here now, even talking about what they'd once had, was because of him, and she didn't know how she ought to feel about that. She only knew that the rage she felt about her brother's death was a constant undercurrent, pulling her back in whenever she tried to escape it.

'We never could have seen this coming, not in a million years. If he was here now I'd slap his stupid face until my fingers broke! How could he die like this? Why couldn't he have taken more care? Why couldn't he have left well alone?'

Jude wrapped his arm around her shoulder and pulled her close. She wanted to beat him off, to fight her way out of his embrace, and yet she wanted to disappear into it too, to lose her soul in his so she could forget where she ended and he began and maybe then the red-hot pain would be lost too.

'You're angry?' he asked.

'Of course I'm angry! I hate James for this. I hate what he's putting my mum through, what he's doing to us all, and I can't even tell him! I have all this rage and frustration burning me up and it has nowhere to go.'

'Maybe you could try me?'

'What?'

'Send it my way. If it helps then I can take it.'

'It's not your fault.'

'It doesn't matter.'

'It's too much to ask of you.'

'Nothing you could possibly ask of me would be too much,' he said, his voice low and earnest. 'Whether we're together or apart, you mean the world to me.'

'How can I after the way I behaved?'

'You had good reason to behave that way and I deserved everything. I should have recognised how my friendship with Harriet might have made you feel and I should have tried harder to put it right when we split up. I was too stubborn to see what a mistake I was making, what I was losing. Believe me, there's not a day that goes by when I don't want to punch myself in the face for being such an idiot.'

'I would have done that for you,' Lizzie said.

He gave a wry smile. 'Have I convinced you yet that there's never going to be anything more than friendship between Harriet and me? We have Artie and that will never change, but we've both changed as people, and what I might have once wanted is not what I want now.'

'You wanted her.'

'I can't lie – I did. But now it's you and only you. I'm not saying this because I expect you to fall back into my arms, and I know it's probably not the time to discuss it, but I just think it's important that you understand. And if we're never more than friends from this point on, I'll understand why, even though I would wish for something more. In any capacity that you feel comfortable with, I want you in my life. That's all, Lizzie – just that.'

She looked across the pub gardens, out to the trees, the wind tearing the last of the russet leaves from their branches just beyond the boundaries, and she was suddenly taken by surprise as a lone tear fell from her eye. All these weeks she hadn't cried once – how strange that she would start now. Jude reached across and caught it with a gentle thumb. And then she turned her face up to his and they met in a tentative kiss.

'I'm sorry,' Lizzie said, hastily moving from his arms.

'It's my fault,' Jude said. 'I shouldn't have…'

From nowhere, Lizzie began to cry properly this time, fat uncontrollable tears that rolled down her face. She cried for James and she cried for her family, she cried out of guilt and she cried all the pent-up tears that had refused to fall for all the weeks since that dreadful phone call on the day they'd moved into the mill. But mostly she cried because she now knew that she'd been so wrong to cut Jude out of her life. Gracie, Florentina, her mum – they had all lost the man they'd loved and they'd had to make the best of that. But Lizzie had Jude – he'd been right there all along and she'd rejected him. She'd thrown away so readily and carelessly the one thing that any of the women who lived with her in the mill right now would have treasured. It had taken a tragedy of unimaginable magnitude for Lizzie to see the truth, and she didn't know how to feel about that. The only thing she knew for sure now was that she never wanted to be without Jude again.

'Oh God, Lizzie… tell me, what can I do to help?' Jude said desperately. 'Whatever it is I'll do it.'

She turned a pleading face to him. 'Just hold me. I can't do this alone anymore.'

Chapter Twenty-Six

It felt like spring today, for the first time this year. During the dark months of winter, it had seemed like they'd never feel the gentle heat of a warm sun again, but today, everything was bright and full of hope. Daffodils crowded around the base of the mill, a vibrant trimming of yellow against the cream of the stone, while bluebells nodded in the shade of the newly budding pear trees where birds had begun to build their nests.

Lizzie was standing in the garden looking up at the mill. Everyone was gathered for the big moment – Gracie, Gwendolyn, Florentina, Charlie and Jude (they'd even brought the doddering George the dog for a rare trip out to join in), Harriet and Artie. Even Derek and Caroline had rolled up in their 4x4 minutes earlier after Lizzie had seen them in the village that morning and told them the mill was almost ready to start working again. They all waited, breath held, and then the old sails of Magnolia Mill creaked and groaned and began to turn for the first time in decades. Lizzie squealed and threw herself into Jude's arms.

'They're going, they're going!'

'I can see they're going,' he said with a broad grin. He turned to Charlie, who had George sitting patiently by his side on a slack leash, looking quite bored with the windmill and more interested in when his next nap might be. 'What do you think? Pretty cool, huh?'

'Amazing!' Charlie breathed, staring up as if he'd never seen anything more amazing in his life.

Lizzie gazed up again and decided quickly that she hadn't seen anything more amazing in her life either. 'I wish Dad could have seen this.'

'He'd be so proud of you,' Gwendolyn said. Lizzie turned to see her smiling with quiet pride. It was four months since James's funeral, and while they'd had a tough Christmas, it seemed Lizzie's mum was coming through the worst of her grief now. She was often quiet and reflective, and Lizzie knew she was probably thinking of James, but she had allowed herself to look to the future a little more. They all had. 'We all thought you were mad,' her mother continued, 'but your dad would have had faith from the start, and he would have been right to.'

Florentina nodded agreement, but she kept whatever thoughts she had on the matter to herself.

The specialist who'd seen the mill back to its former glory emerged from the front door, beaming. 'Not bad, eh?' he called, walking across the grounds to join them. Hands in his pockets, he stood and watched for a moment with the rest of them.

'It's amazing!' Lizzie squeaked, and if her voice got any higher it might only be stray dogs that would answer it. 'I can't believe it!'

'Ready to get making some flour?'

'Absolutely!'

'We are not quite ready yet,' Florentina said, her face wrinkled in a good-natured warning. 'I think we might need grain…? Let's not get ahead of ourselves.'

Lizzie grinned. 'Yes, boss! It's a good job I have you keeping me on the straight and narrow.'

'It has nothing to do with straight and narrow; I have money tied up in this.'

'Me too,' Gracie said.

Lizzie laughed. 'You don't have money tied up in it.'

'Well, then I have emotional investment. And I for one am glad Florentina is keeping you in line.'

'Well, she'll be keeping you in line too when you start working here,' Lizzie said.

'Steady on,' Gracie replied with a laugh herself now. 'Let me have my baby first before we start talking about working.'

'Can I still work here?' Charlie asked. Lizzie gave him a warm smile.

'You'll be my number one, right-hand man.'

Charlie looked uncertainly at Jude, who laughed. 'She means of course you'll be working here.'

'Selling the bread?' Charlie asked. 'I'm good at selling bread.'

'Since when have you ever sold bread?' Jude threw his brother a sideways look.

'Shut up,' Lizzie said, digging Jude in the ribs with her elbow. 'Charlie will be my top bread salesman – you'll see.'

'Oh, and what will I do?' Jude asked.

'You can be the tea boy.'

Charlie giggled and Jude gave a mock stern look, which only made Charlie giggle harder. Lizzie smiled. She couldn't recall a time when life had looked quite this rosy, but it felt like it had been a long time coming. But then her gaze fell on Harriet, who was watching the sails as they travelled on their graceful, sweeping arc with Artie on her hip, pensive and silent and looking for all the world like someone who felt like an outsider.

Over the months since James's death and Lizzie's reconciliation with Jude, there had been some progress on the relationship between her and Harriet too, but it was still new and awkward at times. Harriet seemed to have finally accepted that something had changed between her and Jude, and she accepted the importance of Lizzie in his life, and she'd certainly been more considerate and respectful of how her own behaviour might impact that relationship.

Lizzie wondered if perhaps Jude had spoken frankly to her about it or whether Harriet had simply come to realise herself that she had to change if she was going to keep Jude's friendship, and – more importantly – his good-natured co-parenting of Artie.

Lizzie wanted to say something reassuring now, to let Harriet know that she'd never be excluded from life at the mill, especially now that Jude was set to move up there, but she couldn't find the words. She didn't want Harriet to think that she was losing Jude's friendship, or that Artie would be losing his father. It almost felt like a complete reversal of their fortunes, and Lizzie recalled how hard it had been feeling like the outsider. Later, she decided, she'd try to talk to her and put things right.

Her thoughts were interrupted by Caroline tapping her on the arm. She turned to see her and Derek smiling broadly.

'Congratulations,' she said. 'I don't mind telling you I doubted your sanity, but you've done it.'

'You thought there was a new mad lady at Mad Lady Mill?' Lizzie said with a smile.

'You might have just turned Piriwick's fortunes around by getting this up and running again,' Derek put in.

'Really?' Lizzie asked.

'There'll be tourists bringing money into the village now.'

'Not *that* many, surely? Not just to see my little mill.'

Derek shrugged. 'Time will tell.'

Lizzie frowned. She'd never really considered what impact Magnolia Mill might have on the surrounding area once she'd restored it. She hoped, if Piriwick's fortunes were to change with those of her mill, Piriwick wouldn't mind too much.

'I'm sure the extra visitors will be welcome,' Caroline said, seeming to read Lizzie's thoughts. 'Nobody in their right mind would turn their noses up at a little extra trade.' She reached to kiss Lizzie on the cheek. 'We'll be off. Thank you for letting us see your big switch on.'

'You mean my big lever pull,' Lizzie said with a little laugh. 'Thank you for coming.'

As Derek and Caroline bid their goodbyes and started to walk back to their car, Florentina looked at her watch. 'I really ought to be driving back too.'

'It'll be dark soon,' Lizzie said. 'You're welcome to stay over tonight if you'd rather – your old room is still made up.'

Florentina shook her head. 'Thanks, but I've waited long enough to get my little house back so I'm all for making the most of it now.' She turned to Lizzie's mum. 'Are you heading home soon too? I could give you a lift.'

'That would be good, thank you,' Gwendolyn said. 'Leave the young ones to it.'

'Oh yes,' Lizzie said, 'leave the young ones to their debauched, rock-and-roll milling lifestyle.'

'You might laugh but I think it's quite bohemian,' Gracie said. 'Who else around here is milling wheat?'

Lizzie chuckled. 'Who else around here wants to? But I appreciate the sentiment. I suppose it is going to be a bit of an alternative lifestyle in some people's eyes. To me it just seems normal.'

'Trust me, it's not normal,' Gwendolyn said with a smile. 'But we wouldn't have you any other way.'

The restorer took off his thick gloves and spoke. Everyone turned to him, having quite forgotten he was there in their playful bickering. 'I'll leave you to it. You've got my card if you need any help.'

Lizzie nodded. 'Thank you so much for everything.'

'Thank you for giving me the opportunity of working on her – she's quite a beauty.'

'She is,' Lizzie agreed. 'Although I'd never really thought of Magnolia Mill as a girl before.'

'Don't you think she feels like a girl?' Gracie said.

'Do you?'

'Now that you come to mention it, yes.'

'Well, if you're happy with that then so am I.'

Lizzie took a moment to walk the restorer back to his van. They exchanged a few more pleasantries on the perfection of Magnolia Mill and what her plans were now that it was ready to start working again, and then she made her way back to the little crowd gathered in the grounds, still watching the sails sweep through a blue sky.

'We think we ought to have a party,' Gracie said.

'*You* think we ought to have a party,' Florentina said.

Lizzie arched an eyebrow at her sister. 'You always think we ought to have a party.'

'Life's short and sad enough – why not party when you can?' Gracie folded her arms emphatically across her now huge belly, as if it were the simplest, most obvious wisdom in the world. When Lizzie thought about it, perhaps it was.

'Amen to that,' Jude said with a grin.

Lizzie let out a sigh. 'OK, when are we having this party?'

'There's no time like the present,' Gracie said.

'But Florentina and Mum are going home and Derek and Caroline have already gone.'

Gracie turned to her mum. 'You could stay for a little longer after all? Or stay over until tomorrow?'

'I suppose we could,' Florentina said uncertainly, looking to Gwendolyn for agreement.

'Oh, please say yes, Mum!' Gracie begged.

'Surely you don't want to be on your feet catering, the size you are now,' Gwendolyn replied.

'What's that supposed to mean?' Gracie asked, her smile turning into a scowl. 'I'm not fat!'

Lizzie giggled. 'I'm not sure that came out in a very complimentary way, Mum.'

'I only mean you're very pregnant to be rushing around hostessing parties,' Gwendolyn said patiently.

'I've got three weeks yet.'

'You *have* got a big belly,' Charlie said.

'Charlie!' Jude admonished.

'I bet you were as big as this when you were pregnant with Artie,' Gracie said, looking to Harriet now as an ally. 'And I bet you still got on with things.'

'Well,' Harriet said uncertainly, 'I didn't really throw parties…'

'But you could have if you'd wanted to.'

'I suppose so.'

'There you go.' Gracie looked at her mum with a triumphant expression.

'If you insist, then I suppose I'll have to stay,' Gwendolyn said. 'But if it sends you into early labour, don't come crying to me.'

'Of course it won't—' Gracie began, but then she stopped dead and looked down. 'Oh.'

'Bloody hell!' Lizzie said under her breath.

'I don't think baby wanted to miss the party,' Jude added as they watched the water run down Gracie's leg.

'Yep,' Lizzie replied, 'that would be Gracie's baby then.'

'Does this mean we can't have the party now?' Charlie asked.

'I think I've probably got hours,' Gracie reassured him. 'I'm sure we could manage a little nibble and a drink.'

Lizzie stared at her. 'You're actually kidding – right?'

'It says on that pregnancy blog that just because your waters have broken, doesn't mean the baby will come straight away.'

'I don't think we ought to be taking that risk,' Jude put in gently.

'And he should know because he was there when Artie was born,' Lizzie said. She looked at Harriet for agreement, who nodded.

'But what about the mill?' Gracie asked.

'Never mind the mill now,' Lizzie said. 'Sod the mill!'

'But, Lizzie—'

Gwendolyn clapped her hands for attention, and Lizzie looked up to see a light in her mum's eyes that hadn't been there for a long time. It was purpose and usefulness, and it made Lizzie's heart soar to see it.

'Don't just stand there everyone!' she cried. 'We've got a baby coming!'

Chapter Twenty-Seven

It had been a long night of waiting, but at 5.14 the following morning, Alexander James Lovell took his first breaths, weighing a satisfying eight pounds on the nose. Mum and baby had both been sleeping by the time Florentina had taken Gwendolyn home to freshen up so they could come back later for official visiting hours. Harriet had taken Charlie and George the dog home while Lizzie and Jude waited for the birth, aware that neither Charlie nor Artie would make it through the night without falling asleep. Now, Lizzie was dozing on a hospital chair in the corridor next to Gracie's room. She awoke to a gentle nudge from Jude.

'You fell asleep too?' he asked, stretching out.

'Oh, we're just great bodyguards, aren't we?' she replied with a tired smile.

'Maybe we ought to head back to the mill for a rest. We're clearly fit for nothing here and I'm sure Gracie and Alexander will be able to manage without us for an hour.'

'But what if they discharge Gracie? I won't be here to take her home.'

'Then she can call. We'll keep a phone close and on full volume just in case. Besides, I'm sure she can wait for an hour, even if they do discharge her. Or maybe Florentina will come to pick her up.'

Lizzie shook her head uncertainly. 'If it's only going to be a couple of hours more then I'd rather stay.'

'Let me go and ask one of the nurses to see if they know.'

Jude got up and Lizzie was about to ask him not to bother them when her attention was caught by a figure marching up the corridor towards them. His face was almost obscured by a huge bouquet of white and pink roses and carnations, but Lizzie would have known that walk anywhere.

'Frank!' she breathed.

Jude's head snapped up. 'Gracie's ex?'

In the seconds it had taken for Lizzie to express her surprise, Frank had reached them.

'Lizzie.' He nodded, his dark eyes as arrogant as ever, but Lizzie thought she detected something else in there, something she hadn't seen before. Was he nervous? Feeling a little vulnerable and unsure of himself? She shook herself – she must be more tired than she'd thought. 'Gracie through here?' he added, nodding at the door to her room.

'Well, yes, but... I don't think it's a good idea to go in.'

'She'll want to see me.'

'I don't think she will,' Jude cut in. Frank stared at him, the old steel in his expression back again.

'And you are...?'

'A friend of Gracie's.'

'Well, I'm the father of her child so I rather think I win,' Frank said.

'I'm not looking for trouble, I just know what Gracie has been saying for the past nine months and it's that she doesn't want to see you.'

'She must have changed her mind because I happen to know that she does.'

'Hang on...' Lizzie shook her head. 'Frank, how did you know Gracie is here?'

'She phoned me. I've been driving like a bat out of hell for the past couple of hours. And you have no idea how hard it is to find somewhere that sells decent flowers at this time of the morning. I had to phone a florist and make them open up.'

Lizzie blinked. What on earth he could have said to make a florist open up especially for him she couldn't imagine, but it sounded like the Frank she knew only too well. 'She phoned you? When?'

'I suppose it must have been during labour. There was quite a lot of squealing and panting.'

'And she just told you about her baby? Just like that?'

'*Our* baby.'

'Why?'

'Because I have a right to know.'

'I don't mean that. I mean, why now? Like Jude said, she didn't want anything more to do with you after... well, you know—'

'My indiscretion?'

'I was going to say shagging about. Let's call a spade a spade, that's what I say.' Lizzie glanced at Jude who gave her a quick, surreptitious grin.

'I'm not with that particular girl anymore.'

'That doesn't make a bit of difference. I just don't understand what's changed for Gracie.'

Frank gave a vague shrug. 'She said she didn't feel she could keep it from me any longer and she thought I had a right to know that I was going to be a father. I think she rather wanted me here for the birth.'

'And why weren't you?'

'Because I only picked up the message on my answer machine a couple of hours ago. I jumped in my car and drove straight here – after the detour for flowers – and this is me, fresh from a night at the theatre with some clients. I realise that I must have completely missed the birth.'

'I'm sure Gracie could have managed without the flowers.'

'Yes, but it's what one does in these situations, isn't it? Bring flowers, I mean. So I missed the birth?'

'You did.'

'Was it…' Frank paused. He looked unfamiliar, uncertain again. 'Was it awful? Was she in a lot of pain?'

'Well, you do expect a certain amount of pain when you give birth. That's what all the squealing and panting is about. But it was beautiful and Alexander is beautiful.'

He nodded slowly. 'Can I see her? Please? I just want to leave these and then I'll go.'

'She's asleep right now.'

'Oh. So I can't go in?'

Lizzie looked at Jude for some kind of sign. What would he do? What was the right thing to do in this situation? Gracie had clearly relented and decided to tell Frank, but did that mean she really wanted to invite him back into her life? Or had she just been feeling emotional and irrational while in the throes of labour? Lizzie hadn't even realised she'd had access to a phone, and she had to wonder at what point in the proceedings this had happened, but it was a question she'd have to clear up with her sister later.

'Lizzie, perhaps you could go in and see if Gracie is awake and if she wants to see Frank?' Jude offered. 'If you'd care to wait for a minute,' he added, turning to Frank himself.

'I would be more than happy to,' Frank replied smoothly. He was doing his best to look as if he had the situation under control, and he was used to having any situation under control, but Lizzie could tell that he was bluffing this time. It gave her a strange sort of satisfaction that probably wasn't entirely appropriate, but she decided to enjoy the feeling anyway.

Leaving Jude with Frank in the corridor, Lizzie slipped into Gracie's room and closed the door quietly behind her. Gracie was peaceful, her breathing deep and regular. In the cot next to her bed, Alexander snuffled and opened his eyes. Lizzie couldn't help but take a closer look. There was something addictive about the way he smelt and she could have watched him stare up at her all day.

'Hey there, mister,' she cooed. 'Your daddy's here; he wants to see you, but your mummy's asleep. So what do you reckon I should do?'

'I want to see him.'

Lizzie looked up to see that Gracie was awake.

'I'm sorry, I didn't mean to disturb you.'

'It's OK.' Gracie pushed herself up on her pillows. She looked exhausted and bedraggled, but she radiated happiness. 'I called him because I decided you'd all been right all along and he ought to know. But that's all it is – just so he knows.' She gave a tired grin. 'That and the fact that he's going to owe me lots of money to bring Alexander up.'

Lizzie smiled. She knew Gracie didn't really mean the thing about the money, though there was no doubt that on a practical level she was probably going to need it. 'So you're actually admitting we were right? That's a turn-up for the books.'

'Yes. I suppose it is.'

Lizzie frowned. 'You don't want him back, do you?'

Gracie shook her head. 'Surely you don't think I'm that stupid?'

'No,' Lizzie replied, laughing now. 'I don't think you're that stupid at all.'

'I don't ever want him back, but I have to give him the opportunity to be a part of his son's life if he wants it. It's bigger than just us, isn't it? What if Alexander finds out I cut his dad off when he's older? What if it upsets him? And there's Frank's family to consider too – his parents would want the chance to be grandparents. Think how angry they'd be finding out in years to come they'd had a grandson whose childhood they'd totally missed.'

Lizzie leaned to kiss Gracie on the forehead. 'For the record, you're doing the right thing.'

'I know that – it's why I'm doing it.'

'Want me to come in with him and stay while you talk?'

'I can manage. It's probably better if we talk alone.'

'Want me to wait outside?'

'You look as if you've been outside all this time. Why don't you go home and get some rest?'

'I want to stay in case you're discharged.'

'It'll be later. The last nurse who came in said the next ward round won't be until this afternoon now so I'm not going anywhere until then. Go home, Lizzie, you look terrible.'

'Thanks so much. This coming from the woman who's just given birth. I really feel good about myself now.'

'Silly.' Gracie gave her a warm smile. 'I only meant you look tired and I'm not surprised. Go and have a sleep.'

Lizzie glanced at the door uncertainly.

'Go!' Gracie insisted, her smile spreading. 'Everything will be fine here. I'll call you later.'

Lizzie began to back away towards the door. 'Don't let him charm you,' she said sternly.

'I won't.'

'But he has flowers. *Lots* of flowers. And he says he's driven like a demon for two hours. It's pretty romantic.'

'It might be but shagging the office intern isn't. Don't worry; my heart is steel where Frank is concerned.'

'If I hear he's wormed his way back in...'

'You won't because it won't happen. But I will be reminding him that he does have a lot of birthday and Christmas gifts to buy for his son over the next couple of decades, and they'd better be bloody good ones!'

'God yes, of course!' Lizzie turned and pulled at the door handle. But then she stopped as Gracie called her back. 'What?'

'Thank you.'

'No problem.'

'No, not just for this. For everything, ever. You're the best sister a girl could ask for and I love you.'

Lizzie's eyes misted. 'I love you too. And everything has always been my pleasure. For what it's worth, you're not quite the best sister a girl could have – clearly that's me – but you're pretty close.'

Gracie tipped her head this way and that, as if weighing up the truth of Lizzie's assertion. 'Fair.'

Lizzie laughed through her tears. 'I'll send the new daddy in. And you'd better phone me the minute you're allowed to go home.'

*

'It makes you feel a lot easier that Frank knows about his son now, doesn't it?' Lizzie said to Jude as they arrived back at a dark and silent Magnolia Mill. Now, at the mill, it was just Lizzie and Jude. Usually, that would be a perfect excuse for a steamy assignation, but after the night they'd had, all they both wanted to do when they got into bed was sleep.

'I'd have missed so much if I'd missed out on Artie growing up.'

'But your situation isn't quite the same as Frank's.'

'True.'

'And Frank probably doesn't care.'

'That's also true, but if he doesn't even know he has a son then he isn't being given a chance to care, or to change everyone's opinion of him. You never know, he might be a great dad – it's often the ones that come to fatherhood unexpectedly that rise to the challenge. Either way, it's only fair to let the man decide. Gracie said herself that she thought it would be unfair to Alexander if he was never given the chance to get to know his dad and that he might come to resent that.'

Lizzie went to boil some water. The room was silent for a moment, save for the hissing of the kettle as it started to heat up. But then Jude broke it.

'How would you feel about having a baby?' he blurted out.

Lizzie spun around. 'What?'

'You and me, I mean. How would you feel about it?'

'I don't know. It's a weird question to ask.'

'Not really, as we're all about the babies at the moment.'

'There's one reason right there not to have one. Gracie will have her hands full and will need all the help she can get, and that's without getting the mill business up and running. Even if I thought you were remotely serious I don't have time to have a baby.'

'I am serious. I've never been more serious in my life.'

'Jude, you haven't even moved in here yet.'

'That's only a matter of time. Once I'm here… we're practically married then.'

'You don't need to be married to have a baby anyway – you of all people should know that.'

Jude's hand clutched at his breast. 'Ouch.'

'I wasn't being snarky when I said that.' Lizzie gave him a reassuring smile. 'I'm tired and it came out wrong. Too tired to be having a conversation like this. I think you're tired too and that's why you started it. In the morning you'll wonder what the hell you were thinking bringing it up.'

'I won't. I want to have a baby with you.'

'I'm not saying never,' Lizzie said gently. 'I'm saying some day. Can you live with that?'

'I guess so.'

'Waiting a while won't be all that bad. Isn't it usually the women who get broody when there's a new baby? At least, that's what you men are always saying.'

Jude broke into a lopsided grin. 'And I suppose the practice baby-making might be fun.'

'See, there you go. Every cloud and all that. So you're OK? You're not upset?'

'I'm not upset. In the end I'm happy that we're where we are and I can work to any timetable you give me. So… about that moving in…'

'You can do that any time you like; you know that.'

'How about tonight?'

'We don't have Charlie's room ready yet,' Lizzie said with a giggle. She reached for two mugs from the cupboard. 'Be serious.'

'Then that's my first job, tomorrow morning as soon as I wake up.'

'I don't have time for any of that tomorrow morning; Gracie and Alexander will be home.' Lizzie smiled. Gracie, baby Alexander, and soon Jude and Charlie, all calling Magnolia Mill home. She liked the sound of that.

Jude took the mugs from her and placed them on the worktop, wrapping his arms around her and dipping in for a kiss. When she pulled away, her insides were on fire.

'Wow. Where did that come from?'

'Aren't my kisses always good?'

'Well, yes, but you haven't usually been up all night waiting for a baby to arrive.'

'It's your doing – you get me all hot under the collar. And we're alone for once. We might not get many more hours alone when everyone's back here.'

'True.'

'So…' His voice was hot and lazy as his hands crept to the front of her blouse and he began to pop the buttons. 'How about we make the most of this hour alone?'

'I thought you were tired?'

'I was.'

Lizzie's smile was slow as he kissed her again. Suddenly, she wasn't quite so tired either.

A Letter from Tilly

I want to say a huge thank you for choosing to read *The Mill on Magnolia Lane*. If you did enjoy it, and want to keep up to date with all my latest releases, just sign up at the following link. Your email address will never be shared and you can unsubscribe at any time.

www.bookouture.com/tilly-tennant

I'm so excited to share *The Mill on Magnolia Lane* with you. It's my tenth novel for Bookouture and I can't believe I'm saying that! I truly have the best job in the world, and I've been so proud to share every new book with my lovely readers.

I hope you loved *The Mill on Magnolia Lane*, and if you did I would be very grateful if you could write a review. I'd love to hear what you think, and it makes such a difference helping new readers to discover one of my books for the first time.

I love hearing from my readers – you can get in touch on my Facebook page, through Twitter, Goodreads or my website.

Thanks,
Tilly

www.tillytennant.com

tillytennant

@TillyTenWriter

Acknowledgements

The list of people who have offered help and encouragement on my writing journey so far must be truly endless, and it would take a novel in itself to mention them all. However, my heartfelt gratitude goes out to each and every one of you, whose involvement, whether small or large, has been invaluable and appreciated more than I can say.

There are a few people that I must mention. Obviously, my family – the people who put up with my whining and self-doubt on a daily basis are top of the list. My mum and, posthumously, my dad, who brought me up to believe that anything is possible if you want it enough, no matter how crazy or unlikely it seems. My ex-colleagues at the Royal Stoke University Hospital, who let me lead a double life for far longer than is acceptable and have given me so many ideas for future books! The lecturers at Staffordshire University English and Creative Writing Department, who saw a talent worth nurturing in me and continue to support me still, long after they finished getting paid for it. They are not only tutors but friends as well.

I have to thank the team at Bookouture for their continued support, patience, and amazing publishing flair, particularly Lydia Vassar-Smith – my incredible and patient editor – Kim Nash, Noelle Holten, Peta Nightingale, Lauren Finger and Jessie Botterill. Their belief, able assistance and encouragement means the world to me. I truly believe I have the best team an author could ask for.

My friend, Kath Hickton, always gets a shout out for putting up with me since primary school. Louise Coquio also gets an honourable mention for getting me through university and suffering me ever since, likewise her lovely family. And thanks go to Storm Constantine for giving me my first break in publishing. I also have to thank Mel Sherratt and Holly Martin, fellow writers and amazing friends who have both been incredibly supportive over the years and have been my shoulders to cry on in the darker moments. Thanks to Tracy Bloom, Emma Davies, Jack Croxall, Clare Davidson, Angie Marsons, Christie Barlow and Jaimie Admans: not only brilliant authors in their own right but hugely supportive of others. My Bookouture colleagues are all incredible, of course, unfailing and generous in their support of fellow authors – life would be a lot duller without the gang! I have to thank all the brilliant and dedicated book bloggers (there are so many of you but you know who you are!) and readers, and anyone else who has championed my work, reviewed it, shared it, or simply told me that they liked it. Every one of those actions is priceless and you are all very special people. Some of you I am even proud to call friends now.

Last but not least, I'd like to give a special mention to my lovely new agent, Madeleine Milburn. I'm still not sure she's realised what she's getting herself into by taking me under her wing but I'm glad she has!